Praise for *New York Times* bestselling author Diana Palmer

"Palmer proves that love and passion can be found even in the most dangerous situations."
—*Publishers Weekly* on *Untamed*

"You just can't do better than a Diana Palmer story to make your heart lighter and smile brighter."
—*Fresh Fiction* on *Wyoming Rugged*

"Diana Palmer is a mesmerizing storyteller who captures the essence of what a romance should be."
—*Affaire de Coeur*

"The popular Palmer has penned another winning novel, a perfect blend of romance and suspense."
—*Booklist* on *Lawman*

"Diana Palmer's characters leap off the page. She captures their emotions and scars beautifully and makes them come alive for readers."
—*RT Book Reviews* on *Lawless*

Dear Reader,

I can't believe that it has been thirty years since my first Long, Tall Texans book, *Calhoun*, debuted! The series was suggested by my former editor Tara Gavin, who asked if I might like to set stories in a fictional town of my own design. Would I! And the rest is history.

As the years went by, I found more and more sexy ranchers and cowboys to add to the collection. My readers (especially Amy!) found time to gift me with a notebook listing every single one of them, wives and kids and connections to other families in my own Texas town of Jacobsville. Eventually the town got a little too big for me, so I added another smaller town called Comanche Wells and began to fill it up, too.

You can't imagine how much pleasure this series has given me. I continue to add to the population of Jacobs County, Texas, and I have no plans to stop. Ever.

I hope all of you enjoy reading the Long, Tall Texans as much as I enjoy writing them. Thank you all for your kindness and loyalty and friendship. I am your biggest fan!

Love,

Diana Palmer

NEW YORK TIMES BESTSELLING AUTHOR

DIANA PALMER

LONG, TALL TEXANS:

Brannon

John

Previously published as
The Texas Ranger and *The Founding Father*

 HARLEQUIN SPECIAL RELEASE

SPECIAL RELEASE

ISBN-13: 978-1-335-08040-0

Recycling programs for this product may not exist in your area.

Long, Tall Texans: Brannon/John

Copyright © 2020 by Harlequin Books S.A.

Brannon
First published as The Texas Ranger in 2001.
This edition published in 2020.
Copyright © 2001 by Diana Palmer

John
First published as The Founding Father in 2003.
This edition published in 2020.
Copyright © 2003 by Diana Palmer

This edition published by arrangement with Harlequin Books S.A.

For questions and comments about the quality of this book, please contact us at CustomerService@Harlequin.com.

Harlequin Enterprises ULC
22 Adelaide St. West, 40th Floor
Toronto, Ontario M5H 4E3, Canada
www.Harlequin.com

Printed in U.S.A.

CONTENTS

A prolific author of more than one hundred books, **Diana Palmer** got her start as a newspaper reporter. A *New York Times* bestselling author and voted one of the top ten romance writers in America, she has a gift for telling the most sensual tales with charm and humor. Diana lives with her family in Cornelia, Georgia. Visit her website at dianapalmer.com.

Books by Diana Palmer

Long, Tall Texans

Fearless
Heartless
Dangerous
Merciless
Courageous
Protector
Invincible
Untamed
Defender
Undaunted

The Wyoming Men

Wyoming Tough
Wyoming Fierce
Wyoming Bold
Wyoming Strong
Wyoming Rugged
Wyoming Brave

Morcai Battalion

The Morcai Battalion
The Morcai Battalion: The Recruit
The Morcai Battalion: Invictus
The Morcai Battalion: The Rescue

Visit the Author Profile page
at Harlequin.com for more titles.

BRANNON

CHAPTER ONE

THERE WERE FRAMED black-and-white photographs of Texas Rangers on the walls of the San Antonio Texas Ranger office. Like sepia ghosts of times gone by, they watched over the modern complex of telephones and fax machines and computers. Phones were ringing. Employees at desks were interviewing people. The hum of working machines settled over the office, oddly comforting, like an electrical lullaby.

Sergeant Marc Brannon was sitting kicked back in his swivel chair, his wavy blond-streaked brown hair shimmering under the ceiling lights as he pondered a stack of files on his cluttered desk. His narrow, pale gray eyes were almost closed as he thought about a disturbing recent mishap.

A close friend and fellow Texas Ranger, Judd Dunn, had been almost run over by a speeding car a few weeks earlier during a temporary assignment to the San Antonio office. There were rumors that it had something to do with a criminal investigation into illegal gambling that the FBI was conducting on local mob boss Jake Marsh in San Antonio. Dunn had been working with the FBI on the case, but shortly thereafter, Dunn had transferred down to the Victoria office, citing personal problems. Brannon had inherited the Marsh investigation. The FBI was also involved—rather, an agent Brannon knew was involved; a Georgia-born nuisance named Curtis Russell. It was curious that Russell should be working on an FBI case. He'd been with the Secret Service. Of course, Marc reminded himself, men changed jobs all the time. He certainly had.

Apparently, Russell was knee-deep in the Marsh investigation. Attorney General Simon Hart had spoken with Brannon on the phone not two days ago, grumbling about Russell's tenacity. The former Secret Service agent was now in Austin giving the local officials fits while he dug into state crime lab computer files on two recent murders that he thought were tied to Marsh. And who knew, maybe he was right. But pinning anything on the local mobster was going to take a miracle.

Marsh had his finger in all sorts of pies, including blackmail, prostitution and illegal betting, mostly in San Antonio, where he lived. If they could get something on him, they could invoke the state's nuisance abatement statute, which permitted any property to be closed down if it were used as a base of operations for criminals. Since Marsh was known to be involved in prostitution and illegal betting at his nightclub, all they had to do was prove it to oust him from the premises. Considering the real estate value of that downtown property, it would hit Marsh right where he lived. But knowing he was conducting illegal operations and proving it were two whole different kettles of fish. Marsh was an old hand at dodging investigators and searches. Doing things by the book sure seemed to give career criminals an advantage.

Pity that you couldn't just shoot the bad guys anymore, Brannon thought whimsically, eyeing a hundred-year-old framed photograph of a Texas Ranger on horseback with a lariat pulled tight around a dusty and wounded outlaw.

His lean hand went to the dark wood butt of the Colt .45 he wore in a holster on his hip. Since Rangers didn't have a specified uniform, they were allowed some personal choice in both dress and weaponry. But most of the men and women in the office wore white shirts and ties with their star-in-a-circle signature badge on the shirt. Most of them also wore white Stetsons and boots. To a Ranger, they were neat, conservative, polite and professional when they were on the job. Brannon tried very hard to adjust to that image. Well, he tried to, most of the time. He was more cautious about his job now than he ever had been before. He'd made the mistake of his life two years ago, misjudging a woman he'd grown to…care for, very much. His sister said that the woman didn't blame him for the mess he'd made of her life. But he blamed himself so much that he'd quit the Rangers and left Texas for two years to work with the FBI. But he'd learned that running from problems didn't solve them. They were portable. Like heartache.

He could still see her in his mind, blonde and sassy and full of dry wit. Despite the miseries of her life, she'd been the brightest, most delightful person he'd ever known. He missed her. She didn't miss him, of course. And why should she? He'd hurt her terribly. He'd ruined her life.

"Nothing to do, Brannon?" a female Ranger drawled as she passed him. All the women thought he was a dish, lean and slim-hipped, broad-chested, with that square sort of face that once graced cowboy movie posters. He had a sensuous mouth under a nose that had been broken at least once, and an arrogant sort of carriage that excited more than it intimidated. But he wasn't a rounder, by anybody's estimate. In fact, if he dated, he was so discreet that even the office gossip couldn't get anything on him.

"I am doing something," he drawled back with a twinkle in his eyes. "I'm using mental telepathy on escaped criminals. If I'm successful, they'll all be walking into law enforcement offices all over America as we speak, to turn themselves in."

"Pull the other one," she chuckled.

He sighed and smiled. "Okay. I just got back from testifying in a court case. I've got half a dozen cases to work and now I have to decide on priorities," he confessed. He flicked a long finger at the file stack. "I thought I might flip a coin…"

"No need. The captain has something urgent for you to do."

"Saved by new orders!" he joked. He jerked forward and his booted feet slammed to the floor. He got up and stretched enormously, pulling his white shirt with the silver Ranger badge on the pocket tight over hair-roughened, hard chest muscles. "What's the assignment?"

She tossed a sheet on his desk. "A homicide, in an alley off Castillo Boulevard," she told him. "White guy, mid-to-late-twenties. Two detectives from CID and a medical examiner investigator are already on scene, along with a couple of EMTs and patrol officers. The captain said you should go right now, before they call a contract ambulance to transport the dead body."

He scowled. "Hey, that's in the city limits. San Antonio PD has jurisdiction…" he began.

"I know. But this one's tricky. They found a young white guy with a single gunshot wound to the back of the head, execution-style. Remember what's on Castillo Boulevard?"

"No."

She gave him a smug look. "Jake Marsh's nightclub. And the body was found in an alley two doors down from it."

He broke into a smile. "Well, well! What a nice surprise to drop in my lap, and just when I was feeling sorry for myself." He hesitated. "Wait a minute. Why's the captain giving it to me?" he asked suspiciously, glaring toward the head Ranger's closed door nearby. "The last assignment he gave me was looking into the mysterious death of a mutilated cow." He leaned down, because he was a head taller than she was. "They thought it was *aliens,*" he whispered fervently.

She made a face. "You never know. Maybe it was!"

He glared at her.

She grinned. "He's just ticked because you got to work with the FBI for two years, and they turned down two applications from him. But he said you could have this murder case because you haven't embarrassed him this month. Yet."

"It won't be uncomplicated. In fact, I'll bet a week's pay that by dark it's going to turn into a media feeding frenzy," he said.

"I won't take that bet. And, by the way, he said you should stop getting gas at that new all-female gas station downtown, because it's giving the department a bad name."

He lifted both eyebrows. "What's he got against women pumping gas?" he asked innocently.

"Gas isn't all they're pumping." She flushed when

she realized what she'd said, gestured impotently at the assignment sheet and exited in a flaming rush.

Brannon grinned wickedly as she retreated. He picked up the sheet and went out of the office, grabbing up his off-white Stetson on the way.

IN AUSTIN, a slender woman with her long blond hair in a bun, wearing big gold-rimmed glasses over her twinkling dark brown eyes, was trying to console one of the state attorney general's computer experts.

"He really likes you, Phil," Josette Langley told the young man, who was in the first month of his first job out of college. He looked devastated. "Honest he does."

Phil, redheaded and blue-eyed, glanced toward the door of Simon Hart, Texas Attorney General, and flushed even redder. "He said it was my fault his computer locked down while he was talking to the vice president online about an upcoming governors' conference. He got knocked off the network and couldn't get back on. He threw the mouse at me."

"Lucky you, that it wasn't attached to the CPU at the time," she said with a wicked grin. "Anyway, he only throws things when Tira's mad at him. It doesn't last long. Besides, the vice president is his third cousin," she pointed out. "And mine, too, come to think of it," she added thoughtfully. "Never mind, Phil, you have to learn to just let it wash over you, like water on a duck's back. Simon's quick-tempered, but he gets over it just as fast."

He gave her a baleful look. "He never yells at you."

"I'm a woman," she pointed out. "He's very old-fashioned about yelling at women. He and his brothers were raised strictly. They don't move with the times."

"He's got four brothers and he says they're all just like him. Imagine that!" he said.

She remembered that Phil was an only child, like herself. "They're not just like him. Anyway, they live in Jacobsville, Texas. The married ones are a lot calmer now." She didn't dare allow herself to think about the two remaining Hart bachelors, Leo and Rey. The stories about their homemade biscuit-craving and the things they did to satisfy it was becoming legendary.

"The bachelor ones aren't calm. One of them carried a cook out of a Victoria restaurant kicking and screaming last week, and they sent the Texas Rangers after him!"

"They sent Judd Dunn," she replied. "He's our cousin, too. But it was a joke, sort of. And she wasn't exactly screaming… Well, never mind. It's not important." She was talking too fast. She felt her face go hot at the mention of the Texas Rangers.

She had painful memories of one particular Texas Ranger, whom she'd loved passionately. Gretchen, Marc Brannon's sister, had told her that Marc Brannon had gone on a drunken rampage two years ago, just after they broke up and ended up on opposite sides of the courtroom in a high-profile murder trial. Marc had left the Rangers shortly afterward and enlisted with the FBI. He was back in San Antonio now, back with the Rangers again. Gretchen also said that Marc had almost driven himself crazy with guilt over an even older incident when Josette was fifteen and he was a policeman in Jacobsville. Odd, she thought, remembering the painful things he'd said to her when they broke up.

Josette had told Gretchen that she didn't blame Marc for his lack of belief in her innocence. Part of her didn't.

Another, darker part wanted to hang him by his spurs from a live oak tree for the misery of the past two years. He'd never really believed her story until their last disastrous date, and he'd walked out on her without another word, after making her feel like a prostitute. She'd loved him. But he couldn't have loved her. If he had, he'd never have left Texas, not even if the murder trial had set them at odds.

She cleared her throat at the erotic images that flashed through her mind of her last date with Marc and turned her attention back to poor, downcast Phil Douglas.

"I'll square things with Simon for you," she promised him.

"I really like working here," he said eagerly. "You might mention that. And I promise I'll fix the computer next time so that his e-mail won't ever lock down again. I'll put it in writing, even!"

"I'll tell him, Phil. Right now, in fact. I have to see him on a question one of the district attorneys faxed in this morning. Chin up, now. The world hasn't ended. Everything passes with time—even things you think will kill your soul."

And she should know, she thought, but she didn't say it out loud.

When she walked into Texas Attorney General Simon Hart's office, she found him scowling at the telephone as if he'd just taken a bite of it and found it rotten.

"Something wrong?" she asked as she paused in front of his desk.

He shifted, the artificial hand resting on the desk looking so real that sometimes it was hard to remember that he was an amputee. Simon was big, dark-haired, pale-eyed and formidable. His gorgeous redheaded wife, Tira, and his two dark-haired young sons smiled out from a jumble of framed photographs on a polished table behind him. There was one of him with his four brothers just after he'd been elected attorney general. His brothers were giving him apprehensive glances. She smiled. Disabled or not, Simon was a force to behold when he lost his temper.

"That was the assistant district attorney in San Antonio," he said, indicating the phone. "They've got what looks like a mob-related hit in an alley just a few steps from Jake Marsh's nightclub." He glanced at her. "A local mob figure," he added. "Ever heard of him?"

"The name rings a bell, but I can't place it. That case won't concern us, will it?" she asked.

He was tracing a pattern on his desk. "As a matter of fact, it might. It depends on whether or not we can tie Marsh to the murder. I don't have to tell you how hard the district attorney in San Antonio has been trying to shut him down. The D.A. phoned the deputy chief of police and cleared it to have the Texas Rangers send an officer over there to assist in the investigation. If the case can be tied to Marsh, we'll be looking at multiple jurisdictions and we'll end up in a high-profile case. In a senate election year here," he added solemnly, "crime will be a campaign issue. I don't want Texas in the spotlight again. Neither does the D.A. in Bexar County, so she's making sure every step is documented and backed up."

He was holding something back. She could see it in the way he looked at her.

"You know you can't hide things from me," she said abruptly. "What is it you don't want to tell me?"

He shook his head and laughed. "I forgot that uncanny ability of yours to sense what people are feeling. Okay. They're sending Marc Brannon to look into it," he told her finally. He held up a hand when she froze and started to speak. "I know there's bad blood between you, but Marsh is notorious. I want him as much as the D.A. does, so I'm going to send you over there to run liaison for my office during the investigation. I've got a bad feeling about this one."

She wasn't listening. She had a bad feeling about it, too. Her heart was racing. Two years. *Two years.* "You'll have a worse feeling if you send me there. Can you see me and Brannon working together? It will only be possible if they confiscate all his bullets and make me leave my stun gun here in Austin."

He chuckled. Despite her tragic life, she was strong and independent and dryly funny. He'd hired her two years ago when nobody else would, largely thanks to Brannon, and he was glad. She had a degree in criminal justice. Her choice of jobs was to be an investigator in a district attorney's office. Fate had landed her here, working on the Prosecutor Assistance and Special Investigation Unit for Simon. She could be loaned out to a requesting district attorney, along with other investigative personnel and even prosecutors, providing resources for criminal investigation.

It was a harrowing job from time to time, but she loved it. She had access to the respected Texas Crime Information Center. It boasted a statewide database on wanted persons and provided real-time online information to law enforcement agencies. Josette counted it as one of her biggest blessings during investigations, particularly those involving cybercrime.

"It's nothing definite yet," Simon added. "They're

still at the scene. The murder may not even be connected with Marsh, although I hope to God it is. But I thought I'd prepare you, just in case you have to go out there."

"Okay. Thanks, Simon."

"We're family. Sort of." He frowned. "Was it your third cousin who was related to my stepgrandmother...?"

"Don't," she groaned. "It would take a genealogist to figure it out, it's so distant."

"Whatever. They can't accuse me of nepotism for hiring you, but we're distant cousins anyway. Family," he added, with a warm smile. "Sort of. Like the staff."

"I'm glad you think of them like that, because 'Cousin' Phil wants you to know that he likes his job and he's sorry he messed up your e-mail," she told him, tongue in cheek. "And he hopes you won't take away his job with the Internet Bureau."

His light eyes flashed. "You can tell Cousin Phil to kiss my...!"

"Don't you say it," she warned, "or I'll call Tira and tell on you."

He ground his teeth together. "Oh, all right." He frowned. "That reminds me. What do you want in here, anyway?"

"A raise," she began, counting on one hand. "A computer that doesn't crash every time I load a program. A new scanner, because mine's sluggish. A new filing cabinet, mine's full. And how about one of those cute little robotic dogs? I could teach it to fetch files..."

"Sit down!"

She sat, but she was still grinning. She crossed her legs in the chair across the desk and went over the question she'd been faxed from a rural district attorney, who'd asked for a legal opinion. For Simon's sake, she acted unconcerned that fate might fling her in the path of Marc Brannon for a third time.

BUT WHEN JOSETTE left Simon's office, she was almost shaking. It had to be an easily solvable murder, she told herself firmly. She couldn't be thrown into Brannon's company again not when she was just beginning to get over him. She went through the rest of the day in a daze. There was a nagging apprehension in the back of her mind, as if she knew somehow that the murder in San Antonio was going to affect her life.

Her grandmother, Erin O'Brien, had been Irish, a special woman with an uncanny ability to know things before they happened. The elderly lady would cook extra food and get the guest rooms ready on days when the Langley family dropped in on "surprise" visits. She could anticipate tragedies, like the sudden death of her brother. When Josette's father had stopped by her small home to tell her the bad news, she was wearing a black dress and her Sunday hat, waiting to be driven to the funeral home. It was useless to try to watch murder mysteries with her, because she always knew who the culprit was by the end of the first scene. Erin was Josette's favorite person when she was a child. They shared all sorts of secrets. It had been Erin who told her she would meet a tall man wearing a badge, and her life would be forever entangled with his. When Marc Brannon had rescued her, at the age of fifteen, from a wild party and near-rape, Erin had been waiting at her parents' home when Brannon drove her there in the Jacobsville police car, with her arms open. Marc had been fascinated by the old woman, even that long ago. Erin's death before the family moved to San Antonio had devastated Josette. But, then, so had losing Marc two years ago. Her life had been an endurance test.

That evening, she went home to her tomcat Barnes in her small efficiency apartment and deliberately got out her photo album. She hadn't opened it in two painful years, but now she was hungry for the sight of that tall, elegant, formidable man in her past.

She'd loved Marc Brannon more than her life. They'd come as close to being lovers as any two people ever had without going all the way, but he'd discovered a secret about her that had shattered him. He'd dragged himself out of her arms, cursed her roundly and walked out the door. He'd never looked back. Scant days later, Josette had gone to a party with an acquaintance named Dale Jennings and a wealthy San Antonio man had died there. Josette had accused Marc's best friend, and a candidate for lieutenant governor, of the murder, citing that he was the sole heir of the old man. Brannon had used her past against her in court to clear his friend. They hadn't spoken since.

It had been a fluke, that whole situation. She couldn't really blame Brannon for defending his best friend. But if he'd loved her, he couldn't have walked away that easily. And he wouldn't have treated her like trash, either.

Most people around San Antonio said that Brannon wouldn't know love if it poked him in the eye. It was probably true. He was a loner by nature, and he and his sister, Gretchen, had suffered terrible poverty in childhood. Their mother had died of cancer two years ago, not long after Josette had split up with Marc. Gretchen had been wined and dined and then horribly jilted by an opportunist when he discovered that she inherited little more than debts. Like her, both Brannons had known betrayal.

Barnes purred and rubbed against her arm, diverting her from her sad thoughts. She petted him and held him close. His loud purr vibrated against her skin and gave her comfort, like the weight of his big, furry body. He was a battle-scarred alley cat who'd needed a good meal and a bath. Josette had needed something to come home to after a hard day's work. She'd never been able to walk past anything that was hurt or deserted, so she'd loved Barnes on sight. She'd taken him to the veterinarian for a checkup and shots and then she'd taken him home with her. Now, she couldn't imagine life without him. He filled some of the empty places inside her.

"Hungry?" she asked, and he rubbed harder.

"Okay," she said, sighing as she got to her bare feet and stretched lazily, her slender body twisting with the motion. Her hair was down around her shoulders. It fell like a golden cascade to her hips in back. Brannon had loved her hair like that. She grimaced. She had to stop remembering!

"We'll split a hamburger, Barnes. Then," she added with a wince, "I have to comb through a thousand files and download a dozen pages into the laptop for Simon. After that, I have to write a summary and take it back to Simon so that he can compose an opinion on it. Then I have to fax it to the district attorney." She looked down at Barnes and shook her head. "Oh, for the life of a cat!"

CHAPTER TWO

NOTHING ABOUT A crime scene ever got easier, Marc Brannon thought as he knelt beside the body of the shooting victim. The man was young, probably no more than late twenties, and he was dressed shabbily. One bare arm bore a tattoo of a raven. There were scars on both wrists and ankles, hinting at a stint in prison. There was a pool of blood around his fair hair and his pale eyes were open, staring blankly at the blue sky. He looked vulnerable lying there; helpless and defenseless, with his body wide-open to the stares of evidence-gatherers and curious passersby. Evidence technicians went over the scene like bloodhounds, looking carefully for trace evidence. One of them had a metal detector and had just found a slug which they hoped would be from the murder weapon. Another technician was videotaping the crime scene from every angle.

Brannon's big, lean hand smoothed over the neat khaki of his slacks while his keen, deep-set silver-gray eyes narrowed in thought. Maybe Marsh had nothing to do with this, but it was curious that a dead body would be found so close to his nightclub. No doubt Marsh would have an iron-clad alibi, he thought irritably. He had dozens of cronies who would give him one whenever he needed it.

Deep in thought, Brannon watched the lone medical

examiner investigator work. She was going very slowly and methodically about securing the body. Well, she should. It could turn out to be a very high-profile case, he reminded himself.

The homicide detective for the central substation, Bud Garcia, waved at Brannon before he spoke to the patrol officers who'd apparently found the body. Brannon sighed as he joined the medical examiner investigator beside the body, out of the way of the evidence technicians who were busily garnering trace evidence close to the body. Brannon had an evidence kit himself, but he would have felt superfluous trying to use it with so many people on the case. There were continuous flashes of light as the corpse was photographed as well as videotaped.

"Hi, Jones," he greeted her. "Do we know anything about this guy yet?"

"Sure," she replied, busily bagging the victim's hands. "I know two things about him already."

"Well?" he prompted impatiently, when she hesitated.

"He's male, and he's dead," Alice Jones replied with a wicked grin as she put the last bag in place with a rubber band. Her hair, black and short, was sweaty.

He gave her a speaking glare.

"Sorry," she murmured dryly. "No, we don't have anything, not even a name. He wasn't carrying ID." She stood up. "Care to guess about his circumstances?"

He studied the body. "He's got abrasions on his wrists and ankles. My guess would be that he's an escaped prisoner."

"Not bad, Ranger," she mused. "That would be my

best guess, too. But until we get him autopsied, we're going to have to wait for our answers."

"Can you approximate the time of death?"

She gave him a long, appreciative look. Her eyes twinkled. "You want me to jab a thermometer in his liver right here, huh?"

"God, Jones!" he burst out.

"Okay, okay, if you have to have a time of death, considering the state of rigor, I'd say twenty-four hours, give or take two either side," she murmured, and went back to work. "But don't hold me to it. I'm just an investigator. The medical examiner will have to go over this guy, and he's got bodies backed up in the morgue already. Don't expect quick results."

As if he didn't know that. Evidence processing could take weeks, and frequently did, despite the instant results displayed on television police shows.

He swore under his breath and got to his feet gracefully. It was a hot September day and the silvery metal of his Texas Ranger badge caught the sun and glittered. He took off his Stetson and swept the back of his hand over his sweaty brow. His blond-streaked, thick and wavy hair, was momentarily visible until he stuck the hat back on, slanting it across his eyes.

"Who called you in on this?" the medical examiner investigator asked cursorily as she worked to prepare the body for transit.

"My boss. We're hoping this may be a link to a guy we've been trying to close down for several years without success, considering where the body's located. Naturally my boss sent someone experienced and capable and superior in intelligence to investigate." He looked at her mischievously.

She glanced appreciatively up at her rugged companion, appraising his lean physique and commanding presence. She gave a long, low whistle. "I'm impressed, Brannon!"

"Nothing impresses you, Jones," he drawled.

He turned around and went to look for Bud Garcia, the homicide detective. He found him talking to another plainclothes detective, who had a cell phone and a notepad.

"Well, that sure fits the description," Garcia was agreeing with a satisfied smile. "Right down to the raven tattoo. It's him, all right. What a lucky break! Thank the warden for me."

The other officer nodded and spoke into the cell phone again, moving away.

"Brannon, we've got something," Garcia said when he saw the taller man approaching. "Wayne Correctional Institute down near Floresville is reporting a missing inmate who fits this man's description exactly. He escaped from a work detail early yesterday morning."

"Have you got a name?" he asked.

"Yeah."

"Well?" Brannon pressed.

"It's Jennings. Dale Jennings."

It was a name that Brannon had reason to remember. And now the face that seemed so familiar clicked into place. Jennings, a local hoodlum, had been convicted of murdering a wealthy San Antonio businessman two years before. He was also alleged to have strong ties to Jake Marsh and his underworld. His photograph had been in half the newspapers in the country, not to mention the front page of several tabloids. The trial had been scandalous as well. Josette Langley, the young woman who had been Jennings's date the night of elderly Henry Garner's murder, insinuated publicly that the person who stood to gain the most from the death was Brannon's best friend, who was Bib Webb, now Texas Lieutenant Governor.

But Webb's attorney had convinced the prosecutor that it was Jennings who committed the murder and that Josette's testimony on Jennings's behalf was filled with lies. She had, after all, been proven a liar in a rape trial some years earlier. Her past was what had saved Webb from any charges. Silvia Webb, Bib's wife, had seen old man Henry Garner outside and waved to him just before she left to take Josette home. She also said she'd seen a bloody blackjack on the passenger seat of Jennings's car. Both she and Bib Webb had an alibi for the next few minutes, during which Garner was said to have lost his life on the pier of the private lake at Webb's estate.

When Silvia came back from taking Josette home and saw Garner's car still in the driveway, and empty, and nobody remembered seeing him recently, she called the police to report it. Several guests remembered hearing her make the call, and sounding disturbed. The guests were forbidden to leave the party while they searched for the old man, whom they found floating near the pier, dead. It looked like an accidental drowning, one newscaster said, and it was rumored that the old man had been drinking and walked off the pier, hitting his head on the way down. Still, no one was allowed to leave the scene until the police and the EMTs, along with the coroner, were finished. Witnesses were questioned.

Even so, it just might have passed for an accident. Except that Josette, who heard the breaking story on television later that night, called the police and told them that Garner hadn't been drinking at all, that she hadn't seen him outside when she and Silvia left the party, and that there had been no blackjack in Dale Jennings's car. She knew because she'd ridden in it to the party.

A lump was found on Garner's head when they pulled him out of the water. There was a blackjack lying visible on the passenger seat of Dale Jennings's car. He'd protested wildly when the police took him away.

Josette was positive Bib Webb was involved. Despite the ironclad alibis of Bib Webb and his wife, who stated that Jennings had a motive—an argument the day before with Garner over his salary. It turned out that Garner had been paying Jennings to be his combination handyman and chauffeur. It was alleged that Jennings was helping himself to the old man's possessions as well. They found a very expensive pair of gold cuff links, a diamond tiepin and a lot of cash in his apartment, which added to the sensationalism of the trial. Jake Marsh had been pulled in and questioned repeatedly because of some nebulous work Dale had done for him. But there was no hard evidence and Marsh walked away without a blemish, to the dismay and fury of Bexar County prosecutors and State Attorney General Simon Hart.

Brannon stuck his hands into the pockets of his khaki slacks. They clenched as he recalled Josette's face in another courtroom, years ago, when she was only fifteen and trying to convince a hostile jury that she'd been drugged and nearly raped by the son of a wealthy Jacobsville resident. Josette's life had been a hard one. But it wounded him that she could have accused Bib Webb, his best friend, of something as heinous as murdering a helpless old man for money. It was so obvious that Jennings had done it. He even had the murder weapon in his car, blatantly in sight on the front passenger seat, still bearing minute traces of blood and tissue, and hair, from poor old Garner's head. The medical examiner positively identified the blackjack as the weapon used to stun the old man before he was pushed into the water.

"You know the Langley woman, who works in Simon Hart's office, don't you?" Garcia asked suddenly, dragging Brannon back to the present. The two men had known each other since Garcia was a patrolman and Brannon a fledgling Texas Ranger.

Brannon nodded curtly. "We both come from Jacobsville. Josette and her mother and father moved to San Antonio some years ago. I heard that her parents were dead. I haven't seen her in two years, not since she moved to Austin," he added, reminded unwillingly that he'd broken off their relationship the week before Garner had died.

"No reason to, I imagine," the officer said carelessly.

Brannon's eyes went back to the body on the ground. "This does look like a professional hit," Brannon said out of the blue, studying Dale Jennings's body, with his hands bagged and his white, still face vanishing under the zip of the dark body bag. "One downward-angled gunshot to the back of the head at point-blank range. His knees were covered in red mud, just like this." He moved the dirt caked on the pavement with the toe of his boot. "He was probably kneeling at the time."

"That was my first thought, too. And it's a pretty big coincidence that Marsh's nightclub is only two doors that way," the detective agreed, nodding toward the street that fronted the alley.

"If Marsh is involved here, I'll find a way to prove it," Brannon said bitingly. "He's walked away from murder and attempted murder, drug-dealing, prostitution and illegal betting on sports for years. It's time we made him pay for the misery he's caused."

"I'll drink to that. But we can't just walk in and arrest him without probable cause. Not that I don't wish I could," Garcia confessed ruefully.

"Well, there's no time like the present to get started. I'm only in the way here as it is. I'll go back to my office and fill Simon Hart in on what we know." He pursed his lips. "He's going to be madder than a teased rattlesnake."

Garcia chuckled. "That he is." He looked toward the body. "Did the guy have any family?"

"A mother, I think. Did they find the slug?"

"They found a slug. Ballistics will have to tell us if it's the right one. I'd bet on a nine-millimeter handgun myself, but that's why we have the Bexar County Forensic Science Center."

"And the department of public safety's own lab," Brannon felt obliged to mention.

"Which is a very good one," Garcia agreed, smiling. "Say, wasn't Jennings convicted of murder a couple of years ago?" he added suddenly.

"Yes. In a trial that almost implicated our brand-new lieutenant governor, too," Brannon told him. "It almost cost him the election. Both contenders were first-time state office seekers. But the other guy dropped out a week before the election, and Bib won. He's a good man."

"Yes. So he is."

"I had a nice, easy month all planned," Brannon sighed. "Now here I am up to my armpits in a dead body and a two-year-old murder case that the press will resurrect and use to embarrass Bib Webb. It couldn't be worse timing. He's just won his party's nomination for that senate seat that the incumbent resigned from because of a heart attack. The publicity could kill Bib's chances."

"Life, they say, is what happens when you have other plans," Garcia said with a grim smile.

"Amen," Brannon agreed heavily.

He went back to his office and phoned Simon Hart with the news. An hour later, he was on a plane to Austin.

SIMON HART LISTENED to Brannon's report in his spacious office in Austin. He'd requested the Ranger's help on the case as soon as he knew who the victim was. Brannon had a good track record with homicides and the Texas Ranger post in San Antonio was where he was stationed, anyway. Brannon had legal authority to investigate in multiple jurisdictions, and that complication existed. Jennings was killed in Bexar County, but he'd been in a correctional facility in Wilson County. Simon was certain that the murder was going to make national headlines. There was a sad lack of sensational news lately and the media had to fill those twenty-four-hour news channels with something. Sure enough, the murder had led the noon news on local channels. The body was barely in the morgue before the wire services and national television broadcast the story that the victim was tied to a murder case two years ago in Austin,

Texas, that had involved the state's lieutenant governor,
Bib Webb. God knew, the media loved political scandal. But with luck, they just might get Jake Marsh for
murder at last.

Simon had asked Brannon to fly to Austin and fill
him in on the preliminaries. "I had Bib Webb on the
line early this morning," Simon told Brannon while he
sipped coffee. "Not only is he running for the U.S. Senate, but his construction company is involved in a major
project outside San Antonio, a prototype agricultural
complex with self-contained irrigation and warehous-
ing. He's invested millions of his own money in an effort to help the drought-ridden ranchers. This case is
already affecting him, and this is a bad time. Wally's
worried," he added, mentioning the governor, who was
a close friend. "Campaigning is seriously underway for
the November election. Wally's been stumping for Bib."

"Yes, I know. I had lunch with Bib last week." His
gray eyes narrowed. "Could this rehash of the case be
engineered to hurt him in the polls?"

"Of course it could," Simon said with a grin. "You
know how dirty politics is. But I don't think sane people commit murder to cause a scandal."

"There are a lot of insane people running loose in
the world," Brannon reminded him amusedly.

Simon shifted, moving the prosthesis he wore in
place of his left arm onto the desk while he lifted his
coffee cup with the right. He and Brannon were dis-
tantly related, both with ties in Jacobsville. Simon's
four brothers lived there. Brannon had grown up there,
and he still had a ranch in Jacobsville where his sister,
Gretchen, had lived until her marriage to the ruling
Sheikh of Qawi in the Middle East. She and the sheikh

had a son now, and they were becoming well-known in international circles.

"Have you heard from your sister, Gretchen, lately?"

Brannon nodded. "She phones me every month to make sure I'm eating properly. She doesn't think much of my cooking," he added with a fond smile at the thought of his baby sister.

"Does she miss Texas?" Simon asked.

"Not visibly. She's too crazy about her little boy and Philippe," he murmured, naming her husband. "I have to admit, he's unique."

"Why did you leave the FBI?" Simon asked abruptly, something that had bothered him lately.

"I got tired of living out of a suitcase," Brannon said evasively. "Two years was enough."

"I never could understand why you left the Rangers to begin with," Simon replied, sipping black coffee. "You had seniority, you were in line for promotion. You tossed all that to go haring off to Washington. And then you only stayed there for two years."

Brannon averted his eyes. "It seemed like a good idea at the time."

"And it didn't have anything to do with the Jennings murder trial or Josette Langley?"

Brannon's jaw clenched so hard that his teeth ached. "Nothing."

"You work out of San Antonio, and she works here in Austin." Simon persisted. "Under ordinary circumstances, you won't have to see her, if you don't want to. At least, not after she investigates this murder for me."

The odd wording of the remark went right by him. "I'll do my job, regardless of the people I have to do it with," Brannon said finally, and his pale eyes dared his cousin to pursue the conversation.

"Okay, I give up. But you'd better know that I'm sending Josette to San Antonio tomorrow."

Brannon's eyes glittered. "What?"

"She's the only freelance investigator I have who's cognizant of all the facts. Wayne Correctional Institute is near there, where Jennings was located before he managed to get released…"

"She was involved in the case!" Brannon burst out, rising to his feet. "Two years ago, she did her best to get Bib arrested for old Garner's murder!"

"Sit down." Simon stared at him with steady, cold silver eyes.

Brannon sat, but angrily.

"There are other people who maintain to this day that Jennings was nothing more than the fall guy in that murder," Simon told Brannon. He held up a hand when Brannon started to speak. "Jennings and Josette had been invited to a party on Garner Lake with Bib Webb and Silvia and Henry Garner the night Garner died. Jennings was a nobody, but he had ties to the local San Antonio mob headed by Jake Marsh, and he'd threatened Garner over money. Recreational drugs were ingested at the party, the punch was spiked—even Bib admitted that, and I know Webb's your friend. It might have passed off as a simple drowning except for Josette's accusations and the knot on Garner's head that was first thought to have occurred when he fell. Josette was the one who insisted that Garner hadn't been drinking and didn't accidentally fall off the pier."

"She accused Bib because she didn't like him or his

wife," Brannon insisted. "She was angry at me, to boot. Accusing Bib was one way of getting back at me."

"Marc," Simon said quietly, "you know what sort of upbringing she had. Her father was the youth minister of their church and her mother taught Sunday school. They were devout. She was raised strictly. She doesn't tell lies."

"Plenty of girls go wild when they get away from home," Brannon pointed out stubbornly. "And I'll remind you that she slipped out of her house to go to that wild party when she was fifteen, and accused a boy of trying to rape her. The emergency room physician testified that there was no rape," he added, and was visibly uncomfortable talking about it. "She was almost completely intact."

"Yes, I know," Simon said with a sigh. "Presumably her assailant was too drunk to force her." He glanced at Brannon, whose face was strained. "We have to solve this murder as quickly and efficiently as possible, for Webb's own sake."

"Bib is a good man with a bright political future ahead of him," Brannon said, relieved at the change of subject. "He's already ahead in the polls in the senate race, and it's just September."

"You mean, Silvia has a bright political future ahead," Simon murmured dryly. "She tells him what to wear and how to stand, for God's sake. She's the real power behind his success and you know it. Amazing insight, for a woman so young, with no real education."

Brannon shrugged. "Bib's not a self-starter," he admitted. "Silvia's been his guardian angel from the beginning."

"I suppose so, even if he did rob the cradle when he

married her." He leaned back. "As I said earlier, I want this case solved quickly," he added. "We've already been in the public eye too often because we have a Texan in the White House. We don't need to be the focus of any more media investigations of our justice system."

"I agree. I'll do what I can."

"You'll work with Josette," Simon added firmly. "Whether or not you have to grit your teeth. You both know this case inside out. You can solve it." *If you don't kill each other first,* Simon thought.

BRANNON WAITED FOR the elevator in the hall, leaning against the wall to observe a silk plant. There was a fine film of dust on it, and one petal was missing from the artificial rose. He wondered why the artificial flowers and plants in government office buildings never seemed to get dusted.

The sound of the elevator arriving diverted his attention. He straightened up just as the doors slid open to admit a single occupant to the floor.

Big dark brown eyes met his and went even darker with accusation and resentment in an oval face that had not even a touch of makeup. Her long blond hair was in a tight braided bun atop her head. She wore no jewelry except for a simple silver-and-turquoise cross suspended from a silver chain. Her shoes were gray, to match the neat, if outdated, suit she wore with a simple pink blouse. She was only twenty-four, but there were lines in that ordinary face, visible even through the big, gold-framed glasses she wore. His heart ached just at the sight of her.

Her full mouth parted on a shocked breath, as if she hadn't expected to see him. Certainly he'd hoped to get out of the building without running into her. Her gaze dropped to the badge on his shirt pocket.

"I heard you were back working for the Rangers, in San Antonio," Josette Langley said. Her face lifted as if with some effort and he noticed that her slender hands were clenched on the stack of files she was carrying. They were working hands; her short fingernails showed no polish, no professional manicure.

He shoved his hands into his pockets and clenched them as he looked down at her. She was only medium height. Her head came up to his nose. He remembered her dark eyes twinkling, her full lips parted and gasping with joy as they danced together at one of her college parties so long ago. He remembered the softness of her eyes when she smiled at him, the feel of her sweet, bare body warm and close in his arms, the innocence of her mouth when he kissed it for the first time, the feverish response of her body to his ardent caresses…

"Simon says he's assigned you to this case," he said curtly, refusing to permit his mind to look back in time.

She nodded. "That's right. I usually do liaison work, but I know more about Dale Jennings than most of the other investigators."

"Of course you do," he drawled with venomous sarcasm.

"Here we go again," she said with resignation. "Well, don't stand on ceremony, Brannon, get it off your chest. I tell lies, I damage careers…maybe I cause computer crashes, but the jury's still out on that one."

He felt disoriented. He'd expected her to bite her lip and look tormented, as she had two years ago when he'd glared at her in court during Jennings's trial. He reminded himself that she should be tormented. She'd led him on without a qualm, when she knew she couldn't be intimate with a man. And her public accusations could have landed Bib Webb in jail. But this was a different Josette, a strong and cool woman who didn't back down.

"I'll need whatever information you have on Jennings," he said abruptly.

"No problem. I'll send it to the San Antonio office by overnight delivery before I leave the office today," she said. She indicated the stack of files. "In fact, I've just been downstairs copying the information so that I could do that." She smiled with forced pleasantry. "Unless you'd rather lug it back on the plane?"

"I wouldn't. How very efficient you've become, Miss Langley."

"Haven't I, though?" she replied pertly. "Look out, Brannon. One of these days I may be state attorney general myself, and wouldn't that tie a knot in your ego? Now, if you'll excuse me?"

Josette turned and started to walk away. The elevator had departed while they were talking. It was on the tenth floor. He pushed the down button viciously.

"Did Jennings have any family?" he asked abruptly.

She turned to look at him. "He has a mother who's a semi-invalid. She's on disability and she has a bad heart. Just recently she lost her home because of some scam she fell for. She was supposed to be evicted this week." Her dark eyes narrowed. "Her husband is long dead and she has no other children. She and Dale were very close. It goes without saying that her son served two years in prison for a crime he never committed while the real culprit escaped justice and inherited the fortune he needed to finance a senate campaign…!"

"Not another word," Brannon said in a soft, deep tone that made chills run down her spine.

"Or else what?" Josette challenged with uplifted eyebrows and a cool smile. When he didn't reply, she shrugged. "I hope someone had the decency to inform Mrs. Jennings of her son's death. Just so that she won't have to find out on the six o'clock news with footage of the coroner's office carrying him off in a body bag."

Brannon's heart jumped. He hadn't asked if anyone was going to call Jennings's next of kin. Damn it, he should have been more efficient. Whatever Jennings had done, his mother wasn't a criminal.

"I'll make sure of it," he said abruptly.

Her eyes softened, just a little, as she matched the memory of that lean, formidable face against the man she'd first known so many years ago. It made her sad to realize what his opinion of her must have been, even at the beginning. He wouldn't have walked off without a goodbye if there had been any feeling in him for her. He'd hated her the night they'd broken up. He'd hated her more when she accused his friend Webb of being behind Garner's murder. Probably he still hated her. She didn't care.

"Thanks," she said and turned away.

"Have you come across any clue in those files that would point to a potential execution?" he asked deliberately.

Josette came back to face him at once. "You think somebody put out a contract on him," she said confidently, her voice deliberately lowered.

Brannon nodded. "It was a professional job, not some drive-by shooting or a gang-related conflict. He was on work detail and escaped, apparently with help from some unknown accomplice, made his way to San Antonio, and ended up with a single gunshot wound to the back of the head at point-blank range, just around the corner from our most notorious mobster's nightclub."

"But what would be the motive?" she asked curiously. "He was in prison, out of the way. Why would somebody break him out just to kill him? They could have done that at the prison."

"I don't know," he had to admit. "That's what I have to find out."

"Poor Dale," she said heavily. "And his poor mother…!"

"What's in those files?" he asked, deliberately changing the subject.

"Background checks on all the people who called and wrote to him before his escape, and dossiers on mob figures he was rumored to be connected with," she said. "We'll speak to these people, of course, and the police are going to canvas the area where he was found to see if they can turn up any witnesses."

"Which they won't find, if it was professional."

"I know."

"Why did you choose law enforcement for a career?" he asked unexpectedly.

Her dark eyes narrowed on his face. "Because there are so many innocent people convicted of crimes," Josette said deliberately. "And so many guilty people go free."

Brannon stiffened at the innuendo. "Jennings was a mobster and he had a record," he reminded her.

"He had a felony battery conviction, and first offender status," she corrected. "He was just a teenager at the time. He got drunk, got into a fight and got ar-

rested. He didn't even go to jail. After a year's probation, he was turned loose. But that, and his connection
with Jake Marsh, went against him when he was arrested for Garner's murder."

"He was cold sober when Garner drowned," he countered. "They did a breath-analyzer test on him and it
registered zilch. Jennings had opportunity and the
means—Garner was elderly and couldn't swim. Being
knocked over the head and pushed in the lake in that
condition would have been instantly fatal, especially
where he went off the pier. It's twenty-feet deep there."

"Where's the motive?" she persisted.

"Garner owed him money, he said, and he couldn't
get his check," Brannon replied with a cold smile. "Garner had fired him, and they'd already had one argument. They may have argued on the pier. Your memory
of the events was questioned. You were drunk, I believe?" he chided.

Josette was still ashamed to admit that she'd been
stupid enough to drink spiked punch. Not being used
to hard liquor, the vodka had made her disoriented and
weak. When she was fifteen, she'd unknowingly been
given LSD in her soft drink and almost ended up raped.
These days she never took a drink unless she was completely confident of where it had come from. "I wasn't
totally sober," she admitted in a guilt-ridden tone. "But,
then, neither were most of the people at that party. Silvia said she saw Mr. Garner at his car before she took
me home and even waved at him. I didn't see that. She
said it was because I was drunk."

"You didn't say that at the trial," he reminded her.

"I didn't have time to say much at the trial," she replied. "I was immediately subpoenaed as a prosecution

witness because I hadn't seen Dale or Mrs. Webb at the time Garner was allegedly murdered, which was before she took me home, not after! And I didn't see Henry Garner at his car as we left. I tried to point out that Dale hadn't had a blackjack in his car when we arrived. But the prosecuting attorney took me apart, with your helpful suggestions about bringing up my testimony at the rape trial when I was fifteen," she added pointedly and saw his eyelids flinch. "He destroyed me on the witness stand. I heard later that you and Bib Webb told him about the rape trial. I thought you wanted to help me." She managed a bitter smile. "You taught me how to dance. You were friends with my father. When I went to college in San Antonio, you were always around. We went out for months together, before Mr. Garner… died." She drew in a long breath. It hurt to remember how Marc had been with her. She'd thought they were in love. She certainly had been. What a joke! "But none of that mattered, did it? You believed that I lied to implicate Bib Webb. You never doubted it."

"Bib Webb is one of the most decent human beings I know," Brannon said icily, refusing to face a truth that he knew for certain now about her credibility.

"Even decent people can get into a circumstance where they'll do something crazy. Especially if they're desperate, or drunk. You of all people should know that people on drugs or alcohol frequently forget everything that happened until they sober up," she added, pleading her case fervently. It was the first time he'd really spoken to her alone about what happened. He seemed to be listening, too, even if he didn't believe a word she said.

"Silvia wasn't drunk enough to forget what she saw," he told her. "She'd only had one drink. And she said she saw Garner by his car when she left the party to take you home."

"That's right. She *said* she saw him there."

"What's the difference?" he asked, out of patience. "You won't change my mind."

"I know that," Josette agreed finally. "I don't know why I try." She added, "I'll overnight the information in these files to your San Antonio office before I leave today, so neither of us will have to lug it to San Antonio." She turned away. "If you have any questions, I'll be here tomorrow morning and in San Antonio tomorrow night, at the Madison Hotel. You can reach me there."

He was still stinging from the encounter. "If I have any questions, you're the last person I'd ask," he said coolly. "I wouldn't trust you as far as the street."

"That never changes, does it?" She laughed. "But your low opinion of me doesn't affect anything anymore. Basically," she added with a pointed glance, "I don't give a damn what you think of me. Go stick that in your pipe and smoke it, Brannon."

Josette walked down the hall and he watched her go, infuriated that she wouldn't admit the truth. Maybe her pride wouldn't let her. He thought about her father, who was disgraced because of her rape trial, and her mother's fatal stroke after the Jennings trial. He felt sorry for her parents, but there had been nothing he could do for them. He thought of their last date, and her ardent response until he was out of his head with desire, until he found her so intact that he had to stop. He'd really hated her for that, although the time that passed had made it harder to believe that she'd set him up. She'd been as involved as he was. Maybe even more. But no matter how hard he worked at it, he simply couldn't forget that she'd tried to have his best friend arrested for Henry Garner's murder. He turned back to the elevator and reluctantly pressed the down button again. He didn't like leaving with unanswered questions between them. He wanted... He sighed. Maybe he just wanted to sit and look at her for a while. The sight of her opened old wounds, but it also made a warm place in his heart.

He turned from the elevator and went back down the hall.

CHAPTER THREE

SIMON HART STUDIED Josette quietly as she walked into his office and put the file folders down on his desk. She explained the information she'd gathered for the investigation.

"I know this may be painful for you," he told her quietly. "Since you were dating Jennings two years ago."

"We were friends, that's all," she assured him. "I'm sorry he was killed, and in such a way. I never thought he murdered Henry Garner in the first place."

"You paid a high price trying to defend him," Simon said solemnly.

"Yes, but I'd do it again. He was innocent. Someone framed him. The only thing that puzzles me is why he didn't try harder to fight the conviction. It was as if he just gave up the minute he got in the courtroom," she recalled pensively.

"Did you see Marc Brannon on your way in here?" he said abruptly.

Her heart jumped. "I saw him." She forced herself to smile carelessly. "He still can't believe that his best friend, Bib Webb, would be involved in anything underhanded. That was what put us on opposite sides of Dale's trial. Marc's loyal, I'll give him that."

"Too loyal. He can't be objective."

"It doesn't matter. Everyone who could be hurt al-

ready has been," she said philosophically. "Now there's
a new murder to solve."

He motioned her into a chair. "I want to know what
you think."

She leaned back in the chair and crossed her legs,
frowning thoughtfully. She was still shaken by Marc's
unexpected appearance, but her mind was sharp and
she focused on the matter at hand. "According to my
research, Dale Jennings has a mother, a widow. She's
practically an invalid. Just recently she fell for some
sort of financial scam. She lost her life savings and
her home. She was going to be evicted this week. Dale
knew. I can't help but think his murder has something
to do with that. Maybe he was trying to get money for
her in some way."

"You think he was blackmailing somebody, and his
victim hired a killer to stop him?"

Josette nodded slowly. "It's conjecture, of course.
But what if he had information that would hurt somebody? Bib Webb, for example. And what if he demanded
money for his silence? Webb stands to lose everything
if he's involved in another scandal. Nobody would believe that he was an innocent bystander if he was connected with a second murder. Besides, he's ahead in the
polls in the senate race. Being proven guilty of murder
would sure sour his chances of election."

"He's the lieutenant governor, and a successful businessman," Simon reminded her.

"Only successful because his partner, Garner, died,"
she reminded him right back.

"Yes, and Garner was a widower with no children.
Webb was named sole beneficiary."

"He inherited those millions and used his inheritance to buy into a successful agricultural concern and the balance went into the coffers for his political campaign. He won the lieutenant governor race two years ago, although a lot of people said he won it by default, by having his staff dig up dirt on his opponent and forcing him out of the race with it."

"That was never proved," Simon reminded her.

"I know. But Jake Marsh's name was mentioned, and not only in connection with Dale. Now, Webb is well on his way to the nomination for the United States Senate. He's a rising star."

"There's one little hole in your theory, Josette. Murderers don't usually stop at one murder, unless they're crimes of passion," Simon remarked, thinking out loud.

"Nobody stood in Webb's way until now. If Dale Jennings had something on him, some sort of proof, what would a man in Webb's position do?"

"First, he'd make sure proof existed."

"I don't know how there could have been any tangible proof since nobody saw Mr. Garner's murder. The only real evidence was the blackjack they found in the passenger seat of Dale's car. I never saw it, but he didn't deny that it was his. He never pointed his finger at anybody else. I don't see what could have spooked anybody into killing him. No, if there was blackmail, there had to be something else, something that would prove Webb guilty of something besides Garner's death. But the burden of proof will be on us. Otherwise Dale's death will be another senseless, unsolved homicide."

"Okay. Take the ball and run with it. But you have to work with Brannon." He held up a hand when she started to protest. "I know, he's a pain in the neck and he's prejudiced against you. But he'll balance your prejudice against Webb. Besides, he's one of the best investigators I've ever known. I got involved in this to put Jake Marsh away. That's still my primary goal. I think he's involved. If he is, the investigation is going to get dangerous. Brannon," he mused, "is good protection. He's a master quick-draw artist, and he can even out-shoot my brother Rey."

"Rey won medals in national skeet-shooting competition," Josette recalled.

"He's still winning them, national and international ones, too, these days." He stood up. "Keep this conversation to yourself," he added sternly. "The governor and Webb are good friends. Webb has powerful allies. I don't want to get anyone in San Antonio in trouble. We're investigating a murder that we hope we can link to a notorious mobster who's probably paid off a lot of people. Period."

"I'll be discreet."

"I hope you and Brannon and the San Antonio CID can turn up something on Marsh. And the sooner the better," Simon added with a wry smile. "Because I'll go loopy if Phil Douglas has to take over your job as well as his own."

"Phil's a nice boy, and a good cybercrime investigator," she defended her colleague.

"He's a computer expert with a superhero complex. He'll drive me batty."

"You're the attorney general," Josette reminded him. "Send him on a fact-finding trip."

"There's a thought. I've always wanted to know what the police department's computer system looks like in Mala Suerte."

"Mala Suerte is a border town with a population of

sixteen, most of whom don't speak English. Phil isn't bilingual," she pointed out.

Simon smiled.

Josette held up a hand. "I'm history. I'll report in regularly, to keep you posted."

"You do that."

She nodded, picked up her files and left.

But once she was outside in the hall, the pleasant expression left her face and she felt as if her knees wouldn't even support her. Running into Marc unexpectedly like that had shattered her. It had been two years since she'd set eyes on him, since the trial that had made him her worst enemy. She felt drained from the conflict. She only wanted to go home, kick off her shoes, and curl up on the sofa and watch a good black-and-white movie with her cat, Barnes. But she'd have to pack instead. Tomorrow, she had to go back to San Antonio and face not only a murder investigation, but the pain of her own past.

Josette walked back into her office and stopped dead. Marc Brannon was still around and he was now occupying her desk chair. His Stetson was sitting on one of the chairs in front of her desk. Marc was sitting behind her desk, in her swivel chair, with his size thirteen highly polished brown boots propped insolently on her desk. Her heart jumped up into her throat for the second time in less than an hour. Despite the years in between, she still reacted to his presence like a starstruck fan. It made her angry that she had so little resistance to a man who'd helped ruin her life. His angry words from two years ago still blistered her pride, in memory.

"I thought you left," she said shortly. "And I don't remember inviting you into my office," she added, slamming the door behind her.

"I didn't think I needed an invitation. We're partners," Brannon drawled, watching her with those glittery gray eyes that didn't even seem to blink.

"Not my idea," she replied promptly. She put the files down beside his boots and stood staring at him. He didn't look a day older than he had when she'd first met him. But he was. There were silver threads just visible at his temples where his thick blond-streaked brown hair waved just a little over his jutting brow. His long legs were muscular. She knew how fast he could run, because she'd seen him chase down horses. She'd seen him ride them, too. He was a champion bronc buster.

"You think Bib Webb hired a hit man to kill Jennings," he said at once.

"I think somebody did," Josette corrected. "I don't rush to judgment."

"Insinuating that I do?" he asked with an arrogant slide of his eyes down her body. He frowned suddenly as it occurred to him that she was dressed like an aging spinster. Every inch of her was covered. The blouse had a high collar and the jacket was loose enough to barely hint at the curves beneath it. The skirt was slightly flared at the hips, so that it didn't pull tight when she walked. Her hair was in a tight bun, despite the faint wisps of blond curls that tumbled down over her exquisite complexion. She wasn't even wearing makeup, unless he missed his guess. Her lips, he recalled, were naturally pink, like the unblemished skin over her high cheekbones.

"No need to check out my assets. I haven't gone on sale," she pointed out.

Brannon raised both thick eyebrows. That sounded like banked-down humor, but her face was deadpan.

Josette moved closer to the desk. "I've just explained my theory to Simon."

"Would you care to share it with me?" he invited.

"Sure," she said. "The minute you get your dirty boots off my desk and behave with some semblance of professional respect." She didn't smile as she said it, either.

Brannon pursed his lips, laughed softly and threw his feet to the floor. He'd only done it to get a rise out of her.

He got up and offered her the swivel chair with a flourish. He sank down gracefully into the chair next to the one his hat was resting on and crossed his long legs.

She sat down in her own chair with a long sigh. It had been a hard day and she only wanted to go home. Fat chance of that happening now, she thought.

"Anytime," he invited.

"Dale Jennings's mother was in serious trouble," Josette said without preamble. "She's sick and living on a small disability check. She's only in her mid-fifties, not old enough to draw other benefits." She leaned back in the chair, frowning as she considered the evidence. "She'd lost her small savings by listening to a fast-talking scam artist who convinced her that he was with a federal agency and she had to turn over her savings account to him in repayment for back taxes she owed."

"Of all the damned outrages," he said, angered in spite of himself.

That comment moved her. Brannon, despite his rough edges, was compassionate for the weaker or less fortunate. She'd seen him go out of his way to help street people, even to help young men he'd arrested himself.

She had to force her eyes away from the powerful, lean contours of his body. She was still fighting a hopeless attraction to him.

"By the time she found out that no federal agency was asking for her savings," Josette continued, "it was too late. Some people believe anything they're told, even from people who don't prove their credentials. She didn't even ask for any identification, I understand."

He grimaced. "Did she own her home?"

"She was barely a year away from paying it off. When she couldn't make the next two payments, the bank foreclosed. She's staying at a homeless shelter temporarily." She studied him. "Now put yourself in Dale's shoes," she said unexpectedly, "and think how you'd feel if you were in prison and you couldn't do anything to help her."

Brannon remembered his own frail, little mother, who'd died an invalid. His thin lips made a straight line across his formidable face.

Josette nodded, realizing that he understood. She remembered his mother, too. "I'm not pointing fingers at anybody right now," she said before he spoke. "I'm telling you that, first, somebody helped him escape prison detail. Second, somebody had proof or was keeping proof hidden of a crime that involved a person of means. Dale must have thought his chances of blackmailing the guilty party were pretty good. That doesn't explain what he hoped to do on the outside. But he was killed, and in a very efficient manner. Whoever killed him had to know that he'd escaped from that work detail, and exactly where they could find him. I'm assuming that the person who had him killed was satisfied that he had concrete proof of something illegal, and that Dale was helped to escape so that he could present whatever proof he had and be dealt with efficiently."

"Any prison has inmates who'll kill for a price, guards and wardens notwithstanding," he reminded her. "They didn't have to get him out of prison to have him killed."

"True, but maybe he was lured out to present his proof in person, to make sure that he really had it." Josette leaned forward and clasped her hands on the desk. "Then, what if they thought he had the proof on him, and he didn't?"

"We don't know that. We didn't find anything on the body, no ID of any sort, not even a pocketknife. If it hadn't been for the information about the Wayne escapee fitting Jennings's description exactly, and that raven tattoo on his arm to clinch it, we might have spent weeks trying to identify the body."

She nodded. "So either the perpetrator took the evidence with him, or he didn't get it and there's still somebody out there, who was helping Jennings," she emphasized, "and who now has the evidence and may still use it. Money is a powerful motive for murder. What if Marsh had him killed, for some reason?"

Brannon frowned. "He's had people killed before. There could be a hit man on the loose, and whoever he's working for may dig deep enough to find Jennings's source."

"That means we have another potential murder waiting to happen unless we solve the crime in time," she agreed.

He studied her quietly. "You've learned a lot in the past few years."

"Simon taught me," she said simply. "He started out

as an investigator while he was in law school. He's very good."

"You haven't said anything about Bib Webb," Brannon said.

"I said I don't have a potential perpetrator," she replied quietly. "And that's true. I'm approaching the case with a completely open mind. But there's a lot of investigative work to do. I'll give my information to the local district attorney's office in San Antonio, and we can do interviews with the most prominent people in the case. But I want to talk to Dale's mother in San Antonio, the evidence technicians and police in San Antonio, and the prison warden at the Wayne Correctional Institute near Floresville. And to any cell mates Dale may have had or anyone who corresponded with him. Especially somebody who knows computers."

He watched her, brooding, with one eye narrowed. "Why do you dress like a woman out of the fifties?" he asked unexpectedly.

"I dress like a professional on the state attorney general's staff," Josette said, refusing to be baited.

"What's your next move?" she asked.

"I'm going to see Mrs. Jennings, and then I'm going to try to get a line on the hit man."

Josette raised an eyebrow. "Have a good relationship with Jake Marsh and his local stable of bad boys, do you?" she drawled in a good imitation of his own sarcastic tone.

Brannon stood up. "I have informants, which is probably about the same thing."

"Did anybody question Marsh about the body being found near his nightclub?" she asked.

"The very day we found the body. He's out of town.

But his assistant manager seemed shocked!" He said that with a disbelieving expression. He studied her quietly. An impulse had brought him back into her office, when he'd meant to go straight to the airport. Two years, and she still haunted him. Did she hate him? Gretchen said she didn't. But Josette had learned to hide her feelings very well. He'd thought to surprise her into a reaction. The one he got wasn't what he was expecting. Or the one he was hoping for.

Brannon watched her rise from her chair with that same easy grace he'd admired so much when she was still in her teens. She wasn't pretty, not in a conventional way, but she had a sharp intelligence and a sweet nature.... Sweet nature. Sure she did. He recalled the vicious things she'd sworn to about Bib and his expression closed up.

Josette came around the desk and right up to him, unafraid. "I'm not prejudging. That means you can't, either," she said deliberately. "I know what that—" she indicated his Ranger badge "—means to you. My job means just as much to me. If we're going to work together, we have to start now. No acid comments about the past. We're solving a murder, not rehashing an incident that was concluded two years ago. What's over is over. Period."

His gray eyes narrowed so that they were hidden under his jutting brow and the cream-colored Stetson he slanted at an angle over them. Until he'd seen her again, he hadn't realized how lonely his life had been for the past two years. He'd made a mess of things. In fact, he was still doing it. She held grudges, too, and he couldn't blame her.

"All right," Brannon said finally.

She nodded. "I'll keep you posted about anything I find, if you'll return the courtesy."

"Courtesy." He turned the word over on his tongue. "There's a new concept."

"For you, certainly," Josette agreed with an unexpected twinkle in her eyes. "I understand the Secret Service tried to arrest you when your sister came home to your ranch in Jacobsville the last time, and they threatened to charge you with obstruction of justice for assaulting two of them in the yard."

He straightened. "A simple misunderstanding," he pointed out. "I merely had to mention that I was related to the state attorney general to clear it all up."

That sounded like the dry humor she'd loved in him so many years ago. "Simon uses his new cousin-in-law, the Sheikh of Qawi, to threaten people."

He leaned down. "So do I," he confided with a grin.

That grin was so like the old Brannon, the one she'd loved with all her heart. She let the smile she'd been suppressing come out. It changed her face, made it radiant. His breath caught at the warmth of that smile.

"If I run into any uncooperative officials, I'll use it myself. He's my cousin-in-law, too," Josette recalled.

Brannon cocked his head and smiled quizzically. "I forget that we're related."

"By an old marriage way back in our family tree," she agreed. "And it's a very thin connection with no blood ties." She turned away and walked ahead of him to her office door. "I'll make arrangements to see Mrs. Jennings day after tomorrow."

He gave her a long scrutiny, remembering her at fifteen, shivering in a blanket—at twenty-two, passionate and breathless in his arms. Then he remembered what he'd said to her, afterward. He hated his memories.

She glanced at him and saw the resentment and bitterness on his face. "I don't like you, either, Brannon, in case you wondered," she drawled.

He shrugged. "Doesn't bother me," he lied.

"Not much does."

He nodded curtly, closed the door behind him and she stood in the middle of the room listening to his footsteps die away down the hall. She hadn't realized until then that her heart was doing a rhumba in her chest. She moved back to her desk and stared blankly at the stack of file folders. When her heart threatened to break, there was always work waiting to divert her attention. At least, there was that.

THAT EVENING, she curled up with her cat, Barnes, on the sofa and tried to get interested in a popular detective show, but her mind wouldn't cooperate. She stroked the big cat's fur lazily while he nestled against her and purred. She'd have to board him at the vet's while she was in San Antonio. She didn't like the idea, but she didn't have anyone she could ask to keep him for her.

As she stared blankly at the screen, she remembered the fateful party that had cost Dale Jennings his freedom.

She'd met Dale at a coffee shop around the corner from the college she'd attended. Dale drove a fancy late-model sports car, and he was personable and charming. He also knew Bib Webb, and was helping him with his campaign for the lieutenant governor's race in his home district, which was San Antonio. Webb was in partnership with Henry Garner, a wealthy local man who'd made a fortune selling farm equipment. Webb and his wife, Silvia, shared a palatial mansion on a private lake with Henry Garner in San Antonio, in fact. Garner was a lonely old man and welcomed the companionship of Webb and his wife.

A number of influential voters and members of high society were invited to the Garner home for a party on the lake two months before the election. Dale, who was keeping Josette company since Marc had quit the Rangers and left town, invited her to attend the party with him.

It didn't occur to her at first that it was odd for someone like Dale, with rough edges and only a high school education, to be invited to a high-society party. In fact, she asked him bluntly how he'd been invited. He'd laughed and told her that he was old Henry's chauffeur and bodyguard, and he'd been invited by nobody less than Silvia Webb to the party. Henry wouldn't mind. Silvia didn't care if he brought a friend, either. Josette had a passing acquaintance with Silvia Webb, whom she saw infrequently at the same coffee shop where she'd met Dale. There was a tall, shady-looking man who came there to meet Dale occasionally, too. She'd never known his name.

Josette was grateful for an opportunity to go to the party, expecting that Brannon would be there, and she could parade in front of him with Dale. It would have helped her shattered ego, because Brannon had dropped her flat after their last, tempestuous date. But when she and Dale arrived at the palatial lake house, Brannon hadn't been there.

Silvia Webb's reaction to Dale's date had been less than flattering. Her beautiful face had undergone a flurry of emotions, from amusement to calculation and then to polite formality.

Silvia had pulled them over to introduce Josie to her husband, Bib, who gave Josette a look that made her want to strangle him and then he asked amusedly if she was a missionary. Her single party dress was high-necked and very concealing, and she'd been insulted by the remark. Webb had been drinking. A mousy little brunette was standing nearby, watching him adoringly. Silvia ignored her.

Dale had laughed with Bib Webb, which didn't endear him to Josette, before Silvia herded them toward a dusty-looking old man in a dark suit holding a can of ginger ale. He had receding white hair and gentle eyes. This, Silvia had muttered, was Henry Garner. While Josie was returning his greeting, Silvia drew Dale away with her into the crowd.

Henry Garner was a kind, sweet man with a dry wit. Josie had liked him at once, when she saw that he was drinking ginger ale and not alcohol. She explained about her strict upbringing, and he grinned. They found a quiet place to stand and talk while the party went on around them and guests got less inhibited.

Bib Webb was dancing with the little brunette, his face quiet and intent as he stared down at her. He was saying something, and she looked worried. He glanced around covertly and then pulled her closer. She looked as if she were in heaven. When he turned her, as they danced, Josie could see that his eyes were closed and his eyebrows drawn down as if in pain.

Henry Garner noticed Josie watching them and distracted her, talking about the lieutenant governor's race and asking about her party affiliation, success-

fully drawing her attention away from Bib Webb. When
Garner asked her gently if she wasn't thirsty, she agreed
that she was. She couldn't see Dale Jennings anywhere.
She asked Garner if he wanted some punch, but he
chuckled and said no at once. She didn't question why.
She was still disappointed that Brannon hadn't shown
up. She'd wanted him to see that her heart wasn't breaking. Even if it was.

Josie went to the punch bowl, and Henry Garner
made a beeline for Webb and the brunette. He said
something to them. Bib Webb smiled sheepishly and
the brunette moved away from him to where the band
was playing. Odd, Josie thought, and then dismissed
the little byplay from her mind. She thought she heard
Garner's voice raise just a note, but she didn't think
much about it. She got a cup of the pretty red punch
with ice floating in it and took several long swallows
before she realized that it wasn't just punch.

Unused to alcohol, it hit her hard. She felt disoriented. She looked around for Dale, but she still didn't
see him anywhere. One or two of the older men started
giving her pert figure speaking looks, and she felt uncomfortable. Looking for a port in a storm, she made
her way back to where Henry Garner had been, only
to find him gone.

Bib Webb was sitting down in a chair, looking worried and a lot more sober than he'd been acting before.
He was sitting beside the little brunette, who had a
small hand on his, and was talking to him earnestly. He
looked as if the world was sitting on him. But when he
saw Josie, he smiled politely and nodded. She shrugged,
smiled and moved back into the crowd.

She was feeling sicker by the minute and she couldn't

find Dale. All she wanted was to go home. Mr. Garner hadn't been drinking, so perhaps, she thought, she could ask him to drive her home. She made her way to the front door and walked out onto the porch. Down a double row of steps, past a deck and a garden path was the pier that led out onto the lake. She couldn't see all the way to the edge of it, but she knew Mr. Garner wouldn't be out there. She turned and went down the side of the house. On the way, she ran into Silvia.

The beautiful woman was a little disheveled and the hand that pushed back her windblown hair was trembling. But she forced a smile and asked how long Josie had been stumbling around outside in the dark.

It was an odd question. Josie admitted that she'd had some spiked punch and was sick. She wanted Dale or Mr. Garner to drive her home.

Silvia had immediately volunteered. She'd only had one wine spritzer, she assured Josie and herded her toward a new silver Mercedes. She put the young woman in the car and pointedly remarked that Henry Garner's car was still sitting there, but he'd told Bib he was going out for some cigars. She waved, but Josette couldn't see anybody to be waved at.

She drove Josette home. Late that night, the local news channel was full of the breaking story of the apparent drowning of philanthropist Henry Garner, whose body had been found by a guest—floating in the lake. A news helicopter hovering over the Garner and Webb estate fed grainy film to the studio for broadcast. Police cars and ambulances were visible below. It was an apparent accidental drowning, the newswoman added, because the gentleman was drunk.

Still unsteady on her feet, but certain of her facts,

Josette had immediately phoned the police to tell them
that she'd just been at that party. Henry Garner had
been drinking ginger ale, he wasn't drunk, and he and
Bib Webb had apparently been arguing before Garner
vanished from the party. The tip was enough for the
local district attorney's office to immediately step into
the investigation.

A blackjack with blood on it was discovered in the
passenger seat of Dale Jennings's car at the scene, where
police were holding guests until they could all be interrogated. Against the wishes of Bib Webb, an autopsy
was ordered, which was routine in any case of sudden, unexplained violent death. The medical examiner
didn't find a drop of liquor in Garner's body, but he
found a blunt force trauma wound on the back of the
old man's head.

The "accidental" drowning became a sensational
homicide overnight.

The best defense attorney in San Antonio was at Bib
Webb's side during a hastily called press conference,
and Marc Brannon got emergency leave from the FBI,
with Webb's help, to come back to San Antonio and
help investigate the murder. In no time at all, Dale Jennings was arrested and charged with first-degree murder. The blackjack in Jennings's possession was said to
be the instrument used to stun Garner; it had traces of
Garner's hair and blood on it, despite obvious efforts
to wipe them off. Silvia Webb added that she'd seen
Jennings near the lake, and the blackjack in Jennings's
car, just before she'd come back to the house and had
taken Josette Langley home.

Jennings didn't confess or protest. His public defender attorney entered a plea of not guilty, evidence

was presented, and Josie had to admit that she hadn't seen Dale during the time the murder was apparently committed. But she had been in Jennings's car on the way to the party, and she hadn't seen any blackjack, and she said so on the witness stand.

She also said that Bib Webb had a better motive for the old man's death than Dale, and that he'd argued with Henry Garner that same evening. But Webb spoke to the prosecutor privately during the lunch break and gave him an ace in the hole. When she was fifteen, Josie had slipped out of her parents' home to attend a wild party given by an older classmate. She'd ingested a drug and a senior at her school had tried to seduce her. She had been so frightened, she'd screamed and neighbors called the police. Her parents got an attorney and tried to have the boy prosecuted, but his attorney had the deposition of the emergency room physician on call the night of the incident—who testified that there had been no rape. The arresting officer, a former Jacobsville police officer named Marc Brannon, had been instrumental in getting the boy acquitted of the charges.

Brannon had told Bib Webb's attorney this, and Webb had given it to the prosecution to use against Josette's defense of Jennings. Josette Langley, it seemed, had once made up a story about being raped. Ergo, how could anybody believe her version of events at the party, especially when she'd been drinking, too?

The sensationalism of the story was such that reporters went to Jacobsville to review the old rape case, and they printed it right alongside the Garner murder trial as a sidebar. Jennings was convicted and sent to prison. Josette was publicly disgraced for the second time, thanks to Brannon. For a woman who'd made only one real mistake in her young life, she'd paid for a lot of sins she hadn't committed. Consequently, she'd given up trying to live blamelessly, and these days she gave people hell. Her experience had made her strong.

But she still thought of Brannon with painful regret. He was the only man she'd ever loved. There had never been another man who could even come close to him in her mind. She sighed as she remembered the way they'd been together two years ago, inseparable, forever on the phone when they weren't exploring the city. He'd helped her study for tests that last year in college, he'd taken her to Jacobsville to go riding on the ranch. When it all blew up in her face, she thought she might die of the pain. But she hadn't. The only problem was that Brannon was back in her life, and she was going to have to face those memories every day.

Well, if it was going to be rough on her, she was going to make sure it was equally rough on him. She thought about giving Marc Brannon hell, and she smiled. If any man ever deserved a setback, that strutting Texas Ranger did. She was going to prove that Dale Jennings never killed Henry Garner, and she was going to rub Brannon's nose in it so hard that he'd be smelling through his ears for the rest of his life!

Josette ran a gentle hand over Barnes's silky fur. "You know, if men were more like cats, we'd never have wars," she murmured. "All you guys do is eat and sleep and sleep some more. And you don't drive trucks and wear muddy boots and cowboy hats."

Barnes opened one green eye and meowed up at her.

She turned her attention back to the television set. "Too bad these writers never saw the inside of a courtroom," she murmured as a defendant in the series grabbed a bailiff's gun and started shooting jurors. "If a defendant ever tried to disarm *our* bailiff in superior court, he'd have his fingers bitten off on the way!"

CHAPTER FOUR

BEFORE HE GOT on his plane back to San Antonio, Marc stopped by Bib Webb's second home in Austin. The Webbs lived there except during holidays and weekends, when they were at Bib's San Antonio home.

Silvia beamed when the butler showed Marc to the living room, where they were sharing cocktails with three other couples. Blonde, beautiful and vivacious, she was a woman most men would covet. Marc liked her, but he found her a bit too aggressive and ruthless for his own taste. She was an asset to Bib, of course, who wasn't at all pushy or aggressive by nature.

"Marc, I didn't know you were in town!" she exclaimed.

"I'm doing some investigative work for Simon Hart," he drawled with a grin. "You look prettier than ever," he added, brushing his hard mouth against her blemishless cheek.

"And you always look like a male model, darling," she purred. "What sort of investigative work?" she added coquettishly, hanging onto his arm with her free hand while she sipped a martini held in the other.

"A murder."

She paused with her eyes on her glass. "Anyone we know? I hope not!"

"Dale Jennings."

There was a tiny tremor in the liquid of the crystal glass she was holding. She looked disconcerted. Probably, Brannon thought, her memories of Jennings were as uncomfortable as his own.

She gazed up at him, then quickly composed herself. "Dale Jennings!" She put a hand on her low-cut bodice. "Jennings. That terrible man…! Bib!" she called to her husband, drawing his attention. "Someone has killed that Jennings man in prison!" she exclaimed, turning all eyes toward her.

"Not in prison, Silvia," Marc said easily.

Her perfect eyebrows arched. "Excuse me?"

"He broke out. Or, someone broke him out," he replied carelessly as Silvia let go of his arm and moved to sit on the arm of the chair Bib was occupying.

"He killed Henry," Bib recalled with cold eyes. "I'm not sorry he's dead!"

"How did he get out of prison?" Silvia persisted.

"I have no idea." Marc refused the offer of a drink and was introduced to the people Bib was entertaining. He didn't know them, but he recognized the names. They were very wealthy people from Austin.

"Can you spend the night?" Bib asked Marc.

Marc shook his head. "I have to be in San Antonio tomorrow morning. I'm going to be working the Jennings case along with the detectives in San Antonio. Simon's sending a liaison investigator from his office out to help."

"Why?" Silvia asked suddenly, wide-eyed. "Jennings was a nobody! Why should the Texas Rangers and the attorney general be involved?"

"He wasn't a nobody," Bib reminded her quietly. "He killed Henry. And Henry Garner was a very prominent man." He studied Marc. "There's something else about this, isn't there?"

Brannon nodded. "There may be some mob involvement. Specifically, Jake Marsh."

"Marsh." Bib ground his teeth together. "Well, that tears it. If he's implicated, it will really make headlines all over again, right?" he asked his friend with a grimace of distaste.

"It's already doing that," Marc agreed, reading the undisguised worry in his friend's handsome face. Beside him, Silvia looked as if she'd been frozen in place. He knew she hated bad publicity. "Don't worry, Bib. It'll be a nine-day wonder. Nothing more," he assured his friend.

"I hope so," Bib said heavily. His eyes lowered and he toyed with a tiny piece of thread on a jacket button. "It brings back so many terrible memories."

"Oh, that's all behind us now," Silvia said at once, and smiled, but not with her eyes. She got to her feet abruptly, and a little clumsily. "Marc, you have a good trip back to San Antonio. And, you will let us know how it goes?"

"Certainly." He was curious about why Silvia seemed so eager to get rid of him. "Bib, how about walking me out?"

"I'll come, too," Silvia said at once, apologizing to their guests.

That was one of many things about Silvia that Marc didn't like: she hung on to Bib like ivy. The man couldn't get out of her sight. It had been like that since she was sixteen and seduced Bib into marriage, so that she could escape the unbearable poverty of her childhood. She never talked about it. Her father had fallen down a well and died just after the unexpected accidental death of her younger brother. Neither death had seemed to bother her much, although Marc was apparently the only one who'd noticed that, despite Silvia's tragic past, she was curiously impervious to grief.

"You haven't told us all of it," Bib said when they were out on the porch. His pale blue eyes narrowed. "There's more, isn't there?"

Marc stuck his hands deep into his pockets. "The investigator Simon's sending out to coordinate efforts with the Bexar County District Attorney," he began reluctantly. "You might remember her. Josette Langley."

Silvia's face flushed. "That bitch!"

Bib looked weary. "Sil, it was a long time ago…"

"That woman accused you of being the murderer! Do you think I could ever forget? She'll stir up trouble, she'll make false accusations, she'll go to the media…!" Her voice rose, becoming shrill.

"Calm down," Bib said quietly, looking her straight in the eyes. He put a gentle hand on her nape and smoothed it up and down. "Calm down. Take deep breaths. Come on, Sil."

She did what Bib told her to. She still looked glassy-eyed, but she was quiet. Bib reached into a crystal bowl on the side table next to the open front door and produced a mint in a fancy wrapper. He placed it in her hands and waited while she unwrapped it and popped it into her mouth. Candy calmed her in these odd outbursts. Once he'd thought she might be diabetic, but bloodwork disproved that theory. She refused to see a psychologist, despite his best efforts. She was violent in these rages, dangerously so. Once, she'd killed a favorite dog in one of them. In a way, Bib was glad they couldn't have children. She was too unpredictable.

Bib turned back to Marc, who was scowling worriedly. "Miss Langley was talking to Henry, before he was killed. She was a quiet woman, not the sort to enjoy a party. I couldn't understand why she was dating Dale in the first place. He did work for Henry, against my advice. He was in close with Jake Marsh in San Antonio. I had problems with a campaign worker who was in Marsh's pocket during the lieutenant governor's race. I'm sure Marsh put Dale up to what he did," he added bitterly.

"That was never proven," Silvia said sweetly. "I always thought the man was working on his own. I'm sure he had no real connection to Marsh."

"Then why was his body found near Marsh's nightclub?" Marc wondered aloud.

"Those sort of people can get killed anywhere," Silvia said carelessly. "I wouldn't waste state money on an investigation like that. He was a nobody."

Bib ignored her. "That campaign worker," he told Brannon, persisting. "Jennings had recommended him, to work on my campaign for lieutenant governor. The man went behind my back and apparently dug up a scandal to force my opponent out of the race. I'm almost positive it was why he pulled out of the race at the last minute, but I never could prove it. I didn't like Jennings around Henry, and I said so that night at the party when Henry was killed. We argued." He grimaced. "I hated parting from him on an argument. You know how Henry was," he added with a wan smile. "He trusted people."

"That's how you get killed in the modern world,"

Silvia said with a high-pitched laugh. "You can't trust anybody these days."

Bib continued to ignore her and stared at Marc. "How did Jennings die?"

"Single gunshot wound to the back of the skull."

Bib's intake of breath was audible. "Dear God!"

"Oh, what does it matter how he died? He was a murderer," Silvia said with regal nonchalance. "I don't feel sorry for him. Is that why the state attorney general's sticking his nose in, because it was execution-style?"

Marc didn't reply for an instant. "That, and because Marsh is involved in a lot of illegal activities. He's been trying to shut him down for years. Now we're involved in a high-profile murder. Everyone wants to make sure the investigation is done properly."

"And Simon's letting that Langley woman mess it up. How stupid!" Silvia said.

"She has a degree in criminal justice, and she's worked for Simon for two years," Marc said, defending her against his will.

"She's personally involved in this case. So are you. Neither of you should get involved." She turned to Bib. "Call someone important and tell him to pull Marc and that woman off the case!"

That went right through Marc. "Do it," he invited, silver eyes glaring at her, "and I'll call a press conference myself and tell the world why I'm off the case."

Silvia gasped. "Well! And I thought you were our friend!"

"I am your friend," he returned curtly, looking at Bib, not at her. "But the law is the law. I won't have interference in a case this sensitive."

Silvia glared at him. Her hand, holding the glass,

shook. She slammed it down on the porch, shattering it. "You stupid idiot!" she raged at Bib. "You're such a wimp! You never do anything right!" She whirled and went back into the house with her eyes flashing. She muttered curses as she slammed the door furiously.

She wasn't quite normal, Marc thought, and not for the first time.

Bib just shook his head. "Seven years of that," he murmured heavily. "She's a good politician's wife, and she loves television appearances and society bashes. But there are times when I wish I'd married someone less explosive. I'm afraid I fall far short of Silvia's expectations. She'd have left me long ago if I'd been poor or had a dull social life."

"She loves you," Marc said, although he wasn't convinced.

"She owns me," Bib laughed hollowly. "Well, I'd better go back inside and kiss a little more butt. They're potential contributors to my senate campaign." He lifted both eyebrows. "Going to vote for me?"

"No," Marc said, deadpan. "You're corrupt."

Bib laughed with pure delight. "We're all corrupt," he agreed. He studied the other man curiously. "This must be painful for you," he added perceptively. "You and the Langley girl were an item back then."

Marc didn't say a word.

Bib shrugged. "Okay. I'll let it drop. We'll be heading up to our place in San Antonio this weekend. Drop by for a drink if you have time." He leaned closer. "Sil's going to Dallas to shop on Saturday morning. We can sneak down to the corner coffee shop and eat doughnuts while she's gone!"

"Won't she let you have them?" Marc asked, surprised.

Bib patted his flat stomach. "I have to have a nice, lean figure for the publicity shots," he confided. "I can't have anything sweet if she's within smelling distance." He shook his head. "Dear, dear, the things we give up for public office."

"You're a good politician," Marc replied. "You have a conscience. And a heart."

"Liabilities, old friend, nothing but liabilities. I lack the killer instinct in campaigns. Fortunately, Silvia has it. You have a safe trip back to San Antonio."

"Sure. You take care, yourself," he added quietly. "There may be more to this case than meets the eye. Do you have a bodyguard?"

He nodded. "T. M. Smith. He was army intelligence in Operation Desert Storm. He can deck most men in hand-to-hand, and he's a crack shot."

"Keep him close. Just in case," Marc added, and smiled to soften what sounded like an order.

Bib shook hands with him. "Do you ever miss the old days, when we hung around the record shop hoping to meet women?"

"I miss sleeping a whole night," Marc said enigmatically, and grinned. "See you."

He got into his black sports utility vehicle and drove away, the smile fading from his lips as he pulled out onto the highway. Silvia's attitude bothered him. She was a strong-willed woman, and most of the time she was an asset to Bib. But he couldn't help recalling her violent outburst when he mentioned that he was investigating Dale Jennings's murder—or that it had been

Silvia's testimony that had resulted in Dale's conviction for Henry Garner's murder.

Marc had been so upset over Josette's accusation about Webb and the revelation about the truth of her rape charges at the age of fifteen, that much of the murder trial had escaped his notice. He'd misjudged her and caused her untold misery and shame about that long-ago rape trial. Despite his anger at her allegations against Bib Webb, he'd been devastated at having misjudged her so badly. But any idea he'd had about apologizing had gone by the board. She'd looked at him in that courtroom at Jennings's trial as if she hated him. Probably she did. He'd just walked out on her, with no explanation at all.

Worse, he'd been more than a little in love with her just before the Jennings trial got underway. He hadn't been as angry about her allegations as he had been angry at himself, for being such a poor judge of character. He'd gone through the trial in a fog and, afterward, he'd left town, to spend two miserable years with the FBI.

Now he was home again and the whole damned mess was being resurrected. Josette had no time for him. He could see the contempt in her eyes when she looked at him, feel her anger. He didn't blame her. She had every right to consider him the enemy. She would do her best to put Bib Webb under investigation, and he would do his best to stop her. After all that time, they were still on opposite sides.

He stopped at a traffic light and a passing glance at a young girl in a long, flowered dress reminded him of his last date with Josette. She'd just graduated from college and he'd been there, along with her parents, for the ceremony. That night, he'd taken her out to a very fancy restaurant. She'd worn a long black silk dress with exotic flowers hand-painted on the fabric. Her long blond hair had been in a neat chignon at the nape of her neck. She'd looked absolutely exquisite.

After dinner, he'd taken her back to his apartment. Up until then, there had been brief, clinging kisses and love play that neither of them carried to the inevitable conclusion. He still hadn't believed her rape story, although the woman he was getting to know didn't seem the sort to tell lies. He'd reminded himself that plenty of women who looked innocent, weren't.

His suspicions increased when she went with him to his apartment. She hadn't protested being alone with him. He'd put on some slow dance music and shed his dinner jacket, moving her close to his crisp, white cotton shirt. Against it, he could feel the soft press of her breasts under the thin fabric. He hadn't felt a bra, and that had aroused him, quickly and uncomfortably.

But instead of backing away, to keep her ignorant of the effect she had on him, he'd let her feel it. He could still remember being surprised at the faint shock in her wide, dark eyes, the tremor that ran through her. She'd started to speak, but he bent and took the husky words right inside his hungry mouth.

He was slow, and deliberate, and thorough in his ardor. Her innocence was no match for his years of experience with women. He had her on his couch in no time, bare to the waist. While his mouth fed hungrily on her small, firm breasts, his hand had been under that silky fabric and the soft cotton briefs she wore under them.

She'd been fascinated by what he was doing to her.

He could see it in her eyes, feel it in the nervous hands that clung to him as he undressed her. His shirt had been off, drawing her fingers to his broad, hair-roughened chest while he suckled her.

He'd wanted her for months. During that time, he hadn't seen any other woman. He was aching, and he'd abstained while they were dating. It was inevitable that he was going to lose control.

His hand went between them to the fastening of his slacks and undid it, so that he could push them away. His knee had edged between her soft thighs and his mouth had moved back to cover hers, tenderly. When she felt him at the veil of her innocence, she stiffened a little, but her body was hot with desire, her hands were biting into his back, her mouth was moaning under the devouring pressure of his hard lips.

"Oh, God, I need you," he ground out as his lean hips began to push down. "I need you so much."

She cried out.

"Too fast? I'll be careful," he said at her lips. "It's been a long time, hasn't it?"

"Marc... I haven't ever been with anyone!" she sobbed.

He only laughed softly. She'd been with the boy she accused of raping her when she was fifteen. She was no innocent. But he was careful with her just the same. He didn't want to turn her off, not when his own body was racked with desire.

He wrenched off the trousers and his boots while his mouth worked on her soft belly. He aroused her all over again, determined to make her want him as much as he wanted her, to stop her feeble protests, her lies.

She was shivering, begging him, when he finally slid

between her long, trembling legs and positioned himself against her. He looked into her wide, dazed eyes.

"I'm going inside you," he whispered blatantly. "I'm going deep inside you, Josie. Now. Now...now!"

His body was shuddering with each quick, hard motion of his hips, and he felt the pleasure rising in him. But he couldn't penetrate her. She was sobbing, shivering, her voice at his ear whispering ardent encouragement, her hands on his buttocks, pulling, pleading.

"Damn it...!" he growled, frustrated, blind with desire. He gathered his strength and pushed as hard as he could.

She cried out and came right up off the couch, frantically pushing at his hips, her eyes blind, not with desire, but with honest, terrible pain.

It took him several seconds to realize what was wrong. He was shivering with desire, aching for satisfaction. But her body resisted him, and suddenly he realized why.

His lean hand moved suddenly. He touched her intimately, and found a barrier so formidable, so noticeable, that he froze above her in total shock.

"You're a virgin," he whispered, wild-eyed.

She swallowed, embarrassment flooding her. She looked down, at his blatant arousal, and gasped. She'd obviously never seen a man...like that!

"Damn you!"

He dragged his body away from hers, too far gone to care that she was shocked by his nudity. He dressed in silent rage, barely aware that she was crying and had pulled her dress up over her to conceal her own nudity in shame.

"Of all the low-down, dirty things to do to a man,

that is the lowest!" he accused. "Get dressed," he said tersely, leaving the room.

He waited in the kitchen while she dressed, too overcome with shock and anger to think rationally. His body was in anguish. Josette had led him on deliberately, knowing that she couldn't be intimate with him. That barrier wouldn't break without some surgery. She had to know it. Then it hit him, like a board in the face. She was a virgin. There was absolute proof of it.

That was when he knew the boy in Jacobsville had lied on the stand when he was accused of raping a fifteen-year-old Josette. That was when he knew, with absolute certainty, that she'd been assaulted with the intent of rape. But the barrier had stopped him. As it stopped Marc, that night...

A horn blew, bringing him back to the present. The light had changed and he was sitting there, staring into space. He grimaced at his memories and put his foot down on the accelerator, shooting forward.

He could still see Josette's shocked, shamed face. She'd cried and cried, still aroused, and ashamed as well, fascinated and humiliated. Nothing he said then could have erased that expression from her face, and he knew it, and didn't speak. He'd said far too much already, things he couldn't even take back now. She hadn't been able to meet his eyes, and tears poured down her cheeks. He wanted to explain why he'd been angry, why he'd said such terrible things to her. But she wouldn't speak, wouldn't listen, wouldn't look at him, and the words died unspoken.

It had occurred to him then that she was probably remembering the rape attempt, that his ardor had reminded her of the most distasteful experience of her life. He'd lost control of himself almost at once, something that had never happened before. She'd let Marc undress her and touch her, and she'd been willing, apparently, to give herself to him. Except that she knew she couldn't have intimacy with any man. So maybe she was a tease. Maybe she was getting even with him, finally, for testifying against her when she was fifteen. That growing suspicion had kept him quiet when she came to the kitchen doorway, fully dressed.

He'd taken her home in a painful silence. He wanted to apologize for helping the boy's defense attorney get her case thrown out of court when she was fifteen. He wanted to apologize for not believing her.

Those harsh words he'd spoken to her, even in memory, had the power to make him sick. She was a virgin, and he'd treated her like a criminal. He should have known that she wasn't the sort of person to lie. When had she ever lied to him, during their months of dating, enjoying each other's company? He'd misjudged her horribly, and then her strict upbringing had probably left her with feelings of guilt because she'd let him go so far. Her natural, sweet ardor was a gift. He wanted to tell her that. He wanted her to know that he didn't blame her for what had happened. But he didn't trust people. She might have done it deliberately. He couldn't be sure she hadn't. He cut off the engine in front of her home and faced her.

But before he could say anything, she'd turned her head toward him. "Don't ever call me. Don't ever come near me again," she'd choked, her voice breaking on the words as she glanced in his direction, but not meeting his gaze. "It was just sex, wasn't it? It was just sex you wanted, all along, and you thought I'd be easy because you thought I was easy at fifteen!"

He remembered glaring at her with mingled frustration and anger. "You're a damned disappointment, that's what you are, Josette. You led me on deliberately tonight, knowing I couldn't have you. It was revenge for not believing you in Jacobsville, wasn't it? It was payback, pure and simple."

Her face had flamed scarlet. "You started it!"

He didn't like remembering that. "You didn't fight very hard, did you? But don't worry, I won't be back. I don't have any desire to see you again. You never were woman enough for me in the first place!"

And he left her, with those cold, heartless words, driving away before she even reached her front door.

After that, he'd gotten drunk. A few days later, he'd resigned his Ranger job and accepted one with the FBI. Josette had accepted a date with Dale Jennings to go to a party Bib Webb was throwing. In fact, Silvia Webb had put her on the guest list at Jennings's request. Soon afterward, there was a trial, a speedy trial because Bib Webb's opponent had suddenly dropped out of the race at the last minute and Webb had been elected lieutenant governor.

During the trial, Josette was made out to be a liar. Marc hadn't provided that information about the rape trial. But Bib Webb had remembered hearing about it, and told the prosecuting attorney. Josette thought it was Marc. He hadn't gone near her because he couldn't bear the condemnation in those soft, dark eyes every time she looked at him. Then, the longer he'd waited to apologize, the more impossible it had become. In the end, he didn't contact her again. Not at all. He just left town for good.

Actually he needn't have left San Antonio, because soon after the trial, Josette moved to Austin to work for Simon Hart, to get away from the publicity. Her mother had died of a stroke a couple of months later, and her father had died of a heart attack not long after that. There were no siblings.

She'd mourned both of them bitterly, and alone, because she had no family left.

Now here she was, back in Marc's life, and he had to try to keep his head around her, and not let her know how powerfully she still affected him. He wondered if she'd had something going with Jennings—or anyone else—since the trial. She seemed very self-confident, self-assured, businesslike. But the one time he'd gone close to her—deliberately, because he had to know if he still affected her physically—he'd seen her blouse shake with the force of her heartbeat.

She was still vulnerable to him; a little, anyway. But she didn't want to be. Even if she didn't hate him, she was so remote she appeared disinterested. He wondered if he was ever going to get close to her again, especially now, with the two of them on opposing teams outside the investigation.

He *knew* that Bib Webb would never be a party to corruption or murder. He just didn't know how to make Josette see it. She was prejudiced, and maybe with good reason. Silvia had been vicious, sniping at her in the press and quoting things that her husband hadn't actually said about Josette's penchant for lying. It had turned Josette against Bib, and maybe that had been Silvia's intent all along.

When Silvia had seduced Bib into marrying her, against Marc's advice, years before to escape poverty, she'd been pregnant. But she'd lost the child while she was out of town. She was ambitious from the start, and she loved money. It was her own ambition that had first pushed Bib into partnership with childless widower Henry Garner, and her ambition that had been responsible for his election to lieutenant governor. It was her ambition that had him running for a U.S. senate seat that he'd privately told Marc he didn't really want.

Bib's idea of heaven was to spend his life selling farm equipment or working with the horses on his ranch. He loved the ranch. He loved the open country. He was more a cowboy than a diplomat or a politician, but that would never have suited Silvia. She wanted expensive clothes and jewels and the cream of society in her living room sipping imported champagne. Marc wondered how different his friend's life might have been if he'd never married Silvia.

But it wasn't possible to relive the past. If he could do that, he wouldn't have made the mistake of his life trying to seduce Josette Langley on his sofa.

MARC LEFT HIS rental car at the airport and boarded the plane back to San Antonio, finding that he was the only passenger seated in that particular set of seats over the wing. He didn't mind that. He wasn't in the mood for a talkative companion.

He put his hat in the extra seat and leaned back with his arms folded and his eyes closed as the big plane took off and shot up into the blue sky.

Funny how many of his most vivid memories were tied up with Josette Langley and her family, he recalled.

He and her father had first become acquainted when he was a patrolman with the Jacobsville police force. He'd been trying to get a repeat DWI offender into an alcoholic rehabilitation clinic. The man had been a member of the Langleys' church, and Josette's father had intervened on his behalf. Marc and Mr. Langley had a lot in common, because Langley had started out to be a career policeman. But he felt the call to preach, and he'd quit his job and gone to a seminary to complete his education. Marc came to the house often to see Josette's father, and he got to know Josette as well. He thought of her as a cute and mischievous child; or, he had, until he'd seen her undressed in the company of a half-naked boy one unexpected night.

The boy had been very convincing. Josette had sneaked out of her house to meet him, he told Marc; she'd wanted him. She came on to him. But when he agreed and got enthusiastic, she started fighting and screamed rape, wasn't that just like a girl? Marc, to his shame, had believed him. He'd even felt sorry for him. So, despite his affection for the family and his friendship with Josette's father, he'd helped investigate the incident. The intern at the hospital where Josette had been taken that night gave a taped deposition, which stated emphatically that there had been no rape—although not the reason why there hadn't. It had convinced Marc that Josette was afraid to tell the truth about what had really happened, for fear of hurting her parents. That was a common enough response for a girl who'd never done anything wrong in her life; in fact, Marc had recently seen such a case in court. The girl had tearfully admitted fault and apologized, and the case was thrown out of court.

So, remembering that trial, Marc had testified for the boy, repeating what he'd said at the scene. The boy had won. Josette was publicly branded a liar. Her parents were humiliated. The whole family was disgraced. And when Josette tried to finish school in Jacobsville, the taunts and cruel jests of her fellow students, male and female friends of her attacker, had made it impossible for her to continue.

Her father had moved his family to San Antonio, taking a lesser job in order to give Josette some peace. He and Marc didn't see each other anymore. Then Marc was assigned to the San Antonio Ranger post, during Josette's senior year in college. Marc had taken a course in criminal justice that had landed him in a class of hers when she was twenty-two.

It had been difficult at first for her to speak to him at all. She hadn't forgotten or forgiven what he'd done to her at the trial. But she was attractive and he was drawn to her against his will. With gentle teasing and comradery, he'd worked his way back into her life, despite the disapproval of both her parents. He was never allowed in their home. Her parents had forgiven him, of course, but they didn't like the idea of Josette being friendly with him. They could never trust him again after his betrayal at the rape trial. They had never believed Josette guilty, despite the trial and the boy's assurances.

Marc had ignored that disapproval. He'd taken Josette to dances, to picnics, to the theater at the college. He'd brought her little presents and phoned her late at night just to talk. She'd fallen head over heels in love with him. His own emotions were confused and hard to define.

And then he'd invited her to a dance, the night after

she graduated from college—and he'd attended graduation, even though he sat apart from her family.

That last date they'd shared had changed everything. Marc's painful discovery about her had prompted him to write her a letter, a long and rambling letter of apology. He'd almost mailed it. Then Henry Garner had been murdered and Marc had been assigned to help solve the case. Josette had been right in the middle of it, as a guest at the party.

After the story of Josette's rape trial hit the papers, Marc threw away the letter. He knew she'd tear it up, unread. She'd blame him for that publicity, assuming that he was the only person who'd remember it, without knowing that Bib Webb knew.

Marc had left town after Jennings's conviction, devastated. He couldn't bear to know that he'd destroyed Josette's life by believing the culprit and denying her innocence. A young girl, drugged and almost raped, had then been subjected to sordid gossip and accused of lying, so that the perpetrator went free and lived to gloat about it.

Marc had done that to her. He'd helped cost her father his good job as youth minister of a Jacobsville church. And he'd not only destroyed her young womanhood, but he'd come back into her life just long enough to make her trust him and then he'd betrayed her all over again by accusing her of making false accusations against his best friend.

They were false, of course. He knew Bib Webb hadn't killed old man Garner. Bib loved the old devil as if he'd been his own father, who'd deserted Bib and his little sister when Bib was seventeen. Bib had raised the girl and then had to watch her die of a drug over-

dose when she was just eighteen. Bib's life had been
rocky and painful until old man Garner came along and
took him in. Silvia had reminded him of his sister in
those days, being poor and unsure of herself and hope-
lessly infatuated with Bib. He'd married her seven years
ago, and Bib had grown gray in the years between. He
looked a decade older than Marc.

The flight attendant passed him with the drinks cart,
but he shook his head and she moved on by. He felt
her eyes on him and had to hide a smile. The Texas
Ranger badge and accoutrements did that to a lot of
women. They saw the uniform and were drawn to the
man wearing it. He wasn't bad-looking, and he knew
it, but he wasn't overly interested in responding these
days. Until Josette Langley had walked back into his
life unexpectedly that morning outside Simon Hart's
office, he'd thought he was dead from the neck down.
It was discomforting to know that she affected him in
the same old way. And in the same old places.

He had to remember that he was involved in a murder
investigation. Lives would be ruined when the culprit,
whoever he or she was, was found. He had to have an
unbreakable chain of evidence that led to the perpetrator, and he had to do some quick investigative work to
make that happen.

This was going to be a front-page case until it was
solved. Inevitably it would subject Bib Webb to unpleasant publicity, as well as Josette and Dale Jennings's
mother, and anyone else who'd had ties with the old
case. He had to make sure that he didn't slip up. He had
to be methodical, and not let his old feelings for Josette
get in the way of good police work.

He wondered how it was going to be for her, having

to suffer his company when he was the one man in the world she had reason to hate. He felt sorry for her. He felt sorry for himself. He had plenty of regrets.

Two rows up from him, a woman was cuddling a toddler, who was grasping her hair and gurgling as he smiled up at her. Marc smiled involuntarily, thinking of his young nephew whom he'd only seen in newsreels and in the photos Gretchen had sent him copies of. He wanted to see the child, to hold him, to see his sister's eyes in that young face. He would have bet that she and her husband Philippe spent a lot more time watching the baby than they spent watching television.

He'd have liked a child of his own. He was beginning to see the long, lonely years ahead. He wondered if Josette ever thought about kids. He grimaced. With her distaste for anything intimate, he doubted she'd let herself think of kids. It was a shame, too, because she had such a sweet, nurturing personality. She was forever doing things for her parents, for neighbors, for kids she didn't even know. He remembered taking her to an amusement park once, and she'd found a little boy crying with a cut knee. She'd dug a bandage out of her pocketbook and put it in place, drying the tears and even buying him an ice-cream cone. By the time his frantic parents found him, he was laughing and holding Josette's hand as if it were a lifeline.

He hated that memory. It had been the day before her graduation, before he took her to the dance. It had been the last full day they ever spent together. It was his last chance, and he didn't know until it was too late.

He thought of the lonely years he had left and almost groaned out loud. He had to keep his mind on the case, not on the past; even if they did end up being one and the same thing.

The past was inextricably linked to what was happening now. He and Josette had to find a killer before he decided to target another unknown victim. And they had to find him fast.

CHAPTER FIVE

SAN ANTONIO WAS bigger than Josette remembered. She'd attended college here. She'd fallen in love here. Now she was up to her neck in a murder investigation, facing an enemy whom she'd loved with all her heart before he betrayed her.

Her knowledge of the Jennings trial gave her an edge that most investigators wouldn't have. Still, she didn't want to step on any toes, especially those of the local police department. But it was a crime that could reach all the way to state government, and that required cooperation and sensitivity from all the agencies involved.

It was going to be a tricky investigation. The murder victim had escaped from prison, where he was serving a long sentence for killing Bib Webb's elderly business partner. How he escaped, and why he was killed execution-style, were questions that currently had no answers. Josette was expected to help find those answers.

She looked around the district attorney's office with a smile, because it reminded her of her own office—cramped and bogged down with file folders. It was a nice, modern office, but she had yet to meet any district attorney who didn't have a caseload that he or she could never catch up with. It was almost a hallmark of the profession.

A door opened and a trim young woman with dark

hair and eyes motioned her inside another office, also
stacked with files too numerous to fit inside the two
filing cabinets.

"I'm Linda Harvey, one of the assistant district attorneys," the young woman said pleasantly. "I'm the
one who requested your help. We spoke on the phone."

"I'm glad to meet you. I'm Josette Langley. I was
just noticing the overflow," she added with a smile and
a handshake. "I feel right at home."

Linda Harvey just shook her head. "I expect to go
to my grave with a box of unfinished case files," she
admitted. "If you want coffee, there's an urn right outside the district attorney's door, just put a quarter in the
box and help yourself."

"Thanks, but I've had two cups to wake me up. Any
more and I'll be flying around the room."

Linda chuckled. "I know what you mean. Have a
seat." She dropped into her own chair. "I understand
from Simon Hart that you were personally involved in
this case."

"Far more involved than I wanted to be," Josette confided. "The murder victim was my date on the night he
was supposed to have killed Henry Garner. I couldn't
give him an alibi, but I never thought he was guilty."

"I've read the file" came the quiet reply. "You suspected that Bib Webb was somehow involved."

Josette grimaced. "*That* didn't win me any points,
I can tell you. I only mentioned that he was the man
with the most to gain from Garner's death, which was
a fact. The media blew it into an accusation and went
to town speculating on Webb's involvement, which was
dynamite, considering that he was running for lieutenant governor at the time."

"Yes," Linda said, frowning thoughtfully. "His opponent dropped out at the last minute, leaving him a clear field. I always thought the timing was interesting, especially since Webb fell behind in the polls after the trial." She smiled at Josette. "As I recall, the prosecution was pretty rough on you when you tried to testify for Jennings."

"They dug up a rape case I'd been involved in when I was fifteen," she said, obviously surprising the other woman. She nodded. "Yes, I was pretty sure that would be in my file." She leaned forward. "That boy did try to rape me," she said firmly. "I didn't realize until much later that he'd slipped something into my Coke. It was like a forerunner of the date-rape drug."

The other woman let out a breath. "I wondered if it wasn't something like that," she confessed. "I'm glad you were honest with me. In fact, what I heard bothered me so much at the time that I tracked down that attorney, and had him tell me himself why the case was thrown out of court. He was very apologetic. He was young and the boy had family and friends who convinced him the boy was the wronged party."

Josette took a slow breath. "How nice of him. And only nine years too late."

"Women are still getting a rough deal in a lot of places," Linda said quietly. "But at least he's off the streets—for good. The year before last, he had raped a young woman and strangled her almost to death in Victoria. He died trying to run away from the police in a high-speed chase."

Josette grimaced. "I know. I had a lot of calls from people in Jacobsville afterward. Including one from the district attorney who prosecuted the boy. He believed in me, right up until the verdict and even past it."

"At least you were exonerated," Linda said. "You've done well, despite everything."

Josette shrugged. "I had motivation. I wanted to be able to do something for other innocent victims."

"You're a trained investigator. Why aren't you working on a district attorney's staff? In fact, why aren't you a district attorney? We have a female one here."

"I know," Josette said with a grin. "If I still lived here, I'd have voted for her on qualifications alone."

"She's a tiger. So am I," she confided. She leaned forward. "Is there some particular reason you're marking time in state government?"

She was persistent, Josette thought. She smiled sadly. "Just after I graduated from college, Dale Jennings's murder trial made national headlines. I was an instant notorious celebrity, past and present, and made out to be a liar. Nobody wanted to hire me except Simon Hart. I've known him most of my life. He was the only person who was willing to take a chance on me."

"Tough," Linda said quietly. "I'm sorry. All the same, if you ever change your mind, we're not prejudiced here. We'd be happy to have you."

"Thanks," Josette said. "I'll remember that."

"I'll be happy to have you on this case. If you need anything, anything at all, you just ask."

"I may need more than you want to give," Josette said quietly. "This is a high-profile case, involving a member of state government. That's one reason we've got Marc Brannon of the Texas Rangers involved. We're going to have to cross a lot of jurisdictional lines. With luck, we may get our hands on your local mob boss,

Jake Marsh. But it may also involve prosecuting someone pretty high up."

Linda nodded. "None of us here are afraid of bad
publicity."

Josette let out a sigh of relief. "That's just what I
wanted to hear. Thanks."

Linda stood up. "You'll have to share an office with
Cash Grier, but he's not so bad, despite what you'll
hear about him from Brannon. They used to work together. Sort of."

"I'll remember. Thanks for the help."

Linda smiled. "That's what we're here for—doing
the job."

BY THE END of the day, Josette knew several people on
the staff and felt vaguely comfortable in her new office.
She hadn't met Grier and she hadn't seen Brannon. She
assumed he'd be working out of the local Ranger office.
That was a relief. She didn't know how she was going
to manage being close to him day after day.

But when she got back to the room she'd rented at
the Madison Hotel for her stay in San Antonio, she
had a surprise waiting. Brannon was sitting in a late-
model unmarked sport utility vehicle, black, with an-
tennae all over it.

She hugged her purse to her chest as she stood beside her car and waited for him to get out of his own
vehicle, watching him with a carefully noncommittal
expression. That was difficult, when her heart was trying to escape through her ribs.

He leaned against her car, his arms folded, and stared
down at her in that arrogant manner of his. He was the
most attractive man she'd ever known. He was also

sensually intimidating, and in her case, she was certain he did it on purpose. He knew very well how she'd felt about him before she accused his best friend of murder. He was rubbing it in.

"I thought the Rangers issued you a car," she drawled.

"I'd rather drive my own," he replied shortly. "How'd your day go?"

"I moved in with an assistant district attorney," she said without preamble. "I assume you'll be working out of your own office?"

He nodded.

"Did you get the files I sent?"

He nodded again.

She lifted an eyebrow and cocked her head at him. Her dark eyes twinkled. "I speak sign language, if you'd rather not answer me directly."

He chuckled. "You haven't changed."

She adjusted her gold-rimmed glasses. "Oh, I've changed, Brannon," she said. "But I try not to let it show." She turned. "If you'd like to discuss the case…"

"I would. But not in a hotel room," he added coldly, stung by her remoteness.

She didn't look at him. "Fine. I'll take a minute to check my messages and be right back."

That irritated him. He couldn't seem to make her angry. He wasn't sure why he wanted to. Her calm demeanor made him uncomfortable. She was so damned self-confident.

Ignoring him, she went into her room, called the desk and found no messages, refreshed her makeup and went right back outside, locking the door behind her. She'd taken barely five minutes.

Brannon was obviously surprised. "Five minutes. For a woman, that's a world record."

"For a man, it would be a miracle," she murmured dryly. "Where do you want to go, and I'll meet you there."

"Don't be absurd." He opened the passenger door of the SUV.

She gave it a doubtful look. "Got a ladder?"

"It's not that high to climb up into," he said shortly.

She shrugged and got in with as much grace as possible. He closed the door behind her with exaggerated patience.

When he was behind the wheel, he fastened his seat belt and checked to make sure she had her own in place before he started the truck and pulled out into traffic. He drove like he did everything else, with ease and mastery. She looked at his beautiful lean, brown hands on the steering wheel and remembered how they felt on bare skin...

She shifted in her seat and looked out over the golden grass as they passed pastures scattered with pumper wells, small grasshopper-shaped machines that brought up oil from beneath the grazing pastures. Cattle plodded around beside them with magnificent unconcern.

"Those tanks barely look half full," she remarked, eyeing the concrete depressions that caught rainwater, called "tanks" in Texas.

"The drought is hitting everybody hard. Of course, some people do get rain, as long as they don't need it," he added.

He glanced at her from under the broad brim of his Stetson. "I spoke to the D.A. before I got off duty. She says they like you over there."

"Shocking, isn't it?" she replied drolly.

"That isn't what I meant."

She glanced toward him with a bland expression. "What do you want to talk about?"

"How a convicted murderer got put on a work detail," he said.

She pursed her lips, watching fences and cattle and grasshopper-shaped oil pumpers fly by. "Now there's a valid question. I didn't think to wonder about it, either, but it's not exactly standard policy to let murderers pick up trash on the roadside."

"Exactly." He glanced at her. "Something more—the Wayne Correctional Institute isn't a federal prison, either, it's a state prison. Jennings was sent to federal prison."

"So, what was Jennings doing in Wayne at all, right?"

"Right." He pulled off the highway toward a truck stop. "Coffee and a burger suit you? That's about all I can afford until payday."

"I pay my own way, Ranger, so suit yourself," she said without embarrassment. "Have you talked to the warden?"

"Not yet. But it's pretty obvious that somebody pulled strings to get Jennings transferred there."

She whistled softly. "Some strings!"

"I'm waiting."

"For what?"

"For the obvious inference—that the Texas lieutenant governor probably has contacts who could manage it."

She gave him a steady glance. "Why state the obvious?"

DIANA PALMER

"Bib didn't kill Henry Garner, or Dale Jennings," he said firmly.

"Nobody could ever accuse you of being disloyal to your friends," she remarked. "But I'm keeping an open mind on this case, and you have to do the same," she added firmly, her eyes steady on his face. "We're both prejudiced in favor of the people we think are, or were, innocent. That has to make us extra cautious about any accusations."

"You're very broad-minded for a woman with your past," he said curtly. "And I don't mean that in a derogatory way," he added quietly. "I can't quite figure you out."

"No need to try," she assured him. "We're doing a job together, nothing more. When we get the culprit, I'll go back to Austin and do what I do best."

"Which is?" he prompted.

"Providing a liaison from Mr. Hart's office to district attorneys around the state. I'm very much at home with my nose stuck in a filing cabinet or my ear glued to the telephone."

"That isn't what you trained to do at college."

She shrugged. "I'm not suited to fieldwork" was all she was going to admit. "If you don't mind, I'm rather tired. I'd like to get the preliminary discussion out of the way and go back to my room. It's been a long day."

He didn't reply. He pulled into the truck stop and cut off the engine. She noticed that he didn't offer to open the passenger door for her. Brannon had been raised with exquisite manners by his late mother, and while he was Mr. Conservative with the image he gave as a Texas Ranger, he was emphatically not politically correct in some areas. It was as much his nature to open doors for women and walk on the traffic side of them as it was to rest that cannon of a .45 caliber revolver he wore on his hip on an empty cylinder. So not offering to open her door was meant to sting. She opened it herself and ignored the intended insult.

He led the way to a booth in the back of the restaurant, with no diners nearby. A waitress came at once, young and pretty and clearly delighted to have Brannon at her table.

"What can I get you?" she asked enthusiastically.

Brannon grinned at her. It changed his whole appearance. He looked handsome and roguish all at once. It was the way he'd looked at Josette two years ago. "Coffee with cream, a rib eye steak, medium rare, and a house salad with Thousand Island dressing."

"No problem." She looked at Josette with a toned down mutation of the smile. "And you, ma'am?"

"Coffee, black, and the house salad with ranch dressing on the side."

"It'll be right up. I'll get your coffee now." She gave Brannon another shyly fascinated smile and hurried away.

"That silver star gets them every time," Josette drawled, nodding toward his circle and star Texas Ranger badge.

He leaned back with one long arm over the vinyl of the booth, stretching the fabric of his shirt over those hair-roughened muscles that she remembered with such painful vividness. "If there weren't a few women left who liked men, the next generation would be sparse." He smiled coldly. "Not all of your gender are happily following their radical leaders and their man-hating agenda. Makeup-free lemmings," he added to get a rise out of her, "playing follow-the-leader off a cliff."

"Some men inspire women to start revolutions, Brannon," she pointed out.

"Oh, I don't know. I closed a door in a woman's face just yesterday." He smiled, watching her, waiting for a reaction.

He was absolutely gorgeous, she thought, watching him. He didn't look like the sort of man who liked to play, but he did. She remembered him with some teenagers on campus during an impromptu game of basketball; throwing sticks for one of his dogs on his own ranch. He could be as mischievous as any one of his cowboys. But there were only traces of that man in him now. He wasn't just making conversation. He was probing for weaknesses. So Josette was not going to get into a verbal sparring match with him. He could keep his good-old-boy prejudices until hair grew out of his ears, for all she cared.

"I want to know how Jennings got out of a maximum security prison, into a state facility, and then placed on a work detail," she said instead of gracing his remarks with a reply. Her dark eyes met his gray ones evenly. "Whoever was behind it, that would take more than mere influence. Money changed hands. A lot of money."

"I'm still looking for a motive," he said, irritated that she wouldn't rage at him. He hated that even, calm tone. The woman he'd known two years ago, even with her tragic background, had been feisty and happy and full of the joy of life. Her eyes had made love to his every time he'd looked at her. Now, they were empty eyes. They were painted windows with the curtains drawn.

"If we can find the evidence, we can find the murderer," she returned, pausing while the waitress returned with two mugs of steaming coffee and four little round tubs of half-and-half for Brannon. The waitress gave him yet another deliberate smile.

Brannon took time to return the smile, and wink. The waitress blushed, a breathless little giggle escaping from her lips before she continued to the next table, where another couple was just settling in. The back of the booth bowed behind Josette and she shifted, uncomfortably close to the table edge. It didn't bother her that he was flirting with the waitress. It didn't!

With an amused glance, Brannon busied himself with the cream and sugar, doctoring his coffee until it was just the right color and sweetness. He tasted it with his spoon before he placed the spoon carefully down on a napkin and lifted the mug to his lips.

"The motive is pretty obvious," he said after a minute, setting the mug down carefully on the Formica tabletop. "Jennings had something incriminating in his possession."

"I agree." She sipped her own black coffee thoughtfully, noting the rich, strong taste of it with pleasure. In so many restaurants, coffee was like lukewarm brown water. She often imagined the cooks putting coffee into a cloth sack and dragging it across the surface of water in a coffee urn. The image amused her and she smiled to herself.

"Something funny?" he asked.

She'd forgotten how observant he was. Nothing made it past those quick pale eyes. She recalled that he'd spent the past fourteen years of his life in law enforcement.

"I was thinking about the coffee, actually," she confessed, and told him what she'd been thinking.

His firm lips pursed in a faint smile. "That's why I like to eat here," he remarked, raising the mug deliberately. "Even when the food isn't perfect, the coffee always is." He took a sip and put the mug back down. "I went to see Mrs. Jennings this morning," he added unexpectedly. "She's in a downtown mission. She doesn't even have the price of a phone call."

His expression told her how he felt about that. Despite his faults, Brannon had a soft heart.

"Dale didn't give her anything to keep for him, did he?"

"Now that's an interesting question," he replied. "Because the house she'd owned was ransacked just before she was evicted. She was taken to the mission by a social worker. The woman was going to drive her back to her old home and help her collect her things, but when they got there, the house was already destroyed in a fire. Not a toothpick was salvaged."

Josette frowned. "Just in case they missed something, they covered all their bases. If the evidence was there, it went up in smoke."

"I don't think they know where it is," he replied. "If Mrs. Jennings didn't have it, she still may know where it is, even if she wouldn't admit it when I asked her. The fire could have been a not-so-subtle warning that she'd better cooperate. I talked to the police chief here and asked him to have his men keep an eye on the mission when they could. They don't have a budget for full-time surveillance," he added impatiently. "They hardly get enough to cover the bare necessities."

"It's like that everywhere," Josette said. "If we spent two percent as much money on law enforcement and poverty as we do on financial aid to other countries, we wouldn't have any crime."

"And no little kids would have to go hungry," he said. He shrugged. His pale eyes caught hers and he didn't smile. "Both of us know about poverty."

She smiled wistfully. "Don't we, though? And now your sister Gretchen's the equivalent of a queen."

"She carries it well," he pointed out with a sigh. "Wealth and power haven't changed her. She's doing a lot of good in Qawi for the underprivileged, and the UN recently asked her to do fund-raising work for them."

"She'll be a natural."

It disturbed him how much Josette knew about his family, his history. She probably knew that his father drank like a fish and had the business sense of a frog, too. Only his premature death in a corral had saved the family ranch from certain bankruptcy. There were no real secrets in his hometown of Jacobsville, Texas.

"What are we going to do about Mrs. Jennings?" Josette asked abruptly. "She's bound to be a continuing target if the perpetrator didn't get what he or she was looking for."

He nodded. "If I were the perpetrator, I wouldn't assume that something I couldn't find was in a house, even if I torched it. I'd find a way to make Mrs. Jennings talk."

She grimaced. "That's not a heartening thought. Got any ideas, beyond scanty surveillance?"

"Glad you asked. You can have Mrs. Jennings move into your hotel with you for the next couple of weeks and keep an eye on her," he said.

"Great idea. But who's going to pay for that? Our budget won't stand it," she said, aghast.

"Get Grier to talk to the D.A. for you. If he takes the trouble to ask for things, they usually give it to him without any argument."

"Grier?" she asked, knowing the name rang a bell but unable to place it.

"Cash Grier. He's the cybercrime expert with the D.A.'s office here." He eyed her curiously. "You haven't met him?"

"No. They put me in the office with him at another desk and said I'd work out of it, but that's about all they said. Well, except that I mustn't believe everything I heard about him. He was out of the office all day."

"You'll hear plenty. He worked for us, just briefly, but he hated the commanding officer, so he quit."

"That makes two of you," she couldn't resist saying.

He didn't tell her the real reason he'd left the Rangers. His temporary commanding officer two years ago was the obvious one—most of the men had hated him. "Buller made a lot of enemies. He was allowed to resign, just after he lost Grier and me both at once," he said shortly. "Damned paper-clip-counting bureaucrat. The high-ups wanted to know why we had such a turnover in this office, so after I left, the staff told them. Straight up. Buller wasn't fired, but he was cautioned that if he didn't voluntarily resign, he'd regret it."

"Ouch. I guess he had skeletons in his closet."

"Buller was the single bad apple we ever had in our outfit," he said proudly, "and he was barely there two months, just filling in. But we all have skeletons," he said quietly, and without meeting her eyes. He finished the last swallow of his coffee. It left a faint, pleasant bitterness on his tongue.

"Somebody has a big skeleton, and if we don't find

it, Dale Jennings is going to have a lot of company, wherever he went in the hereafter."

He nodded. "I phoned Jones over at the medical examiner's office, but she's got bodies stacked up. She said the staff's on overtime and it will be another twenty-four hours before the forensic pathologist gets to work on our DB. That means it'll be in the morning before we get much about Jennings's autopsy."

"Jones." She pursed her lips. "You wouldn't mean, by any chance, Alice Mayfield Jones from Floresville?"

His eyebrows arched. "You know her?"

She chuckled. "She was at college with me," she said. Her somber expression lightened just for a few seconds. "She was a great prankster."

"She hasn't changed much," Brannon told her.

His salad, and hers, arrived, and so did his steak. For a few minutes they ate without speaking. Both refused dessert, and over their second cups of coffee, they got back to the subject of Jennings.

"I think that Jennings's murder is connected to Henry Garner's," Josette said.

"Why?"

"Because of the amount of money involved."

"Don't say a word about Bib Webb," he cautioned coldly.

"You stop that," she said irritably, glaring at him. "Everybody, and I mean everybody, is a suspect. You have to be a law enforcement officer in this investigation. Period. You can't afford to be prejudiced. Not in your position."

He almost ground his teeth, but he had to admit that she had a point. "Okay," he conceded.

Her eyes softened. "I know he's your friend," she

said gently. "I know you don't want to do anything that might hurt him."

He hesitated. "You don't know him the way I do," he said quietly. "He loved Henry Garner. The old man was more like a father to him than his own father ever was. Bib's father deserted the family when he was just a kid. He had to support his mother and sister before he was even out of high school. After his mother died, he looked after his sister, until she died of a drug overdose. Not one single person had ever done a damned thing for Bib—except Henry. He couldn't even come to Henry's funeral," he added.

Josette nodded. She'd known that. She assumed it was guilt, of a sort.

"It wasn't publicized, but we had to have a doctor come out to sedate him," he added.

"Because of the grief," she began.

"Hell, no!" he shot back. "Because he was raging like a homicidal maniac! He thought it had to be some of Jennings's mob contacts, that Jennings had arranged the murder because he knew Henry was going to fire him. He wanted to throttle Jennings with his bare hands. It took two shots of Valium to put him to sleep, at that. And when he came around, he couldn't stop crying for another two days. He hated Jennings."

Josette didn't mention the obvious, that it gave him a motive for Jennings's death. But something about the episode unsettled her. She remembered Bib Webb's wife, Silvia, at the funeral, dressed in a black Versace suit, smiling at the other mourners.

"Webb's wife has very expensive tastes," she remarked without thinking.

"Silvia lost her brother and her father just before she

started going out with Bib. She was on the street and she didn't even have the price of a pair of shoes when she was sixteen, and Bib married her."

"That's young to marry," she said warily.

"He thought she was twenty. At any rate, she was old enough to be pregnant with Bib's child," he replied. He didn't like Silvia, and it showed.

"I didn't know they had a child," she said.

"They don't. She miscarried," he replied. "At barely two months. She went on a shopping trip to Dallas and apparently fell down some stairs at the hotel where she was staying. She said the doctor told her she could never have other children because of the damage it did."

Josette almost said, how convenient, but she was having enough trouble with Brannon as it was. She really couldn't picture Silvia as a mother; the woman was too selfish.

"She's very possessive, isn't she?" she murmured absently. "The night of the party, she hardly let her husband out of her sight for a minute."

"She's like that." He studied her, toying with his empty mug. "She was with him all evening, I suppose?"

"Actually she wasn't," she said honestly. "Dale went outside and I didn't see him or Silvia for several minutes. When they came back, separately, Dale was preoccupied and Silvia's hair was windblown. I remember that your friend Bib was dancing with a neat little brunette in a rather conservative dress, and Silvia almost made a scene over it when she saw them."

"Becky Wilson," he murmured, remembering Webb's personal assistant. She was usually invited to parties, over Silvia's constant objections. "Was this before or after you talked to Henry Garner?"

"After," she said. "I went to get some punch to drink and started talking to another woman guest at the punch bowl. A few minutes later, I looked around to see where Mr. Garner was, but I couldn't find him. Just after that I realized that the punch was spiked. I got very sick and Silvia offered to drive me home." Her eyes were sad. "I liked Mr. Garner. He was honest and gentle and kind. All he talked about was Bib Webb and what a hard life he'd had. He really loved him."

"It was mutual," Brannon said roughly. "Why were you with Garner? Wasn't Jennings your date?" It was difficult to talk about that. At the time, when he knew from court testimony that she'd accepted a date with Jennings only days after they'd broken up, he'd been devastated.

"Dale and I were acquaintances and he needed a date for the party," she said honestly, having decided that lies were no way to deal with problems. "I went just to make up the numbers. Dale was pleasant enough, and I didn't know about his mob connections until that night. Henry Garner told me about them."

"Told you what, exactly?" he asked, perking up.

"That he'd come to the party exclusively to fire Dale because of a theft at his house. He'd put something up in his safe and it had been removed."

Brannon almost held his breath. "Bingo!" he exclaimed.

CHAPTER SIX

"I DON'T UNDERSTAND," Josette said, frowning.

Brannon leaned forward, his big, lean hands clasped together around his empty coffee mug. "Listen to what you said, Josette—Garner was going to fire Jennings because he thought Jennings stole something from him. What if Garner was killed not because of his wealth and its beneficiaries, but because he had evidence of some criminal dealings? What if the murderer killed him to silence him, and then couldn't find the evidence he had?"

"Oh, that's chilling," she replied. "That's really chilling."

"It puts a whole new light on things," he agreed. "Maybe we were looking in the wrong direction altogether at Jennings's trial."

"I don't believe Dale did it," she began.

"And I don't believe Bib did." He cocked an eyebrow and his eyes lost their hard glare. "Maybe we're both right."

She nodded slowly. Then she nodded enthusiastically. "Maybe we are!"

Brannon warmed to his subject. "Suppose Henry Garner had evidence of wrongdoing, and threatened to go to the police with it. He was killed and the murderer couldn't find the evidence. Suppose Jennings did steal it, and hid it, figuring he'd use it for blackmail instead of bringing the culprit or culprits to justice."

"That's a lot of 'supposes.'" But she began to see the light. "And Dale Jennings denied that he'd committed the murder…"

"Only at first," he reminded her. "He denied it and then, all of a sudden, he had his lawyer plea-bargain for a reduced sentence by admitting to a lesser charge than murder one. Why?"

Her eyes brightened. "Someone offered him something," she guessed. "Money."

"Money. That's a good place to start looking." He twirled his empty mug on the table, thinking. "But if there was a payoff, why wait another two years to kill him?"

"His mother," she said at once. "She'd just been swindled out of her life savings and was left homeless and impoverished, and an invalid. He might have contacted the perpetrator and demanded more money. This time maybe he offered to give up the evidence. Maybe he'd only asked for a moderate amount before and when he heard about his mother's condition, he asked for more money. A lot more. For his mother."

"Not bad," Brannon mused. His pale eyes twinkled at her, as they had in the old days, before they were enemies. "Ever thought of devoting yourself to law enforcement as a career?"

She gave him a "duh" stare and finished her own coffee. "I think we're onto something. Where do we start?"

"At the most likely place. Let's find out who was in contact with Jennings in prison besides his attorney."

She pulled a small notepad out of her purse and flipped the pages. "I have a list of his correspondents and the names of people he phoned—addresses and telephone numbers." She handed it to him.

He gave her a narrow glare. "You should have been a doctor. Nobody could read this!"

"Everybody's a critic," she murmured, taking it back. "First name on the list is Jack Holliman. He lives in Floresville, southeast of here in Wilson County. He's Dale's uncle."

Brannon raised an eyebrow. "Convenient, that he lives so close to the prison."

"Probably too convenient, but we have to start somewhere." She picked up her ticket and got to her feet. He did the same. They paid for their meals in silence before they walked back out to his utility vehicle.

MINUTES LATER, they pulled into the long driveway of a small ranch. The fences were falling down. The dirt road was full of potholes. When they pulled up at the small house, they could see the peeling paint and missing porch rails.

As they got out of the car and started up the steps, a shotgun barrel snaked out the cracked door and there was the sound of a trigger being cocked. Josette hesitated.

Brannon never missed a step. "Texas Rangers!" Brannon announced in a curt tone, and kept walking. "If you pump any buckshot into me and I don't die on the spot, you'll live to regret it!"

The hammer quickly uncocked and the door opened. A little old man, bent with age and white-haired, peered at his shirt through pale blue eyes. "Yep, that's a Ranger badge, all right," he said in a thin, raspy voice. "Well, come in. I reckon you won't be trying to plug me," he added with a laugh.

The inside of the house was as gloomy as the outside. It smelled of pipe smoke and burning wood and sweat. It was hot, but the old man seemed not to notice. He sat down gingerly in a rocking chair graced by an embroidered cushion and a faded, colorful afghan. He motioned his visitors to the only other two chairs in the room, cane-bottomed and flimsy-looking with cushions that looked as if they hadn't ever seen soap. In fact, so did the old man.

"We're looking for Jack Holliman," Brannon said, easing down into the chair and leaning forward, his steely-gray eyes unblinking.

"That's me," the old man said heavily. "I guess you came about my nephew, Dale." The old man grimaced. "Hell of a way for a man to die, warn't it?" he drawled. "Shot like a dog in an alley. He was the last family I had, except for my sister."

"Dale Jennings was your only nephew?" Josette asked.

"Yep," he said. "My kid sister's only child. His pa's been dead since he was ten. His ma couldn't fix what his pa did to him." His pale blue gaze dropped to the worn rug on the floor. "His pa was always in some sort of trouble, right up till the day he died. He taught the boy how to break the law."

"Do you know of anyone who might have wanted to kill your nephew?" Brannon asked quietly.

"No," he said at once. "I know they all said he killed that Garner fellow, but I never believed it. Dale might forge a check or steal a credit card, something like that, to get money for his ma, but he never would have killed anybody. He was the sort who'd stop to help a hurt animal and give everything he had on him to pay a vet to save it."

"I know," Josette said quietly, and without looking at Brannon. "He and I were acquaintances," she elaborated. "I never thought he was a murderer, either. Now I want to know who killed him. If you can think of anything that might help us track down the person who shot him, we'd be grateful."

The old man pursed his thin lips and nodded slowly. "I wrote to him in prison. He was a bad letter writer, but he did send me a card last month. I'll get it." He got up with obvious pain, grimacing as he went to a small table and opened the drawer. He pulled out a card-size envelope with his address on the front and handed it to Josette.

She opened it. The card, a landscape, was written in bad handwriting. The note was very brief, mostly asking about the old man and recalling the last time he'd been to see him, before he was arrested for Garner's murder and a horseback ride he and the old man had taken to a bubbling spring in a pasture.

"He never stopped talking about that last time we rode together," he recalled sadly. "I remember he brought his own saddle, had it made special, so he could ride when I did." He smiled sheepishly. "Since I got down with my hip, money's been tight. I kept two horses, but I only had the one saddle." He sat back down with a sigh. "Still got the one he brought," he recalled. "It's fancy, even got hand-tooled saddlebags." He shook his head. "He always loved this old place, loved the country. He stayed in town to look after my sister, when she was so bad sick. He might have been wild, but he always looked after his mama. Would have left the ranch to him, if things had been different. I just sold off my horses last week. I guess I'll sell the saddle as well. Nobody needs it anymore."

Brannon turned the card over in his hands and then passed it over to Josette.

"I can't get in touch with my sister," the old man said. "Not since she told me about Dale. Would go to the funeral, but there ain't nobody to drive me. She said she'd call me up and tell me about it, after. But now I can't call her. The phone at her house is disconnected. Is she all right?"

Brannon and Josette exchanged wary glances.

He looked so frail that they hated telling him.

"She's all right," Josette said at once. "But her house caught fire and burned. She has a nice place now, in a retirement village. I'll get her telephone number, or one of her neighbors', and send it to you."

He sighed wearily. "Thank you, girl," he said in a defeated tone. "Looks like everything's going. Never thought getting old would be like this, that I'd be so crippled I couldn't do anything for myself." His pale eyes met Josette's. "Don't take life for granted, young lady. Squeeze every drop out of it, while you can."

She smiled. "I try to."

Brannon took the card back from her. "I don't guess you know any of Jennings's friends or co-workers?"

"Co-workers? Never knew the boy to have but one job, working for that old man who got killed," Holliman said. "He sure was proud of that job. The last time he was up here, though, he said something strange," he remembered, frowning. "Said he'd done something he wished he hadn't. Wanted to protect the old man from some sort of threat," he continued. "He said he hoped he'd done the right thing." He glanced at Brannon. "Any idea what that meant?"

"Not yet," Brannon said, getting to his feet. "But I will have. That's a promise. We'll be in touch about your sister. She's all right."

Holliman slowly got to his feet. "Thanks for stopping by. Uh, sorry about the shotgun," he added. "Dale told me to keep my doors locked and watch if strangers came around. Never knew why, but it seemed like good advice, just the same."

"No problem. No need to walk us out," Brannon added. "I'll lock the door as we go. You do have a phone?"

The old man pointed to it. "Not that it would be much use if anybody meant me harm, way out here in the sticks," he added meaningfully. "But I got my shotgun."

Brannon gave him an even look. "Got a dog?"

"Can't take care of one."

"Keep that shotgun close, and your doors locked," Brannon told him. "I'll ask the sheriff to get his deputies to increase their patrols out this way."

Holliman smiled. "Thanks, son."

Brannon glanced at the wall and hesitated with the doorknob in his hand. "Jennings is being buried tomorrow at 2:00 p.m. If you want to go, say so. I'll come and get you."

The old man swallowed hard. "You'd do that for a stranger?"

Brannon touched an old, worn pistol and holster that Josette hadn't even noticed, hanging on a nail beside the door. Hanging on the nail with it was a faded, worn silver Texas Ranger badge. "We aren't strangers," he said quietly.

Holliman nodded. "Then I'd like to go. Thanks."

"No problem. I'll be here at one-thirty."

"Thank you for giving us so much of your time, Mr. Holliman," Josette said.

"Not much else to do with it, except talk," he replied, and grinned.

She smiled back and waited for Brannon on the porch, while he pushed the lock and closed the door firmly behind him.

"I didn't even notice the holster," she confessed. "You're observant."

"You might be forgiven for not thinking so, considering the mistakes I've made," he said tersely.

She let that go. "Do you think someone might hurt him?" she asked as they got back into the black SUV.

"A murderer who's killed twice won't hesitate. After all, he can only be executed once," he replied as he started the vehicle. "We've seen evidence of how desperate he is to get whatever Jennings had on him. Anyone who's connected with Jennings, in any way, is in danger. And I still think Jake Marsh is up to his neck in it."

She wrapped her arms around her chest. It wasn't chilly, but she was remembering poor old Mrs. Jennings. "Dale's mother's house has been ransacked and she's been burned out. Surely the murderer won't bother her again."

He gave her a quick glance as he pulled out onto the highway. "He will if he thinks she knows something. That's just Marsh's style, if it is him."

"Lord," she whispered huskily, looking out the window. "What a fearful thing, to be old and helpless and have nothing."

"To date, we've been living in a country that punishes age."

She smiled sadly. "I guess."

"Hell of a shame, a man like Holliman, who spent his life protecting other people, has to live like that," he commented as they drove along. His face was somber. "There are hundreds like him, not just in Texas, but all over the country, men who put their lives on the line every day to save others. And this is how they're repaid, with retirement and Social Security that isn't even enough to pay for their medicine, most of the time."

"That isn't right."

"Don't get me started," he cautioned. He made another turn, and they were on the road back to San Antonio.

There was a long, tense silence. Josette felt worn and wrinkled. The past two days had been so rushed that she'd hardly slept. It was beginning to catch up with her.

He noticed her lack of animation. "We'll go see Mrs. Jennings tomorrow, after the funeral," he said. "Meanwhile, I'm going to talk to the warden at the state prison."

"Do you think he'll know who pulled the strings to get Jennings assigned there?" she asked drowsily.

"Not really. But he may have contacts who can find out," he replied. "This whole thing is fishy. I don't see how a system with so many checks and balances can let a convicted murderer slip through the cracks."

"Money talks," she murmured, closing her eyes.

He glanced at her, noticing the new lines in her young face. Her traumatic life was written there. She'd made one error in judgment, and it had tormented her ever since. He hadn't helped, with his certainty that she'd tried to frame the local politician's son for rape. He was sorry that he'd helped get the boy off. It was something he wasn't ever going to be able to justify, especially considering the fact that he'd seen her at that party, half naked and cowering and sobbing, so sick and afraid that she wasn't even coherent. He hated his own treatment of her later even more.

"Did you ever find out what the boy gave you at that party when you were fifteen?" he asked, thinking aloud.

"Yes," she murmured, too drowsy to protest the question. "The forerunner of the date-rape drug."

He stiffened. "Of all the mistakes I've ever made in my life, I regret helping that boy get off the most. I should have known better."

"It's all ancient history, Brannon," she said impassively. "We can't change anything."

"I wish to God I could," he said harshly. "I rushed to judgment about you. I've ruined your life."

"I helped," she returned without looking at him. "I deliberately left the house at night to go to what I knew would be a wild party. I was rebelling against my stodgy old parents. And guess what? They were right all along. I was too young to handle experienced boys and alcohol and drugs. Because of what I did, their lives were ruined, too. Dad couldn't keep his job in Jacobsville. We had to move, and he had to take a big cut in salary. They died a lot younger than they probably would have," she added gruffly. "All because I didn't like having rules when nobody else did."

His jaw clenched. He felt as guilty about that as she did. She'd been too young to know better, and he'd been a young police officer who was still learning how to size up suspects. He hadn't done a very good job with Josette's assailant.

His hands contracted on the steering wheel. "What I hate most is that if it had been Gretchen, I wouldn't have been so quick to believe him."

"Your sister had better sense than I did, at the same age," she mused. "Gretchen was always mature for her age. I guess that was because your mother was ill so much. You lost your father when you were young, didn't you?"

"Yes. We lost him," he said in an odd tone. "Gretchen looked after our mother when she was in the terminal stages of cancer. I felt bad about that. I was with the FBI then, and working undercover. I couldn't even come home."

"I never understood why you left the Rangers," she commented. "You never wanted anything as much as that job, and then just as you were getting promotions, you quit. Just like that."

"I quit because of you."

She blinked. Perhaps she was hearing things. "Excuse me?"

"Even though you seemed to be a decent sort of woman, there was always a part of me that thought you'd been lying about the rape—that you were scared and accused the boy to exonerate yourself." He stopped at a red light, and his eyes under the brim of his hat pinned her face. "Then I made love to you."

She felt her whole body go hot with the memory. Her face was rigid, but her hands, on the briefcase in her lap, jerked.

"What a revelation that was," he said curtly. "He

couldn't have raped you if he'd tried, not in the condition you were in."

"Could we not talk about that, please?" she asked tightly, averting her face.

He glared at the traffic light, which was still red. "That was when I knew just how faulty my judgment really was," he continued, as if she hadn't spoken. "I helped the defense attorney put the final nail in your coffin, when you were the real victim. Everything you suffered, everything your parents suffered, could be laid right at my door. I couldn't live with knowing that. I had to get away."

"You did a good job of that," she said stiffly. "You called me names, took me home and walked away. The next time I saw you was in court, at Dale Jennings's trial." Her expression cooled.

"Then the prosecuting attorney took me apart on the witness stand and branded me a liar."

"Bib gave that information to the D.A.," he said at once. "He remembered it from early in our friendship, because it had bothered me and I talked about it. But I wouldn't have used it against you. Especially," he added harshly, "not after what I knew about you. I didn't know they even had knowledge of it until I heard it in court. And then it was too late to stop it." He noticed that the light was green and put his booted foot down on the accelerator gently. He felt gutted as he remembered the pain he'd felt at the trial. "After the prosecution took you apart on the witness stand, you wouldn't even look at me. I couldn't blame you for that. I'd done enough damage already. Afterward, it was one more reason to get out of San Antonio."

"You could have stayed," she said, her voice strained. "My parents and I moved away."

"Another move, another job, and your father's heart couldn't take it."

"Life happens, Brannon," she said wearily. "Maybe if it hadn't been this, it would have been something else. My father was fond of saying God always has a reason for things, that He tests us in all sorts of ways—that He even uses other people to do it sometimes. That's why we shouldn't hold grudges, he said." She shrugged and shifted the briefcase. "I don't blame you for what happened. Not anymore."

Which was far more than he deserved. But what she wasn't saying was poignant—that she still cared about him. How could she, after what he'd done?

They were back in the city. He turned onto the street where her hotel was located and pulled up in the courtyard.

"Do you want to go to Jennings's funeral tomorrow?" he asked.

"Yes," she replied at once. "I'd like to see if I recognize anybody in the crowd."

He smiled faintly. "That's why I want to go."

"I figured that. I'll see you…"

"I'll come by for you about one," he said. "Then we can go out and pick up Holliman."

She hesitated. Her fingers traced a pattern on the leather surface of her case.

"It's the logical way to do things, Josette," he said quietly. "We have to work together."

"I know." She opened the door. "Okay. I'll be in the lobby at one."

"Maybe by then, I'll have a new lead, at least."

She studied him through the open door as she held it in one hand. "I don't have to tell you that it needs someone with influence to accomplish a murder like Dale's."

"I'm not stupid," he agreed. His gray eyes narrowed. "Do you carry a piece?"

She glared at him. "No, and I won't. I've got a nice little electronic device in my purse that packs a powerful punch, and I'm no wimp under fire. I'll get by."

"A gun is safer."

"Only if you're not afraid of it," she reminded him. "And I am afraid of guns. You watch your own back, Brannon. I've had a lot of experience taking care of myself."

"So you have."

She closed the door and turned to walk into the hotel. He noticed that she smiled at the doorman, who went to open the door for her with a matching smile. Josette had always been like that, gentle and friendly and compassionate. It made him sick to remember his treatment of her.

He pulled out of the driveway and back onto the street. He really should go by the office, but he wanted to talk to the warden of the nearby state prison. He pulled over into a parking spot and used his mobile phone to get the number and dial it. He made an appointment with the warden, who had the afternoon free, before he pulled back out into the street and turned on the road that led to Floresville.

JOSETTE WENT INTO her hotel room and collapsed on one of the two double beds. She was worn to the bone. A bath was just what she needed, to soothe her aching muscles.

She uncoiled her hair and let it loose. Unfurled, it reached down to her hips in back. It was dark blond, soft, faintly wavy. If only she'd been pretty, too, that hair would have made her like a siren, she theorized. But, then, the only man she'd ever wanted to attract was Brannon, and that door had better stay closed.

She touched her throat and closed her eyes. Even after two years, she could feel Brannon's hard, warm mouth on her throat, working its way down over her collarbone. Her pulse raced. She'd tried so hard to put the painful memories away, but they were tenacious. Josette looked at herself in the mirror. Her eyes were huge, soft. Her mouth was just faintly swollen. She looked…sensuous.

Josette turned away from the mirror, hating her own responses. Brannon didn't want her. He never had. He had a terrible opinion of her; he'd said himself that she wasn't woman enough for him. Why couldn't she get over him? Despite the men she worked around, there had never been another one who attracted her. No matter how hard she tried to get interested in other nice, single men, there was only one in her heart, despite the misery he'd caused her.

She stripped off her clothing and went into the bathroom to shower. Minutes later, when she came back out, in her bathrobe and rubbing her hair dry, the message light on the phone was blinking.

Josette sat down on the bed and lifted the receiver to call the lobby.

It was the secretary at the D.A.'s office. "Miss Langley?" the pleasant voice asked. "I just wanted to give you this new address for Mrs. Jennings. The social worker found her a nice little apartment out at Pioneer

Village near Elmendorf—one of our local retirement complexes."

"That's nice," Josette said warmly. "I was worried about her at the mission. She's not really able to take care of herself..."

"That's just what the social worker said" came the reply. "She's very happy at her new address. Have you got a pen and paper?"

"Yes. Right here." She fumbled for them in her purse. "Okay." She wrote down the address as the woman dictated it. "Has she got a phone?"

"Not yet," the secretary said. "But her neighbor, Mrs. Danton, said she'd be glad to take messages for her. Here's the number." She gave that to Josette, too.

"Thanks," Josette told her. "Brannon and I are going with her brother to the funeral tomorrow. I'll phone Mrs. Danton tonight and ask her to ask Mrs. Jennings if she'd like us to pick her up, too, since she hasn't got any way to go. Her brother was upset because he hadn't heard from her."

"Mr. Holliman? Oh, yes, Grier in our office is a veritable ongoing documentary of his life. It seems that Mr. Holliman was *the* Texas Ranger around these parts in the fifties and sixties."

"I'd love to hear about him," Josette said, smiling to herself. "Thanks for the information."

"My pleasure. See you."

Josette hung up and put the pad in her purse. She was already thinking ahead to tomorrow. She hadn't really wanted to go to Dale's funeral. It wasn't that long ago that she'd lost her parents, both of them within just two years. But it went with the job. She was just going to have to face it.

CHAPTER SEVEN

THE WARDEN OF the Wayne Correctional Institute near Floresville was a heavyset, taciturn man named Don Harris. He offered Brannon a chair, crossed his hands neatly on his desk and let Brannon tell him what he wanted.

He pushed a button on his intercom. "Jessie, get me the file on Dale Jennings and bring it in here, would you?"

"Sir, you can pull it up on your computer," she began.

"Oh. Oh, so I can. Never mind." He hung up, disconcerted as he turned to the computer on the side of his desk and punched in information with two fingers. "Hate these damned things," he muttered. "One day somebody will pull the plug and shut down civilization."

Brannon chuckled heartily. "I couldn't agree more. That's why I keep hard copy of every case file I've got, no matter what the experts tell me about zip files and hard-drive backups."

The warden smiled, the first warm expression Brannon had seen on the man's face since he walked in. "Good for you." He looked at the screen. "Yes, here it is. Jennings was transferred down here two weeks ago from the state prison in Austin…"

"State prison in Austin?" Brannon shot to his feet,

went around the desk and looked over the warden's shoulder, with a murmured apology.

There it was on the screen—Jennings's file. Except that it had been altered. It didn't show a murder conviction. According to the file, Jennings was in for a battery charge, serving a one-year sentence in a state prison.

"That's been altered," he told the warden flatly. "Jennings was serving time for felony murder. He was in federal prison in Austin, not a state facility. The charge that's showing is an old one, from his teens. He got probation for it."

The warden looked sick. "You mean, I let a convicted murderer out on a trustee work detail?"

Brannon touched his shoulder lightly. "Not your fault," he said reassuringly. "The files were obviously doctored. Jennings's escape was carefully arranged. Apparently we're up against a computer hacker as well as a crafty assassin," he added curtly.

"I'll lose my pension," the warden was murmuring.

"Oh, no, you won't," Brannon told him. "I'm working for Simon Hart, the state attorney general. I'll make sure he knows the situation. You can't possibly keep up personally with several hundred inmate histories. It's not your fault."

"It's my prison," Harris said harshly. "I should be able to do it."

"None of us are superhuman," Brannon said. "I'd like hard copy of that file, if you don't mind."

"I can do that, at least," Harris said, crestfallen. He pushed the button to print out the file and rose to get it from a tray across the room. He waited for it to finish, and collected the pages into a new file folder, presenting them to Brannon. "Get the person who did this," he said.

"See that?" Brannon asked, indicating his Ranger badge. "We never quit."

The warden managed a smile. "Thanks."

"We're all doing the job. Thank you."

He took his file and left.

THE SUN WAS out for Jennings's funeral. It was a warm day, and there wasn't much traffic as Josette sat beside Brannon, with a mothball-scented Holliman seated in the back, as Brannon pulled up at the cemetery minutes before Jennings's funeral.

Brannon helped Holliman out and escorted the old gentleman to the graveside, with Josette bringing up the rear.

There weren't a lot of people present, and most of them were law enforcement. Brannon recognized the sheriff, the local police chief, a couple of plainclothes detectives and Mrs. Jennings, in an obviously borrowed black dress. Josette had phoned Mrs. Danton and had her ask Mrs. Jennings if she wanted Brannon to drive her to the funeral. But Mrs. Danton phoned back and told Josette that the sheriff had already offered to transport the little old lady.

It was easy to see that the burial was being paid for by the taxpayers, since Mrs. Jennings very obviously had nothing left after the fire. There was a hole and a coffin, but none of the niceties that would have gone with a proper funeral.

Josette looked at the simple pine coffin and remembered, all too well, her parents' funerals. At least they'd had insurance, so there was a service in church and then a drive to the cemetery for burial. Poor Dale Jennings had only a hole in the ground.

She remembered him, tall and fair and a little cocky, only four years older than she was. His brashness and the abrupt way he had with people made it hard for him to make friends. But Josette had seen through the protective shell to the man underneath. Not that she was blind to his lack of honesty, which was all too apparent. When he'd asked her to a party at Webb's, she'd debated about going. But Marc Brannon had just walked out on her and her ego was badly bruised. She'd expected Brannon to show up at his friend Bib Webb's party, and that was the only reason she'd accepted Dale's invitation. What a difference there might have been if Brannon had come that night.

She stared at the coffin with sad eyes. It seemed such a waste. If only Dale had stayed in prison. Even if it was for his mother's sake, his own greed had seen him done in by a bullet. Blackmail was repulsive, regardless of the reason, Josette thought. There was a price for such underhanded conduct, and Dale had paid it.

She thought of her father, an honest man who'd never done a thing to hurt any other human being. Then she thought of Dale, in that lonely grave on the outskirts of the cemetery, in a mound of earth that would only be marked by a simple white card in a metal holder with a plastic face. Over the years, it would fade until it was no longer recognizable. And it would be as if Dale Jennings of San Antonio, Texas, had never even been born.

A movement caught her eye, and she watched as Jack Holliman went right to his sister and hugged her close.

"They killed my baby, Jack," the white-haired old woman said huskily, tears pouring down her lean, pale face. "Shot him down in the street like a dog."

"I know. I'm sorry. I'm so sorry." He patted her back awkwardly.

Two men were standing by the coffin. One, well-groomed and wearing a nice suit, had to be the funeral director. The other, a slight man with thinning hair and about Dale's age, clutched a Bible. The minister, she assumed. Josette noticed the funeral home director looking impatient, and she turned and started moving the elderly couple toward the grave. There wasn't even a tent to shelter silver hair from the blistering sun, or folding chairs to take the weight off arthritic legs.

The coffin was a cheap one, and the service was very brief. The minister was soft-spoken and a little nervous as he spoke about Dale Jennings, whom he said he never met. He read a couple of lines of scripture, endearing himself to Josette when he stumbled over the pronunciation of some of the words. Then he led a prayer, still inarticulate, and folded his Bible against his hip before he walked over to offer his condolences to the elderly people, with the crisp black cover of the Bible held tightly in his hand. A wide gold ring on his little finger caught the sun and sparkled.

That was when Josette noticed that he was dressed very much like Mrs. Jennings and her brother, in clothes which were functional rather than decorative. She realized also that he'd probably offered to conduct the service out of his own generosity rather than for any monetary concession. She decided that she'd dig into her own purse for that compensation, but she was a minute too late. She saw Brannon pause beside the minister and place a bill gently in his hands. She had to turn away so that Brannon wouldn't see the mist over her eyes. He had a big heart. It was one of so many things she loved about him.

Josette composed herself and turned her attention to the small crowd as Brannon paused to talk to the sheriff. Brannon, too, was looking around for anyone in the small crowd who shouldn't have been there. But it would have been too obvious for the killer to join in.

"Unless you think the sheriff or one of those detectives is the culprit, we're out of luck," Brannon murmured to her.

"I don't want to get old, and I don't want to die poor," she said stiffly.

"Don't look at me," he returned, shifting his gaze to Holliman. "I expect I'll end up packed in mothballs like that suit Holliman's wearing, greeting visitors with a shotgun and spending the hour before I eat trying to remember where I put my false teeth."

"Oh, that was wicked," she said softly, trying not to smile. It wasn't an occasion for humor.

"Notice the minister isn't standing too close to him," he pointed out. "The smell of the mothballs is overpowering." He looked down at her with concern she didn't see. "This must be rough for you."

Her gaze flew up to his. It embarrassed her that he knew. She moved one shoulder in her neat black suit. That and a navy blue one were the only clothes she'd packed, besides her gown and robe. There wasn't much of a choice of outfits.

"You've lost your parents, too," she pointed out.

"With more distance between their deaths, though," he replied. His face was hard as he looked toward the grave. "And I didn't care that my father died."

She'd never heard him mention his father, in all the

time she'd known him. She remembered a few low whispers around Jacobsville, that the Brannon kids had a tough life, but she'd assumed it was because their mother was widowed and sick a lot.

"Didn't you love him?" she asked involuntarily.

"No."

A single word, endowed with more sarcasm and bitterness than he might have realized.

She waited, but he didn't say another word. The minister moved on and he went to escort the old people back to the truck.

"We'll drive you to your apartment, Mrs. Jennings, and save the sheriff a trip," he told her, revealing that he knew how she'd arrived.

The sheriff thanked him and made their goodbyes, along with the detectives. Brannon helped the old people into the truck and got in beside Josette. Minutes later, they disembarked at the small efficiency apartment the social worker had found for Mrs. Jennings just off the Floresville road near Elmendorf.

"It ain't much," she said wearily as she pulled out her key. "But it's a roof over my head."

She unlocked the door and invited them inside. "I'll make some coffee."

"No, you won't," Josette said. She drew Brannon to one side and slipped him a ten-dollar bill. "Would you go get them a bucket of chicken and the fixings, and some cups of coffee?"

He pushed the money back into her hand and closed her fingers around it. "You're still a sucker for lost causes," he said huskily. "I'll get the chicken, and the coffee. You see what you can find out from her. Back in a minute."

She watched him go with a sense of breathlessness. He still got to her. It was disturbing.

She sat down on the sofa next to Mrs. Jennings and passed her a tissue. The old woman had been very dignified and quiet at the funeral, but it was all catching up with her now. She dissolved into tears. Mr. Holliman was trying his best not to be affected by it, sitting stoically in his chair until his sister calmed down.

"He was good to me," she told Josette in a husky old voice. "No matter what else he did, he was a good son."

"He didn't kill anyone, Mrs. Jennings, least of all Henry Garner," Josette said firmly, and with conviction. "I never doubted that for an instant. I just couldn't convince anyone else, with so much evidence against him."

"He never had no blackjack," the old woman said harshly. "Never liked physical violence at all."

"No, he didn't," Holliman added firmly. "I couldn't even teach the boy to shoot a gun. He was scared of them."

"I know he did some bad things, Miss Langley," Mrs. Jennings continued, wiping her nose with the tissue, "but he wouldn't hurt an old man."

"I'm certain of that," Josette replied. She leaned forward. "Mrs. Jennings, did Dale ever leave a package with you, something he wanted you to put up and keep for him?"

Old man Holliman shifted in his chair. Mrs. Jennings frowned, brushing at her mouth, and avoided Josette's eyes. "He did once say he had something that needed a safe place. But he never brought it to me," she said.

"Did he say what he did with it?" Josette continued, warming to her subject.

"No. He just said that woman wanted it."

"Woman?" Josette asked quickly. "What woman?"

"Don't know much about her," the older woman told her. "He mentioned her once or twice, said she was helping him with this new job he'd got. He thought she was real special, but he wouldn't bring her to see me, even when I asked. He said she was real shy, you see. He was talking about marrying her, but he said he didn't have enough money to suit her. He was always talking about getting enough to make her happy. He said she wanted him to keep that package in a real safe place. She wanted him to let her keep it, but he wouldn't give it to her. He said she'd be in danger if she had it. I asked," she added, glancing at Josette, "but he wouldn't tell me what it was."

This was something new. It was exciting to Josette that what had seemed a dead end was beginning to show promise.

"Did he say where the woman lived, what she did for a living?" Josette pressed.

"No. But he was seeing her before that mess he got into, and he worked here in San Antonio. I guessed she was a local girl. Oh, and he did say she loved peppermints. He was forever buying her fancy ones, whenever he went to the drugstore to pick up my medicine for me."

Peppermints. Josette dug out her pad and pen and wrote it down.

"Did he ever mention a man named Jake Marsh?" she persisted.

Mrs. Jennings and the old man exchanged a look, but the old woman just shook her head. "Not that I recall. He just talked about that woman."

"A bad woman can be the ruin of a good man," Holliman said sadly.

"No doubt about that," Mrs. Jennings retorted.

"Can you remember anything else he might have said about her?" Josette pressed.

"Well, he didn't say a whole lot about her," she repeated. "Not even what she looked like, although my Dale liked a good-looker. I don't think he would have been interested in an ugly girl."

"No, I don't either," Josette replied, but she was wondering about that, because he'd asked her to the Webb's party the night of the murder. Josette had a passable figure, but her face was just ordinary, not pretty, and she wore glasses. Funny, she hadn't thought of that until now.

"Didn't recognize that minister," Holliman murmured. "Did you?"

His sister shook her head. "I asked the funeral home director if he could find somebody," she replied. "He didn't even have to look. That young fellow volunteered to do it. Nice young fellow."

Holliman was about to say something when the front door opened and Brannon came in with a big sack of food, and a boxful of coffee cups. By the time they finished the meal, the thread of conversation was lost.

LATER, BRANNON TOOK Holliman home before he drove Josette back to her hotel and told her what he and the warden had discovered.

"We've got a guy in our office, back in Austin," she told him. "Phil Douglas. He gives Simon headaches, because he's so overeager, but he's a real hacker. There's nothing he doesn't know about computers. Maybe he could track down whoever changed those records."

"We've got people working on it, but you might give him a shot at it," Brannon replied immediately. "It had to take someone specialized. I know computers, but I couldn't get into protected files, even with my clearance."

"Neither could I," she agreed. "Something else—Mrs. Jennings said Dale was involved with a woman when Garner was murdered. She said he was obsessed with getting enough money to keep her happy, and that there was some sort of package involved. But Mrs. Jennings never saw it."

He'd already parked the truck near her hotel room. He leaned back in the seat and folded his arms over his broad chest. "A woman. Did she know what this woman looked like?"

"No. He didn't tell her much, just that the woman was smart and that she liked fancy candy."

"It's probably a dead end."

"That's what I thought," Josette agreed. She turned her purse over in her lap. "That was nice of you, slipping the minister money for preaching the funeral. I was going to do it, if you hadn't. He was sweet."

"Not long at the job, either, apparently," he mused, smiling. "His Bible was brand-new."

"He did a good job, for somebody who didn't know Dale."

He studied her from under the brim of his dress Stetson. "I hate funerals."

"Me, too, Brannon," she confessed. "But this one went with the job. I felt sorry for his mother and his uncle."

"They're good people. Sometimes the worst offenders come from the best families."

"I've learned that."

He studied her openly, one eye narrowed. "Tomorrow, I'm going to check out bank records and see if Jennings made any large deposits recently. You might phone your office and get that computer expert to work."

"I will. Thanks for driving today."

He shrugged. "I don't really feel comfortable riding with anyone else."

"I noticed. You were always like that. You can't give up control, can you, Brannon?" she added.

His face hardened. "I never had any when I was a kid. My father told me what to do, where to go, how to breathe. Gretchen was only ten, too young to understand much about how things were, but I wasn't. My mother couldn't call her soul her own. He upset her constantly. I kept him away from Gretchen. She never even knew how dangerous he was."

"At least he didn't take a short quirt to her," she said, recalling something that had happened to her friend Christabel at the age of sixteen.

He nodded. "Judd Dunn sent Christabel's father to jail for that, after he'd beaten him within an inch of his life. Christabel's protests and her mother's didn't faze him. Christabel almost died from the attack. Her back was in ribbons when her father got through with her. All because she tried to stop him from beating a horse."

"Are she and Judd still married?" she asked, because Judd was a good friend of his, and a fellow Texas Ranger.

"Yes." He smiled involuntarily. "And still not living together. She's, what, almost twenty-one now?"

"She was sixteen when he married her, for no other reason than to take care of her and her mother," she agreed. "Her father had no sooner got out of jail than he got drunk again and wrecked his car. He died of his injuries, so Judd still has the responsibility for the ranch, not to mention Christabel and her mother. You'd think he'd be glad to let her take over the ranch, and have the marriage annulled. She wrote me that a man she knows wants to marry her."

"That's what Judd told me," he commented, pushing his hat back on his head. "But he doesn't approve of her choice, and I wouldn't give a fig for Christabel's chances of an annulment."

She wondered about that. She didn't add that Christabel had also written her that she was either going to make Judd wild for her and seduce him, or make him give her up. It would be interesting to know who won that contest of wills.

His pale eyes slid over her body in the neat-fitting dark suit, down the long skirt to her ankles and back up to the high-buttoned white blouse she wore with the suit. "You always button the collar of your blouses," he commented. "And wear skirts down to the ankles. I wish you'd stayed in therapy, Josette. You don't move with the times."

"My life was ruined because I tried to."

The statement was bitter, full of self-recrimination. He laid his arm across the back of his seat and his pale eyes narrowed. "You don't have to sacrifice your principles to fit in these days," he said. "A lot of women prefer being celibate to risking their lives, and they're not afraid to say so. Sex is dangerous. Even men think twice before they indulge."

She averted her eyes to the windshield. "You, too, I guess?" she asked, and could have cursed herself for that involuntary question.

"Me, too," he said at once. "I don't want some fatal disease or a chronic condition doctors still can't cure."

"That doesn't stop a lot of men."

He was still watching her. He noticed the twinge of color on her high cheekbones. "You don't even date, do you?"

She thought about denying it, but there was really no point. "Not much," she said frankly, meeting his eyes. "I still don't have a clue about how men think, and I don't want to be accused of—teasing." She bit off the word as if it tasted bad.

He averted his face. His jaw clenched as his own words came back to haunt him.

"Surely you remember?" She clutched her purse. "You were eloquent about women who—how did you put it?—led men on and wouldn't deliver."

He grimaced. There was an audible sigh as he curled one big hand around the steering wheel and stared out the windshield. "I guess I was. I was shocked. Furious. All those years, I thought I was right when I helped get that boy off. To be confronted with positive proof that you were the real victim was painful." He slanted the hat back over his eyes, as if to hide them from her. "But I had no right to say those things to you, or to leave without a word, after we'd been going together for months."

"We never went together," she said in a monotone. "You took me out places. That's all it was."

"Until that last date, maybe." His jaw clenched again with emotion. "I don't like being wrong."

"Most of us make mistakes as we go along. Not you,

of course," she added with veiled sarcasm. "You never make mistakes, do you, Brannon? People are good or bad. No gray areas. No intangibles."

"I've been in law enforcement since I was eighteen," he said curtly. "The law is the law. You either break it or you don't."

She sighed. "Yes. I guess you're right. I'd better go in. I'll phone you tomorrow afternoon."

"I'll be out most of the day," he said tersely.

"Then I'll leave you a message, Brannon," she said sweetly, opening the door.

He turned his head and looked at her, saw the lines in her face, the dark circles under her eyes, the weariness. "Get some rest."

"I'm fine." She closed the door firmly, turned and went into the hotel. The doorman grinned at her and rushed to open the door. She didn't look back.

Brannon pulled out into the street with mixed emotions. He remembered the feel and taste of her in his arms. They were old memories but they were vivid when he was with her. He wondered if she remembered the magic they'd shared that one evening, before their lives were torn apart a second time. He'd never been able to get past it. Other women were good companions, but Josette was under his skin.

He thought about his father, about the misery the man had caused him and his mother with his incessant raving, his constant criticisms, his demands for perfection, even when he was sober. He'd grown up hating his father for being so inflexible, so judgmental and righteous. Abuse can come in many forms, and one of the worst was verbal. Only now did it dawn on him that he was becoming like his father. He did, as Josette had accused, see things only in black and white. He didn't allow for gray areas. There was only the law.

As he drove back to his own apartment, he considered that. His painful childhood was something he felt comfortable discussing with Josette, but he'd never talked about it to his own sister. Gretchen had been treated gently, cared for, loved by Marc and their mother. She had little memory of their father's brutality, because he was drinking regularly and had calmed down somewhat by the time Gretchen was old enough to be aware of his problems. He'd died while she was in grammar school. But Brannon's memories were much more painful. In many ways, they'd shaped him into the man he'd become.

On the other hand, Josette was better able to understand that sort of pain, because she'd experienced it in her own life. They shared a history of turmoil and unrest. A lot of her problems were probably his fault. But circumstances had been unkind to both of them.

INSIDE HER HOTEL ROOM, Josette was thinking the same thing. She felt drained from the conversation, from the long day, from the case, from the past—she was simply exhausted.

She had room service send supper to her room, which took up most of the rest of the daylight. After she leisurely ate her meal, she took a bath and wrapped up in her chenille robe, her long hair dripping around her shoulders in a wavy golden curtain until she wrapped a towel tightly around her head to absorb the moisture. She sat on the bed to go over her case notes.

The file on Dale Jennings was thick, and references to Jake Marsh turned up every few pages. She couldn't forget that Dale had helped one of Marsh's friends get a job working in Bib Webb's campaign. There had to be something to that.

She'd taken a lot of time gathering this much evidence and printing it out. She didn't want even one loose end that she didn't tie up. Furthermore, she was going to share it with the police and the district attorney's office, so they had access to everything she'd dug up.

The most noticeable thing about the file was the lack of anything that pointed to that missing piece of evidence Dale had held on to. There was no mention of a safety-deposit box, or a key. There was nothing to point to a hiding place.

She remembered what Brannon had said, about the transfer to a state prison, and her eyes narrowed in thought. Perhaps if Phil Douglas, back at the office in Austin, could find a starting point, he could turn up something besides the name of the person who'd gotten Dale out of federal prison. She made a note on the canary legal pad to that effect.

When she finished, she put the file along with the legal pad and pen on the bedside table and propped herself against the headboard with both plump pillows. She wasn't really sleepy, and her mind was whirring around so fast that she couldn't hold a single thought in it. She turned on the television, but there wasn't anything interesting on, except the weekly political faux pas. In an election year, one-upmanship on the nightly news was definitely the thing.

She turned off the television in disgust. What was there to do in a hotel miles from her apartment? She missed Barnes, her cat. Usually he slept curled up next to her on the bedcover.

She wondered if Brannon had a cat these days. He used to have a mangy old yellow tomcat that slept on the kitchen floor at night. It had been Gretchen's pet, but Brannon had fed it, and when nobody was looking, he played with it. He called it John, after the fictional John Reid, the original "Lone Ranger" of television legend. He'd always wanted to be a Texas Ranger, Gretchen had told her once. He knew the tiniest details about the first Rangers. He'd worked hard at law enforcement, just to have a shot at a job with the exclusive law enforcement group. It was a difficult job to get, too. There were only fifteen Ranger sergeants in Company D, Brannon's company, that operated out of San Antonio, and they had to cover forty-one counties. They worked with many other law enforcement agencies to solve crimes, because their authority was literally borderless—a Ranger could go anywhere in Texas to assist in criminal investigation, and infrequently even went overseas in such endeavors.

Gretchen had wondered if Brannon's infatuation with law enforcement had been because of his father. As a young boy, Marc felt he had no power at all. He was at the mercy of a verbally abusive father, and Marc was the only protection his mother and Gretchen had. While old man Brannon might not beat his son, he was apparently good at mental cruelty, which was, in its own way, equally destroying to a young ego.

She remembered how often Brannon went out of his way when he was on the Jacobsville police force to keep young offenders on the right track. He was a caring man. And he liked cats. She smiled, thinking sadly of poor Barnes, sitting in the vet's boarding room while she was away.

She knew Brannon had good horses and beef cattle at his Jacobsville ranch, the one that his manager kept solvent for him. He was an expert horseman, another Ranger skill that he'd mastered long before he pinned that star on his shirt. He could spin a lariat, bulldog, ride bareback—do most anything that equestrian skill demanded. She remembered horseback rides with him in San Antonio during those wonderful, idyllic days before Henry Garner's murder. She liked to ride, too.

Her mind, oblivious to the present as she wandered through happier times, was intent on the good memories. It was so intent on them that she forgot her wet hair was still done up in a towel. She was about to cut out the bedside lamp when a sharp knock came at her door.

CHAPTER EIGHT

JOSETTE GOT OUT of bed and padded to the door in her bare feet, keenly aware that she was wearing nothing but a robe over bare skin. She hesitated, remembering all the reasons she shouldn't open that door. Her purse with the stun gun was halfway across the room, and she didn't have a firearm. For all she knew, the murderer could be on the other side of the door.

Her heart pounded. Her mouth was dry. The knock came again, far more insistent. She went close and looked out through the peephole. It was Brannon, disheveled and dusty, with a cut beside his firm, chiseled mouth.

With a sigh of relief, she opened the door at once and let him in. "What in the world happened to you?" she exclaimed.

He wiped the cut beside his mouth. "I got jumped at my apartment as I was getting out of the truck," he said, traces of anger still evident in his deep voice. "I didn't know if they had a double header in mind, so I came to check on you."

"You could have phoned," she pointed out.

"A lot of good that would have done if they'd already managed to get into the room," he said sarcastically.

The concern, which was obviously genuine, made her feel warm inside. She stared at his face. She winced as she reached up to trace beside the cut. "Well, at least they didn't seem to do any permanent damage to you. How many were there?"

"Two."

"Recognize them?"

He shook his head. "Too dark, and they were wearing face masks."

"Why would they jump you?" she wondered aloud.

"At a guess, it was a warning that we're getting too close to something they want to stay hidden," he told her. His eyes narrowed. "Wet hair?"

She nodded. "I was going over my notes before I dried it. I forgot all about it," she added with a sheepish smile, as she recalled where her mind was when she was about to turn out the light.

He went and put on the chain latch and made sure the door was locked before he sailed his Stetson into the chair next to it. Then he caught her hand and pulled her into the bathroom.

She didn't need to ask why. He stood patiently while she got a washcloth and soaped it, reaching up to clean the wound on his face. He'd been in a fight with a suspect while they were dating. She'd patched him up then, too, flattered and secretly amused that he came to her for bandaging that he could easily have done himself.

"We don't even have an antiseptic or a bandage," she murmured as she bathed the cut.

"I'll get one when I get home. Thanks."

He washed his hands and his face before he wiped them on a towel and turned toward her, reaching for the towel wrapped around her head. "What are you doing?" she protested.

He wrangled the towel off her hair and plugged in the

hair dryer that came with the room. "Nice thing about hotels these days," he murmured, "they furnish everything you need to travel in style. Stand still."

He'd let her clean him up. So she let him dry her hair. It was odd, the feeling of nurturing it fostered in her. Of course, Brannon had always been special to her. That never changed. The feel of his big fingers in her hair was hypnotic, soothing. The nearness of his lean, fit body was disturbing. It had been a long time since she'd been this close to Brannon. She remembered the feel of those hands on bare skin, the faint spicy scent that clung to him, the fresh odor of the soap he used. He was familiar to her as no other man had ever been. She closed her eyes and let the memories wash over her of the last time they'd been close, before he'd walked out of her life.

She'd genuinely believed that he was intensely serious about her in those days. Brannon had never been a ladies' man. He didn't notch his bedpost. He was somber, and quietly deliberative about things, and he was decidedly old-fashioned in his attitudes. He had a tender side, but it was shown rarely, and only to people he trusted. But Josette hadn't understood how hard it was for him to trust. Her judgment had been faulty there. His loyalty to an old friend superseded his trust in a woman he didn't know intimately.

She had to remember that, and hold on to her pride. It was hard, standing so close to him that she could feel the warmth of his body. She wanted so badly to press herself into his arms and forget the past. The comfort of those strong arms had been the crowning glory of her life during those sweet months they'd gone together in her last year of college.

"You seem to shrink every time I see you," he murmured, noticing the disparity in their heights.

"I wear two-inch heels to work," she replied.

"So do I," he murmured dryly.

She looked down involuntarily and noted the riding heels on those hand-tooled cowboy boots he wore. She chuckled softly. "I guess so. But you're still wearing them. I'm not."

He ruffled her hair as the warm air blew it up in wafts of pure gold. "I always loved long hair," he mused.

"You could let yours grow," she pointed out.

"It's not the same." He turned her so that he could dry the back. Over her head, he met her eyes in the mirror. "I still remember you at fifteen," he said quietly. "You don't look much older, now."

Her face flamed. "That isn't a memory I like," she said, averting her eyes.

"Did I ever tell you that just before the rape trial, I'd just seen a man go to prison for a rape he didn't commit?" he asked out of the blue.

"What?"

"He was a nice, clean-cut young man who worked in an office and had a new assistant who seemed to dote on him. One day she went home from work and called the police and told them he raped her."

"Did he?"

"No. She wanted his job. She got it, too. He went to jail."

"But that's so unfair!"

"It was. He would have stayed there, too, but she made the mistake of bragging to a friend about her crafty promotion, and he went to the police. There was a new trial and he testified. The young man was cleared and she was fired. But he was never the same again. He said he couldn't ever trust another woman."

"I guess not." She sighed, meeting Brannon's pale eyes in the mirror. "No wonder you didn't believe me that night. Some people are worse than snakes, aren't they, Brannon?"

"You never use my first name anymore," he said quietly. "Why?"

"We're business colleagues," she said, avoiding his piercing gaze. "I want to keep things at a professional level."

"Most co-workers are on a first name basis these days."

Her face was stiff. She felt him let go of her hair and she pulled away, running her fingers nervously through the silky length of it. "Thanks."

He turned off the dryer and laid it aside. Before she could move, he had two great handfuls of that golden wealth and was lifting it to his mouth. His eyes closed, brows drawn down over his eyes as if he were in pain.

She was uneasy. She caught his hands, as if to remove them, but they turned and caught hers instead, leading them to his shirt. She felt the metal badge on the left pocket cold against her fingers, smelled the scent of her own shampoo and his cologne mingle.

"I was wrong about you. So wrong. I couldn't even apologize," he said as he bent. "Maybe I'm more like my father than I realized, Josie…"

The sound went into her mouth as his lips covered it gently. There in the silence of the room, she felt the heat and power of him as his arms enfolded her against the length of his powerful body and held her there.

She should struggle. It would be more dignified than

moaning under the warm, sweet crush of his lips. Her hands clenched his shirt, still crisp and clean-smelling despite the long day and the fight he'd been in. Pictures ran through her mind of Brannon in an alley with a bullet in him, like poor Dale. Her arms went under his and around him and she moaned again, frightened of what she imagined.

He bent suddenly, lifting her into his arms. With his mouth still covering hers, he carried her to the first of the two double beds and sank into its softness with her under him.

"No," she whispered breathlessly.

"Yes." He kissed her again, his arms making a cage around her. "I know what you are," he breathed into her mouth. "We both know I couldn't seduce you if I wanted to, so relax."

It was disturbing that he knew, or thought he knew, such intimate things about her. "You aren't supposed to know that," she whispered shakily.

He smiled against her mouth. "I know everything about you. I always have." He brushed the hair back from her face and lay propped on one elbow, just looking into her soft eyes. "I hated the FBI," he murmured in a deep, intimate tone.

Her eyebrows lifted. "Then why did you stay with it for two years?"

He shrugged. His fingers touched her softly swollen mouth. "I thought I could leave Texas and get rid of the bad memories. But they followed me."

"Memories are portable," she agreed.

He sighed, brushing her hair back from her face. "You look tired."

"I am," she said, aware of that gentle, caressing hand

at her throat, tangling in the softness of her hair. "I'd been putting in twelve-hour days lately on a new project Simon had initiated, to put information on state felony cases into a central database."

"I thought you weren't a computer whiz," he mused, smiling.

She smiled back. "I'm not. That's where our head computer guy, Phil Douglas, excelled. He investigated cybercrime and did most of the correlation for the database. I did the legwork and made the contacts."

"Like your job, do you?" he asked.

"I might as well. I make a comfortable living."

"So do I, but I'll never be a millionaire," he added. "Not unless cattle prices skyrocket and the price of feed plummets before winter."

"The drought has been hard on ranchers and farmers."

He nodded. "I'm breaking even. I'll settle for that, if it means I can keep the ranch in the family."

"You don't have children," she pointed out.

"Gretchen does," he replied. "Their son is almost two years old now."

"Yes, but she's the equivalent of a queen, too," she returned. "Will her children want to come to Texas to live? Her son inherits the throne of Qawi."

He didn't like that question. He grimaced. "I might have kids of my own one day," he argued.

"Only if the tooth fairy brings them," she said under her breath.

His eyebrows arched. "Oh, that was a low blow."

"You said you never wanted to get married," she reminded him.

"I'm thirty-three, almost thirty-four," he replied.

"And two incomes would come in handy. I could buy a good seed bull and breed my own strain of cattle."

"And give up working for the Texas Rangers?" she teased.

"There's a Ranger post in Victoria," he countered. "And Judd Dunn works there now. We were partners until I left the outfit. We could be again."

"Victoria's close to Jacobsville," she remembered.

"Exactly." He traced one of her eyebrows. "Do you want children?"

"Someday," she said. She shifted on the bedspread. "I guess."

"You've got some bad memories to get past, I understand that," he said slowly. "In your case, it would have to be with a man you trusted very much. Unless you've had that minor surgery in the past couple of years, I assume you haven't found a man you trusted enough."

She felt the heat in her cheeks. She didn't want to tell him that there was only one man alive she'd ever want intimacy with. Neither did she want to admit what she'd had done, just after their last disastrous date…

"The therapist said I hadn't really dealt with it yet," she evaded.

"She's right," he said, recalling the pretty brunette psychologist Josette had seen. "You should have stayed with her for a while."

"I didn't want to remember the past," she said uncomfortably.

"Neither did I," he said flatly. "But you don't get over things by dwelling on them. Sometimes it helps to relive bad memories, so that you can put them away."

"Mine are pretty awful," she said heavily.

"I know." His eyes narrowed. "Were you tempted to get involved with Jennings?"

"No," she said honestly. "I knew him from the coffee shop near the campus, and we were casual friends. It would never have been more than that. I never knew why he invited me to that party."

"I'll bet I know why you went with him," he said. "I'd just walked out on you without a word. You were hoping I'd be at the party, too, weren't you, so that you could flaunt Jennings?"

She grimaced and then she laughed softly. "That's just what I hoped, actually. I must be very transparent."

He lifted up a little and pointed at his badge. "I'm a Texas Ranger. I have experience in deduction."

She made a face at him. "Don't read my mind."

"I assumed Jennings was guilty because of what I knew about his mob connections," he told her. "But I'm beginning to wonder."

"I was so certain that Dale wasn't guilty, and that your friend Bib was. Now, the further we get into this case, the more certain I am that he wasn't guilty, either."

"Just as I am, about Jennings. It's so easy to rush to judgment."

She reached up and shyly traced around the cut on his face. "Good thing you have such a hard head," she commented with a faint smile.

"One of my assailants won't be smiling straight for a while," he replied, irritated at the memory. He searched her eyes slowly. "You keep your doors locked tight when I leave here," he said firmly. "And don't open that door to anybody you don't know, regardless of the reason. Got that?"

"Are we going to do the protective male thing?" she said wickedly, and smiled. "Oh, that's so sexy!"

"Cut it out," he muttered, ruffling her hair again. "It's the understaffed thing. I can't solve this case alone, and they won't give me any more people."

"Which means you're stuck with me." She looped her arms around his neck. Amazing, how comfortable she felt lying like this with him, when she was the most standoffish woman in the world with men.

"That works both ways," he taunted.

"Well, then, you have to be careful, too, and keep an eye behind you," she cautioned. "That's the protective female thing," she added.

He drew a strand of her long hair across her lips and bent to kiss her through it. "Even if you do have half a dozen good reasons to, I'm glad you don't hate me, Josette," he said huskily.

"I wouldn't know how to start."

He moved her hair aside slowly, and his mouth toyed softly with her upper lip, while the tip of his tongue probed under in lazy darting thrusts. She wondered if it was meant to make her feel hot all over. Probably it was. She wished she knew more about men.

He nibbled her lip before he coaxed her mouth to open. Then he kissed her again, with an oddly hesitant tenderness, his big, lean hand lying warm and strong against her cheek. It moved slowly down to her collarbone and teased around the opening of the robe. But when he heard her jerky intake of breath and felt her hands clench behind his head, he stilled.

He knew that it wasn't fear. He could feel the soft rush of her breath, feel the tension in her body, almost hear her wild heartbeat. She was involved already. So was he. But it was too soon. He'd been relentless the last time, overwhelming her protests. This time, he had to go slow. He had to treat her like a priceless treasure, and not make her feel uneasy because she wanted him. It flattered him that she could still want him, with their past. He had to be tender with her, now more than ever, and patient. Very patient, despite the ache in his loins.

So he lifted his mouth slowly from her clinging, soft lips and gave her a long, searching look. Then he pushed himself away with a long, jerky sigh and got to his feet in one fluid, graceful movement. He gazed down at her with muted delight. Now she looked frustrated. *Very* frustrated. Good.

"You're leaving?" she asked abruptly, propping up on her hands. Her eyes widened. "You're leaving *now?*"

He straightened his shirt and string tie, and picked up his hat. "What would be the point of staying?" he asked with faintly amused eyes and a soft chuckle. "I don't have anything in my wallet to use. And even if I did, if I tried to do what you're thinking of right now, we'd both end up in the emergency room!" He pursed his lips at her faint gasp. He pursed his lips and gave her a wicked grin. "Of course, we could rush right over to the hospital and ask if there's a gynecologist on call for emergency minor surgery...?"

She colored when she realized what he meant. She got to her feet and stuck her hands deep into the pockets of her robe. "You can stop right there, you sex maniac!" she said haughtily. "I don't sleep around, minor surgery or not! And I don't give a damn who says it's perfectly okay in a modern woman!"

He smiled, without sarcasm or mockery. "That's more like the woman I remember. I always admired that about you," he said, with a faint glitter in his gray eyes. "You never followed the crowd."

She shrugged. "My father was never one to keep his opinions to himself," she said, and smiled. "He taught me to be politically incorrect!"

He chuckled, remembering some firm lectures he'd heard from the reverend in the old days.

There was an odd little silence. "Thanks for stopping to see about me."

He moved close to her and tilted her chin up to his eyes. He noticed that she didn't have her glasses on. She'd left them on the vanity when he'd started drying her hair. "Can you see me?" he asked suddenly.

"You're a little blurry," she confessed.

He smiled. "And it makes you feel vulnerable." He nodded when her shocked expression blossomed. "Yes, I remember. You didn't have your glasses on that night, when I found you huddled in a corner of that boy's room, and the first thing you said to me was that you felt completely vulnerable because you couldn't see anything clearly. Then, years later when we were dating, you wouldn't wear glasses when you went out with me. Or contact lenses," he added.

She smiled. "I always thought I looked better without glasses. I can't wear contacts," she said, "because I kept getting infections. I'm not meticulous enough about keeping them clean."

"Excuses, excuses," he chided, chuckling.

"Your vision is perfect, isn't it?"

He nodded. "So far. When I get old, I expect I'll be decked out in reading glasses."

She changed the subject. "Did you ask the police to keep an eye on Mrs. Jennings?"

He grimaced. "I meant to," he said at once. "But I got sidetracked." He moved away from her and picked up the phone. He dialed a number and explained the situation to the duty officer, adding a thank-you before he hung up.

"He'll take care of it," he told her. He shook his head. "I phoned the sheriff about Holliman and his place, but I forgot Mrs. Jennings."

"You've been busy," she replied.

"Not that busy." He moved back to her. "I'll pick you up for breakfast in the morning, and we'll go see some of Jennings's correspondents."

"Okay." She smiled at him hesitantly. "You be careful going home."

He touched her nose. "You be careful here. Remember what I said."

"I will."

He opened the door and waited outside until she closed and locked it. She peered out the venetian blinds as he got into the big black SUV and drove off. Now she was worried about him. If two men had jumped him and been routed, what if the killer sent more back after him? She grimaced. This case was turning into a nightmare.

She perched on her bed and stared sightlessly at the case files that had been quickly tossed aside by an impatient Marc Brannon. Her heart rippled with delight as she felt all over again the warmth of his hard mouth on her own, the feel of his long fingers on her bare skin. She shivered with desire. It was happening all over again. She was still in love, living for a sight of him, a phone call, a touch. She closed her eyes tight. She didn't dare walk that road twice. He'd turned and walked away from her two years ago without a single look over his shoulder. Which meant that he could do it again. She couldn't live through a second rejection. So she'd better remember the pain as well as the pleasure, and not get in over her head.

THE NEXT MORNING, she phoned Simon Hart and filled him in on what was happening, especially about the computer break-in.

"I don't like that," he said curtly. "I really don't like that."

"Well, we've got our own hacker right in your office," she reminded him. "Phil Douglas could solve this case before lunch. He's the best cybercrime expert we have."

"I sent him down to Mala Suerte, remember?" he said with a groan.

"Then get him back! It won't take him an hour to find out who hacked into the files and got Dale transferred."

There was a hesitation. "We do have other, more experienced, people in the cybercrime unit."

"Simon, you're hedging," she said.

He made a rough sound in his throat. "Well, the FBI borrowed him on another case."

"You never loaned me to the FBI," she said, disconcerted, "and I've been there two years. Phil's only been there eight months!"

"I didn't want to get rid of *you*," he emphasized. "Okay. I'll phone their office and have him sent back."

"He's very good at his job," she added.

"I was getting even," he blurted out.

She paused. "Huh?"

"Do you remember that agent, Russell, who's been giving us so much trouble over Jake Marsh?"

"The same one Marc almost decked at his ranch when his sister was there with the Sheikh of Qawi?" she asked.

"Yes," he replied. "Anyway, Russell heard about this case and came in here like a pit bull, trying to get help to prove that a local mob boss had Jennings killed. Russell has been trying to get the goods on Jake Marsh for two previous unsolved murders in San Antonio."

"Jake Marsh is our main suspect, too," she agreed, "but nobody seems to know where he is right now. But despite the best efforts of the forensic people and the evidence technicians, we can't tell anything more than the caliber of the gun Dale was killed with—a nine-millimeter pistol."

"That's discouraging. If you had good evidence, I could inflict Russell on you. Anyway, he has suspicions, but he needed a cybercrime expert to go through the law enforcement database for him and run checks on mutual acquaintances and previous charges. I loaned him Phil."

"You might hit pay dirt by letting Phil work for Russell. We need all the help we can get. I would like to know who perpetrated that prisoner transfer."

"So would I, and the more people working on it, the better. I'll get the crime lab guys over at the FBI office on it, too," he said with a chuckle. "If they can borrow our people, we should be able to use theirs. This is a capital crime, after all."

"Thanks a lot, Simon. I'll be in touch."

"Meanwhile, I'll get in touch with the state judicial board and get them to launch an independent investigation into the Jennings release."

"Good idea."

She hung up, more puzzled than ever. So the FBI was

in on this, too, were they? Well, it did involve a candidate for national office, it was murder and there were rumors of mob ties. Jake Marsh's name kept turning up around every corner. She'd have to remember to tell Brannon that. If only they could find Marsh!

WHEN BRANNON SHOWED UP to drive her down to Floresville to talk to Jennings's correspondent, she told him what Simon had said on the way down.

"Jake Marsh, again," he murmured, frowning. "I know Simon wants to put him out of business as much as we do."

"Yes. Your old pal Russell does, too," she added.

"Curt Russell." His eyes began to glitter. "I still don't understand what he's doing on this case. Last time I looked, he was Secret Service."

"Well, he told Simon that the FBI sent him, so I guess he's changed jobs. He's after Marsh," she told him.

"He thinks Marsh was involved in Jennings's murder." He nodded thoughtfully. "So do we. But we still don't have a motive."

"Not unless that information Dale had concerned Marsh and some of his dealings. If he had concrete proof of wrongdoing," she said with a curious frown, "that would certainly make a motive for murder."

"It would," he agreed tersely.

He led the way to the parking lot out back, where he'd left his black SUV. On the way, a small, towheaded boy in jeans and a long-sleeved shirt and sneakers was wandering along between the endless rows of cars in the huge lot and bawling his eyes out. He couldn't have been more than four years old.

"Hey, partner," Marc called softly and picked the little fellow up. "What's the matter?"

"Lost Mama" came the plaintive sob. Little pudgy fists wiped little wet eyes. "Lost Mama!"

"Well, we'll just find her for you," he said, cuddling the child close.

Josette's heart twisted. She'd seen Marc with children before. They changed him. The implacable law enforcement officer with his wild temper and furious expressions was suddenly every woman's ideal of the perfect father for her children. She looked at him and knew how he'd be with his own child. She wanted to throw herself down on the concrete and squall her own eyes out, just to get those lean, muscular arms around her so securely.

"He can't be four yet," Josette said as she joined him. She smoothed the silky, clean hair of the little boy and smiled. "What's your name, little guy?"

"Jeffrey," he sobbed. "I'm three years old." He held up four fingers.

Marc and Josette exchanged amused smiles.

From the hotel's side entrance came the sound of excited voices. "But he was right here!" a woman sobbed. "I just turned my back for a second...!"

"You never pay him any attention!" a sharp male voice countered. "You couldn't even postpone a phone call long enough to watch our son."

"Somebody miss a kid?" Marc raised his voice.

Two neat people, one in a business suit and one wearing ranch clothes, came quickly toward them. The man was irritated. The woman was blonde and small and frantic.

"Jeffrey!" she sobbed, holding out her arms. "Oh, thank God! If he'd gone in the street...! Thank you, thank you!" She grasped her child tight in her arms and covered his wet face with kisses.

The man with her gave Marc a slow, quiet glance. "Thanks," he said tersely. "We'll get him home now."

"Children wander far, and they do it quick," Marc told the woman flatly.

She swallowed. "Yes. I'm sorry. It won't happen again." She gave the dark man beside her a worried glance. "We'll go now."

The man nodded politely and followed along beside her, but he looked like a storm about to break.

"There goes a marriage," Marc mused, watching them. He shook his head. "Sometimes it's just too much distance."

"And others, it's too little communication," she replied.

He turned to her. "That's a fact. Especially with you and me. We should have been totally honest with each other. If we had, we might be friends now, instead of reluctant co-workers."

She searched his eyes. "You really like children, don't you?" she asked.

He smiled. "Love them," he admitted.

"Me, too."

He slid his hand down to link with hers. Thrills of pleasure ran up and down her slender body.

"We'd better go," she said.

He nodded, and he walked beside her. But he held her hand all the way to the SUV. She didn't try to pull it away. Maybe he could help her forget how cruel he'd been in the past, if he went slowly and carefully, and didn't rush her. He had to hope so. He felt alive again. It was a good feeling.

CHAPTER NINE

SANDRA GATES WAS about Marc Brannon's age, with bleached blond hair and purple fingernails and the social graces of a small dog. Her trailer was jammed up against two equally sad-looking ones in a trailer park outside Floresville. She wasn't pleased to see Marc and Josette. She let them inside only when Marc threatened to get a search warrant.

They sat down gingerly on the sofa, which was covered with clothes and newspapers and discarded candy wrappers. While Marc was detailing the reason for the visit, Josette unobtrusively slipped one of the candy wrappers into her pocket, on a hunch.

Sandra sat back in her chair, her lower lip prominent. "I was just a friend of Dale's," she said with cold emphasis, waving a languid hand. Josette noticed that she wore a diamond dinner ring on her right hand. If it was a cheap ring, it certainly didn't look it. "I had nothing to do with his death," she added. "Nothing at all!"

"We aren't accusing you of anything, Miss Gates," Josette said quickly. "We only want to know if he wrote you anything about being transferred to the Wayne Correctional Institute."

She eyed them warily for a minute and her gaze went to the window before she took a slow breath and, without looking directly at them, answered, "Sure, I knew he was being transferred. He wrote me about it."

"Did he tell you how he managed it?" Brannon asked evenly, observing her responses with keen gray eyes.

She glanced at him, startled, and then averted her eyes again. "What...do you mean by that?"

"Wayne Correctional Institute is a state prison, Miss Gates," Brannon replied. "Jennings was in federal prison in Austin until about a week or so before he was killed, when he managed to get transferred over here and assigned to an outside work detail."

She folded her arms and gave him a cold glare. "He didn't say anything about that to me," she said. "I only know that it was easier to go see him here. I mean, it would have been easier for me to go see him, if he hadn't got killed."

Brannon looked at her meaningfully. "I know that you knew him before he went to prison, Miss Gates, and that you visited him both in Austin and San Antonio."

She looked irritable. "So I did. So what?" Now her legs were crossed and one foot started kicking impatiently.

He ignored the question and looked around, his pale eyes lighting on a very expensive computer and printer setup. Considering the poverty around her, that was odd. So was that diamond she was sporting.

"Do you like computers?" he asked pleasantly, changing the subject. "I'm barely computer literate myself, but we have to use them, like every other law enforcement office in the country."

She seemed to relax a little. "Yes, I love computers. I took courses at the local vocational technical school in computer programming." She pointed to a certificate on the wall over her computer. Brannon got up and sauntered over to look at it, leaning toward it with one big, lean hand on the desk. His eyes shot down to the computer. It was an expensive one, and she had several CD-ROM disks lying around it, one of which was a photo program. Another was a sophisticated spreadsheet program.

He stood up. "Impressive," he said, and walked back to the chair. "How long did it take you to get through those courses?"

"A year and a half," she said and smiled jerkily. "My tips paid for that diploma. I was a waitress at a truck stop just outside San Antonio."

"I used to be a busboy when I was in my middle teens," Brannon told her easily, and with a smile. "You don't make much at those jobs without tips."

"You don't make anything," she muttered. "I was so damned tired of being poor…" She laughed nervously. "Not that I'm rich now, but I design game software. My new one won an award from one of the computer magazines," she said, naming it with obvious pride. "I've come a long way."

"Obviously," he said. "That's an expensive computer. Top-of-the-line."

Now she was nervous and on her guard again. "I have to have good equipment or I couldn't make a living." She uncrossed her legs and got to her feet. "I've got a lunch appointment," she told them, quickly checking the watch on her wrist. "Sorry to rush you off, but I'm out of time."

They got up. "No problem," Brannon told her with a courteous smile. "Thanks for your help, Miss Gates."

"I didn't know anything!" she protested.

"And I'm sorry about Jennings," he added, noting the faint flicker of her eyelids. "For what it's worth, I don't think he killed Henry Garner."

She colored. Her lower lip trembled before her teeth caught and stilled it. Her face tautened. "He was such a loser," she said huskily. "Such a stupid, trusting fool…!"

"He wasn't all bad," Josette ventured. "He had some wonderful qualities."

"A lot of good they do him now," she said coldly. "The world is full of people who use other people and get away with it."

Josette started to ask a question, but Brannon caught her hand in his and pulled her out the door behind a pleasant goodbye to Miss Gates.

WHEN THEY WERE in the sports utility vehicle and headed back to San Antonio, Josette asked Brannon why he'd pulled her out the door so abruptly.

"Because your next question would have been, who did she know that used other people and got away with it, and that would have been counterproductive," he explained. "She's in this up to her neck. If she was making that much money, she wouldn't be living in a downscale trailer park, driving a rusting old car and wearing shoes that look three years old. Designing software wouldn't explain that two-carat diamond or the computer and the printer. And I saw some software on her desk that sells for six hundred a pop."

"You think Dale Jennings bought her the ring?"

"If it's real—and it looks real—yes, I do," Brannon said. "And I'd bet money she's the one who hacked into the computer system and got Jennings sent down here."

"That's what I thought, too, but we can't prove it."

"Not yet, anyway." He shook his head. "She's one cool lady. You need to get the local D.A.'s cybercrime specialist on this one, and that guy Phil at your own office, too. I'll just mention it to our resident expert as well. She's not going to be easy to catch, at that, no matter how many people we put on the job. I imagine she's had a lot of practice at erasing her electronic footsteps. But we might find out something."

"Such as, who paid her to get Dale transferred," Josette guessed. "Because she wouldn't have gone to that risk just for the pleasure of his company."

"But she would have for a payoff," he agreed at once. "I don't think she realized she was doing it so that he could get executed, though," he added shrewdly. "And she did seem to care about him. But I don't think Jennings was the only person paying her off. She may have been played for a sucker as well."

"Mrs. Jennings told me that Dale was going with some woman who liked expensive peppermint candy. So I took this," she showed him a wrapper.

Brannon gave it a curious look. "This is imported. Expensive taste for a woman who lives in a used trailer."

"Isn't it, though?"

"You said that Jennings's girlfriend liked expensive mints. Did Mrs. Jennings say anything else about her?"

"Not much. It was just a comment she made, that I remembered."

"I'm glad. Every clue helps."

"Why didn't you want her to get suspicious?" she asked curiously.

"Because I'm going to get a court order for a wiretap on her phone," he said simply. "There's enough evidence, even circumstantial, to involve her in this case.

Besides, if Sandra Gates really is mixed up in this, she's in danger. The murderer is not going to want her to tell what she knows to the police."

"So she's expendable."

"Exactly."

Josette dug into the file in her briefcase and thumbed through it. "There's another person here we need to question. He's an associate of Jake Marsh's," she said, frowning as she read over her notes. "This man, Johnny York, has an arrest record as long as my arm, but only one conviction. He was arrested on suspicion of murder last year, but he was released for lack of evidence. He's on probation for an assault conviction. According to what I've found out, he has one favorite haunt. He likes to play pool. So, we might stop by the pool hall on Mesquite Street and talk to him."

"He won't be there at this hour of the day," he assured her. He pulled over to the curb and used his onboard computer to input York's name.

"That's our state crime database," she murmured with delight.

"Yes, it is, and I couldn't do my job without it, either." A huge file of data came up on the screen. There was a photo. The man was ordinary-looking, with thinning hair and small eyes. Funny, how familiar he looked. He scrolled down to York's home address and smiled. "Isn't modern technology great?" he murmured with a grin. "We could have spent hours trying to run down this information by questioning people who know him."

"It really does save time," she replied. "Where does he live?"

"About six blocks from here. He's probably still asleep. We'll wake him up."

It took less than five minutes, even in morning traffic, to get to the address on the screen. As Brannon and Josette got out of the car, a curtain was pulled back and then released at the front of the house. As they approached the steps, they heard a door slam.

"He's trying to make bush bond!" Brannon said shortly. "Stay back. He may be armed." He drew his own pistol and started quickly around one side of the house.

Josette felt her heartbeat shaking her as she disobeyed Brannon's orders and went around the opposite side of the house. Brannon was trying to head off a criminal by himself. Josette was an office person, not a field agent. Nevertheless, she might be able to spook the man enough to run him back toward Brannon. And even if he had a gun, surely he wouldn't be so desperate as to shoot an unarmed—

As she thought that, a gunshot sang out. Brannon! She rushed around the corner of the house just in time to see a small, balding man who looked strangely familiar whirl at her approach. She felt a stinging pain in her upper arm and heard a firecracker pop half a second later. Funny, her arm felt very heavy.

There was another shot and the man spun around, dropping his gun. Brannon was on him seconds later, whipping him to the ground, jerking his hands behind him. He cuffed him and stood up, reminding Josette absently of the way he used to compete in bulldogging competition in rodeo; she'd seen him throw and bind the legs of calves just that quickly. She wondered why her mind was stuck on such an irrelevant thing, and why she felt so funny.

Brannon glanced toward Josette just to make sure

she was okay. But there was a growing red spot on the beige jacket she was wearing, and she looked as if she were about to faint.

Muttering curses, he reholstered his pistol and rushed toward her, with his mobile phone already out and activated. He phoned 911 as he ran, giving their location, their situation, and a demand for an ambulance and backup.

He caught Josette just as she started to fall. He whipped off his string tie before he eased her to the ground and unbuttoned her jacket, slipping it off her wounded arm.

She lay looking up at him blankly. She began to shake uncontrollably. She laughed. "I feel funny," she said unsteadily.

"Lie still," he replied, his expression set and grim as he tore the sleeve of her jacket to get a look at the damage. Thank God it wasn't through the bone, but it was a nasty wound just the same. It had entered and exited through the inside of the biceps, leaving blood pumping out from what had to be a torn artery. He made a tourniquet of his bolo and a retractable pen from his pocket to help stop the flow of blood while he put pressure on the wound to stop the profuse bleeding. "Come on, come on, damn it!" he cursed, looking around for the ambulance with furious pale eyes. He didn't hear a single siren yet.

Josette felt pain where his hands pressed. The driveway was gravel, and it was cold and uncomfortable under her back. She looked up at Brannon's dark, lean face with a sense that she was somewhere else seeing them together on the ground.

"It hit…an artery, didn't it?" she asked. Her voice

sounded strange. Her tongue was so thick, it was hard to talk at all.

"Yes, it did," he said. He was still pressing down hard where the bullet had entered and exited. There was blood all over his hands, all over her jacket and blouse, all over the ground beside her. It ran into the soil and gravel and she could smell it. There was a metallic smell to blood, she thought, growing weaker by the moment.

"Of all the idiotic things you've ever done in your life…! Hold on, Josie," he said softly. "Hold on." He lifted his head again. "Where is that damned ambulance!" he raged, because his best efforts were barely suppressing any of the red flow. She could bleed to death if it wasn't stopped soon.

Her eyes searched his face. He seemed paler than normal, and his eyes were glittery with fury and impotence. "Marc," she whispered, drifting in and out now from blood loss, "why didn't you say goodbye?"

He was still looking for the ambulance. At last, there was the faint sound of sirens approaching. "What?" he murmured, fixated on his task as he knelt beside her, the suspect already forgotten in the terror of the moment.

"Not a note or a phone call. You just…walked away… and never even looked back. I wanted…to die." She grimaced and groaned, trying to twist away from his hands. "Don't!" she choked. "It hurts!"

"Better hurt than dead," he said through his teeth.

"Think so? I wonder." She bit her lip to keep from crying out.

Marc muttered curses at the slowness of the paramedics, finally yelling at them with language he was going to regret later. She smiled softly at the memory of

his temper from days past. She closed her eyes, oblivious to the sounds of activity around her, and gave in
to the pain.

SHE WAS VAGUELY aware of the hospital, but she was
pleasantly numb from whatever they had pouring into
her from an IV bag. Brannon was still right beside her
as she was moved into a cubicle. A doctor entered and
examined the wound and pronounced it nonlethal. She
was given a local anesthetic and antibiotics were added
to the drip. The doctor went to work on her with a surgical needle and sutures. The whole time, Brannon stood
beside her and held her other hand tight in his.

"You got him, didn't you?" she asked drowsily.

"I got him. He was brought in with you," he said.
"They'll be transferring him up to a secure area when
he's had his bullet removed. He fared worse than you,
believe me."

"You always were a good shot," she sighed. "And
nobody could beat you at a quick-draw. Don't you still
hold a record of some sort for that?"

"You were lucky," he replied, ignoring the praise and
the question. "You're still going to learn plenty about
bullet wounds before this is over."

"She is, indeed," the young doctor replied while he
worked on her. "She's going to be sore and sick for a
couple of days, and on antibiotics for the next ten days.
Is there someone who can stay with her tonight?"

"No," she said.

"Yes," Brannon said at the same time.

The physician made a sound in the back of his throat.
"We can admit you," he offered.

"No chance," she told him. "It's just a scratch."

"You won't think so when the painkiller wears off," the doctor murmured. "I'll give you a prescription for one and another for the antibiotics before you leave." He glanced at Brannon. "We'll have to fill out a report on this."

"She's with the state attorney general's office," he replied. "A trained investigator, and she can't use a gun. Something she should have thought of when she went around the house to try to help me flush out a suspect." He grimaced. "Don't ever do anything like that again, Josie," he added gently.

"I won't, Brannon," she said. "But I'm tough. Besides, think of the boost this will give my memoirs!"

"It was my fault for putting you in danger in the first place," he continued doggedly. "That being the case, I'll take care of you until you're back on your feet." He held up a hand when she protested. "You'd do exactly the same if it were me."

She sighed. "Point taken."

AFTER JOSETTE WAS sewn up, and waiting for the physician to write out her prescriptions, Brannon went down the hall to the surgical wing where his prisoner was being tended.

Brannon recognized the young Bexar County sheriff's deputy who patrolled the south end of the county that bordered on Wilson County. He was waiting outside the swinging doors. He glanced at Brannon, grinned and extended his hand.

"Nice work, Brannon," he told the Texas Ranger. "We've been after this little weasel for months. We convicted him for aggravated assault when he was trying to shake down a liquor store owner. He got caught drinking and driving and went underground before we could arrest him."

"He shot my partner," Brannon said angrily. "She wasn't even armed."

"That wouldn't stop York," he replied. "He's the poor man's cleaner locally—he'll do anything for money, including murder. He's suspected of being one of Jake Marsh's hired guns. In fact, San Antonio PD would finger him for Jennings's murder, if he could be connected with the case any way at all."

"Give us time," Brannon said. He hesitated. "There was a photo of him in the file I accessed on my computer. He sure looked familiar."

"You were at Jennings's funeral yesterday, weren't you?" the deputy asked.

"Yes."

"Remember the minister?" he mused.

Brannon took a sharp breath. "Damn! And I thought the minister was just new and nervous. What the hell was he doing there?"

"At a guess, getting a good look at someone he's been hired to shoot" came the reply. "God knows who."

Brannon shoved his hands into the pockets of his khaki slacks. He was thinking. If the little man was a hired killer, and he was at the funeral, the murderer had already picked his next target. If he and Josette hadn't played a hunch and decided to pay York a visit this morning, he might have succeeded. But, if the deputy was right, who was the target? And why?

HE WAS STILL no closer to answers when he helped Josette into the SUV and drove back to his apartment.

She was too groggy and sick to want to talk. He carried her up the steps into the apartment building, into the elevator despite curious glances from other passengers, and got out on his floor.

On the way to his apartment, he met one of the security people. "Hey, Bill, how about taking my key and unlocking the door for me?"

"Sure thing," the other man replied, with a curious look at Brannon's burden.

"We just came from the hospital," Brannon began.

"Hell of a place to pick up women, Brannon," the other man mused. "But if that's the only way you can get one..."

"Put a sock in it," Brannon said with a chuckle. "She's been shot. I can't leave her alone and she has no family."

"Shot?" The other man unlocked the door, opened it and handed Brannon back his keys. That was when he noticed the white bandage on Josette's arm, where that sleeve of her jacket was off. "Shouldn't she be in the hospital?"

"S'only a flesh wound," she murmured, with her cheek tight against the hard beat of Brannon's heart under his shirt. The Ranger badge was uncomfortable, but it seemed to be everywhere she moved her face, cold and hard. "He didn't mean to..." she added in a slur.

"Now, you're *shooting* women?" the security man asked with wide eyes.

"I didn't shoot her, you idiot! A suspect got her. But I got him," he added with a gleam of triumph. "And he's in surgery right now."

"Sorry, kid," Bill told Josette, who was watching him with eyes barely open. "Maybe when you're better, they'll give you five minutes alone with him."

"Don't I wish," she murmured. "And two stun guns, one for each hand… I'm so sleepy, Brannon."

"Okay. I'll have you inside in a jiffy. Thanks, Bill."

"Anytime." Bill opened the door and put the keys in the hand that was supporting Josette's rib cage. He smiled at Josette, lifted amused eyes back to Brannon's and walked off.

BRANNON CARRIED JOSETTE into the spare bedroom and laid her gently on the brown-and-beige geometric pattern of the coverlet while he took off her shoes and skirt. They were followed by her jacket and the ruined blouse under it, leaving her in a full slip, bra and panties. He tried not to pay too much attention to her very nice figure while he was doing what was necessary.

He lifted her long enough to uncover the sheets before he put her back down on them and pulled the covers over her, noting the faint smell of roses that clung to her creamy skin.

He propped his hands beside her head on the pillow and studied her. Her long blond hair was half in, half out of a bun, hanging in strands all around her oval face. He took her glasses from their perch on her nose and laid them on the bedside table. He smoothed back her hair and then, impulsively, pulled out all the hairpins that kept it in place. The wealth of golden hair came cascading down into his hands.

"It will tangle while I'm asleep," she murmured.

"Let it. You have the most beautiful hair I've ever seen." His hands speared through it, arranging it around her face on the pillow. He smiled gently. "Tired?"

"Very." She drew a long breath. "Sorry to be so much trouble."

"You aren't. I'll have to go back to work, but I'll be here about five-thirty. Just sleep. You need to get better before we go any deeper into this investigation."

"Okay." She searched his eyes slowly. "It wasn't your fault."

His face set in harsh lines. "I should have known you'd try to play hero."

"Don't blame yourself."

"You're the one who got shot. It should have been me."

She managed a smile. "You're only jealous. It's bullet envy."

"There's a genuine delusion!"

"I'll be fine," she added drowsily.

"Of course you will. But for a couple of days, you need to rest that arm and let your body get over the shock. You lost a lot of blood." He bent down impulsively and brushed his hard mouth over her soft one. "Get some sleep, honey. I'll see you this afternoon. Want me to put something to drink by the bed?"

Had he called her "honey?" Surely not. "Could you? Something cold?"

"Orange juice?" he asked, remembering how much she liked it while they were dating.

Her eyes lit up. "Yes, please."

He went to get it. By the time he came back and set it on the bedside table, she was sound asleep.

He stood watching her for a long time with a strange expression. He'd never brought a woman home with him before. He couldn't explain what impulse had led him to make himself responsible for Josette. But she did look so right there, in that bed, asleep. She needed nurturing, taking care of. It touched him to realize that he was needed, on a very personal basis. Since his mother's death and his sister's marriage, he hadn't had anyone to take care of. He missed that. He liked being needed. Not, he added silently, that he was going to tell Josette that!

SHE DIDN'T WAKE UP for several hours. She was aware of pain in her arm, a fullness and throbbing that were decidedly unpleasant. She sat up with an effort and looked on the bedside table. Brannon had left her a carafe of orange juice and two bottles of pills, one for pain and the other a powerful antibiotic. She took both and swallowed them with the cold, delicious juice. It felt good going down. She put the glass next to her forehead and drank in the cooling contact. She must have a fever, she decided, and wondered if Brannon had anything she could take for that.

She made her way into the master bathroom and looked in the medicine cabinet for an analgesic. Finding it, she shook two tablets into her hand and went back to the bedroom.

She laid down for a few more minutes, but she was far too restless to sleep. She got up and looked around for something to put on. She'd have to get Brannon to go by her hotel and get her clothes, or she wouldn't have anything to wear. She thought about some of Brannon's colleagues walking into the room and finding her in her slip. That wouldn't do his reputation much good.

In the end, she drew out a worn old pair of clean denim jeans, Brannon's of course, and a tan-and-white checked long-sleeved shirt with a pocket missing. She left her hair loose because she couldn't find her hairpins, using Brannon's combs to try to get some order out of the tangles. Then she went to the kitchen, her arm still in its sling, and began to look for food.

Evidently he could cook, because he had a nicely stocked refrigerator. She made biscuits from scratch and put them in the oven to bake. While they were cooking, she put a small chicken on to cook in the oven with them, and busied herself preparing beans and potatoes on the burners.

THE BISCUITS CAME out perfect. The chicken took longer. By exactly five-thirty, she had everything ready on the stove and two places set at the kitchen table.

Brannon walked in carrying a bucket of chicken. He stopped at the kitchen doorway, his eyes on the table. He took a whiff. Something smelled delicious.

"Is that chicken?" he asked, indicating a casserole. "It smells fabulous!"

"I cook it with rosemary," she told him shyly. "Sorry the chicken is redundant."

"And you made biscuits." He put the bucket of chicken on the counter and went to the stove to look at the meal she'd prepared. "You shouldn't have gone to this much trouble, but I do love homemade biscuits," he murmured with a gentle smile. "I haven't had a decent one since we were dating. I used to stop by for breakfast some mornings, because you always cooked them at home."

"Yes." The memory made her sad. She'd thought they were going to have a future together back then. He'd even teased her about moving in with him so that he could have fresh biscuits every morning.

"That was an idiot comment," he muttered. "I didn't mean to bring back unpleasant memories."

"They weren't all unpleasant," she remarked. "Here, sit down and butter a biscuit before they get cold."

He seated her, and then himself, but he noticed that she only took a little taste of chicken and a single biscuit. "Aren't you hungry?" he asked, concerned.

"Not really. I'm a little nauseous still. I hope the biscuits are okay," she added. "I had to make them with one hand, and I couldn't roll them out."

He took a nibble of one. "They're delicious."

She smiled. "I'm glad. You never used to eat proper meals. You were forever snacking, because something always came up when you were working."

"That goes with the turf," he reminded her. "I can't remember the last time I had a single uninterrupted meal." He took a forkful of chicken to his lips and savored it.

"Are you happy, now that you're back with the Rangers again?" she asked conversationally.

"I love the Rangers," he replied. "I always have. I suppose I'll keep working for them until I'm old enough to retire with a pension. But I'll still have the ranch. It brings in a nice profit. I put the money right back into livestock and mechanical improvements. What's left over, I invest. I've made some good choices. So good, in fact, that I could probably quit working whenever I felt like it."

She smiled. "You aren't cut out to sit around on a ranch and let everyone else do the work."

"You've got that right. At least drink some more juice," he chided when she left her glass and started to stand up. "And don't even think about doing the dishes. That's my job. Tomorrow night, I'll cook."

"Can you?" she asked.

"I'm no gourmet chef, but I make a mean meat loaf."

"My favorite!" she exclaimed.

He gave her a speaking look. "One of the only two restaurants you'd let me take you to had meat loaf on the menu. I haven't forgotten."

"I love it."

"Meat loaf and peach cobbler," he murmured, smiling reminiscently. "And crepes and chocolate malt shakes." The smile faded. "I wish we could go back in time. I've made serious mistakes. I don't suppose I'll ever be able to make up for them."

She avoided his eyes. "The past is best left alone. What did you find out about the shooter?"

He told her, adding the bit about York being the nervous minister at the funeral of Dale Jennings.

"I thought he looked very nervous for a minister, but I assumed he was just new at the job! What was he doing there?" she exclaimed.

"Probably," he said flatly, "getting a good look at his next target."

CHAPTER TEN

JOSETTE FELT HER heart drop. "Do you think he killed Dale?" she asked bluntly.

"I don't know. It's possible. But what connection could Jennings have had to York, or to Jake Marsh, for that matter? Were they in on some blackmail scheme with him? Or are they in cahoots with somebody else? Despite all the investigating we've done, we haven't answered many questions."

"I know." She looked at him worriedly. "York's in custody now, though. He can't hurt anybody else."

"York is like Marsh—he's slippery," he replied. "York got loose once and he can do it again. Apparently he's being paid well enough to make the risks worthwhile. He probably has a new identity and a plane ticket hidden and ready to use, once he gets rid of the target. Or targets." He grimaced. "This whole damned case is like a well. You go down an inch and discover you've got several yards below to explore. Somebody has a lot to lose, and is willing to kill however many people it takes to keep a secret."

"Mrs. Jennings has been targeted once already," she pointed out. "If the perpetrator thinks she knows more than she's telling—and I think that myself—she's still in danger. Maybe not from York, but from somebody else."

His gray eyes narrowed as he watched her across

the table. "You shouldn't have done so much," he said gently. "Go to bed. I'll clean up in here."

"I do feel a little woozy," she murmured, smiling faintly as she got to her feet. "I'll be better tomorrow."

He made a noise, but it didn't sound like he was agreeing. She went back into the room he'd given her and sat down heavily on the bed, feeling weak and shaky. A minute later, he came in with a pajama top and tossed it to her. It was brand-new and looked as if it had never been worn.

"I keep a pair in case I get shot and have to go to the hospital," he murmured dryly. "Otherwise, I don't wear any."

She flushed, looking at the top, which would probably come down to her knees.

"I'll wear the bottoms while you're here," he added. "Tomorrow, I'll go by your hotel and pick up some things for you. And tell the clerk to hold your room."

"Thanks."

"No problem. Try to get some sleep. Good night."

"Good night."

He closed the door. She changed into the pajama top and climbed under the covers. In scant minutes, she was dead to the world. But it didn't last long. She woke in the night, feverish and frightened.

Brannon opened the door and moved to the bed, feeling the fever with a cool hand against her forehead.

"Hot," she whispered hoarsely. "So hot!"

He turned on the bedside light and went to get a wet cloth. He bathed her face and hands with it and lifted her head so that she could swallow the analgesic to take the fever down. Then, afraid to leave her alone in a room, he got under the covers and pulled her close, holding her while she shivered with the fever.

"Oh, Marc," she whispered in her delirium. "Marc, why did you leave?"

His teeth ground together as she relived that last, disastrous date with him that had put an end to their relationship. She wept and shivered until the analgesic finally kicked in, and she slept, her face bathed in tears.

BY THE TIME she woke, Brannon was already up and dressed. She didn't even realize he'd stayed with her all night. But with morning, she didn't feel better. Her arm throbbed, no matter how she held it or rested it, and she was still feverish. All that long day, Brannon didn't leave her. He bathed her heated face and her hands, dispensed aspirins and antibiotics and painkillers to her, and finally stretched out on the cover and pillowed her head on his chest while she wept from the misery of it all.

"I guess you've been shot," she said wearily when the pain had eased a little.

"Twice," he said. "Once in the leg—missed the bone, fortunately—and once in the shoulder."

"Who looked after you?" she asked absently.

There was a pause. "I looked after myself," he said.

"Did Gretchen know?"

"I don't tell my sister things that will upset her," he said stiffly. "She had enough responsibility, looking after our mother and the ranch. Mother's cancer was rough on Gretchen. That's why she went on holiday overseas after our mother died, and it's how she met her husband."

"I always liked Gretchen," she sighed.

"She liked you, too."

"How's the hit man?"

He chuckled, surprised at the reference. "In a room, under heavy guard, being relentlessly questioned by Grier. I wouldn't wish him on my worst enemy."

"I haven't met him yet."

"You haven't missed much. He probably has a badge sewn on his underwear and a tattoo on his butt. He's the type."

"Not a Ranger badge, though," she murmured drowsily.

"Those are hard to get. But actually, he had one, until two years ago."

Her eyes closed. "I'll be better tomorrow."

He smoothed her disheveled hair, liking the faint scent of roses that clung to it. She was warm and vulnerable in his arms. He felt peace. Odd, when he'd never felt it with anyone else. He liked holding her while she slept. But he wasn't going to tell her that he'd spent the previous night with her, or what she'd whispered in the grip of fever.

"Go back to sleep," he said softly.

She felt him move and her fingers clung to his shirt. "Don't go," she whispered, too weak from pain to pretend she didn't mind being left alone.

His chest rose and fell heavily, but he sank back down and her body relaxed against him. Seconds later, she was asleep again and, like the night before when she lay so close in his arms in the darkness, he was fighting once again a two-year-old hunger that had never diminished. Only when the first light broke through

the window did he leave her and go back to his own
bed. It was best for now if she didn't know that she had
company at night.

THE NEXT MORNING, she was up before Brannon. She
dressed and began making breakfast. It was ready when
he came out of his bedroom, wearing jeans and nothing else, yawning.

He stopped short at the sight of her putting butter on
the table and blinked. "I thought I told you to stay in
bed," he remarked, coming closer.

She was trying not to stare. His wavy blond-streaked
brown hair was disheveled, and his chest was sexier
than a TV commercial. She'd seen his chest before,
with broad, hard muscles covered with a tangle of soft
hair that wedged from his collarbone down into the low
waistline of his jeans. She'd touched it as well, that last
memorable evening they'd spent together; touched it,
kissed it, nibbled it…

She flushed and averted her eyes. "I'm much better," she said. "It's sore, but I can handle that. The fever
seems to be gone."

"Does it?" He was beside her before she had time to
be shocked, one lean hand pressed to her cheek.

Her heart stopped and ran away. He saw her pulse
rampaging in the artery of her neck. The shirt she was
wearing—his shirt—was throbbing from the force of
her heartbeat. His fingers spread gently on her cheek
and his thumb rubbed softly over her swollen lips, sensitizing them in a silence broken only by the insistent
sizzle of bacon in the iron skillet on the stove.

"The bacon," she choked.

His eyes held hers for one long minute before he

dropped his hand and moved to the table. The impact of those soft, dark eyes made him ache. He'd done nothing but hurt her in the past, but she still wanted him. He wondered what she'd say if she knew how hungrily her hands had explored his chest while she slept in his arms for the past two nights. It had kept him awake until dawn. Of course, he was used to grabbing catnaps and functioning with them.

With unsteady hands, Josette took a spatula and piled the bacon onto a platter lined with paper towels. She then moved the pan off the hot burner to an unlit back one. She put the bacon on the table beside the eggs she'd just scrambled and the basket of hot biscuits. She poured coffee into two mugs and put them on the table.

"I'm going back to work today," she said huskily.

"You're not."

She glared at him. "I don't get paid for lying around in bed…!"

"You have sick days just like any other government worker," Brannon said calmly, while he buttered a biscuit. "I'll bet you haven't taken a sick day off since you've been in Simon's office," he added, staring straight into her eyes.

She averted her gaze and grabbed a biscuit. "I don't get sick."

"Neither do I, as a rule, but a gunshot wound isn't exactly sick. You'll stay home today," he added, impatiently taking the biscuit she was trying to butter with one hand away and buttering it himself.

She took the biscuit from his outstretched hand with a mutinous expression. "All right," she said curtly. "One more day."

"We'll see."

Her gaze fell reluctantly to his chest and darted away. He wasn't overly muscular, but he was well-built and fit physically. She didn't doubt that he could hold his own in a free-for-all. He was certainly efficient when he went after someone, and she remembered amusedly how he'd tackled the man who shot her.

He finished his eggs and bacon and biscuit and sat back with his coffee cup in his hand, and watched her try not to look at his chest. It amused him that she was still shy.

"You could take off your shirt, too," he remarked as he sipped coffee. "We could compare wounds."

"You've already seen mine," she pointed out, trying not to react.

"And a lot more," he added with a wicked grin.

She flushed, almost overturning her coffee cup. "That's enough, Brannon."

"We're back to that, are we?" he said wistfully. "I suppose you don't think we know each other well enough for first names anymore."

She put down her cup audibly and wiped her mouth with her napkin. "I'm going back to bed, since you won't let me out the door."

He stood up, blocking her way. His big, warm hands caught her face and held it up to his pale, glittery eyes. "Don't box it up inside you," he said curtly. "You still resent the fact that I walked away from you without a word."

"Yes, well, some memories are more vivid than others." Her voice sounded odd. The touch of those strong hands on her face made her melt inside.

"I testified for the prosecution at your rape trial," he continued, his tone blunt and uncompromising. "On the basis of the boy's assurances and the deposition of a resident in the emergency room. How do you think I felt when I knew, *knew,* that you were telling the truth that night?"

She searched his eyes. "It was a long time ago," she said heavily.

"Not for me. I made a mistake—a hell of a mistake. Instead of support and justice and sympathy, you were treated as if you'd committed the crime. It scarred you. You're still carrying the wounds, and they're not easily treated, like the one in your arm."

Her gaze fell to his chest, but she didn't really see it. "I can live with my scars."

"Well, I can't," he said flatly. His eyes were flashing like sunlit silver. "I can't bear them! You dress like a dowager. You don't date—yes, I know," he added when she looked up, surprised. "Simon told me. He said you cut men dead if they so much as smile at you. You had therapy, but only for a couple of weeks, because your father didn't believe in that sort of thing. Now here you are, twenty-four years old and as sexless as that table over there. And it's my fault. It's my fault, Josette!"

Her eyes closed. Most of it was true, she supposed. She hadn't wanted to think about the past. But the past and the present were linked together like a circle, forming a chain that was endless.

His warm hands went to her waist and contracted. "I couldn't deal with it, so I quit the Rangers, joined the FBI and left Texas. But even that didn't work. The memories went along." His hands drew gently over her small waist. "Gretchen said you didn't blame me."

She searched his hard face, surprised by the indecision there, when he was always such a forceful person.

Her lips parted on a soft breath. "I didn't," she said. "I was in Jacobsville selling my father's last bit of property there. I ran into her at the bank." She looked down at his broad chest. "She said it wasn't because I accused Bib Webb of old Mr. Garner's murder. I thought it was, you see. I thought you blamed me for accusing him, and you couldn't bear the sight of me afterward…"

"Dear God." He drew her to him and held her as gently as he could, allowing for the wound in her left arm. His lips moved in her long, soft hair. "People disagree with me all the time. It doesn't usually inspire me to quit my job and leave the state."

She smiled to herself. "I'll remember that."

He smoothed the length of her hair, enjoying the softness of it. "I left because I knew how badly I'd misjudged you. Despite the relationship we were developing in San Antonio, I still had doubts," he confessed quietly. "If you were the sort of woman who'd accuse an innocent boy of rape… Well, it was a question of trust."

"You thought you might end up in court as a defendant," she said flatly and with a hollow laugh. She pulled away from him and moved to the doorway.

"I don't trust people," he said harshly. "I never have! Most people are only kind when they want something. I thought you were too good to be true. Given your past, or what I thought was your past, I erred on the side of caution. And then, that last night, I lost my head completely." His eyes closed. "When I left you, I drove around for hours, trying to accept how mistaken I'd been about the whole situation. I remembered the verdict, when the boy was acquitted largely due to my testimony and that of the intern. You sat there so stiffly, so proud, so wounded, and you didn't cry. You held up your head and you walked out with your parents as if you were the victor. That memory was what hurt the most."

She met his eyes. "We'll always be on opposite sides, Brannon," she said, and she didn't smile. "You don't trust people. Neither do I. Not anymore."

"At least you were exonerated when that creep was killed in that high-speed car chase after raping and nearly strangling that woman in Victoria," Brannon said, trying to find some good in the awful situation.

"Not that it mattered anymore," she replied. "I have a good job, nice co-workers and a future in state government to look forward to."

His eyes narrowed. "And how about a family? Kids?"

She turned away. "I don't want to marry."

His face contorted, because he knew why. He'd only just realized it. A woman like that, with her tortured past, had given in to him completely one dark night. She wouldn't have been capable of sleeping around after her experiences. The only reason she could have had to give in to Brannon that night, that disastrous night, was that she loved him. It was the only possible explanation for what had happened. She'd loved him. He'd found her virginal and was so shocked by it that he'd jerked back from her as if she were diseased. He'd rearranged her disheveled clothing, stuck her in his car and driven her straight home. He left her at her front door, and stalked away. Except for one fumbling phone call to check on her, later that night, he walked away and never said another word to her, until they met outside Simon Hart's office two years later.

He shoved his hands into the pockets of his jeans, his expression harder than ever. "We could have solved a lot of problems that night if either one of us had been honest about what we felt."

She turned. "I felt ashamed."

His jaw tautened. "Not until I stopped," he drawled with self-recrimination in his tone.

She flushed to the roots of her hair and started walking back down the hall.

He followed her into the bedroom.

"I'm not going to argue with you!" she raged. "I'm hurt. You just leave me alone!"

There was a suspicious brightness in her eyes. "You aren't walking away this time," he said, and moved closer. "Never again."

She put up both hands at his approach, wincing as the left one protested.

"Idiot," he murmured as his arms enfolded her against his bare chest. "You're vulnerable."

"I don't want your arms around me!" she fumed.

"Funny, because you've slept in them for the past two nights."

"Wh-what?" she exclaimed, staring up at him.

He pushed the long, soft hair away from her cheek. "If I'd been shot and raging with fever, would you have been in here asleep with me in the other room?"

"Of course not," she said without thinking.

"Exactly."

"But it would have been impersonal," she said doggedly.

"It was mostly impersonal," he agreed.

"Mostly?"

His fingers trailed down her neck, making chills where they touched. "It's difficult for a man to be totally impersonal when he's hard as a rock."

She didn't believe she'd heard him say that. Her eyes were like saucers.

"I thought of it as penance," he murmured, amused by her shock. "Retribution. You kept stroking my chest and kissing it and whispering how much you wanted me. I'm only human, Josie."

"I never!" she exclaimed, horrified.

He lifted an eyebrow and smiled slowly. He looked rakishly handsome when he did that. "No, you didn't, but it was going through my mind all night how sweet it would be if you did." He shrugged. "I haven't had a woman in a long time. I'm very easily aroused when I've abstained for this long."

She met his gray eyes evenly, fascinated.

He could see the question that she didn't want to ask. He touched her lips with his mouth, tenderly brushing them apart. "Two years," he whispered into them. "I haven't had sex in two years, Josie. Not since that night I lost my head with you."

While she was trying to get her mind to work, one of his lean hands eased up under the shirt she was wearing with nothing underneath. His fingers began to stroke her naked breast while his mouth played tenderly with her soft lips and teased it into submission. He nibbled the upper lip while his thumb and forefinger found a hard nipple and caressed it softly.

He felt her body tauten against him, heard the soft, shocked moan that went into his mouth. "Yes," he whispered, and his mouth ground hungrily into hers.

Both hands were under her shirt. Then they were on the buttons. While he kissed her, he opened the shirt. He drew back, so that when he pulled the edges aside, her pert, pretty little breasts were bare, their dusky nipples hard, her body trembling with desire.

His lean hands held her narrow waist. His eyes blazed as he looked at her body. "Not even the dreams were this beautiful," he ground out.

He bent, and she felt his mouth ease down very tenderly on her nipple. She jerked. His head lifted a fraction of an inch. "I won't bite you," he whispered. "I only want the taste of you."

Her breath was audible. His mouth eased closer, enveloping her. She felt his tongue smoothing against the hard nipple. Her whole body arched. There was a raging heat in her abdomen, a sudden moisture in another place. Her trembling hands caught in the thick waves of his hair.

His free hand was at the fastening of her jeans. She caught it, holding his wrist, digging in.

He sighed against her breast, but he didn't insist. Seconds later, his head lifted and he drew her bareness against his own, letting her feel the thick hair on his chest brushing her sensitized nipples while he looked into her wide eyes.

"You haven't had that minor surgery we discussed," he guessed.

She swallowed hard, trying to get her breath. She was standing half nude in his arms, feeling his body so intimately against her own that she could feel the strength and power of his arousal starkly against her lower stomach.

"I told you...years ago," she managed to say shakily, "that I didn't have affairs. I still don't."

His pulse was hammering at his throat. His eyes were blazing with desire. His body was rigid.

"I know. I'm living in the dark ages," she said sarcastically, trying to pull away.

"Chastity isn't something you need to apologize for," he said quietly, watching her. "I respect it."

She looked down at her bare breasts pressed hard to his bare chest. "Sure you do."

He smiled gently. "This is foreplay," he said in a soft, teasing tone. "Perfectly permissible, even among some of the most devout people."

Her hands met on his broad chest. "Let me go."

He did, slowly and with obvious reluctance. He brought the edges of her shirt back together after one long, last look at her breasts. "I've never seen a Greek statue who could compare with you," he murmured as he refastened buttons. "You have the most beautiful breasts I've ever seen."

"You mustn't say things like that to me," she choked, embarrassed.

"You can say them to me anytime you like," he offered.

She coughed. "You don't have breasts."

A slow, wicked smile split his lips. "I have something else you could comment on…?"

She pushed at his chest, hard. "You stop that!"

He laughed, not at all put out by her bad temper. He swung her up gently in his arms and deposited her in the bed, leaning over her to search her angry face. "You might ask me why I haven't had sex for the past two years."

"Does it have anything to do with a social disease?" she asked pointedly.

He grinned. "Nope."

She averted her eyes to his mouth. It was slightly

swollen. Such a masculine mouth, and it could wreak the most delicious havoc on a woman's lips...

"You shouldn't tempt me while you're lying on a convenient flat surface, Josie," he mused, bending to kiss her very gently. He stood up and moved away. "Now stay put. I've got to go out for a while, but I'll be back before you miss me. I'll put on the dead bolt when I leave. Don't open the door for anyone. Understand?"

"I understand."

He moved toward the door.

She sat up, breathless. "Marc."

He turned, his eyes softly inquisitive.

"Why...haven't you had a woman for two years?" she asked huskily.

He searched her eyes. "Oh, I think you know, Josie." He turned and went out, back to his bedroom. Scant minutes later, he called goodbye as he was closing the outer door. Josette was still sitting up in bed, trying to reason out that cryptic remark. She was no closer to solving it when she drifted back to sleep.

CHAPTER ELEVEN

WHEN BRANNON CAME BACK, he brought her case files and some of her clothes. He acted as if he hadn't said or done anything unprofessional, and he was polite and gentle, but completely remote. She wondered if he regretted what had happened. She didn't get the chance to ask, because he no sooner delivered her things than he went right back out again.

When he was through with work for the day, he found her on the telephone with her notes spread out on the bed and a pad and pen close by. The pad had scribbling all over it. She'd changed clothes, too. She was wearing a pair of gray sweatpants with an oversize long-sleeved cowl-necked pullover, and her hair was back in its neat bun.

She glanced up at him while she talked, curious about the odd look on his face as he went toward the kitchen.

When she finished her conversation, she hung up, picked up her notepad and walked into the kitchen in her socks.

He was making sandwiches with a package of sandwich meat, a loaf of bread and a jar of mayonnaise.

"Ham and cheese or salami?" he asked.

"I fixed myself a salad just before you got here," she

said. "That's all I usually have for supper. Breakfast is my big meal."

He only nodded and continued what he was doing.

"I've been trying to run down leads," she said. "Simon managed to get Phil returned by the FBI, so I called Phil in Austin and got him busy on Sandra Gates's background. Then I phoned the assistant district attorney and told her the direction the investigation is going. She's going to put her cybercrime expert in touch with Phil. That would be Grier, I guess?"

He nodded again.

"Are you even listening?" she asked, exasperated.

He finished his two sandwiches and put everything back in its place before he looked at her. His eyes were harder than she'd seen them in a long time.

"Are you making a statement?" he asked, nodding toward the way she was dressed.

"A statement?" she asked blankly.

"You're dressed like a bag lady," he said flatly. "Text-book unisex clothing."

"What did you have in mind?" she returned hotly. "Were you expecting to find me in a pert little see-through negligee, panting for you to walk in the door?"

His eyes narrowed. "No," he said quietly. "That's the last thing in the world I'd expect to see with you."

"Then what's wrong?"

"You can't forget, can you, Josie?" he asked in a soft, weary tone. "You won't do anything to encourage me—not even leave your hair down."

She stared at the notes in her hand. After a minute she lifted her eyes back to his. She couldn't manage words. Her misery was plain in her dark eyes.

He leaned back, watching her. "Even a man with an

enormous ego would need encouragement with you," he said softly. "But *you* aren't confident enough, are you? You're still seeing me as the man who walked out on you without a word."

"I suppose that's true," she replied after a minute. "Trust comes hard to me. But there's more to it than trust. You want me. But that's all it's ever been, and all it ever will be. You don't need a woman in your life, Marc. You're self-sufficient. You can do most anything around a house better than I can. You're a born loner." She shrugged, favoring her sore arm. "So am I, really. I like being alone, having my own space, not having to answer to anyone. I don't... I don't want to change my life now. I'm used to things the way they are."

"What do you know about me?"

That was a curious question. She didn't really understand it. "You're a Texas Ranger. You were born in Jacobsville. You were a policeman before you worked highway patrol. You've been a Ranger since you were twenty-six, except for those years with the FBI. You're thirty-three now, and you have a sister who's married to a foreign head of state."

"That's right. All you know are the external facts." He made coffee before he spoke again. "What sort of music do I like? What do I read for pleasure? What are the things I enjoy most? What do I want to do with the rest of my life?"

She could have answered those questions, because she knew most of the answers. But she wasn't setting herself up for another rejection from him. She didn't trust him.

"I don't know," she said flatly.

"Exactly. And you don't want to know." He looked

at her for a long moment. "I betrayed you once, and you can't forget."

"You betrayed me *twice* and I can't forget," she shot back.

His eyebrows lifted. "Twice?"

"You sold me out to the prosecutor at Dale's trial."

"I didn't," he replied. "I told you, Bib brought it up himself, without any inspiration from me."

"But you told him all about my past," she continued.

He couldn't deny that. His face tautened. "Yes, I did," he told her. "And when I realized what he'd done, I told him the truth. He was as upset by it as I was, but neither of us could make it up to you by then. It was too late."

She searched his eyes and saw the inflexibility there. He was remembering that she'd accused his best friend of murder, and she was remembering the stinging commentary in the local newspaper about her background. It opened up wounds she thought were healing and convinced her that they were never going to be able to get past what had happened. It was too late. It was just too late.

"It doesn't matter anymore, Brannon," she said, turning away. "Let's go back to being colleagues and not complicate the issue anymore. I'm sure you have all the women you need in your life, anyway."

There was a hard thud behind her, as if a fist had hit the table. She didn't turn. She kept walking, right back into the bedroom. She put down the pad, picked up the phone and went back to work on the case.

JUST THAT QUICKLY, she and Brannon were enemies again. They were polite and cordial with each other, and nothing more. They returned to work the next day, although

Josette still favored her sore arm. But she was well enough to do what she needed to do. She moved back into her hotel with a gruff speech of gratitude to Brannon for taking care of her, which he ignored.

Two days later, having tried to phone Mrs. Jennings and failing to hear from her or the guard that had been hired to protect her, she got into her rental car and drove down toward Elmendorf where the old woman's apartment was located, and without phoning Brannon first. Mrs. Jennings might be more willing to talk to her if there wasn't anyone else around.

She knocked on the front door, but there was no answer. She went next door, to Mrs. Danton, the neighbor who'd offered to take calls for the elderly woman until her own phone was working.

"No, I haven't seen her since day before yesterday," the thin, elderly neighbor said, and frowned. "But she had company yesterday," she added quickly. "A man and a woman, dressed real nice, in a big fancy black car. The woman had on a hat. I remember thinking what a pretty hat it was and wishing I had one. I used to always wear a hat to church," she added, smiling with reminiscence.

"How long did they stay?" Josette asked with an uneasy feeling.

"Not too long. Maybe an hour. They came out and got into their car and drove away. I figured maybe they were family, because they were carrying some of her things."

"What sort of things?"

"A little wooden box, kind of like a cigar box, and a book of some sort. A Bible, maybe. The man had a cigarette in his hand, but he didn't smoke it. He ground it out on the driveway under his shoe just before they left. Nice shoes he had on, too. Those black wing tips. I always liked to see a man wear those, they look real fancy."

Now Josette felt really uneasy. She went to the driveway in front of the house. Sure enough, there was the cigarette stub. Gingerly she produced a handkerchief and carefully rolled it onto the white cloth with her ballpoint pen, securing it loosely before she tucked it into the briefcase she was carrying. She put it back in the car, along with her purse, and took out her flip phone, slipping it into her jacket pocket.

She went back to the apartment, accompanied by the neighbor, and peered in through the curtains. She couldn't see anything. She went around to the side of the apartment, but there were venetian blinds there, and they were pulled. At the back door, she saw the kitchen through the door, but no person was visible and no lights were on. There was, however, a cracked window. And the scent that reached her nostrils through it was unmistakable to someone raised in ranch country.

She activated the flip phone and dialed the emergency services number and the sheriff's patrol unit for that area, asking them to send not only an ambulance, but a crime scene investigation team as well. Then she called Brannon. He wasn't in his office, but she had them relay a message to him.

"You think something's happened to her, don't you?" the neighbor asked sadly when she closed her flip phone. "Somebody's always falling and can't get up, or being found dead. It's sad that we have to get old and helpless."

"You go on home," Josette said gently. "Thank you

for your help, but you don't need to be here when we go in."

The old woman grimaced. She turned around with her arms folded and went back to her own apartment.

Josette waited outside until the paramedics and a deputy sheriff's car drove up. She went immediately to the young deputy and introduced herself.

"There's a recognizable odor coming from the house," she said flatly, providing information she hadn't wanted to share with the elderly neighbor. "I think she's probably dead. She's connected to a case I'm working with one of the San Antonio Company D Texas Rangers and the local D.A.'s office. If she is dead, it's going to be a homicide."

"You sure of that?" the deputy asked, a little dubiously.

"Dead sure," she replied.

They had to force the front door. The smell came and hit them in the face the instant it opened, because the heat was unseasonable and there was no ventilation, no air conditioner working, inside. Mrs. Jennings lay face-up on the hall carpet just outside the kitchen doorway, her eyes wide-open, her mouth open, and round burn marks all over her thin old arms and legs. There was a small hole in the bodice of her cotton housedress. There was no weapon visible anywhere around the body. The bodyguard was found in a closet, bound and gagged, but unharmed. He gave a statement, but couldn't provide any leads because he'd been knocked out from behind and never saw the assailants' faces.

A few minutes later, there was the screeching of brakes outside. She walked out onto the pavement in time to see Brannon get out of his SUV, followed by a panel truck driven by Alice Jones from the medical examiner's office.

Josette nodded at Brannon and waited for Alice.

"You working homicide now, Langley?" Alice teased as she lugged her bag up the steps.

"You'd be surprised. Still cutting up people, I gather?"

Alice laughed and hugged her. "It buys groceries. I see Brannon's here, too. He'll want me to jab in a thermometer in front of everybody..."

"For God's sake, Jones, put a sock in it!" Brannon said disgustedly.

"No sense of humor," the coroner scoffed. "No wonder you never made captain."

"I'm not old enough," he said curtly.

"Excuses, excuses," she murmured, and shouldered past them, her mind already focusing on the task ahead.

The deputy gave Brannon an amused look and followed Alice into the apartment.

The apartment had been thoroughly ransacked. It looked as if a tornado had hit the contents of the sparsely furnished rooms. Everything the old lady had was emptied out or scattered. There, in the midst of it, the body lay under a sheet someone had brought out of the bedroom. Her shoes were visible where it didn't quite cover her feet. Josette remembered the woman's affection for her son, and her grief at his death. Maybe she was with him again, now. But she looked so vulnerable lying there like that, so helpless. It made her sad.

BRANNON AND JOSETTE were outside with the deputy and two sheriff's department crime-scene investigators, helping keep the curious away, when Alice came out and pulled them to one side.

"You'll get a complete report after we finish the autopsy," she told them. "But from a preliminary standpoint, I can tell you definitely that she's been dead at least twenty-four hours, and that she was probably tortured before she was shot."

"Cigarette burns," Josette guessed.

"Right on."

"Just a minute, Alice," Josette called over her shoulder as she went to the car to her purse. She drew out a handkerchief and opened it. "I found this on the pavement outside the apartment."

"Hey, Bill!" Alice called to one of the civilian evidence technicians. "Come get this!"

The technician came out, his hands in disposable gloves. He stripped them off and peered over Alice Jones's shoulder at what Josette had. She explained where she found it and gave a description of the visitors to them, adding the name of the neighbor who gave it to her and where she lived.

Pulling an evidence bag from his pocket, the technician carefully eased it inside and closed the edges.

"It's a long shot," Alice said, very professional now, "but in seven percent of the population, we can get a DNA profile from saliva traces. Cross your fingers."

"They're crossed. Nice work, Josie," Brannon remarked.

"Luck," she replied. "Pure luck. If her neighbor hadn't told me about it, I'd have walked right over it. I saw something else. It's an unusual brand of cigarettes."

"I noticed." His face was flinty. "I want these people

locked up. I can't imagine the sort of mentality it takes to torture a helpless old woman!"

"The neighbor said they took a small box and a book, maybe a Bible, out of the apartment when they left. Mrs. Jennings knew something. We'll never know what."

"And I have more news," he told her. "York knocked out an orderly and walked right out by the man we had guarding him in the hospital."

"Oh, great!" Josette muttered. "That's just what we need, a hit man on the loose and a target we can't name still in danger." She glanced toward the apartment. "You don't suppose...?"

"The neighbor's description of the male visitor doesn't match York," Brannon said. His eyes narrowed. "But I checked the files. Jake Marsh always wears wing tips," he added with a determined look.

"Does he have a wife or mistress?" she asked.

Brannon lifted an eyebrow. "I hear he has two wives," he mused. "But nobody can prove it."

"Mrs. Danton said the man had a nice-looking woman with him, in a fancy hat with a veil," she continued.

"Not much to go on."

"Yes. I know." Josette grimaced. "I guess somebody's told poor Mr. Holliman that his sister's dead."

"Not yet," Brannon said. "I asked. I think you and I could handle that chore better than the deputies, because we know him. I'll clear it with them." He went to find the investigator in charge.

"DID YOU NOTICE that all the drawers were pulled out and the contents dumped?" Josette asked as she sat beside Brannon in his big SUV on the way to Mr. Holliman's house.

"Yes."

"Wouldn't you deduce that whatever they were looking for was small enough to fit in a drawer?" she persisted.

He nodded slowly. "Good thinking."

"I'm a trained investigator," she drawled.

"And that's all you want out of life, is it?" Brannon asked carelessly. "To go on working in the criminal justice system until you can draw your pension?"

She frowned. "What's wrong with that?"

"You used to love kids," he recalled quietly. "I remember we'd go to the park and feed the pigeons some days during lunch. Parents would bring their children to swing on the swings, and you'd watch and smile and go dreamy."

"You have to have sex to get children," Josette pointed out.

"That's blunt."

"It's the only language that works with you," she said. She glanced at him and folded her arms over the blue jacket she wore with a white blouse and patterned rayon skirt.

"What's wrong with sex?"

Josette shivered. Every time she thought about it, she saw herself as she was with that boy so long ago, or with Brannon. The things she'd let Brannon do to her were still shocking. And, even in memory, delicious.

"I know your people were religious," he said gently. "But I'll remind you that sex is a big part of life. It's a beautiful experience between two people who care about each other."

"If they're married."

Brannon shook his head, laughing softly. "You've got to be the only woman I know who thinks so."

"I was never one to follow the crowd, as you keep reminding me," she said idly, glancing out the window.

"If you'd have that minor surgery, you could have sex with me," he said outrageously.

Josette leaned back against the seat with her eyes closed. "Then you'd go on to your next conquest. You only want me because you can't have me."

He laughed. "That's really funny."

She turned her head toward him. "Why?"

Brannon pulled onto the long, winding graveled road that led to Holliman's house and looked at her for a long moment before he accelerated. "Because I could have had you whenever I liked two years ago," he replied quietly.

"That is a…!"

"If you're going to say 'lie,' save yourself the breath," he interrupted. "I was the one who pulled back on that last date," he reminded her bluntly. "You were begging me not to stop."

Josette ground her teeth together. "Don't!" she groaned.

"Why are you so ashamed?" he persisted. "Josette, we were two grown adults. You make it sound like a perversion that I made love to you."

Her eyes closed in anguish.

"You enjoyed me. I enjoyed you, too. I've never been so high on such innocent love-play," he added gently.

"Innocent!" she exclaimed, almost choking on the word.

"Innocent," Brannon emphasized. "Surely you know…?"

Her face was like stone. She didn't meet his searching gaze, and she was even more tense than before.

"You don't," he realized, scowling. "Why not?"

"Because everyone in Jacobsville knew that I accused a boy of rape and he was acquitted because they
said I lied about it," Josette replied tersely. "Nobody
would come near me after that. I had a reputation. Even
after we moved to San Antonio, there was a girl who
had family in Jacobsville. She knew about it and told
everyone."

"God!" Brannon exclaimed. "I never realized…!"

"I didn't go to parties, because the boys either made
fun of me or made insinuating remarks," she said huskily. "I didn't go to a single school function right up
until graduation. Then when I went on to college, I
thought it would be all right, but there were people
there who knew me from high school." Josette sighed
audibly. "Until you started taking me out, I hadn't had
a single date."

He was floored. No wonder she'd reacted so strangely
to his ardor that night. He'd literally swept her off her
feet, given her no time to be shocked or hesitant. He'd
aroused her and proceeded to undress her. She'd been in
so deep that she never protested at all. And if it hadn't
been for her shocking condition, he probably wouldn't
have stopped at all, he admitted privately. He'd wanted
her. He'd been prepared. There would have been no
real risk.

His hand smoothed absently over the steering wheel
and he frowned, deep in thought.

"I thought Gretchen would have told you," Josette
said, puzzled by his silence.

"We didn't talk about you after that night," Brannon

replied. "Or before it." He drew in a long breath. "It's far too late to say I'm sorry. But I am. Deeply sorry."

"You didn't know," she said. "It was a misunderstanding all around." She picked at the cuticle around her thumb. "Brannon, were you…going to stop?" she asked.

"No."

Her intake of breath was latent with shock.

"I'm sorry," he said. "That was much too blunt. But it was the truth, just the same. I was in over my head," he amended. "I'd wanted you for a long time. We were alone together in my apartment, and you were so responsive that I stopped thinking in terms of right or wrong. I hadn't planned to seduce you. But I lost control. I never had before."

"Oh."

"And I had company," he added solemnly. "Because you lost control, too, Josie. That's why you can't face what happened. You wanted me so badly that you were sobbing with sheer desire. You begged me not to stop, and I was so sick with realization of what you were and what I'd cost you that I couldn't think past getting out the door."

Brannon stopped at a stop sign and turned to face her fully on the deserted stretch of road. "I compounded every error I'd already made by not explaining why I left. It wasn't only because I was ashamed of what I'd done to you. It was because I felt comfortable coming on to you in a purely sexual way, with your past. I should have been horsewhipped."

"But it wasn't completely your fault," she said. "I…" Josette averted her eyes and clutched her briefcase tightly on her lap. "I…"

"Wanted me," he said for her. "It's not a dirty word. Desire is the way God perpetuates the species. It isn't ugly."

"It is." She choked. "It's ugly and it makes women act like prostitutes!"

"Prostitutes sell their bodies, sweetheart," he said gently. "It's not the same thing. Not at all." He reached out and grasped one of her hands tightly in his. "I wanted very badly to make love to you that night. Not as a one-night stand, or a casual affair, either." Brannon smiled faintly. "It was hard for me to leave you, even to go home at night," he confessed. "I found the damnedest excuses to run into you, on campus, in town. I even started going to church, so that I could see you on Sundays."

Her eyes widened with surprise.

"You didn't notice," he mused. "Your father did. He was still uneasy about having you go out with me, thinking about you the way I did. But he seemed to realize later that it wasn't just physical with me. Or with you."

She hesitated. "It wasn't?"

His fingers tightened around hers. "Josie, you have some wonderful qualities," he said softly. "You have a heart as big as all outdoors. You're generous to a fault. You love people, and they react to you because they can see it in the way you look at them, the way you talk to them. You're honest, you hate lies, you never shirk a job because it might be hard or dangerous, and you're the best company I ever had. I even enjoyed going to the park with you, because I could watch you watching other people. And even then, it didn't dawn on me that what I felt was more than desire."

"Was it?" she asked huskily.

"You know that already," he said. "But you're hesitant to trust me, because you've been let down so badly. You accuse me of living in the past, but so are you. Until you can put away all that resentment and anger, there isn't any hope for a new relationship."

She shifted restlessly. Her arm was uncomfortable, even in its sling. "What sort of relationship could we have?"

He rubbed his thumb over her palm, sensitizing it. "Any sort you want," he said openly. "I want to be your lover. You know that. But I'll settle for whatever you feel comfortable giving me, even if it's only friendship."

Her dark eyes softened on his face, curious and puzzled.

"I'm not putting any pressure on you," he added. "But I'd like to get to know you again."

Josette swallowed. "You live in San Antonio. I live in Austin."

"You could work out of the D.A.'s office here," Brannon pointed out. "I know they have vacancies. Not a lot of people are standing in line for investigators' jobs here. Or I could work out of Victoria and you could get a job with the district attorney in Jacobs County and work out of Jacobsville."

"That would be like a…commitment."

He nodded. "Yes. A commitment."

Josette sighed. "What would you expect?"

"Now, or eventually?"

"Now."

Brannon smiled. "A companion for the symphony and the opera and the ballet," he said. "We used to share a passion for those things."

Her face brightened. "Yes. I enjoyed going out with you."

"I enjoyed just being with you." He brought her hand to his mouth and kissed it hungrily, making her tingle all over. "I won't try to seduce you, either," he promised.

"I'll have to think about it," Josette said after a minute. Her heart was racing. Her body was exploding with sensation and hope.

He saw that expression in her eyes and smiled. "Take all the time you like."

Brannon dropped her hand and moved back onto the road toward Holliman's. It felt like a new beginning. He hoped that this time he wouldn't foul things up.

CHAPTER TWELVE

MR. HOLLIMAN WAS waiting for them on the ramshackle front porch when they drove up. He smiled as they approached him, until he got a close look at their faces.

"Something's happened, hasn't it?" he asked uncertainly, and his expression tautened.

"Yes. I'm sorry to have to tell you that your sister's been killed," Brannon said straight out.

"Been killed?" The old man just stood and stared at them for a minute. "Killed? How?"

"Shot," Brannon said, without going into details. "We don't know who did it. Her apartment was ransacked, so we know the perpetrator was looking for something. Two items were removed, but we don't know if they found what they were looking for or hoped to find it in the items. We assume that it was something of Dale Jennings's that they thought she had. We're investigating."

Mr. Holliman sat down in his chair on the porch, heavily. "I'll have to make arrangements…" He looked up. "Is she at the hospital?"

"Yes. The medical examiner will have to do an autopsy, and evidence will go to the state crime lab for analysis. When the autopsy is finished, they'll make arrangements to release her to a funeral home. You can call Alice Jones at the medical examiner's office. She'll tell you what you need to know."

"I'll do that, and get in touch with the funeral home," he said, lifting his head. "Two funerals in less than a week is a little more than I bargained for." He sighed. "That makes me the last of my family," he murmured sadly. "The very last one…"

"Is there anything we can do?" Josette asked, interrupting him gently.

"Yes." The old man's watery eyes glittered. "You can get her murderer for me," he said coldly. "You can make sure he's punished. Because ten to one whoever killed her also killed my nephew!"

BRANNON DROPPED JOSETTE off at the D.A.'s office. She paused in the open door with the engine running and looked back at him.

"I've been thinking," she said, explaining her silence on the way back. "What if Jennings had a safe-deposit box?"

He nodded slowly. "That's possible. I'll look into it. Call you later."

"Okay."

"One more little thing," Brannon added softly.

Her eyebrows lifted and she smiled. "Yes?"

He leaned toward her. "If you feel sick, or dizzy, get someone to drive you back to my apartment and phone me. I don't want you out of that office alone, for any reason. We're still short one hit man."

York, he meant. Josette stared at him with an odd little smile. He was very protective. She shouldn't like that. But she did. "Okay."

He smiled back at her. "And don't go adventuring."

She moved her wounded arm gingerly. "Too soon for that. See you."

She closed the door and watched him drive away before she went inside to report their progress. She was introduced to Grier, who invited her into his office.

Cash Grier was thirty-eight, tall and lean-faced, with black eyes and long, black hair that he wore in a ponytail. He wore jeans and a black T-shirt under an unconstructed denim jacket, and black boots. Josette was quietly amused at the thought of him as a sort of reversed Texas Ranger. Unlike his colleagues, he didn't like a white hat and conventional haircuts. He was certainly nothing like the conservative detective Josette had pictured. Grier had perfect white teeth, which he displayed only briefly when they were introduced, and a manner that was to the point and professional. He was the computer expert, and within two minutes Josette would have put him on a par with Phil Douglas in Simon Hart's office. Grier knew his job.

"Sandra Gates is responsible for getting Jennings transferred to a state prison, and onto a work detail," he said at once. "I've tracked down every connection she's made in the past three months, including forays into her account at the bank," he added. "She gets paid a flat fee for her software, mid-four figures. But she's got fifty grand in her savings account, and it was all deposited at once, the day Jennings was killed."

"Bingo!" Josette said, smiling. "Can you prove it?"

"I can," he said. "And in fact, I've put together enough evidence for a warrant. There's just one small hitch."

"Which is?"

"She flew the coop," Grier said, leaning back in his

chair, his black eyes under heavy dark brows steady and impatient. "She went to the bank and drew out her money, got a cab to the airport and went to Argentina. Your guy Phil Douglas tracked her there. But we can't extradite her from there."

"At least we know that she's involved in all this," Josette said.

"Yes, but it doesn't help us find her connection to Jennings's murder, or to Jake Marsh. She had no computer contact with anyone except Jennings, in prison, and with the other computers she broke into to make those changes in Jennings's record. She had a clear field there, because the prison where he was staying had just had a systems crash and some prisoners got lost in the cracks."

"That explains a lot."

"It doesn't help my conviction record," Grier said curtly. "I'd like to fly down to Argentina, slip a bag over her head and bring her back for questioning."

"Ask the D.A. for a plane ticket," she suggested lightly.

"I did." He looked absolutely disgusted. "She asked the budget chief. He said I could stand outside with a tin cup and a sign until I collected the fare."

Josette laughed. "Okay, that avenue's cut off," she added. "But we still have Jennings's tie to Jake Marsh, and the hit man, York. Well, we had York. He escaped from the hospital."

"Yeah, I heard about that," he commented, crossing his long legs. "Sloppy police work."

"No fair. The officer guarding the door was knocked out," she explained. "He has a concussion. Nobody expects a man with a gunshot wound to be walking around."

"I would," Grier mused, noting her wounded arm in its sling. "Doesn't seem to have slowed you down much."

"Point taken. The thing is, he's out and we don't know who his target is. We don't think he killed Mrs. Jennings, though. The neighbor described the man as wearing wing-tip dress shoes, and we know that Marsh favors them."

"Yes, and two-thousand-dollar suits," he added. He got up, grabbing his service revolver out of his desk drawer. Grier checked it, made sure the safety was on and stuck it in its holster at his lean waist. He wore his detective's shield in front on his belt, she noted. "I have a contact who's in the local mob. He usually knows what's going down in the underworld. I'll go see him."

"Can I go along?"

He scowled. "Why?"

"I'm closer to the Jennings case than you are," Josette said simply. "I can think of questions to ask that you might not."

He looked absolutely perplexed, and there was an odd glint in his dark eyes.

"I'm not going to storm in and start flashing my credentials," she persisted. "I'll just be an appendage. You can tell him I'm a colleague."

He gave her a curious appraisal. "Brannon know you're going with me?"

Josette glared at him. "I do not report every movement I make to Brannon," she said firmly. "Anyway, he won't mind."

Grier pondered that with narrowed eyes. "Brannon

has a peculiar way with him about women," he persisted. "I've heard him speak of you. He's territorial and he has a temper almost as bad as mine. I don't trespass."

"Yes, but then, you probably don't have to pick up wounded women at the hospital to get them to go to your apartment with you," she replied pertly.

"I don't take women to my apartment," he returned, and he didn't smile.

She cleared her throat. What Brannon had said about this guy having a badge sewn to his underwear was beginning to make sense. "It's a business matter. I'm working with the D.A.'s office, just like you. There's nothing personal about it. Now, shall we go?"

Grier shrugged and stood aside to let her go first.

He drove an unmarked patrol car. Josette glanced at the hubcaps, shook her head and got inside.

He slid in beside her, noted that she had her seat belt on and fixed his in place before he started the car. "Something funny?" he asked.

"Unmarked police cars," she said. "They all have those same round plain hubcaps that regular police cars have. It's a dead giveaway."

Grier made a rough sound and ignored her until he pulled up at a local billiards parlor. She grinned, but he didn't notice.

There were two men around a big pool table, while three others sat at a nearby table playing cards.

"Hello, Bartlett," Grier greeted the elder of the two men, and the shortest. He shook hands with him. "How's it going?"

"Not bad, Grier." He glanced at the woman beside the detective. "Crippling women these days?"

"I didn't shoot her," Grier returned drolly.

Bartlett chuckled. He had a raspy voice, the kind that comes after countless years of smoking. He coughed and went back to his game. He called the shot, and made it.

"Nice shot," Josette mused.

He looked at her curiously. "You play?"

"A little," she said with a smile. "I learned from a girl in college."

"I don't guess you play much now," he said, indicating her arm.

"Only if I could hold the cue stick with my toes," she agreed.

He chuckled. "She's okay," he told Grier. He set up his next shot. "What you want, Grier?"

"A word in private."

"Sure."

He put the cue stick down and moved out into the deserted cafeteria next door with Josette and Grier.

"Is there any word on the street about Marsh being involved in a hit?"

The smaller man's eyebrows lifted. "How'd you know about that?"

"Never mind. What do you know?"

"Well, what I hear is that Marsh had hired this guy he knows to put away a blackmailer for him. Then he finds out the dead guy didn't have the stuff on him, the blackmail stuff. So now he's going nuts trying to find it and zapping anybody who gets in the way."

"You know if he's found it yet?"

"Naw, but I doubt it," the little man drawled. "They say he's got hives worrying that he's going up for Jennings's murder. Not that he did it," he added.

"Who did? York?" Grier asked.

"That would be my bet," the older man replied. "York's been in the game for several years. He may look like a kid, but he'd do anything for a dime. Marsh hires him for the really dirty jobs."

Grier gave Bartlett the description he had of the man who'd gone into Mrs. Jennings's apartment and killed her.

"Not York," he agreed. "But that wouldn't be Marsh's style, either. He don't torture old ladies."

"There was a woman with him, in a fancy hat and veil."

"Marsh has a mistress. I've never seen her. They say she's married to some rich guy that Marsh knows. Word is that she's ready to leave the husband because of something that's going to happen to him."

"Something connected with blackmail?" Grier wondered.

Bartlett smiled. "Now what do you think? You're the detective, aren't you?"

ON THE WAY back to the office, Josette was quiet. The presence of the woman in Mrs. Jennings's apartment was disturbing, since no one seemed to credit Jake Marsh with stooping so low as to torture old women. So—what if the woman had done the torturing?

That made the situation even more disturbing—and more complicated. A rich woman, married to a rich man, who had a connection to Dale Jennings, who had evidence of some sort of wrongdoing. In the middle, Jake Marsh—the local mob kingpin—and a hit man, and two recent murder victims connected to it all.

"Someone," Josette said aloud, "is taking extreme risks to get their hands on a piece of blackmail."

"Someone connected to Marsh and Jennings," Grier added.

"That woman your contact mentioned, Marsh's mistress," she began. "What if she tortured old Mrs. Jennings, trying to make her tell what she knew?"

"I've seen it done."

"Some women are worse than some men," she said.

His hard face got even harder. "I'll drink to that."

Josette had a feeling that he was speaking from personal experience, but he was a colleague, not a confidant, so she didn't press.

"How do we find out who she is?"

"That's the big question."

He pulled up in the courthouse parking lot just in time to find Brannon getting out of his black SUV. He stood with his hands on his hips and glared as Grier got out with Josette.

"Where the hell have you been?" Brannon demanded of Josette in a tone that would have kindled a fire under wet wood.

Grier gave her an I-told-you-so look and walked away with nothing more than a nod to the Texas Ranger.

"I've been out with Grier talking to one of his contacts," she said calmly. She didn't feel calm. He was glaring at her with silvery eyes that glittered like metal shards.

"You can tell me on the way to get something to eat. I'm hungry."

"Listen, Brannon..." she began.

"Aren't you hungry?"

"No." Her stomach growled loudly just as she said it. "Yes," she amended.

"We can eat and talk at the same time."

"Okay."

It was easier to agree than argue, and Josette did, after all, have to tell him what she'd learned. Not that she wanted to spend a lot of time with him in his present mood. Brannon was really intimidating when he didn't smile.

He pulled into a nice-looking building where plenty of cars were already parked, even though it wasn't noon.

"Do you eat here a lot?" she asked.

"All of us do," he replied. "They always have fresh fish, whatever season it is."

He led her inside and they waited until a waitress came to seat them. Josette asked for separate checks. Then she ordered the fish platter and coffee. Brannon ordered the same, substituting iced tea for coffee.

"Okay," he said. "What did you find out?"

She told him, elaborating about Sandra Gates's flight from prosecution and adding her own suspicions about the part the mysterious woman of Jake Marsh's had played in Mrs. Jennings's death.

"That's a lot of generalizations," he remarked.

"I know," she sighed. "If we knew who the woman was…"

"Didn't Grier's contact know anything about her?" Brannon asked far too casually.

She took the question at face value. "Only that she was rich."

"Did he ask you to go with him?" he persisted over a forkful of fish. "Grier knows some dangerous people. It isn't safe to tag along with him."

"Why not? Grier isn't scared of them."

"That's because he's more dangerous than they are."

His eyes narrowed. "You don't know anything about him, do you?"

"He's the resident computer expert," Josette said, nibbling on her food.

He laughed. He finished his fish and fries, and pushed the plate aside, wiping his mouth with the napkin and sipping iced tea before he answered her.

"And you're not going to tell me why that's funny, are you?"

Brannon leaned back and stared at her with faint amusement. "Does he fit your idea of a computer expert?"

She thought of Phil Douglas in her office and compared him with Grier. "Well, no," Josette confessed.

His silver eyes narrowed. "Just don't get too attached to him," he said bluntly.

Her eyebrows arched. "And why not?"

Brannon leaned forward abruptly, so that his face was inches from hers. "Because you're mine," he said flatly.

While Josette was trying to think of a snappy, mature reply, he got up, grabbed the check, and stood aside to let her out while she was still fumbling in her purse for the tip.

She barely managed to get it on the table under her saucer before she was led to the checkout counter. And before she could argue about it, he'd paid that bill, too.

"You have to stop feeding me," she muttered as he led her outside to the truck and drew her around to the passenger side.

"I can't. You're too thin." He paused at the door. The parking lot was deserted. He moved deliberately so that he was standing close to her, both arms on the cab of the SUV behind her.

"Brannon," she protested, but she sounded breathless as her hands went to his shirt.

He searched her eyes for so long that her heart began to flutter in her chest. She knew he could see her ragged breathing and the hot flush she felt on her cheeks. But she had no way of resisting him.

He looked down at her soft mouth hungrily. "All right," he said huskily. "We'll do it your way. Flowers. Candy. Tickets to the symphony concerts."

"Wh-what?" she stammered.

He bent and brushed his hard, warm mouth against her soft one. "I love kissing you, Josie," he whispered. "I always did."

It was hard to resist a man with his skill, moreover, one who could be so tender and teasing. Her hands spread on his chest, feeling the hard muscle underneath. Her eyes closed.

"We're going to get arrested for lewd behavior," Josette moaned.

"Kissing isn't against the law," he ground out against her parting lips.

Brannon levered down against her, his mouth demanding, his body hard and insistent where it flattened against her hips. He groaned softly, and his heavy brows drew together in sweet anguish.

Josette's eyes opened just briefly and she saw his expression, and knew that he wasn't pretending to be affected by her. He really did love kissing her. And that wasn't all. She felt a blatant, insistent pressure against her belly.

"Marc," she whispered, drawing back a breath. "There's a car pulling in."

His eyes looked blank. Glazed. He blinked and drew in a forced breath. Then his head lifted and he glanced at the incoming car's single occupant. Slowly the drawn tension of ardor left his lean face and he smiled quizzically.

Josette was still reeling. From behind her, on the other side of the SUV, came an amused deep drawl.

"*She* said you wouldn't mind if she went along with me. Ha!"

It was Grier's voice, and he was already walking toward the restaurant before either of them could say a word.

"Oh, Brannon," she moaned, pulling back from him with wide eyes, a swollen mouth and a bubble of laughter on her lips.

"Did you tell him that?" he asked softly.

Josette sighed. "Yes, I actually did. But you do mind," she added with sudden realization.

Brannon fingered her soft hair. "I've been in law enforcement almost half my life, yet Grier has done things I never dreamed of." He shrugged. "He hates women, but they follow him like a chicken follows a rattlesnake, with pure fascination."

Why…he was jealous! Why hadn't she seen that before?

He glared at her. "I'm not jealous," he said, reading her expression. "I just don't think it's safe for you to go places with Grier."

She studied him, from his wavy blond-streaked light brown hair to his silver eyes, to his handsome lean, tanned face, to his chiseled mouth and she laughed breathlessly.

"I always thought you knew how good-looking you were," Josette said shyly. "But you don't think of yourself that way, do you?"

He shifted as if uncomfortable. "Looks don't mean much."

She smiled. "You'd be sexy and attractive if you had a big nose and ears like jug handles," she said.

One eyebrow arched. "Would I?"

That faint hint of masculine insecurity made her melt. Did he really need to be reassured that she found him attractive? Impulsively she reached up with her arms and drew his mouth down to hers. She kissed him softly, feeling the delight of it all over her yielded body. Brannon seemed surprised at the move, but he kissed her back tenderly.

"Your only real problem is that temper," Josette whispered. "You make Grier look like a pacifist."

He chuckled, not at all insulted. "I'll calm down in a few years."

"Are you sure about that?"

"They say kids take the rough edges off a man."

"Kids?" She searched his eyes, perplexed, but found nothing there. "Do you have many rough edges?"

He pursed his lips and looked deliberately at her stomach. "We'll have to talk about that one of these days. And about kids. Meanwhile, how about a symphony concert? There's one Saturday night."

Josette hesitated. "We're here on a murder investigation."

"Good. We can investigate the conductor and the

first chair violinist," he replied easily. "They'll make dandy suspects. I'll even file a report, after."

"Brannon!" she said, exasperated.

"Detectives get an occasional night off. Saturday is going to be ours." He kissed her one last time before he opened the passenger door. As he helped her climb up, he noticed several teenagers in a van parked near the restaurant. They were watching the couple at the black SUV with wide eyes and big smiles. The smiles got bigger when Brannon walked around to the driver's side and they saw the cream-colored Stetson, boots and revolver, and the Texas Ranger badge on his shirt.

Brannon almost blushed as he started the vehicle.

Josette, who had been watching the byplay, laughed softly to herself. But she blushed, too.

He glanced at her as she fastened her seat belt. "You still blush. Imagine that, at your age."

"Oh, yeah? Well, you were blushing, too, Brannon!"

"I never blush," he said curtly.

As they passed the teenagers, one of the girls let out a long, enthusiastic wolf whistle at Brannon.

He could hear Josette's soft laughter, but he wasn't going to look at himself in the mirror. He was *not* blushing.

"WHAT ABOUT THE safe-deposit box?" Josette asked when they were back in front of the D.A.'s office.

"Dead end. I checked every bank in town that didn't require a court order, and I'll go back and check the ones that did. But so far, nobody has a record of Dale Jennings renting one."

She thought about that, hesitating about getting out

of the vehicle. "Suppose," she began, "just suppose it was in the woman's name."

"It might be," Brannon said. "But we're no closer to finding her name. Apparently it wasn't Sandra Gates."

"I'll bet Grier can find out who she was," she said without thinking. "He seems to know his way around the underworld."

"Then let him do his own legwork. I mean it, Josie," he said shortly, and his eyes were threatening. "I'm not having you at risk for any case, no matter how important."

"What do you know about the man that you're not telling me?" she demanded.

"Things I can't repeat," he said harshly.

"Things?"

Brannon hesitated and bit off a hard sigh. "Classified things, Josie," he said finally.

Her eyebrows shot up. That could mean anything.

"Just…take my word for it and humor me, could you?" he asked, exasperated, scowling at her. "Listen, having you get shot was hard enough on my nerves. I don't want to risk you twice."

The lines in her face smoothed out magically. "You don't?" she asked absently, because her eyes were locked into his. She tingled all over with the delight of his concern.

Brannon touched a wisp of blond hair that had escaped her braided hairdo. He looked exasperated. "Josie, how would you feel if I'd been shot?"

Her involuntary exclamation was telling. It was as if all the masks had been torn off and she was facing him with her whole heart in her eyes.

His lean hand framed her cheek and his thumb

rubbed softly over her mouth. "At least you still feel something for me," he said huskily.

She started to protest, but that thumb was back across her lips again.

"Don't disillusion me," he whispered, leaning toward her. His lips parted just as they touched her. Brannon had to force himself not to drag out the warm, tender kiss. He lifted his head. As he did, he looked straight into Grier's dark eyes through the open passenger window.

"She said you wouldn't mind if I took her along," Grier repeated, deadpan.

"I mind," Brannon said flatly, his silver eyes threatening, possessive.

Grier pursed his wide, thin lips and just for an instant, there was a glimmer in his dark eyes. "Lighten up, Brannon. I'm just a computer expert now."

"And Putin used to be just a cop!"

Grier burst out laughing before he turned and walked back into the building, both hands stuck in his jeans pockets.

Her mind was whirling. "Putin?"

He gave her a speaking look.

Russia. The premier. A former colonel in the KGB. "Oh. Putin! Vladimir Putin!" she exclaimed. "Right."

"Never mind. Get out and go to work, but not with Grier. I mean it."

"I'm not a waitress."

He blinked. "Excuse me?"

"I don't take orders," she said with a grin, and got out of the SUV.

He leaned toward the open door, where she was silhouetted. "I want kids."

She gaped at him. "So?"

"So take care of yourself and do what I asked." Brannon reached over and pulled the door shut before Josette could ask him to explain that outrageous statement.

CHAPTER THIRTEEN

WHEN JOSETTE FINISHED going through local files, looking up information about Jake Marsh and talking to police officers and detectives who had interrogated him, she was surprised to find Brannon waiting outside the D.A.'s office.

He leaned across and opened the passenger door. "Climb in," he invited. "I'll drive you to your hotel."

It was like old times, when he picked her up after her last college class, or at the library on Saturdays when she was researching project papers. It warmed her heart to see that he was still just as thoughtful.

She climbed in beside him with a delighted, unguarded smile. "Thanks! But, why are you here?"

He gave her a long stare. He sighed and shrugged. "I thought Grier might offer to drive you back," he confessed reluctantly.

She chuckled softly at that involuntary evidence of jealousy. "He went out when I got back from lunch and hasn't returned," she said smugly. "I haven't even spoken to him."

He smiled. "Good." He started the vehicle and carefully pulled out into the stream of traffic.

"I've been looking up information about Jake Marsh," she said as he drove. "One of the patrolmen remembers questioning him about Dale Jennings, about the time of the Garner murder trial. Marsh said that Jennings was a sort of courier for him, delivered messages and that sort of thing, but they cut him loose when he started hanging around Bib Webb's house."

Brannon frowned. "He didn't hang around Bib's. He worked for Henry Garner."

"I'm just telling you what he said," she replied. "It's in the report the officer made after the interview."

"If Bib's going to be back in town this weekend, I'll go see him and ask him about it."

"Good idea."

"Did Jennings ever ask you out before you went to the Webbs' party with him?"

Josette glanced at him warily, because this was sensitive territory. "No. I used to see him at the corner coffee shop all the time. Bib Webb's wife was taking some sort of class on campus that year. I even saw her there. It wasn't exactly a hoodlum hangout, if you get my meaning."

He was suddenly alert. "Silvia had coffee there?"

"Not often," she recalled. "I saw her there once or twice. She was sitting all by herself."

That was disturbing. He didn't remember Bib ever mentioning that Silvia was taking a college class. Since she didn't have a high school education, it seemed a bit far-fetched. "Did she talk to anyone?"

"I didn't really notice," she recalled honestly. "I was usually in a hurry, on my way to class or the library or a lab, or even home. I got my coffee to go, mostly. Once in a while I'd drink it there. I liked those homemade scones they sold. Dale Jennings liked them, too, and we started talking. Just casually. I was surprised when he asked me to the Webbs' party. We didn't really know each other that well."

Brannon didn't enjoy remembering why she'd gone with the man to the Webbs' party. "Did he hit on you?" he persisted.

"Not at all," she said, smiling faintly. "It wasn't ever that sort of relationship. He liked me, but he wasn't even attracted to me. He just needed a date that night, he said."

Brannon frowned. It disturbed him that Jennings might have had ulterior motives for that date. Had he been planning to murder Garner and wanted to use Josette as an alibi? Or had he had darker motives?

"You're wondering why he asked me, aren't you?" she murmured. "I've been wondering myself. Especially since, once we got there, he was never with me."

He scowled. "Where were the Webbs?"

"Bib was dancing with his personal assistant—you remember, that shy little brunette. She was really nervous and uncomfortable. I expect that's why he paid special attention to her. I remember Silvia coming back inside and finding them together and making a terrible scene."

"Becky," he murmured absently. "Becky Wilson. She's on his campaign staff for the senate, too. She's devoted to him. In fact, I think she'd do anything short of murder to protect him."

"I got that impression, too. But I liked her," she recalled.

He gave her a pointed glance. "How did you like Silvia?"

Josette grimaced. "I didn't. And considering the rest of the guest list, I felt as out of place as stale bread," she confessed. "I recognized people I'd only ever seen on the news or at political rallies. Dale said she'd asked him to invite me, but she ignored me completely until I had two cups of that spiked punch and started wobbling. Then she insisted on taking me home. She was cold sober, too." She smiled impishly. "Her husband wasn't. Every time he looked her way, he took another cup of punch. He even gave Becky one, but she had the foresight to smell it and put it down, untouched."

He was trying to remember something; something important. It was there, he just couldn't grasp it.

While he was trying to, his car phone rang. He pushed the speaker button and Jones's voice came clearly over it.

"Brannon, it's Alice Jones at the medical examiner's office. I've got your cause of death."

"Okay, Jones," he said, pausing for a traffic light.

"Mrs. Jennings was killed by severe blunt force trauma to the back of the head. There's an odd indentation in the skull…"

"Oval?" he asked at once. "Like a blackjack might have made?"

There was a pause. "Come to think of it…"

"Jones, check back in the records for the autopsy results on Henry Garner, June, two years ago. You may find a match in that odd indentation."

"G-a-r-n-e-r?" She spelled it out.

"That's it. And let me know what you find, would you?"

"Will do. But don't get used to me calling you like this, Brannon," she added in a husky tone. "You're not bad-looking, and you have that sexy Texas Ranger badge and belt buckle, but you have to remember that

I have hunky movie stars standing in line just to hear the sound of my sultry voice… Hello? Hello?"

Brannon had already hit the switch and was laughing himself sick.

"There is only one Alice Jones," Josette mused. "I miss talking to her since I moved to Austin."

He glanced at her whimsically. "I'll mention you in my will if you can get her to move there, too."

She chuckled. "Sorry. I've got a Phil Douglas in my own office. I don't need an Alice Jones in the Austin medical examiner's office to drive me even battier."

His eyes went back to traffic. "You seem to fit in well with the district attorney's staff here."

Josette nodded. "I can fit in most places. And they're a great bunch of folks to work with. But, I like Austin."

"Why?" he persisted. "Because I'm not there?"

Her hands gripped her briefcase. "You haven't been here for two years, either, Brannon," she reminded him.

"You know why I left," he replied. His silver eyes glanced in her direction and his deep voice dropped softly. "When you feel really reckless, you might ask why I came back."

"Not my business," she said firmly. She wasn't going to open that can of worms.

Unexpectedly Brannon turned off the highway onto the paved service road that led to his apartment building through a back street, his expression taut and uncompromising.

"I want to go home," Josette protested.

"I want to talk."

"Use the phone."

He ignored that. He pulled into his usual parking

spot in the underground garage and cut off the engine,
turning to her.

"Aren't you tired, just a little, of running from the
past?" he asked seriously.

He made her uncomfortable with that level stare,
even though she couldn't see it clearly under the wide
brim of his Stetson in the darkened garage.

"I'm only here to help solve a murder," she said.
"Afterward, I'll go back to Austin, to my own life…"

"You'll go home to a lonely apartment with only the
television for company," he interrupted. "You'll eat TV
dinners or takeout. You'll spend your evenings working through computer files of information, and during
the day you'll talk to other people in law enforcement
and it will be business. Just business. When you go to
bed, maybe you'll dream, but you'll still be alone. What
sort of life is that?"

"Your sort," she threw back curtly.

His face tautened and then relaxed. His shoulders
moved. "Touché."

"You're happy enough," Josette pointed out.

"Do you really think so?" he replied. "I live for my
job. It's all I've lived for during the past fourteen years,
with minor encounters that wouldn't even qualify as romance. Except for the brief time I spent with you two
years ago," he emphasized, "I've lived like a hermit."

Her heart jumped. She couldn't manage a reply.

"And you're still a virgin," he said doggedly. "Why?"

She opened her mouth, but she couldn't get any
words to come out.

"Don't bother trotting out that tired old story that
you have principles," Brannon said before she could

speak. "You want me. You wanted me then, and you want me now."

"We all have these annoying little weaknesses that we can't quite overcome," she shot back with ruffled pride.

He lifted an eyebrow and let his gaze drop to her mouth. "Why try to overcome it?"

"I don't want to have an affair with you."

He shrugged. "I'm not much on affairs, myself."

"That makes it even worse, Brannon," she said icily. "I'm even less in the market for a one-night stand."

"I don't do those, either."

Josette frowned. She stared at him evenly. She couldn't quite grasp what he was saying.

Brannon sighed. "You don't have a problem with abstinence yourself, but it doesn't occur to you that anyone else might have the same ideals—especially a man. Isn't that a little sexist in itself?"

She lifted both eyebrows. "I will never believe that you're a virgin, Brannon," she drawled.

"I'm not," he replied solemnly. "But I'm not promiscuous, either. And, as I mentioned already, for the past two years I haven't touched a woman."

Her worried eyes searched his hard, lean face, looking for answers.

"Why?" she blurted out.

"Why haven't you ended up in some other man's bed?" he threw the words right back at her. "I don't want anyone else." Brannon paused and his eyes narrowed. "And neither do you, whether or not you're willing to admit it to me."

Her body clenched at the insinuation. It might be true, but, then, she didn't have to go around admitting things like that to the one man in the world who'd been nothing but an endless headache to her. Conceit was a character-destroying vice in a man. Besides, he'd be insufferable if she admitted that she wanted only him.

"Why did you bring me here?" Josette asked, avoiding an answer.

He pursed his lips and his eyes began to twinkle. "Because in addition to meat loaf, I can make chicken and broccoli crepes," he said unexpectedly.

It was the last reply she expected. "Excuse me?"

"You always wanted to go to the same French restaurant when we were dating," he reminded her, "because you loved those crepes. The restaurant's gone out of business, but I found the chef and got him to teach me how to make the crepes."

"Why?" she exclaimed.

His lips pursed. "A little flattery, a little exquisite cuisine, a little classic tenor sax music…" He leaned toward her with a suggestive smile. "A little minor surgery…?"

She flushed and whacked him with a newsletter.

Brannon sighed. "Ah, well, there's always tomorrow." He got out of the SUV and went around to open the door for her. "You can leave those files in here," he said, putting her briefcase in the floorboard. "I'm not talking business over my crepes."

He eased her hand into his and held it all the way up the elevator. When he opened the door to his apartment and pulled her inside, he nudged her body up against the closed door and propped his lean hands on either side of her head. He looked down into her eyes for a long time, watching the telltale signs of her attraction as they broke through her reserve.

"Nice," he murmured. "After two years, you still

start trembling when I come close, like this." He leaned down, so that his powerful body was touching hers from breast to thigh. He felt her intake of breath on his lips. "I can feel your heart beating against my chest," he murmured, and his hips began a slow, sensuous revolution against her own. He stiffened with the arousal that was instantaneous.

"Marc!" she exclaimed, embarrassed.

His teeth nibbled at her upper lip and his eyes closed so that he could enjoy the taste of her. "Mint and coffee," he breathed, nudging her lips apart. "You always tasted of coffee and smelled of roses." He levered even closer. His own heart was racing now, and one long leg eased between both of hers. She didn't even protest this time.

Her nails bit into his chest helplessly as her mouth followed the open, teasing pressure of his hard lips.

"Hell, don't play. Touch!" Brannon guided her fingers to the snaps that held his creamy Western-style shirt together.

Josette didn't need prompting after that. Her fingers ripped it open to the shiny silver and gold metal of his belt buckle with the Texas Rangers logo embossed on it. Her hands found thick, rough hair over the warm, damp muscles of his chest and burrowed into it even as her mouth pushed up at his to tempt it into longer, deeper contact.

He smiled as he kissed her with slow enjoyment. "Grier may be something with a K-Bar," he whispered into her yielded lips, "but I'm in a class all by myself with you. Open your mouth a little more, Josie…."

His leg began to move seductively between hers and made her tremble. She kissed him back helplessly, with a tiny little moan of pure pleasure as her arms reached up and around his neck.

"Wait…just a minute…" His hands were busy and all at once, she felt cool air on bare skin. But she was too far gone to care. Brannon looked down at bare silky breasts with hard, dusky little nubs. His hands smoothed over them and she moaned again. "Yes," he breathed, drawing her against his bare chest. "Oh, God, yes…!"

"It's been…so long," she whimpered as he kissed her.

He pulled her up even closer, groaning against her soft, tremulous mouth. "Yes," he whispered huskily. "Too long! Come closer, baby. Come…closer…closer!"

His hands went to her rounded hips and jerked her roughly, hungrily against the visible evidence of his desire. A shock of pleasure shot through his powerful body like fire and he groaned harshly.

Josette felt tears sting her eyes as her hands moved helplessly into his thick blond-streaked brown hair, dislodging his hat as she tore her mouth from his and pulled his head down to her breasts. She arched backward, whispering, pleading.

He couldn't resist her. His mouth opened over a hard nipple and began to suckle her in a hot, tempestuous silence that was like the flash before a thunderclap. She cried out softly as her body throbbed with hunger. It had been two years since he'd handled her like this, since she'd lain in his arms all but nude on his sofa and begged him not to stop.

Brannon lifted his head and looked into her wide, hungry eyes. "I had your clothes off," he said harshly. "Do you remember? I stripped you out of your clothes and you fought mine out of the way. I was over you, my mouth on your mouth, my legs between yours…" His mouth ground hard against hers. "And you cried out. I could barely breathe by then. I was shaking, I wanted it so much. But I couldn't get…inside you! For a few seconds, I didn't even realize why. Not until you started sobbing and begging me to stop. It was like having a bucket of ice thrown on me."

Josette moaned and hid her face against his chest. Her eyes closed as she, too, relived the memory.

"You turned every shade of red when I pulled away and looked at you," he recalled huskily. "I knew then, without a word, that you'd never been with a man. I was so ashamed that I couldn't even speak."

"But you did," she reminded him painfully. "You said…plenty!"

"Josie, I really hope you've seen at least one X-rated movie by now, so that you begin to understand why I was upset!"

She was blushing, she knew she was, but she couldn't meet his eyes. "Well, I do, sort of," she stammered.

Brannon laughed gruffly. His hands moved in her hair, removing hairpins, until the wealth of the golden mass fell around her shoulders. "No, you don't," he murmured dryly. "But I remember too well how it felt to want to repeat it. So this is as far as it goes. For now."

All at once, Brannon moved away from her jerkily, his hands hard on her waist as he held her at a faint distance and dragged air into his lungs, a faint tremor in his body as he fought the demons of his own headlong hunger.

"I'm sorry about that," he added huskily, and he smiled. "I didn't mean to get in over my head so fast."

The apology was unexpected, like his nonexistent restraint toward her. Slowly it began to dawn on her numbed senses that he wasn't playing. Apparently he wasn't exaggerating his length of abstinence, either, because he was visibly shaken.

His very vulnerability made her curious and chased away her own embarrassment at her abandon in his arms. Josette stared at him with quizzical affection, a little shy, even now.

He saw that, and he liked it. She was so capable in her job that she seemed impervious to temptation. She wasn't. If he was a slave of his passion, so was she. He relaxed.

"I realize that you must feel like the main course. But I actually meant it when I promised you crepes," he said dryly.

"That's okay," she replied, and smiled gently.

The smile made his chest swell. Her eyes were luminous, soft, full of secrets. He looked down at her bare breasts, making a meal of them until she laughed a little nervously and started doing up fastenings. He did the same, but without the least sign of anger.

Brannon glanced at her ruefully. Her mouth was swollen from the hard pressure of his lips. She looked disheveled and off balance. She also looked happy. He smiled, too. Perhaps, he thought. Perhaps...

BRANNON DID COOK CREPES, and Josette made a salad to go with them, and an egg custard for dessert. She was walking around in her stockings, he in his socks. He had on jeans and a black T-shirt, and she was in her suit slacks and a scoop-neck beige blouse with her long hair loose down her back. They worked in quiet harmony as if they'd lived together and worked in the kitchen together forever.

She savored every bite of the unexpected treat, surprised at his proficiency. He'd actually made the crepes from scratch, not from a mix.

"You're impressed," he mused with a grin. "I can tell."

"I'm very impressed," she replied, finishing the last bite of her crepe and eyeing the last bite of his with helpless envy.

Brannon chuckled, forking that last bit and offering it at her lips. "No need to thank me," he murmured. "Flattery is quite adequate."

"They really are delicious," Josette admitted sheepishly, and with a smile.

"And just think, if we lived together, I could make you crepes all the time."

She paused with her coffee cup halfway to her lips and stared at him, uneasy and uncertain.

Brannon wasn't smiling. His pale eyes glittered as they stabbed into hers with determination and something else, something even deeper.

The sudden jangling of the telephone was more than enough to shatter the tension between them. He got up, muttering, to answer it.

"Hello?" he said shortly. He hesitated as he listened to whoever was on the other end of the line. He glanced toward Josette and frowned. "Why now? Can't it wait until in the morning?" he asked impatiently.

There was another hesitation. He let out a long breath. "Okay," he replied. "If it's that important. Sure. Twenty minutes."

He hung up, staring at the telephone blankly for a few seconds before he faced Josette. "Bib," he said slowly. "He's at their San Antonio place. He wants me to come over. Some enterprising reporter has a new angle on the Garner case and seems to know the reason behind the murders. The reporter approached Becky with his theory and now Bib's scared to death."

"What does he want you to do, arrest the reporter?" she asked.

"He wants to ask advice. And considering the nature of the story, I think you'd better come along."

"Why?"

"Because the reporter says that someone in the local underworld has found a damaging piece of evidence against him and is planning to blackmail him with it."

Her eyes lit up. "At last! The evidence and maybe even the culprit himself!"

"A break, at least, if we're lucky. Come on."

HE DROVE THEM quickly to the spacious estate where Bib Webb lived when he wasn't in the state capitol. Josette thought, not for the first time, what an empire he'd inherited when Henry Garner was murdered.

There were two cars in the driveway that wound up to the front door. One was a small gray VW Beetle, the other was a stately late-model dark Lincoln.

"Is his wife here?" Josette asked curiously, indicating the VW.

"Silvia drives a Ferrari," he remarked idly, noting the little German-made car. "That's Becky's car."

"Another scandal in the making?" she mused.

"I think you're going to find that Bib's tired of living a lie," he said enigmatically. "A scandal over Becky is the least of his worries right now."

"You're not thinking that he was mixed up in Garner's death at this late date?"

"Not a chance," he replied with conviction.

"Aren't you going to tell me why we're here?" she persisted.

"I'll let Bib do that."

He cut off the engine and came around to open her door for her.

"You have nice manners, Brannon," Josette remarked with a smile.

"My mother was a stickler for them. Just like yours," he added gently.

He took her hand in his and pulled her along to the front door. When he rang the bell, Bib Webb himself opened the door. He was holding a can of diet cola and he looked worn to the bone. His jacket and tie were off, and the top buttons of his shirt were undone. His hair was ruffled, as if he'd been running a nervous hand through it. There were dark circles the size of apple slices under his eyes. He looked miserable.

"Come on in," he drawled. He managed a smile for Josette. "Nice of you to come, Miss Langley, under the circumstances."

"Nice of you not to mind, Mr. Webb," she replied pleasantly.

Becky Wilson was standing nervously in the center of the living room, looking uneasy. She was wearing a long, patterned dress that came to her ankles. It had a neat white collar and long sleeves. Her dark hair was in a bun, and she wore glasses. She was the exact opposite of Silvia Webb, right down to her nondescript flat shoes.

"You know Becky," Bib said, smiling at her.

"Yes. Good to see you," Brannon replied.

"He's going to be ruined, absolutely ruined," Becky blurted out. "What are we going to do?"

Bib held up a hand. "Don't throw in the towel yet," he told her with a faint smile. "First, we explore the options we've got."

"What options, for heaven's sake?" she moaned.

"There are always options," Bib told her gently. "Sit down, Becky."

She dropped into an armchair, but leaned forward as if she couldn't bear to relax.

Bib sat down on the sofa. Brannon sat next to him, motioning Josette beside him.

"What does the reporter have, exactly?" Brannon asked, cutting to the chase.

"He has a sworn statement from an acquaintance of Jake Marsh's, who says he overheard Marsh talking about a ledger that would prove I took kickbacks from mob affiliates to rig the vote and blackmail my opponent into quitting the race when I became lieutenant governor a little over two years ago," Webb said gruffly. "The acquaintance says that Marsh doesn't have the ledger, but he knows who does."

"A ledger. Of course!" Brannon said, glancing at Josette, who looked equally surprised. It would certainly fit the few facts they had so far, including the apparent size of the missing evidence. Brannon frowned. "Is it true?" he asked, concerned. "Did you take kickbacks?"

Bib looked at him wryly. "You've known me for years. Am I the sort of man who would pay for votes?"

Brannon only laughed. "Of course not."

"But I fired a man who was working on my election staff who tried to do that very thing," Bib continued. "That was the week before the party, two years ago. The man was a friend of Jake Marsh, and an acquaintance of Dale Jennings. But I knew nothing about any led-

ger. I did know that Dale Jennings fought with Henry
Garner about an item Henry said was missing from his
safe, the day before Henry was killed. In fact, Henry
and I argued over his keeping Jennings around. Henry
wanted him close until he could make him give the
ledger back. I was sure the man was up to something,
and I said so." He shook his head. "I'd give anything to
take back that argument, even if it wasn't a bad one."

"We've managed to put that much together," Brannon said. "Did you know that Dale Jennings's mother
was killed?"

Bib looked horrified. "The poor woman."

"She was cheated out of her life's savings, evicted
from her home, her possessions were burned and then
she was tortured to death for some information her
killer thought she had."

Bib put his head in his hands. "Dear God!"

"A man and woman were seen going into Mrs.
Jennings's apartment the day before her body was
found," Josette added quietly. "We've tentatively identified the man as Jake Marsh. We've also identified the
contract killer who shot Dale Jennings, and the computer expert who manipulated files to get Jennings
transferred to Floresville and out on a work detail."

Bib's face came up at once. "Who's the killer?"

"A man named York," Brannon said. "We're certain
he's got his next victim targeted. I shot it out with him
and Josie got hit. We had him in custody, but he escaped. We don't know who he'll be going after next."

Bib clasped his hands over his knees, worried.
"Marsh doesn't like loose ends. Anybody who knows
about that ledger is in danger." He toyed with his wedding ring. He glanced at Becky and winced. "That puts

you on the firing line with me," he told her uneasily. "And Silvia as well," he added, but carelessly.

"Speaking of Silvia, where is she?" Brannon asked.

"On another shopping expedition," he said, and took a sip of his drink. "She's buying a new wardrobe so that she can dress the part of a senator's wife." He chuckled hollowly. "I told her I was satisfied being lieutenant governor, but when the incumbent senator announced his retirement halfway through his term of office, she insisted that I run for it. Hell, I've only been in the state house for two years. I don't want to go to Washington," he added, staring at Becky broodingly. "Now, it looks as if I may not even be able to keep the job I've got."

"The reporter promised he wouldn't print the story yet, not until he could confirm it," Becky said heavily. "At least he did come to me first. He could have gone ahead and printed his suspicions. He's not a bad man, and he doesn't want to make a reputation for himself by destroying lives. Besides," she added with a smile as she glanced toward Brannon, "he likes Bib."

"Nobody will like me if such a story gets in print," Bib said heavily. "And I can kiss the senate seat goodbye. Funny thing," he added, with a long look at Becky, "the senate seat was Sil's idea, not mine. She wants the feeling of power it gives her to brush elbows with just the right people and wear clothes expensive enough to make the other women jealous." He shook his head. "I just want out of politics after my term as lieutenant governor is over. I want to experiment with new agricultural machines and tinker with improvements for them. That's all I ever really wanted." He glanced at Brannon. "But I don't want to go out under a cloud of suspicion.

I haven't taken kickbacks. I want you to help me prove it, whether or not the reporter prints what he's got."

"That's a tall order, Bib," Brannon said honestly.

"Somehow or other, it's all tied to Dale Jennings's murder," Bib told him. "And I can't help thinking that Jake Marsh is up to his ears in all of it, somehow."

"I did have that much figured out," Brannon replied. He glanced at Josette. "We've been putting in a lot of overtime on this case. We're making progress. If we could just find the woman…"

Becky opened her mouth to speak, and Bib looked up, silencing her.

Josette frowned as she noticed a small ornate bowl of candy on the coffee table. She got up and moved closer to look at it.

"Oh, those are just mints," Bib said easily. "Help yourself. I can't stand them. Becky orders them from a sweets firm in France."

Josette caught her breath and looked straight at Brannon. They both made the connection at the same time. Expensive mints, Mrs. Jennings had said. The woman who was trying to get that ledger from Dale liked expensive mints…!

Brannon stared at her evenly and shook his head. She got the message. She picked up one of the mints and opened the fancy package, sticking it in her mouth. She glanced at Becky Wilson, who was staring at Bib with her heart in her eyes. Becky wasn't blond. But she could have been wearing a wig…

"Delicious," Josette said, smiling. "Thanks."

"They are, aren't they?" Becky murmured. She was still looking at her boss. She drew in a shaky breath. "Who do you think the killer is after, Mr. Brannon?"

Becky asked worriedly. "You don't think he means to kill Bib?"

"That would probably defeat the whole purpose," Brannon replied. "Think about it. That ledger must have information that could put the killer in prison, or he wouldn't be willing to go to such lengths to obtain it, even to use in a blackmail scheme. I'd be willing to bet good money that it would exonerate Bib even while it condemned someone else. And that's why the killer is so desperate to get it."

"It's probably someone on my own staff," Bib guessed miserably. "But who do I know who's desperate enough to get mixed up in murder to keep the secret?"

Brannon had a good idea. But he couldn't say a word. Not yet.

"We'll keep you posted. Meanwhile," he told Becky, "string that reporter along. Try to keep him quiet, just long enough."

"But where's the ledger?" Bib asked worriedly. "Who's got it? And what's in it?"

"That's what we still have to find out," Brannon said. "But we will. I promise you, we will."

Bib got to his feet, smiling sadly. "You always supported me," he said. "Even when they were trying to make me into a murderer at Dale Jennings's trial. You never believed that I might be involved."

"I know you," Brannon said simply.

Bib extended his hand. "And I know you," he replied. "You're the best friend I ever had. I think I'm going to need one more than ever before this is over."

"I'm not deserting you," Brannon said, grinning.

"Neither am I," Becky said firmly. "And I don't care if Mrs. Webb likes it or not. She should be here instead of on another shopping trip. She's never here! She's never in Austin, either!"

"Becky, don't," Bib pleaded gently. "We both know that Silvia doesn't care what happens to me. She only cares about the wealth and prestige."

"She doesn't care about anybody, except herself," Becky muttered. "You should have had a houseful of kids…"

"I'd love that," Bib mused, and he smiled at Becky in a way that made her flush and avert her face.

"We'd better go," Josette said quickly, sparing Becky's blushes.

"Yes. Take it easy. And don't sign anything," Brannon advised Bib.

"I have a law degree," Bib reminded him.

"I know. But it doesn't hurt to advise people—even lawyers."

Bib nodded. "You be careful, too," he added as he saw them to the door. "Two people are already dead— three if you count Henry. Whoever's doing this won't hesitate over another couple of people if they get in his way."

"I know that," Brannon said. He smiled secretively. "In fact, I'm counting on it. I'll be in touch." He hesitated. "One other thing. Did Silvia ever mention taking college courses?"

Bib laughed heavily. "Silvia? My God, she barely got to ninth grade, and there was no way she'd even talk about continuing her education. It would take away from her time shopping!"

CHAPTER FOURTEEN

NO SOONER WERE Brannon and Josette in the SUV than she turned to him excitedly, fumbling her seat belt in place.

"Silvia didn't go back to school. So why was she at that coffee shop, and on campus?"

"I'd like to know the answer to that, too," Brannon said.

"And what about those expensive mints on the coffee table?" she said, flashing the wrapper that she'd pocketed. "Mrs. Jennings said that her son's girlfriend loved expensive mints, and that she knew about the evidence! Becky orders those mints and you said yourself that she would do anything to protect Bib Webb...!"

"Anything short of murder," he retorted, meeting her eyes in the overhead light as he revved the engine. "And she's not blond."

"She could have worn a wig," she persisted.

"Josie, can you really see Becky holding a lighted cigarette to an old woman's arms?" he asked.

She hesitated. "It's hard to imagine her doing something like that," she had to admit. "But it's obvious how she feels about Bib Webb. And how he feels about her," she added. "People in love do irrational things."

He sighed. "She's loved him for years. She and Silvia have never gotten along. In fact, Silvia's tried repeatedly to get her fired, but Bib won't have it. That's another source of friction between them. Silvia's ambitious. Becky isn't."

"Becky wants children," Josette murmured, remembering the pain and hunger in the other woman's eyes when she'd looked at Bib.

"So does Bib. Silvia can't have kids. She took a bad fall years ago. She said it made her barren."

She pursed her lips. "Do you think it did?"

He chuckled. "I don't think a gunshot would faze her. She's hard as nails and manipulative. Whatever she wants, she gets."

"Maybe Silvia was at that coffee shop for a purpose. Does she cheat on Bib?" she asked.

He glanced her way as he pulled out of the Webbs' driveway onto the highway. "I don't know. Maybe."

"They had a photo of Jake Marsh in the file at the D.A.'s office," she murmured, thinking aloud. "He's very attractive, dresses well, apparently has exquisite manners for a man on the wrong side of the law. And they say he's beginning to get rich, from all the interests he invests in. What if," she continued, "the absent Mrs. Webb has an affection her husband isn't aware of?"

Brannon scowled. He'd never considered that angle seriously, because of Silvia's love of her social status. "She values her position in life above everything else. Would she risk all she's got for a fling with another man? Especially a man like Marsh?"

"Danger attracts some women like honey attracts flies."

He gave her a wicked glance. "Does it? Let's test that theory. How about a nice game of billiards?"

"Oh, no," she groaned. "Not back to the underworld again!"

"You went there with Grier," he pointed out. "Why can't you go with me? I'm just as mean as he is, and I can coax people to talk to me, too."

"I like you better than I like him," she said absently.

"Why?"

Josette met his searching eyes. "He can't cook."

He burst out laughing.

THE BILLIARD PARLOR, despite the hour, was full. If it closed, it closed very late. They found the diminutive Mr. Bartlett bent over a billiard table, making a tricky shot. He finished it, grinned and looked up, right at Brannon.

He put the cue stick down and held up both hands. "I never said a word against the Texas Rangers," he said emphatically. "And I had nothing, absolutely nothing, to do with that attempted hit-and-run on Judd Dunn last month. I don't know who did, either!"

Josie glanced at Brannon and was surprised at his demeanor. He was alternately teasing and mocking around her, but here, among the local underworld element, he looked downright intimidating. He didn't smile as he moved closer to Bartlett.

"I don't know. I swear, Brannon!" the little man repeated quickly.

"I never said you did," Brannon replied, but he kept coming. "Let's take a little walk."

"Not until you swear in front of witnesses that I'm going to be *able* to walk, afterward! I've heard stories about you. I'm not taking any chances."

Josie was intrigued. She'd have to ask someone about those stories, later.

"You'll be able to walk," Brannon assured the man. "No Texas Ranger would ever act like a street tough with any witness. We have a tradition to maintain."

"Okay then."

"What about this game?" a heavyset man complained.

"We'll start over when I'm done" he was told.

Brannon and Josie followed the informant out into the dimly lit back alley.

"What do you want, Brannon?" the man asked uneasily.

"I want to know about Jake Marsh's playmate."

There was a harsh, indrawn breath. "Listen, Grier was down here a few days ago, asking me the same question…"

"And got zilch for his pains," Brannon finished for him. He moved relentlessly closer to the smaller man, his eyes glittering, unblinking. He stopped an arm's length from the little man and looked down at him. "But you're going to tell me what I want to know. You don't want to get mixed up in a murder. That's not your style."

"No," the other man said after a minute. "It isn't. I'm not going to take a fall for Marsh, I don't care what threats he makes. But he's got something on me…"

"It won't do him any good if he's in prison. Now, talk," Brannon interrupted.

"All right." The other man let out a long breath. "He's got some rich woman in his pocket," he said. "He says he's made sure that she has to help him get his hands on that missing ledger. She's got as much to lose as he does if that little package of dynamite shows up in the hands of law enforcement. More, even. He said she wouldn't be rich much longer if that information got into the wrong hands."

"Have you seen her?" Brannon asked curtly.

"Yeah. I've seen her. She's a show horse, I can tell you that. She and Marsh both dress like fashion plates."

Brannon glanced at Josette, who was frowning curiously. That didn't sound like Becky. On the other hand, maybe the blonde computer expert Sandra Gates had a hidden wardrobe, and she really was blonde. And there *was* that expensive mint they found in her trailer…

"Does Marsh stake the blond?" Brannon asked.

"I don't know stuff that intimate," he said. "All I can tell you is that she's as hard as he is. From what I hear, she was the one who tortured the old lady they killed."

That was chilling stuff. Josette remembered the tough little blonde hacker, in her cheap trailer. A woman who'd think nothing of breaking the law to help free a convicted murderer might not stop at torture. But Sandra Gates was in Argentina and couldn't be extradited.

"Have you ever heard of a woman named Sandra Gates?" Josette interjected.

"Gates? Yeah. She can do anything with a computer. Marsh uses her sometimes for investigative work, when he wants to get something on somebody. She's tough as nails." The little man looked worried. "Listen, Brannon, you aren't going to tell Marsh I talked, are you? Because he'd send York after me…"

Another piece in the puzzle. That, and the expensive mint in Gates's trailer, began to fit. A tough woman, he'd also said.

"I don't sell out informants. One more question and

we're through," Brannon told him. "How was Dale Jennings connected to Marsh and the blonde?"

The little man stopped to light a cigarette with hands that shook, blew out a puff of smoke and chuckled. "That's the best part. Jennings was having an affair with her. Marsh found out and had some pictures made that they didn't know about. Marsh said she went white as a sheet when they told her. Seems her husband wants a divorce and she won't give him one." He chuckled again. "If those pictures got out, she'd have to give him one, wouldn't she?"

Josette's eyebrows arched. If those photos were of Sandra Gates, did she have a secret husband? Or Becky Wilson? Now the puzzle started to fall apart again.

"Okay," Brannon told the smaller man after a minute. "That's all I wanted. Thanks, Bartlett. I won't forget this."

"If Marsh finds out…!"

Brannon's fist shot out so fast that Josette never saw it until Bartlett's head rocked back and he was holding his jaw and grimacing. She gasped out loud, but the little man only grinned.

"You can show that to the guys inside," Brannon said pleasantly, and smiled as he nodded toward the closed door of the billiard parlor, "and tell them that I was questioning you about Dunn's close call."

Bartlett laughed through the pain. "Thanks, Brannon. You're all right." He paused. "Just by the by, who did try to run Dunn down? Do you know?"

"No, I don't know. But Judd says he does, sadly for the perpetrator," he added with a chuckle. "Thanks."

"No problem." He smiled, but it was a shaky sort

of smile. He walked past Brannon gingerly, and went quickly back into the billiard parlor.

"Sandra Gates," Josette said as soon as the door closed behind the small man. "She's blonde, she doesn't hesitate to do illegal things, there was an expensive mint in her trailer, she knows Marsh and she was probably Dale's mysterious girlfriend. She could have been blackmailed by Marsh to help him get the evidence. It all fits!"

"It seems to," he agreed. "But if she's got a husband, he's well hidden, and she doesn't live like a rich wife. There's something else not quite right."

"What?"

Brannon shoved his hands into his pockets. "I don't know," he said irritably. "I can't get it in focus." He glanced at her and smiled. "I'm tired. So are you." He hesitated. "Don't take this the wrong way, but I'm going to take you back to your hotel instead of my apartment. We'll both have a good night's sleep, and then in the morning, we'll try to put it all together."

"Spoilsport."

He gave her a long look. "Torture is supposed to be against the law," he reminded her with a wicked grin.

Josette hesitated.

"I'll bring your things by the hotel tomorrow. If you need me, I'm as close as the phone," he continued when she was trying to think of a way to tell him something he didn't know yet.

It probably was a good idea to let things cool down, she decided finally. For a day or so, anyway. "Okay," she agreed. She gave him a mischievous look. "If you're through throwing punches at people for the night."

He helped her into the SUV and drove her back to

the hotel. "I just noticed something. You're not wearing the sling tonight," he noted.

Josette flexed her arm. "The wound isn't all that bad. I hate the sling. It gets in my way."

"If you see any redness, or feel any heat in it…"

"I have a good brain," she pointed out.

He just looked at her.

"I'll keep an eye on it," she said with resignation. "Thanks for the crepes."

"You're welcome. I like them myself." Brannon tugged at the nape of her neck. "Come here and kiss me good-night," he murmured in a deep, soft tone that made her tingle all over.

She laughed with delicious anticipation as she leaned toward him. "Want me to read you a story, too?" she whispered.

He smiled as he bent to her mouth. "Sure. How about a nice Agatha Christie murder mystery?"

"We've got a murder of our own to solve. That would be redundant."

Brannon drew her mouth under his and kissed her softly, nibbling on her upper lip until it parted on a husky little sigh.

"I think this is going to be habit-forming," he murmured.

"Do you?"

He drew her closer, wrapping her up in his arms. "Are you sure you want to go back to Austin?" he persisted, and kissed her insistently.

Her whole body went up in flames from the devouring pressure of his warm, hard mouth. She reached up to hold him while she returned the kiss with more enthusiasm than expertise. He didn't seem to mind.

His lips slid across her smooth cheek to her ear. "San Antonio has a lot to offer," he whispered. "A symphony, a ballet, an opera company…"

Josette touched his mouth with light, caressing fingertips. She didn't know how to answer him, what to say, what to think. He'd been actively hostile back in Austin, but here he was cooking her crepes and kissing her with such tenderness. Just the thought of not having him in her life after this case was depressing. Her eyes mirrored her troubled thoughts.

Brannon made a sound deep in his throat and kissed her again. This time she clung to him as if he was going to his death. She whimpered as the kiss grew more insistent, more ardent. She felt his hand between them, unfastening buttons again. And then it was there, there, inside her blouse, against her bare skin. She sobbed as he touched her with slow, hungry possession, the palm of his big hand warm against the hard, sensitive nipple…

The sound of a car approaching made him lift his head. He looked dazed. His pale eyes went to his hand inside her blouse and his teeth ground together as he withdrew it and rebuttoned the buttons.

"Oh, damn!" she said, and so plaintively that he laughed.

"It's just as well," Brannon said with resignation. "Under the circumstances."

She swallowed. "Actually…well, you could…come upstairs with me," she managed in a strangled tone.

"And do what, Josie?" he asked in a tormented voice. "It's not possible…"

"I had it two years ago," she blurted out.

He frowned. "You had what two years ago?"

She cleared her throat and looked at his chest. His heartbeat, quick and hard, was visible against his shirt. She pressed her nervous hands into the warm fabric. "That…minor surgery," she confessed.

He was very still, and more than a little aroused. His mind wasn't working. He just stared at her, trying to regain his composure.

"Two…years ago?" he whispered.

She nodded. Her fingers traced around the star on his pocket. "I thought…you left because I…couldn't," she said in a strangled tone. "So I had the procedure." Her eyes closed in pain. "But you didn't come back. You didn't call, you didn't write… I even went to the Webbs' party because I thought you'd be there, and I could tell you…" Her voice trailed off.

"Oh, baby," Brannon whispered huskily. He pulled her close and held her tight, tight, against him. "Baby, I'm so sorry! I was too ashamed to come back."

"Ashamed?" she asked blankly.

His big, lean hands spread tenderly over her back as his face pressed into her warm throat. "When I knew what you were, how innocent you were… I wanted to come back. But you looked at me in the courtroom at Jennings's trial with pure hatred in your eyes. After that…" He sighed. "I just got out of town and tried to forget everything."

"I was young and helpless when I was fifteen," she said gently. "I'm not now. You didn't know the truth, Marc. You didn't know. It's all right. I didn't blame you half as much as you've blamed yourself. You're just human."

His arms contracted until the embrace was almost

painful. "I should never have left you," he breathed, searching for her mouth. "Never in this life…!"

Josette smiled under the hard, rough crush of his lips, feeling the lack of control, the passion that he usually kept under such strict control. He wanted her so badly that he couldn't even contain it. That was flattering, that honest desire. Perhaps it wasn't what she really wanted, but living a lonely, sad life without him seemed worse.

When he stopped to breathe, her lips slid to his ear. "You can come up with me," she whispered, giving in to him without a struggle. After their passionate interlude in his apartment, she was on fire for him.

Brannon didn't answer her. His hands made a leisurely trip up and down her spine and he savored the soft feel of her body against him, the faint scent of roses that clung to her smooth skin.

"No," he said finally.

Josette hadn't expected that answer. She frowned. "Why not?"

"Because I'm not willing to reduce what I feel for you to thirty minutes in a bed."

Her heart lifted. She'd been so certain that he'd take her up on it, that he'd jump at the chance to be intimate with her.

She drew back, trying to see his face.

He caught one of the small hands on his shirt and lifted it, palm-first, to his lips. "And you're not willing to do that, either," he said with conviction, staring her down. "Josie, if seduction was all I'd had in mind, I wouldn't have needed to learn how to make meat loaf and crepes," he pointed out with a wry smile. He kissed her palm again. "You'll never know how I felt when I saw you in the hall outside Simon's office in Austin.

Pretending that I was indifferent was the hardest thing I've ever done."

"I thought you hated me!" she whispered.

"I hated myself. In some ways, I still do." He kissed her eyelids closed and his tongue ran softly over her long lashes. "It's been torture having you in the same office with Grier."

"But why?"

"You're the sort of woman he's drawn to." His eyes slid over her delicate features. "You have a quality of tenderness that's very rare."

She touched his hard mouth. "So do you," she whispered.

Brannon drew in a long, heavy breath, and his lean fingers touched the small bandage that remained on her wounded arm. "I've got to do a better job of looking after you."

She smiled. "I can look after myself, usually. But if you want to take care of me, I get to take care of you, too."

The expression made his breath catch. He studied her hungrily. He thought of her in his life, of waking up to her every morning, of carrying her to bed with him every night. He thought of her on the ranch, helping him with routine chores, riding with him, helping feed the occasional stray calf. He'd have someone of his very own, to share the good and bad times with; someone to talk to, someone to comfort him; someone to comfort. And in addition to all that, he'd have her in his bed... It made him ache.

"Deep thoughts?" Josette murmured, tracing his thick eyebrows.

"Very deep." He frowned. "Where are your glasses?"

She grinned. "I can see you."

"Me, but nobody else," he said quietly. "Wear them. You can't look out for what you can't see. And don't bother trying to convince me you've got contacts in," he added when she started to speak. "You haven't."

Josette sighed. "Okay. I'll wear them. I just don't like the way I look."

"I do. Glasses make your big, dark eyes look even bigger," he said softly, smiling. "And sexier, if you want the truth."

"I'll rush right out tomorrow and buy three new pairs," she promised.

Brannon traced her nose, watching her with an odd sense of contentment. "Lock your door."

"Why? Are you planning to kick it down and ravish me?" she teased.

"Don't give me any ideas," he cautioned. "I'm still aroused."

Her full, swollen lips pursed. "Well, well," she whispered, and started moving closer.

His hands stopped her. "The SUV would bounce," he said deadpan. "People would notice. The police would come. They'd probably send Grier. You have no idea what he's capable of, and let me just mention television cameras and at least one local broadcast news reporter who's terrified of him and would do whatever he asked…"

Josette burst out laughing and gave up. "All right, I quit. You're just brutally vivid, aren't you?"

"I'm a Texas Ranger," he pointed out. "See this?" he indicated the silver star in its circle. "Vivid description is part of the job."

She wrinkled her nose at him. "I get the message, loud and clear."

Brannon kissed her one last time. "Make sure you stay locked up tight."

"I will," she replied, opening the door. "But I'd like to know you're locked up tight, too." She glanced back worriedly. "Those men who jumped you," she began. "What if they come back?"

"See this?" he asked, his hand on the butt of his Colt .45.

She threw up her hands. "Be careful, anyway." She pointed at her heart. "See this?" she tossed back at him. "If anything happens to you, it stops beating."

He smiled tenderly. "I think I knew that already, but it's nice to know for sure. I'll avoid bullets. Good night, sweetheart," he added softly.

Her heart jumped. "Good night, Marc," she replied, equally softly and blew him a kiss before she went into the building. Even then, she stood at the door and watched him drive away. He watched her until he turned into the street. After that, going upstairs was agony.

But she was no sooner in her room than the phone rang. She picked it up.

"Miss Langley?"

"Yes?"

"It's Holliman," the old man said. "I been thinking about what you said, about that something or other that my nephew had. I may have an idea. Could you and the Ranger come out here in the morning? No rush. I'd just like to throw a couple of ideas your way, and not over the telephone. It's making some odd noises lately."

"Certainly. We'll see you in the morning," she said and hung up. Odd noises, huh? She wouldn't have put it past Marsh or one of his cronies to bug old man Holliman's telephone.

Finally, she thought, they were getting enough breaks to solve the case. Whoever was responsible for Mrs. Jennings's death could look forward to a long jail sentence, with no hope of being conveniently transferred to a low-security facility.

She hoped Brannon would be as pleased as she was when she told him what was going on the next day.

She slept fitfully, excited about the hopeful new day and a solution to the case.

But if she'd hoped to sleep late, she was doomed to disappointment. The phone rang at 5:00 a.m.

"Hello?" she murmured sleepily.

"San Antonio district attorney's office," a deep, masculine voice replied. "We need to know your schedule for today."

Josette sat up, instantly alert. "Why?" she asked at once.

There was a slight pause. "We don't want to duplicate efforts. We think we've got a break in the Jennings case."

She almost, *almost,* spilled her guts. But there was something that didn't ring true about the call. For one thing, she didn't recognize the voice, and she'd learned to recognize most of them in the local office by now. For another, they wouldn't need to know her schedule. They didn't work that way.

"Well," she said, yawning deliberately, "first I'm going to sleep until eight-thirty, and then Brannon wants me to pick up a witness and get her to go through some mug shots at your office."

There was another pause. "Why?"

"Oh, we think we've got something on the local mob boss," she drawled, wishing she could see the man on the other end. "I'll tell you all about it when I get there."

The line went dead.

She immediately phoned Brannon.

"It's five o'clock in the morning!" he exclaimed when he picked up the receiver, without even asking who it was. "So help me, Grier, if this is you, I'll use you for target practice!"

"It isn't Grier," she murmured softly. "Hi."

There was an indrawn breath. "Josie?" It sounded as if he sat up abruptly. "What is it? Are you all right?"

That concern made her feel warm inside. "I'm fine," she said. "I just had a very interesting call from some-one pretending to be in the district attorney's office. They wanted to know my schedule for the day. I'm just guessing, mind you, but I think we're stepping on some sensitive toes. Wouldn't surprise me if we were actually followed."

"Hmm," he murmured. "Wouldn't surprise me, ei-ther. Want to come out and play follow the leader?"

She chuckled. "I'd love to, if you feed me first. I'm starving, and I want coffee."

She could hear the smile in his voice. "Same here. There's a nice little doughnut shop near my apartment, and no wisecracks!" he added before she could rise to the bait. "I'll run over there and pick you up. Ten min-utes."

Brannon hung up before she could tell him that she couldn't possibly get dressed in less than twenty. But she made it in ten, anyway.

His pale eyes approved of her peach-colored suit and cream-colored blouse, especially since her hair was loose around her shoulders. It was a losing battle to keep hairpins, since he pocketed hers.

"Sexy," he remarked with pursed lips as he climbed into the SUV beside her. "I'm glad we're not having breakfast with Grier."

"I run into that a lot," Josette said in mock seriousness, nodding.

"Into what?"

"Oh, men who covet my suits," she remarked with a wicked glance. "But can you really picture Grier in this shade of pink?" She spread her arms.

He burst out laughing. "I've missed you."

"Good."

He glanced at her. "You're not going back to Austin when we solve this case," he told her flatly.

Her eyebrows arched. "I have a job there."

"You can get a job here," Brannon said easily. "We can share cooking and cleaning and laundry. On the weekends, we can see movies, if it's a month with five weeks." He sighed. "Sometimes money gets tight, especially with winter heating bills." He gave her a slow grin. "Of course, we can save money on heat by sleeping together."

CHAPTER FIFTEEN

"SLEEP WITH YOU?" Her voice sounded odd.

"Oh, it would be strictly platonic," he said carelessly. "You can wear a gown and robe, and I'll wear thick pajamas. I'll never touch you at all. We can live together and be good friends." He smiled slowly. "I'll give you my word as a Girl Scout."

Josette was looking at him as if she feared for his sanity, until that last remark, when he glanced her way with positively wicked silver eyes.

She burst out laughing.

"Don't think that's going to be my last word on the subject," he added. "But you'll have to go through me to get back to Austin. Even if I have to carry you away on my horse and keep you prisoner at the ranch until you agree."

She started to argue, when the radio went off, and he had to pause to answer it. Then they stopped for breakfast. But barely ten minutes into it, Brannon got a call on his handheld unit that Holliman had just phoned the Ranger office to make sure Brannon and Josie were coming to see him, and tell them it was urgent. They left in the middle of second cups of coffee.

THEY MADE IT to old man Holliman's property in less than twenty minutes, but they weren't followed. Brannon made a maze of turns and sudden stops, which produced no stealthy companion vehicles of any kind.

"That's really odd," he murmured as they pulled up in front of Holliman's rickety house. "They have to be watching us, but I don't see the least sign of a tail." He pulled out his Colt, checked it carefully and reholstered it. He glanced at Josie. "When we get out, walk just beside me and head straight for the front door. I can't rule out an ambush. These are desperate people."

"Okay," she said, with no argument. The one thing she knew for certain was that Brannon would keep his nerve, whatever happened. She'd seen him in action before. There was a certain comfort in knowing that he was quite at home handling deadly force, even if it gave her fears for his own safety.

They moved quickly to the house, and Holliman met them on the front steps. He looked as if he hadn't slept a wink and he was clutching the shotgun he'd presented the first time Josie and Brannon had visited him.

He looked around stealthily and motioned them inside. They'd barely cleared the doorway when he closed and locked the door behind them and leaned back against it with the air of a man who'd just escaped death.

"I didn't want to have to tell anybody," he said miserably. "I hoped it would all just go away, that they'd forget about what Dale had. They aren't going to, are they?" he asked Brannon heavily.

"No," Brannon replied tersely. "Too many people have already died protecting it. If you know what it is, you have to tell us. Or very likely," he added evenly, "you'll be next."

"I never thought they'd do such things to my sister," he said, shaking his head. "I was in law enforcement for almost twenty-five years. I never, *never,* knew anybody, no matter how bad, to torture a helpless old woman." His eyes closed and he shivered. He opened them again and gave Brannon a miserable glance. "Should have told you in the beginning. I was trying to protect my sister from something even worse than what she'd already suffered. I was wrong." He took a deep breath. "Dale had a ledger," he said, watching their faces. "You knew already, didn't you?" he asked suddenly.

"We knew that it was a ledger," Josette said. "But we don't know exactly what's in it."

"Proof," the old man told them, "that someone in the lieutenant governor's campaign management paid Jake Marsh to deliver votes in his election to the seat. From what Dale said, they also had something on Webb's wife that was good for a lot of blackmail money. One of the entries in that ledger, Dale said, was for almost a million dollars."

Brannon caught his breath. "Silvia Webb," he said, glancing at Josie. "So that was the blackmail connection!"

"Now I don't know what they had on her," the old man told him. "The ledger only had payoffs made to Marsh, in fairly large amounts, and to at least two professional election people who produced a misinformation campaign that cost Webb's adversary the election. It seems they dug up an old scandal in his family and threatened to reveal it in the press. Since it involved his mother directly, he withdrew at the last minute and Webb won the election by default. The ledger has concrete evidence of it."

"The man Webb fired," Josie said, thinking aloud.

"Yes, but before Bib knew what the man had actually done," Brannon said. He looked back at Holliman. "You should have told us this before."

"Maybe I should," he admitted. "But I still don't know where the ledger is," he added solemnly. "Dale did tell me what was in it, but not what he did with it. I tried to get him to go to the authorities, but he wouldn't. Even after he was arrested and tried, he wouldn't. He said that ledger was his insurance policy, that it would take care of him and his mother well into old age. He didn't even mind going to prison for it, he said, because he knew people who could get him out in a couple of years." He grimaced. "Guess they did, but not in the way he expected."

"Did he mention Sandra Gates or Becky Wilson?" Josie asked.

He shook his head. "He only talked about that Mrs. Webb, and he looked funny when he talked about her."

"Funny, how?" Brannon persisted.

"I don't know. Reverent almost. As if she meant a lot to—!"

The window near Brannon shattered just as a loud pop broke the old man's sentence neatly in half.

Cursing, Brannon had his pistol out in a split second, jerked Josie away from the window and Holliman away from the door. "Get down!" he said sharply.

He crouched by the window and moved the faded curtain enough to allow him to peer out. He didn't see a soul.

"I can still hit what I aim at," Holliman said. "Where do you want me?"

"Watching that door," Brannon told him. He gave the old man a level stare. "Don't let them take Josie."

"They won't," the old man promised him.

"Where are you going?" Josie gasped when he started out of the room.

"Around back. Stay down."

Brannon went around the corner of the house stealthily, his pistol held securely in both hands. He stopped and closed his eyes, listening...listening.

Of all the things law enforcement had taught him, stealth was the most important. He knew that he could trust his hearing, especially in an area as quiet as this, removed from traffic and street noise.

He heard the rhythmic crunch of leaves nearby, followed by a loud snap. Whoever was walking out there didn't know woodcraft. In the forest, the first thing that gave away a human presence was a rhythmic vibration. Forest animals never moved that way, even large ones.

There was also a noticeable scent, like perfume. A woman's perfume. Smell was something else that people unfamiliar with tracking didn't realize. Scent could travel amazing distances, especially when there was a favorable wind.

Brannon moved back the way he'd come and eased slowly into the big barn out back, careful to disguise his steps and walk softly. He moved behind bales of hay that Holliman probably kept for the single milk cow in the barn.

The cow, sadly, noticed him and mooed, hoping for feed.

There were running footsteps. The scent of the perfume came closer. Seconds later, Silvia Webb ran headlong into the barn with a pearl-handled pistol in her black-gloved hands. She was wearing black slacks, a long-sleeve black silk shirt and her blond hair was enclosed in a black cap. Someone who didn't know her probably wouldn't have recognized her. But Brannon knew her perfume, and her build.

"Come out of there!" she raged, looking around with the pistol leveled. "Come out right now!"

Brannon reholstered his pistol and picked up a clod of dirt that was clinging to one of the bales of hay. He waited, counting slowly to twenty.

Then, suddenly, he threw the dirt clod to the side of where Silvia was standing, with force. She whirled when she heard it hit, and Brannon made a dive for her. She never stood a chance. He'd played football in college and the tackle was one of his best skills.

She went down heavily and the pistol flew from her hands as the breath went out of her in a loud rush. Brannon rolled and scooped it up, getting to his feet with lazy grace. By the time Silvia had her breath back, Brannon had the automatic weapon leveled at her chest.

She gasped. It had happened so fast that she didn't have a prayer. She scrambled to her feet, still breathing heavily.

Brannon stared at her, his silver eyes glittering. "You. All the time, it was you. Did you kill Garner, or did you get Jennings to do the dirty work for you?"

She blinked. "Whatever are you talking about?" she asked haughtily.

"Give it up, Silvia," he said coldly. "You can't talk your way out of this."

"My fingerprints aren't on that gun," she said with an equally cold smile. "You can't prove a thing!"

"I can if I get my hands on the package Jennings left here," he assured her with narrow eyes and a mocking smile.

She went very still. "What makes you think it's here?"

"Why else would *you* be around if not to retrieve it?" he countered.

She hesitated. She pulled off the cap and shook her head. She smiled hesitantly. "Now, Marc," she began softly. "Remember me? We're both on the same side, on Bib's side. You wouldn't want your best friend to go to prison?"

"He won't," he said with conviction.

"If they get that ledger he will," she persisted. She moved a step closer. "Listen, nobody has to know. I'll just get it and leave. You can say that it can't be found. Nobody will know better!"

"I'll know better," he told her coldly.

"It will make Bib look like a criminal of the worst sort," she said emphatically. "He'll lose his job. He'll serve time!"

"Bib fired the man that you hired to shoot down his opponent in the lieutenant governor's race, Silvia," he said calmly. "I know his name. I'll find him. He'll talk, with the right incentive."

That was an eventuality she hadn't been prepared for. Her lips parted. She looked briefly uncertain. Then she straightened. "Well, so what if he does? Bib will be the one who suffers, not me!"

"At least two eyewitnesses saw you go into Mrs. Jennings's apartment with Jake Marsh," he said, playing his trump card.

Her mouth flew open. "No! They can't identify me! I was wearing a hat and a veil…!"

"Were you?"

Her fists clenched at her side. She looked murderous.

"I'll have you killed, too!" she screamed at him. Her eyes were glassy, wild. "I'll have you and that Langley woman killed, and that stupid old man as well! You'll all die! I'll make Jake tie you up and then I'll use a knife on you. I know how to use a knife. I watched my father cut off my brother's hand with a hatchet when I was little. My brother was bad. My father said he'd cut my hand off, too, if I didn't do what he said." Her eyes glistened with madness.

Brannon took a harsh breath. He didn't want to hear this. God Almighty, after what Silvia had done, he couldn't imagine feeling sorry for her!

"He taught me that pain makes you strong," Silvia said, alone in her own mind. She laughed. "He showed me how to use a knife. I learned to enjoy it… He said I was like him, I was strong, not weak and pitiful like my brother. He said I was pretty and men would do anything for me. We used to go to town, and I'd lure men in and…" She glanced at him. "I killed him, you know. I killed my father. I'd already told Bib I was pregnant, so he'd marry me. He worked for old Garner, and Garner had millions. My father said we'd all be rich, but he was greedy, so I pushed him headfirst into the old well. They didn't find him for several days. I said he went to visit my cousin. When they found him, I cried and cried, and everybody felt sorry for me. Nobody thought I did it."

She laughed. "He would have been proud, wouldn't he, Marc? He taught me." She blinked. "Bib doesn't know where I am. I told him I was shopping. He always believes me." She frowned. "Jake thinks I don't know what I'm doing, but I do. I killed old man Garner because he knew Dale had taken that ledger. I hit him with the blackjack and then laid it in Dale's car. Dale and I were having an affair, so I had to get rid of him, or Bib might have wanted to divorce me. But Dale didn't mind going to prison if he got paid off, so I sneaked money out of Bib's account, to keep Dale quiet. I didn't know about the photographs," she added with a look of bridled fury. "Then he got really greedy and started making all sorts of threats about publishing what he had on me and Bib. I had Sandra get him transferred and onto a work detail, then I bribed people to let him escape. He promised he'd bring the ledger and some pictures he'd had taken of him and me together…" She shook her head. "So I had to kill him, to protect myself. But the joke was on me, because the ledger he'd brought was blank and there were only two photos and no negatives.

"I had to find the ledger, you know. That old woman wouldn't talk, no matter what I did to her. Jake had gone into the bedroom to look for that ledger. He saw her and he hit me. He never hit me before. He said he wasn't going to get in any deeper, and he made that York man go away, too. He hired York to kill Dale, but I didn't need anybody to do things for me. I can do my own dirty work, like my father did. That's why I told him I'd do old man Holliman. I didn't need York to find that ledger. I'm going to find it. It's here. It must be here!"

She was stark-staring mad, Brannon thought incredulously. It was amazing that nobody had ever noticed and gotten help for her, before she snapped.

He moved closer to her, aware of footsteps coming closer. He took the cuffs off his belt and linked her hands behind her. She didn't even struggle when he snapped them on her wrists.

"Oh, thank God!" Josie said from the doorway when

she saw that Marc was all right. She blinked at his captive. "Silvia?" she exclaimed, stunned.

The blonde turned, glaring at her. "I'm the wife of the lieutenant governor," she said haughtily. "No one calls me by my first name unless I give them permission."

Brannon gave Josie a long, meaningful stare.

"Of course, Mrs. Webb," Josie said, humoring her. She frowned at Brannon. He was looking around the barn with curious intensity.

"The ledger," he murmured. He looked at his prisoner. "Silvia, is it in here? Do you know?"

"Dale wouldn't tell me," Silvia said vacantly. "I went to bed with him and he still wouldn't. Then Dale had a private detective follow us and take pictures," she added. "I didn't know until he showed them to me. He said he'd give them to the press if I didn't get him the money he wanted. That he'd turn the ledger over to the police. It would all have been over, don't you see?" she asked earnestly. "Bib would have lost his job and I wouldn't have been special anymore. We have to protect our family name. My grandmother always said so. She used to cry all the time after my brother died. Daddy killed him, too, you know. He hit him too hard. He was sorry, but we had to make sure nobody knew. So we threw him in with the horses. We said he was careless and got trampled." She smiled at Brannon. "I like to ride horses. Dale and I used to come up here and ride when the old man was visiting Dale's mother. He had this special saddle, handmade." She frowned. "I won't get to go to the governor's ball this year," she said suddenly, her face falling.

Brannon and Josie were exchanging gazes. Brannon

turned. The saddlebags. Old man Holliman had mentioned them. He spared an absent thought for where the old man was, but he was too intent on those saddlebags to concentrate.

He looked against the wall, where the saddles were kept. There were only two. One was old and stained dark from use. A newer one with fancy tooling and blackened silver accessories had a double saddlebag, also handmade.

On a hunch, Brannon pulled the saddlebags down and opened the first one. It was empty. It was probably a futile hope, he thought as he unbuckled the second one.

Then he felt it. A thick package, the size of a legal file, encased in plastic. He brought it out. There was a manila envelope inside a firmly closed flat plastic bag.

He glanced at Josie.

She moved to join him as he unzipped the plastic bag and pulled out the envelope. While Josie held the bag he opened the envelope. Inside were embarrassing color photographs, very explicit, of Dale Jennings and Silvia Webb. Brannon quickly slipped them back into the envelope and pulled out a small ledger. Tucked inside were receipts and at least two handwritten notes, one with Jake Marsh's signature. There were four check stubs, with Silvia Webb's signature on them. And there, in black, was every transaction made by Marsh's associate who'd used blackmail in the election to get Bib Webb's opponent to drop out of the race, complete with names and addresses and dates and amounts. It was dynamite. It was evidence that could send people to prison.

"Bib won't like it," Silvia said with a vacant smile. "He'll lose his job."

"I don't think so," Brannon said coldly.

"Jake thinks he will. Don't you, darling?" Silvia said suddenly, looking at the wide entrance to the barn.

"Yes, I do. Thanks for finding the evidence for me, Brannon" came a slow, dark voice from the doorway.

Brannon and Josie turned to find a handsome man in his late thirties holding an automatic weapon.

"Let's have it," he told Brannon, holding out a gloved hand. "Now."

Brannon let it fall to the ground and both hands went to his sides. "You come get it," Brannon replied.

"I've got the gun, Brannon!" Marsh said.

Brannon didn't look at Josie, but he spoke to her. "Move away, Josie. Now!"

Josie wasn't inclined to argue, even though she was afraid for him. She moved beside Silvia, her eyes wide with fear when she saw Brannon's posture alter just slightly. Surely to God, he wasn't going to try to outdraw a man with a cocked, leveled automatic pistol…!

Brannon was watching the other man. He knew, as Josie didn't, that Marsh would pull the trigger. The man had too much to lose to leave witnesses. Like Silvia, he wouldn't hesitate at gunning down anyone who threatened his freedom. This was going to be a last-ditch stand, and it was a certified long shot that he could draw and fire before Marsh pulled that trigger. But he was adept with his pistol, and he wasn't afraid of bullets. It was the only chance he was likely to get, and he wasn't wasting it.

Suddenly Holliman yelled, surprising Jake Marsh. The old man had snuck into the barn. He had his shotgun.

Brannon drew his pistol. And with such deadly speed, and accuracy, that Marsh crumpled and went down before he even could squeeze the trigger of his own gun. The old man had given the Texas Ranger a split-second edge. In the silence that followed, Josie's gasp was audible.

Brannon went straight toward Marsh without looking anywhere else except at his fallen adversary, unflinching, unyielding, without a second's hesitation. He bent over and jerked up Marsh's pistol while Marsh was holding his thigh and trying to stop the blood flowing from it.

"How did you...do that?" Marsh choked, still disbelieving what he'd seen.

"I hold the record for the quick-draw in southern Texas," Brannon told the groaning man calmly. "I've never been beaten in competition." He gave the other man a cold stare. "Good thing, under the circumstances."

"You shot Jake," Silvia said calmly. Her eyes seemed to be glazed. "I shot Dale, you know. He was blackmailing me with those photos, but just a couple of weeks ago he called me and said he was willing to give them back, and the ledger, if I'd get him some money right away so he could help his mother."

"Oh, God, will you stop talking and get an ambulance?" Marsh groaned.

Brannon reached into his pocket for his flip phone and made the call. Then he noticed Holliman watching Silvia with fury in his eyes.

The old man moved to where Silvia was standing and he lifted his shotgun. "By the time they get here, they'll need two ambulances!" His voice quivered with emotion.

"Don't make me shoot you," Brannon told Holliman,

dropping his hand to the butt of his pistol for the second time in less than five minutes. He crouched slightly, and his silver eyes glittered.

Holliman hesitated, but only for a second. He glared at Brannon, but he lowered the barrel of the shotgun with a resigned sigh. "All right, but it was tempting." He eyed Brannon. "Don't he remind you of a rattlesnake about to strike?" he asked nobody in particular. Holliman looked down at Marsh and up at Silvia, who was smiling and just staring into space. "What's the matter with her?" he asked.

"She's crazy, that's what's…wrong with her," Marsh groaned. "I'm sorry I ever met her!"

"That's no way to talk about the love of your life," Silvia said with a sigh. "And after all I've done for you, too."

"You've got me shot and I'll probably go to prison, thanks to you!"

"Losing a lot of blood, ain't he?" Holliman said with no particular emotion.

"Looks that way," Brannon said carelessly.

"One of you could put a tourniquet on him, for God's sake," Josie said irritably, glaring at them as she bent beside Marsh. "I need a stick and a handkerchief."

"You've got class, lady," Marsh bit off.

"Don't you touch him," Silvia burst out wildly. "He belongs to me!"

"I just went back on the market," Marsh said, wincing as Josie used two handkerchiefs that Brannon tied together for her, and a ballpoint pen, to make a tourniquet around his upper thigh. She tightened it until the bleeding slowed.

"I wouldn't do much of that, Miss Langley," Holliman said.

She glanced up. "Why not?"

"He might live," he said coldly, glaring at the downed man.

Brannon chuckled. "If he dies, you'll miss his trial," he pointed out. "And it's going to be a humdinger."

"Hadn't thought of that." Holliman brightened. "In that case, I'll go phone 911 again, just to make sure... oh. There they come."

The sirens were barely audible when the ambulance roared up in the yard, along with a Bexar County sheriff's car. Odd, Josie thought, because Floresville was just over the border of Bexar County into Wilson County.

A young deputy got out and came into the barn behind the EMTs who went immediately to work on Marsh. Josie and Brannon recognized him as the deputy they'd seen at Mrs. Jennings's apartment after her death.

"Hi, Brannon," he called. "Sheriff's department over here in Wilson is swamped, so I volunteered to take the call for them. Interagency cooperation," he added with a grin. "What's going on?"

"Officer, arrest those people," Silvia said firmly. "I am the wife of the lieutenant governor. These people—" she indicated Brannon and Josie "—have my property and I want you to take it away from them right now!"

The deputy glanced toward the tall man with the silver star on his pocket and the pistol on his hip. He noticed the automatic weapon stuck in Brannon's belt and Jake Marsh's wound. He pursed his lips.

"Been shooting it out again, huh, Brannon?" he mused.

"How did you know that?" Josie wanted to know.

"Oh, we get at least one idiot a year who thinks he can fire before Brannon can draw that hog-legged cannon he wears," he murmured. "Nice to work in the same city as a real live walking legend, sir. I hope to be just like you when I grow up."

Brannon burst out laughing, because the deputy had to be thirty if he was a day. "Don't get ambitious. I'm not resigning so you can get my job."

"Saw right through me," the deputy replied, shaking his head. "There's about a hundred applicants for every Ranger job that opens up, and only about a hundred and seven working Rangers in the whole state of Texas." He sighed audibly. "Oh, well, I can spend my life working as a deputy, I reckon. Great hours, wonderful company—" he glanced at Marsh and grimaced "—and nice benefits if I live to collect any." He glanced at Silvia. "Want me to take this lady in for you?"

"Yes, thanks. I'll come along right behind you with the evidence." He held up the plastic bag. "You're about to see an evil empire fall on a ledger," he added, glancing down at the wounded man, who was being loaded onto a gurney. "Jake Marsh, former mob chief, and very elusive just lately. He'll look good in striped pants."

"I won't…go to prison!" Marsh raged.

"Nor will I," Silvia said haughtily.

"Come along, lady. You can tell it to the judge," the deputy said.

"I'll have you prosecuted!" she shrieked.

"I'll wear my best dress, too," he added as he led her to his patrol car and put her carefully in the back seat.

Brannon laughed grimly. Josie was about to say something, but he stopped her. "We don't want to stunt his emotional growth," he cautioned. "He'll find out who she is soon enough."

Josie slid her hand into his and held on tight. "I'm glad you're okay," she said huskily. "I thought you were going to commit suicide for a few seconds there." She was still shivering a little with reaction, even now.

He slid an arm around her. "You can't kill a Texas Ranger unless you put a stake through his heart."

"That's vampires, sweetheart," she reminded him.

His eyebrows went up. "You're kidding!"

"Will somebody get me the hell...out of here?" Jake Marsh groaned.

"Make sure he goes straight to the prison ward when you get him to the medical center," Brannon told the ambulance men firmly. "I'll radio ahead and have a man waiting at the emergency room door."

The ambulance EMTs, both very young, nodded. "He's not in any condition to cause much trouble," one of them said with a grin.

"If he tries to, point him toward Floresville and shove him out the back door," Brannon told them.

Marsh groaned louder.

IT TOOK THE rest of the day to write up the report, turn in the evidence and talk to the assistant district attorney who was going to be handling the case. Grier sat in with the small group in the meeting room.

"If that isn't the damnedest story I've ever heard," Grier said, just shaking his head. "We've been after Marsh for years with no success whatsoever. The FBI has been after him for years. The state attorney general's been after him for years. And you two just waltz in and put him away!"

"We got lucky," Brannon said easily.

"What about the hit man, York?" Josie asked worriedly. "He's still on the loose, isn't he?"

Grier glanced at the young Bexar County sheriff's deputy who'd been out at the Holliman place. He was now occupying a chair in the office with Brannon and the others, since he'd been involved in the arrest.

The deputy leaned back in his chair with a wicked grin. "No need to worry about York," he murmured. "I was driving down the 410 Loop, minding my own business, when this beat-up old car went by me like I was backing up. Even though it was my lunch hour, I chased it down and stopped it. And lo and behold, there was York himself with a dirty bandage on his bullet wound." He pursed his lips and smiled. "He's sitting down at the county jail even as we speak. And if Marsh sings like I expect him to, we'll have York just where we want him."

"But he didn't kill anybody," Josie pointed out. "Silvia killed Garner and Jennings."

"Yes, but Marsh hired York to kill a man and to try to run down Judd Dunn two months ago when he started investigating the murders that Marsh was suspected in." He grinned slowly. "Dunn has worked day and night to get enough evidence to put him away for good. He's the one who told me about the make and model of York's car. I've been looking for it for the past week. York is just going to love prison," he added with a sigh. "And the men on the inside will certainly love a young, sweet-faced handsome young fellow like him, don't you think?"

Brannon decided that he wouldn't answer that, but he grinned back.

CHAPTER SIXTEEN

THE WORST PART of the ordeal was having to tell Bib Webb what they'd found, and what his wife had done. Brannon took Josie with him, but he phoned Becky Wilson before he left San Antonio and had her come as well.

Bib looked as if he'd been shot. He walked out onto the patio near the swimming pool and stood, with his hands in his pockets, just staring into space.

"Let me have a minute with him first," Brannon told Becky, who was obviously aching to go to the man on the patio.

"All right." Becky sat back down with a sigh and smiled shyly at Josie. "Won't you have a mint?" she offered, and then looked surprised when Josie laughed. Those mints had helped solve a murder.

BIB HEARD BRANNON come up beside him and grimaced. "'There are none so blind…'" he quoted. He glanced at his best friend. "Did you suspect her?"

"No" came the flat reply. "My money was on the computer hacker. Then we found out that Marsh's new 'friend' was married, and she liked expensive mints."

Bib took his left hand out of his pocket and studied his wedding band. "I've been a bachelor since Silvia was about seventeen," he murmured. "She liked sex at first, but I wasn't rough enough to suit her, or reckless enough. She started having 'friends.' I started drinking. It wasn't much of a life. But people get comfortable walking in familiar ruts, and they just keep walking out of habit."

"This trial is going to be very messy," Brannon said after a minute. "I wouldn't bet five cents on your chances for the senate seat when it's over, and that's God's truth."

"I don't care." Bib turned to him. "It doesn't matter if I lose the lieutenant governor's spot. I have a company I love, good employees, and we're branching out into experimental projects that will benefit millions of hungry people in third world countries if we can perfect them. What's that compared to a political job?"

"That sounds like you."

Bib smiled. "That *is* me. All this—" he waved his hand at the opulent living room inside, with its imported crystal and fabric "—is Silvia." He shrugged. "There's nobody I want to get even with. Except maybe Marsh."

"Marsh will serve time, no matter how many good lawyers he can afford. Sadly, so will Silvia, if they don't find her insane. And they might," he added quietly. "You have to be prepared for that. She made a pretty shocking confession about her past. I have to tell what I heard."

"What did she confess?" Bib asked, aghast.

"There's time for that later," he said. No reason he couldn't give the man a few more hours of peace before the media exploded into his life.

Bib worried his hair again. "Well, I'll phone our attorney and see if he can do anything for Silvia. Maybe he can get a psychiatric profile and have her declared insane. There have been signs for a long time. I've been in denial, and pretended I didn't see them. But," he added on a heavy sigh, "it's no use pretending anymore."

"I'll do whatever I can to help."

Bib smiled at him. "I know that. I appreciate it. You're the only friend I ever had who was willing to believe I wasn't guilty of any sort of graft."

"I know you," Brannon pointed out. "And I don't desert my friends. Ever. Let Becky come out and talk to you. She'll save you from the media."

"Yes, she will," he said calmly, and with a smile. "I'm going to marry her, when all this is finally over."

"That doesn't come as a surprise. She'll be good for you, too."

Brannon went back in and spoke briefly to Becky before he sent her out to Bib.

"What do we do now?" Josie asked Brannon, because she felt adrift.

He pursed his lips and smiled slowly. "We have supper, of course. Then we start making plans."

She wondered about that last remark, but she kept it to herself until they'd had a nice, quiet supper and they were sitting in his SUV in the parking lot of her hotel.

"That looked like Grier's car," he remarked as he cut off the engine. "Why would he be here?"

"I don't know. I haven't seen him today." She studied him openly. "You said earlier that we'd make plans. What sort of plans?"

Brannon smiled and touched her mouth gently. "You had surgery just for me. I think that deserves a reward."

Her face began to redden. "If you mean we'll go to bed together…"

He grinned. "Why, you shameless hussy," he teased.

"See this?" He pointed at the star on his chest. "I took a vow of chastity. I don't mess around with women," he added haughtily.

"Oh, everybody who knows you would believe that, I'm sure," Josette said with a wry look.

"I don't mess around with women who aren't named Josette," he qualified lazily. "Furthermore, I expect to be an exemplary husband and father."

She just looked at him. Her eyes were wide, steady and uncertain.

The smile faded. He took her hand in his and lifted the knuckles softly to his mouth. "I love you," he said quietly. "I never stopped. I'm tired of trying to live without you."

She still stared, mesmerized.

"I'm in a dangerous profession, but I won't take unnecessary chances. I can work out of the Victoria office and commute. We'll have the ranch and both our salaries, and we know the best and worst of each other. We'll make it. I know we will."

Josette drew in a long, slow breath, searching his pale eyes. "It's rather sudden," she began.

"I know that. I wasn't suggesting that we jump into bed together tonight and get married in the morning," he said. He looked very somber. "I want you to resign your job and spend three weeks with me at the ranch." He held up a hand. "My wrangler and his wife still live in. We'll have built-in chaperones. You can talk to our local district attorney in Jacobsville about a job, I expect he'd be happy to have the help. I'll get transferred down to the Victoria office. I've already checked, and there's a man who wants to be closer to his parents in San Antonio. He is more than willing to trade jobs."

She just shook her head. "You've given this a lot of thought," she said.

"I've done nothing else since you came to San Antonio to work on this case." Brannon searched her eyes. "It all hinges on whether or not you can forgive me for the past. I know it's a lot to ask. I've made mistakes. Bad mistakes."

She reached up and touched his firm mouth. "We both did. I should have been willing to talk to you when you called me later that last night we were together. I should have called you back and explained what I felt. After the trial, I should have at least tried to talk to you."

"That works both ways," he said curtly. "I didn't even give you a chance. I just left town."

"But now I know why you left," she said. She smiled as his lips pursed against her fingertips. "I've been lost without you," she began, and got choked up.

His arms reached for her. He held her bruisingly close and kissed her so fiercely that it hurt. After a few seconds, his mouth slid against her neck and he held her even closer, a faint tremor in the powerful arms holding her.

"Marc!" she exclaimed, shocked by the way he reacted to her soft confession.

His fingers bit into her back. "I...hated myself," Brannon whispered hoarsely. "I couldn't live with hurting you." His breath sighed out harshly at her ear. "Oh, God, I love you—love you with all I am, all I ever will be! When they lay me down in the dark, the last word I whisper will be your name...!"

Josette kissed him hungrily, stopping the words, stopping the pain. She held on for all she was worth, telling him with her lips that she would never leave him, never stop loving him. Tears poured from her eyes, hot and wet on her cheeks, and still she couldn't let go.

Neither of them noticed that the windows had all fogged up as emotions flared between them. At least, not until there was a firm, and very insistent, knock on the driver's window.

Brannon, half dazed, let Josette move discreetly out of his arms before he lowered the window.

Grier was leaning down with a theatrical disgusted look on his face. "I never thought I'd see the day that a Texas Ranger would get caught making out in a parked car in front of a really nice hotel."

"Well, where else could we go?" Brannon demanded, fierce-eyed. "I can't take her back to my apartment and we can't go up to her hotel room, for obvious reasons! We just got engaged!"

Grier's eyes widened. "You *did?*"

Brannon sat very still. "Now, listen here…"

"Engaged." Grier nodded. He grinned. He chuckled. He turned around and started walking away.

"You're not invited! If you show up at the wedding, you'd better be wearing body armor and a raid jacket!" Brannon yelled at his retreating back.

Grier just kept walking.

With a groan, Brannon powered the window back up and turned to Josette.

"What was that all about?" she asked.

He studied her. She looked delicious with her hair loose around her shoulders and her mouth softly swollen from his kisses, and her blouse half undone. He couldn't stop smiling at the picture she made.

"Hmm?" he murmured absently.

"Marc, what was that all about?" she insisted.

"Grier has this, uh, reputation for going to wed-dings," he imparted slowly.

"Reputation?"

He cleared his throat. "Well, don't worry, because he isn't doing it to ours. Honest. I promise."

"Okay." She opened her arms, just to see what would happen.

He went into them without hesitation, and began to kiss her again. Grier and his reputation were the last thing on his mind in the turbulent minutes that followed. And, just in case, he locked the doors....

SEVERAL WEEKS LATER, Josette was standing with Marc in a small, but beautiful little church in Jacobsville, Texas, having already signed a legal document and taken vows that made her Mrs. Josette Anne Langley Brannon.

She wore a simple white peasant dress with high heels and a hastily improvised veil that had been a lace mantilla. Amazingly, Brannon had even found two unique gold wedding bands that fit at the jewelry shop. She looked at the man she'd just married with her whole heart in her eyes.

"That was a lovely ceremony," Josette told the minister and his wife, who'd acted as witnesses along with their daughter.

"It was our pleasure," the minister told her, shaking hands with both of them. "Are you sure you didn't want something grander? You're both known in Jacobsville. Your mother was baptized here," he reminded Brannon.

"Yes, but my sister is now a queen," Brannon reminded him. "And I didn't want a media frenzy."

The minister cleared his throat. "Of course. Of

course. Well, congratulations! And we'll hope to see you both here one Sunday, if you'd like to visit."

Josette looked up at her husband. "Yes," she said for both of them. "I think we would."

HE HELD HER hand all the way back to the ranch. They'd spent a wonderful three weeks being engaged while they went horseback riding and visiting friends, and generally getting to know each other all over again. They found so much in common that getting married seemed the most natural thing in the world. They even agreed on politics. The one place they drew the line was at sleeping together. And it was Marc who insisted on that condition. They were going to have a conventional wedding night, he informed her. He grinned at her blush and added that he was going to make her very glad that she'd waited for him. Which produced another blush.

He glanced at her while he drove and grinned at her shy scrutiny. They were going to spend a week honeymooning at Marc's ranch, just the two of them. The housekeeper and wrangler had their own little cottage now, that Marc had provided the year before, so the newlyweds had the house to themselves.

Or so they thought. Then they arrived at the ranch. There was a crowd waiting for them.

Marc groaned out loud. "Oh, no. No! Grier, I'll tie you to a horse and send you through a cactus thicket!" he swore.

Beside him, Josie chuckled. "So that's what you meant, about Grier not coming to the wedding."

"He did this to Bud Handley," he said irritably, "and his wife actually shot at him!" His eyes narrowed. "Too bad she missed...!"

"Now, now." She soothed him. "I'm sure they'll go away soon. They just want to congratulate us."

"That's what you think," he muttered, slowing down. "So help me, if I see one damned camera...!"

"There's Grier on the porch! And isn't that Judd Dunn?" she asked suddenly, staring at a tall, lean dark-haired man in jeans, wearing a Texas Ranger star on his shirt pocket. He was dangling a white hat in one hand, with a big booted foot propped against one of the columns on the ranch house's front porch. "But who are those men and women with them?" she added, noting several other assorted uniforms and badges.

"Texas Rangers, local police, sheriff's department, a couple of DEA guys, at least two local former mercenaries," he said through his teeth. "From the look of things, most of the whole damned force!"

"They're here to welcome you back to the community," she exclaimed happily. "How sweet!"

Sweet. Sure. He was remembering that damned smile of Grier's. And wasn't that guy standing by himself Curtis Russell with the FBI? He groaned aloud.

As flattered as he was with the overwhelming welcome, Brannon would have preferred a card. A letter. A phone call. *Anything* except a crowd of law enforcement people on his front porch, on his wedding night!

"Be nice," she chided. "They mean well."

He looked at her as if she'd just burst out in green feathers.

"We'll offer them coffee and cake and they'll leave," she said reasonably.

"Why will they leave?"

She grinned and wiggled her eyebrows. "Well, we don't have any, do we?"

"They'll offer to go and get some!" he raged.

She shrugged. "Then we'll just lock the doors before they get back."

He burst out laughing. "Honey, you're a treasure."

"I married one, too." She moved as close as the seat belt allowed and laid her head on his shoulder. "Marc, did you remember to call Gretchen?"

"I phoned her from the church on my cell phone, while you were tidying up in the ladies' room," he said. "She wasn't in, but her personal secretary will relay the message."

"That reminds me. I'm related to a head of state now!"

She sighed. "I feel as if I should stand up and salute or something."

"Speaking of things that stand up and salute…" he muttered as he pulled the SUV to a stop in front of the bevy of grinning people.

"Congratulations!" Judd Dunn drawled, and moved aside to uncover a huge cooler. He opened it, displaying two magnums of the best champagne.

"Don't forget the food," another Ranger reminded him.

"I haven't forgotten a thing." Judd opened another cooler, displaying chilled shrimp on a platter with an interior bowl of cocktail sauce.

"My favorite food in the whole world!" Josie exclaimed. "You sweet guys!"

"And gals." A brunette popped out, sticking her head from behind one of the really tall visitors. Four other female heads joined it, all grinning.

"And gals!" Josie added on a chuckle. "Thanks so much!"

"I didn't know you liked shrimp cocktail," Brannon said, surprised.

"You should read her résumé at the attorney general's office," the brunette said. "Like we did. She also likes French crepes and meat loaf."

"Yes, I know. I can cook those," Brannon murmured.

The Rangers exchanged wicked grins.

Brannon took off his hat and whacked Judd Dunn with it. "Thanks for the champagne. Now go away!"

"Marc!" Josie gasped, outraged.

He gave her a pointed glare and hit Judd again with the hat.

"Stop that," Grier said in his best law enforcement voice. He moved in front of the other law enforcement people, holding a sheet of paper in his hand. "Lady and gentleman," he read, with a deadpan glance at Brannon. "We, your friends in law enforcement, wish you all the best in your married life. If you are ever in trouble and need help, remember that we are only as far away as your phone."

"My phone is in San Antonio," Brannon said pleasantly. He extended a long arm and pointed. "It's that way."

"I have six more pages to read," Grier announced belligerently.

"I have a shotgun in my den," Brannon replied.

Everybody laughed.

"All right, Grier, you've done your bit. Now we're leaving. We planned to, anyway," Judd told Brannon with a chuckle. "Come on guys and gals, we've got bad men to catch!"

They all formed a line to shake hands and offer congratulations. Josette didn't recognize the names, but she knew she'd learn them over time. She was touched by the crowd's friendliness, and astonished at Grier's.

They drove away, car by car, and Josette turned to her husband with soft, loving eyes after the last one had been waved off.

"We're going to live in a very nice place."

He nodded. He studied her soft, pretty face, surrounded by a cloud of blond hair. He smiled gently. "You make a beautiful bride, Mrs. Brannon."

"You make a handsome groom."

He sighed and turned to the coolers of champagne and shrimp cocktail. "Which would you like first?" he asked, studying them.

She closed both coolers and took his hand in hers. "Later," she said, and lifted her wide, soft eyes to his.

IT WAS STILL DAYLIGHT. Even though the master bedroom was dark, she was a little uneasy with him. Her early memories of intimacy were painful ones, despite her joy in Brannon's touch.

He drew her to him and searched her wide, worried eyes. His fingers drew lightly across her soft mouth. "A man who is a man doesn't tear petals off rosebuds," he whispered. "Do you understand me?"

She smiled slowly. "Yes. I think I do."

He smiled back. "I've waited a long, long time for you, Mrs. Brannon," he said softly. "I promise you, it's going to be worth it. For both of us. Now stop worrying. We're teenagers making out in a big, square parked car. Okay?"

She hadn't thought that intimacy could be fun. He made it sound more like a wicked adventure than an ordeal of embarrassed first times.

She looked around at the room. "A big, square parked car?" she echoed.

"With all the windows closed," he murmured as he brushed his lips against her mouth. "We're going to fog up the windows."

She remembered doing that in his vehicle outside her hotel, and she chuckled as she moved closer to him. "That was a small space. This is a very big room."

"Mmm-hmm," he agreed lazily. "But we're going to generate a lot of heat together."

As he spoke, his hands moved gently up and down her sides, not even touching her intimately. He began to kiss her, very lightly, smiling as he felt her body relax into his.

For a long time, all he did *was* kiss her. Josette sighed as she felt the nonthreatening brush of his hard mouth on her lips. It was like when they'd first started dating. He was gentle and slow, and it was like exploring unknown territory all over again.

But this time, she wasn't locked up in bad memories and afraid of the unknown. She loved this man with all her heart. She wanted a life with him, children with him.

Brannon nibbled her upper lip. "You see?" he whispered. "Slow and easy, Josie. We've got all the time in the world."

She sighed. "I was so nervous," she confessed.

"So was I."

Josette drew back and met his twinkling eyes. "You're not a novice," she pointed out.

"With you, I am," he replied quietly. "In the past, it was a need I satisfied, nothing more." He searched her eyes. "With you, it's an act of love."

Her face mirrored her fascination. She touched his mouth with her fingertips. "I never loved anyone else," she said slowly. "It was…always you."

"Just as it was always you, for me," he replied, bending. "For the past two years, I've gone hungry. You're going to be the most delicious little banquet I ever put my mouth to."

Josette smiled at his wording. Then his hands drew her into full contact with him and she felt the sudden hardness of his desire against her. She hesitated, but only for a few seconds. His mouth brushed her lips apart and one lean hand went slowly under her skirt and up against the silken skin of her thighs. He kissed her more insistently as he found her beneath the trifle of lace she wore and began to discover her intimately.

She gasped and his tongue shot into her mouth. She couldn't get her breath. He'd only touched her like that once, a long time ago. But now he wasn't hesitant or shocked at what he found, because her body was no longer a fortified sanctuary. It was open to his touch, to his desire, and she moaned jerkily as he found a pressure and a rhythm that lifted her in an arch against him.

It was evident that she'd never known physical pleasure. She clung to him, her nails bit into him, and she held on as if she were terrified that he might stop.

"Easy," he whispered as she twisted against him. "This is just the beginning."

"Marc…!" Her voice was tortured. She was blind, deaf, dumb. All she knew was the delight her body was discovering.

Her eyes closed so that she could savor it more fully. She was falling. There was something soft and cool at her back. The pleasure was dark and wicked and…she gasped as the urgency of it increased all at once.

"You're much too intense," he whispered into her mouth, and smiled. "Let me take the edge off that hunger first. Then we'll start again."

Josette didn't understand. She started to speak when a jolt of pleasure lifted her off the bed. Her eyes flew open and met his, but they were sightless, blind with the building ecstasy that made her shiver with each brush of his fingers.

"No…oo!" she choked out, frightened.

His lips pressed tenderly to her eyes, closing them, and his touch became insistent. "I love you more than my life," he breathed. "Let it happen."

Seconds later, she went over some hot, pulsating precipice and began to shudder rhythmically, helplessly. She clung to him, her mouth open against his shirt as she gave herself to the ecstasy of fulfillment.

Afterward, of course, she cried. It was embarrassing and shocking, and her emotions were so scattered that she couldn't tell up from down.

Brannon laughed tenderly, his lips slow and gentle on her face even though his powerful body had a faint tremor. "And now that you have a taste of what you can expect," he whispered wickedly, "we can learn to share."

"Sh…share?"

"Mmm-hmm."

He stripped her out of her dress and underthings and bent to put his mouth hard against her stomach before it moved up and brushed slowly over her taut breasts. "I love the way you taste," he said softly. "Holding back is the hardest thing I've ever done. But it has to be perfect, this time. Absolutely perfect."

Brannon stood up and began to divest himself of his own clothes. Her glasses were on the side table, but he was close enough that she could see him. When he got to the black boxer shorts he wore, her head turned away in faint embarrassment.

"None of that," he said gently. "Look at me, Josette."

Josette knew her face was scarlet as she forced her eyes back up. He was so aroused that it was impossible not to know it. His powerful body seemed poised on a knife edge as he looked down at her.

Amazingly, the sight of him like that made her hungry. She felt her body move of its own accord, and the eyes that met his were misty with desire.

"I don't…understand what's happening to me," she managed to say, shivering.

He smiled slowly. "You will," he said. And he eased down beside her.

CHAPTER SEVENTEEN

IN THE TEMPESTUOUS minutes that followed, Josie learned more about her own body than she'd ever known. His hands were expert as they brought her from one peak of pleasure to another, only to let her down gently at the last minute and start all over again.

"You're killing me!" she protested wildly, as he stopped short again and rolled across the bed with her, one long, hard-muscled leg between both of hers as he bent to her breasts again and suckled her.

His fingers dug in at the top of her thighs and he chuckled against her body as he drew his hair-roughened leg against the inside of her soft one. "That's the idea," he murmured.

"What?"

Brannon nipped her shoulder before his mouth moved back up her chin to torment her swollen, soft mouth. "That's what they call it. The little death."

"Marc," she groaned as his mouth bit hard into hers. Her hands were buried in the damp thickness of his wavy hair and her body was trembling. So was his. She wondered at his stamina, because it seemed a long time since he'd undressed her. He was still fiercely aroused, but when she lifted to tempt him, he only moved away again.

She felt him touching her as the hunger built to flash

point. She steeled herself for another sudden stop, but it didn't happen. This time, he sank into her. She felt him with awe, with wonder, as her body protested just faintly the newness of invasion.

He lifted his head and looked into her wide eyes. His face was clenched and she felt him shiver with every hard downward movement of his hips. Only then did it occur to her that he'd reached the limit of his endurance.

"Help me," he whispered harshly. "I can't hold it for much longer."

"I don't…" she faltered breathlessly.

"Find the position you need," he murmured against her mouth. "Shift your body against mine until you feel the pleasure bite into you…there, sweetheart?"

"There!" she gasped, lifting helplessly in an arch. "Oh…yes…there!"

His mouth opened and began to penetrate hers. He felt her body dance with his, felt her arch up to him, press herself as close as she could get. She was rigid with it, he could feel the pulsation in her even as he felt it begin in himself. He was hot, throbbing, swelling…

He cried out in an agony of release, his whole body flung up into glorious joy and mind-killing satisfaction. He hoped she was going with him, because he lost it entirely. He shuddered again and again and again, groaning her name as the waves of pleasure knocked him almost unconscious.

She felt his pleasure even through the violent satisfaction he gave her. So this was what it was all about, she thought dazedly, clinging to him with bruising fingers. Her mouth opened against his bare shoulder and she shivered with the intensity of it, the beauty of fulfillment. She understood at last what he'd meant when he said he'd given her a taste of satisfaction just as they began. Words couldn't do justice to the sensations that whipped through her slender body. She kissed the taut muscle of his shoulder hungrily as she sank into the mattress with a final, agonizing shudder of ecstasy.

It was hard to breathe. She couldn't stop shaking. Her body was sore, but gloriously pleasured. She felt the dampness of moisture clinging to her skin, her hair. Her fingers brushed lightly against his long, lean back and she felt the same moisture there. She moved, and felt him deep in that secret place and she laughed softly.

"For a nervous beginner, you're a quick study," he murmured into her throat.

She laughed out loud and hugged him close. "Oh, you rake," she whispered lovingly, kissing his throat. "You wonderful, wonderful rake!"

He laughed, too, exhausted but completely relaxed for the first time in years. He rolled onto his back, still intimately joined to her, and held her gently on his body. "Two years of stoic repression. My God, am I glad I waited!"

"So am I." She kissed his chest, the hair tickling her nose where her lips pressed. "We forgot something."

His lean hand smoothed her hair with magnificent unconcern. "What?"

She punched him in the ribs. "You know what."

He only sighed. "It's in the drawer."

"It does us a lot of good in there!"

His mouth traveled over her chin.

"I know that." He sighed. "Kids are great. I wouldn't mind one, even this soon. But we should use more restraint next time."

"Sure," she murmured. Then she laughed. She yawned. "I'm sleepy."

"So am I."

"Shouldn't we…?" she asked, moving slightly.

His lean arm came around her. "Stay right where you are," he whispered. "I don't want you any farther away than you are right this minute."

She smiled and snuggled closer with a sigh. "That goes double for me. Marc?"

"Hmm?" he asked sleepily, his voice deep and soft at her ear.

"I like being married."

She felt the faint rumble of laughter under her. "So do I."

It was the last thing she heard for a long time.

THE HONEYMOON WAS officially over in a week, but people around Jacobsville noticed that it never seemed to end. You never saw Marc unless you saw Josie. She worked out of the D.A.'s office, and he worked out of the Victoria Texas Ranger post, but when they weren't on the job, they were inseparable.

A few months later, Josie was sweeping off the front porch early on a Saturday morning while Marc was getting the men assigned to the day's work when two long, black limousines flying diplomatic flags pulled up in the dusty front yard.

Josie was wearing jeans and a dusty sweatshirt. Her hair was loose and still a little tangled, she had no makeup on, and she was wearing ancient moccasins and socks with holes in them. So, naturally, this had to be Gretchen Sabon and her husband the Sheikh. It was nice to know that she was going to make a suitable impression on her new relation, the head of state of Qawi. They'd wanted to fly to Qawi for the meeting, but their jobs had made it difficult. And there had been another power struggle in Qawi that had only just been resolved successfully. Now the Sabons had apparently taken matters into their own hands and decided to just show up as a surprise. Josie groaned and shook her head. Her hair wasn't even combed!

Marc came striding out of the barn grinning as the tall bodyguard he recognized from Gretchen's wedding got out, waved and opened the back door.

"Hi, Bojo!" Marc greeted the tall man, shaking hands. He opened his arms as Gretchen got out, looking young and happy and very elegant, and went rushing into them.

"Hello, big brother!" Gretchen laughed. "We came to welcome Josie into the family. You remember Philippe."

Her husband was now standing beside her, tall and handsome even with his scarred face, and beaming at his wife. He shook hands with Marc.

"Welcome to the fraternity," Philippe murmured.

"Imagine you, getting married, and to somebody as nice as Josie," Gretchen said warmly. She looked up onto the porch. "Hi, Josie!"

Josie put down the broom, wiped her hands on her jeans and danced down the steps, feeling shy and nervous.

"I wear jeans and sweatshirts around the palace," Gretchen said, realizing at once what the problem was. "And I *never* wear makeup around my husband," she added with a wicked glance at the tall, smiling man beside her.

"It is a waste of time," Philippe drawled. He glanced at Marc and grinned. "As you know, I presume."

"I do." Marc pulled Josie close to his side. "This is your new brother-in-law, Philippe Sabon. He's the ruling Shiekh of Qawi."

"I'm very honored," Josie began.

Philippe took her hand and raised it to his lips with a smile. "It is a pleasure to meet you, madame," he said. "We thought you might like to meet your nephew as well."

He said something in Arabic, and a woman in a hijab and an aba climbed out with a young man of about two years of age held tight in her arms. "Our son, Rashid," he introduced, grinning at the child, who reached for his father and went eagerly into his arms.

"See that?" Gretchen said with a sigh. She shook her head. "His first word was da-da. He cries unless Philippe reads him a story at bedtime. When he gets up, he runs to his father." She threw up her hands. "I'm just a walking incubator around here!"

"Liar." Philippe chuckled, grinning at her. "You are a walking reform committee," he corrected.

"I have only made a few minor changes," she began.

He smiled and kissed his son on the cheek. "Can you make coffee?" he asked his new sister-in-law. "It has been a long and very thirsty trip out here from the airport."

"I make excellent coffee," Josie said, laughing. "I work in the district attorney's office. We live on it."

"Yes, I heard about your new job," Gretchen said, linking arms with her. "I want to talk to you about some legal issues...."

"Oh, my God," Philippe groaned.

Marc patted him on the shoulder. "Now, now, I'm sure it's only things like water pollution and global warming."

"We really need to do more about prison reform in Qawi" Gretchen was saying as she and Josie went into the house.

Philippe exchanged a complicated glance with Marc.

"I've got some aged scotch whiskey in my office," Marc said.

"Yes. And big glasses" came the amused reply.

"Uh, Your Highness…?"

Philippe turned. Curtis Russell was standing just outside the limousine alongside another Secret Service agent and two of Philippe's personal bodyguards.

"Yes?" Philippe asked.

Russell cleared his throat. "About that matter we discussed?"

Philippe sighed. "Complications, complications." He glanced at Marc. "Your bureau chief at the FBI is willing to give Russell a job if you recommend him."

Marc looked as if he'd been asked to swallow a salt block.

"It seems that his last assignment proved unlucky," Philippe continued.

"He was sticking his nose into organized crime the last time I heard anything about him," Marc pointed out. "In Austin, I believe?"

Russell swallowed hard. "I was only showing them how good an agent I'd be. And I did help that guy Phil Douglas get some evidence that helped us track down the Gates woman and bring her back for trial."

"Yes, you did." Marc had to agree.

"Sadly," Philippe interjected, "he identified himself as an FBI agent."

"You're Secret Service!" Marc exploded.

Russell grimaced. "Well, yes, technically, sort of." He coughed. "I was on vacation at the time. I did *used* to work for the FBI, for a year or so." He scowled. "Look here, I'd make a good agent. With all due respect, I'm wasted on visiting dignitaries! I can solve crimes. All I need is a chance!"

Philippe lifted an eyebrow at Marc, who shrugged.

"All right," Marc said. "I'll put in a word for you. With one condition," he added very deliberately.

"Anything!" Russell exclaimed with delight.

Marc's eyes narrowed. "That you work in one of the *other* forty-nine states of the union!"

Russell gave him a tight salute. "You bet. Yes, sir. Florida looks good to me. I love beaches." He grinned.

Marc threw up his hands and went into the house.

THAT NIGHT, after the company was nicely settled in the guest bedroom, with guards outside the door, Marc and Josie lay close in each others' arms while moonlight made stripes across the quilted coverlet.

"Christmas is next month," she murmured with a smile, snuggling closer. "I want a live tree that we can plant."

"Done."

"And some new decorations just for us."

"You can have all the rope and spurs you want."

Josette chuckled. "And a special ornament."

"Hmm?"

"You know, one of those that has our names and the date we married."

"That sounds nice."

"Next year we can add new ones."

He was drowsy. "New ones. Mmm-hmm."

"Like one that says, Baby's First Christmas."

"First Christmas. Nice. I like...what?"

He sat straight up in bed and gaped at her. "Did you say what I thought you said?"

She grinned. "We never did open that drawer next to the bed," she reminded him.

Brannon wasn't listening to explanations. His lean hand pressed softly against her belly and he looked at her as if she'd just solved the mystery of life.

"My very own miniature Texas Ranger, boy or girl." He chuckled softly. "What a Christmas present! Lucky, lucky me," he whispered, and bent to kiss her with breathless tenderness.

She smiled under his mouth and lifted her arms to bring him down to her. "Oh, no," she whispered. "Lucky *me!*"

Outside, the wind was up. It was autumn after all, nippy and frosty and crisp. But inside that room, there was a warmth that all the snow in Alaska couldn't have chilled. It was, Josie thought, going to be the most wonderful Christmas of their lives. And it was.

* * * * *

JOHN

CHAPTER ONE

IT TOOK A lot to make Big John Jacobs nervous. He was tall, rawboned, with deep-set green eyes the color of bottle glass, and thick dark brown hair. His lean, rough face had scars left over from the War Between the States. He carried scars both inside and out. He was originally from Georgia, but he'd come to Texas just after the war. Now he lived in one of the wildest parts of southeast Texas on a ranch he'd inherited from his late uncle. He was building up the ranch frugally, heading cattle drives to Kansas and buying livestock with the proceeds. What he had was very little to show for fifteen years of hard work, but he was strong and had a good business head. He'd tripled his uncle's land holdings and bought new bulls from back East to breed with his mangy longhorns. His mother would have been proud.

He noted the deep cut on his left hand, a scar from a knife fight with one of a band of Comanches who'd raided his property for horses. John and his hired help had fought them to a standstill and put them on the run. His ranch was isolated and he had good breeding stock. Over the years he'd had to fight roaming Comanche raiders and renegades from over the Mexican border, as well as carpetbaggers. If it hadn't been for the mili-

tary presence just after the war ended, courtesy of the
Union Army, lawlessness would have been even worse.

John had more reason than most to hate Union officers. But in the part of Texas where his ranch was
located, to the southeast of San Antonio, the peace
had been kept during Reconstruction by a local com-
mandant who was a gentleman. John had admired the
Union officer, who'd caught and prosecuted a thief
who stole two horses from the ranch. They were good
horses, with excellent bloodlines, which John had purchased from a Kentucky thoroughbred farm. The officer, who rode a Kentucky thoroughbred of his own,
understood the attachment a rancher felt to his blood
stock. John had rarely been more grateful to another
human being. Like John himself, the officer was fearless.

Fearless. John laughed at his own apprehension over
what he was about to do. He didn't mind risking his life
to save his ranch. But this was no fight with guns or
knives. It was a much more civilized sort of warfare.
In order to win this battle, John was going to have to
venture into a world he'd never seen close up. He wasn't
comfortable with high society folk. He hoped he wasn't
going to embarrass himself.

He removed his dress hat and ran a big hand through
his sweaty brown hair. He'd had Juana cut it before
he'd left the 3J Ranch. He hoped it was conservative
enough to impress old man Terrance Colby. The railroad magnate was vacationing in Sutherland Springs,
not far from the 3J. The popular resort boasted over one
hundred separate springs in a small area. John had ridden out there to speak to Colby, without a single idea

of how he was going to go about it. He had figured the details would work themselves out if he made the trip.

He was uneasy in company. He'd had to pawn his grandfather's watch to buy the used suit and hat he was wearing. It was a gamble he was taking, a big one. Cattle were no good to anyone if they couldn't be gotten to market. Driving cattle to the railheads in Kansas was becoming ever more dangerous. In some areas, fear of Texas tick fever had caused armed blockades of farmers to deter Texas cattle from entry. If he was going to get his cattle to market, there had to be a more direct route. He needed a railroad spur close by. Colby owned a railroad. He'd just announced his intentions of expanding it to connect with San Antonio. It would be no great burden to extend a line down through Wilson County to the Jacobs ranch. There were other ranchers in the area who also wanted the spur.

Old man Colby had a daughter, Camellia Ellen, who was unmarried and apparently unmarriageable. Local gossip said that the old man had no use for his unattractive daughter and would be happy to be rid of her. She got in the way of his mistresses. So Big John Jacobs had come a courting, to get himself a railroad…

It started raining just as he got to town. He cursed his foul luck, his green eyes blazing as he noted the mud his horse's hooves was throwing up and splattering onto his boots and the hem of the one good pair of pants he owned. He'd be untidy, and he couldn't afford to be. Terrance Colby was a New York aristocrat who, from what John had heard, was always impeccably dressed. He was staying at the best hotel the little resort of Sutherland Springs could boast, which was none too luxurious. Rumor was that Colby had come here on a hunting trip and was taking the waters while he was in the area.

John swung down out of the saddle half a block from the hotel Colby was staying at, hoping to have a chance to brush the mud off himself. Just as he got onto the boardwalk, a carriage drew up nearby. A young woman of no particular note climbed down out of it, caught the hem of her dress under her laced shoe, and fell face-first into a mud puddle.

Unforgivably, John laughed. He couldn't help it. The woman's companion gave him a glare, but the look he gave the woman was much more expressive.

"For God's sake, woman, can't you take two steps without tripping over your own garments?" the man asked in a high-pitched British accented voice. "Do get up. Now that we've dropped you off in town, I must go. I've an engagement for which you've already made me late. I'll call on your father later. Driver, carry on!"

The driver gave the woman and Big John a speaking look, but he did as he was instructed. John took note of the stranger, and hoped to meet him again one day.

He moved to the woman's side, and offered her an arm.

"No, no," she protested, managing to get to her feet alone. "You're much too nicely dressed to let me splatter you. Do go on, sir. I'm simply clumsy, there's no cure to be had for it, I'm afraid." She adjusted her oversized hat atop the dark bun of her hair and looked at him with miserable blue eyes in a pleasant but not very attractive face. She was slight and thin, and not the sort of woman to whom he'd ever been attracted.

"Your companion has no manners," he remarked.

"Thank you for your concern."

He tipped his hat. "It was no trouble. I wouldn't have minded being splattered. As you can see, I've already sampled the local mud."

She laughed and her animated face took on a fey quality, of which she was unaware. "Good day."

"Good day."

She moved away and he started into the barbershop to put himself to rights.

"John!" a man called from nearby. "Thought that was you," a heavyset man with a badge panted as he came up to join him. It was Deputy Marshal James Graham, who often stopped by John's ranch when he was in the area looking for fugitives.

They shook hands. "What are you doing in Sutherland Springs?" John asked him.

"I'm looking for a couple of renegades," he said. "They were hiding in Indian Territory, but I heard from a cousin of one of them that they were headed this way, trying to outrun the army. You watch your back."

"You watch yours," he retorted, opening his jacket to display the Colt .45 he always wore in a holster on a gunbelt slung across his narrow hips.

The marshal chuckled. "I heard that. Noticed you were trying to help that poor young woman out of a fix."

"Yes, poor little thing," he commented. "Nothing to look at, and of little interest to a man. Two left feet into the bargain. But it was no trouble to be kind to her. Her companion gave her no more help than the rough edge of his tongue."

"That was Sir Sydney Blythe, a hunting companion of the railroad magnate, Colby. They say the girl has a crush on him, but he has no use for her."

"Hardly surprising. He might have ended in the mud

puddle," he added on a chuckle. "She's not the sort to inspire passion."

"You might be surprised. My wife is no looker, but can she cook! Looks wear out. Cooking lasts forever. You remember that. See you around."

"You, too." John went on into the barbershop unaware of a mud-covered female standing behind the corner, trying to deal with wiping some of the mud from her heavy skirt.

She glared at the barbershop with fierce blue eyes. So he was that sort of a man, was he, pitying the poor little scrawny hen with the clumsy feet. She'd thought he was different, but he was just the same as other men. None of them looked twice at a woman unless she had a beautiful face or body.

She walked past the barbershop toward her hotel, seething with fury. She hoped that she might one day have the chance to meet that gentleman again when she was properly dressed and in her own element. It would be a shock for him, she felt certain.

A short while later John walked toward the Sutherland Springs Hotel with a confidence he didn't really feel. He was grateful for the marshal's conversation, which helped calm him. He wondered if Colby's daughter was also enamoured of the atrocious Sir Sydney, as well as that poor scrawny hen who'd been out riding with him? He wasn't certain how he would have to go about wooing such a misfit, although he had it in mind.

At thirty-five, John was more learned than many of his contemporaries, having been brought up by an educated mother who taught him Latin while they worked in the fields. Since then, he'd been educated in other ways while trying to keep himself clothed and fed. His married sister, the only other survivor of his family, had tried to get him to come and work with her husband in North Carolina on their farm, but he hadn't wanted to settle in the East. He was a man with a dream. And if a man could make himself a fortune with nothing more than hard work and self-denial, he was ready to be that man.

It seemed vaguely dishonest to take a bride for monetary reasons, and it cut to the quick to pretend an affection he didn't feel to get a rich bride. If there was an honest way to do this, he was going to find it. His one certainty was that if he married a railroad tycoon's daughter, he had a far better chance of getting a railroad to lay tracks to his ranch than if he simply asked for help. These days, nobody rushed to help a penniless rancher. Least of all a rich Northerner.

John walked into the hotel bristling with assumed self-confidence and the same faint arrogance he'd seen rich men use to get their way.

"My name is John Jacobs," he told the clerk formally. "Mr. Colby is expecting me."

That was a bald lie, but a bold one. If it worked, he could cut through a lot of time-wasting protocol.

"Uh, he is? I mean, of course, sir," the young man faltered. "Mr. Colby is in the presidential suite. It's on the second floor, at the end of the hall. You may go right up. Mr. Colby and his daughter are receiving this morning."

Receiving. Go right up. John nodded, dazed. It was easier than he'd dreamed to see one of the country's richest men!

He nodded politely at the clerk and turned to the staircase.

322   JOHN

The suite was easy to find. He knocked on the door confidently, inwardly gritting his teeth to gear himself up for the meeting. He had no idea what he was going to give as an excuse for coming here. He didn't know what Ellen Colby looked like. Could he perhaps say that he'd seen her from afar and had fallen madly in love with her at once? That would certainly ruin his chances with her father, who would be convinced that he only wanted Ellen's money.

While he was thinking up excuses, a maid opened the door and stood back to let him inside. Belatedly he swept off his hat, hoping his forehead wasn't sweating as profusely as it felt.

"Your name, sir?" the middle-aged woman asked politely.

"John Jacobs," he told her. "I'm a local landowner," he added.

She nodded. "Please wait here."

She disappeared into another room behind a closed door. Seconds passed, while John looked around him uncomfortably, reminded by the opulence of the suite how far removed he was from the upper class.

The door opened. "Please go in, sir," the maid said respectfully, and even smiled at him.

Elated, he went into the room and stared into a pair of the coldest pale blue eyes he'd ever seen, in a face that seemed unremarkable compared to the very expensive lacy white dress worn by its owner. She had a beautiful figure, regardless of her lack of beauty. Her hair was thick and a rich dark brown, swept up into a high bun that left a roll of it all around her head. She was very poised, very elegant and totally hostile. With a start, John recognized her. She was the mud puddle swimmer from the hotel entrance.

He must not laugh, he must not…! But a faint grin split his chiseled lips and his green eyes danced on her indignant features. Here was his excuse, so unexpected!

"I came to inquire about your health," he said, his voice deep and lazy. "The weather is cold, and the mud puddle was very large…."

"I am…" She was blushing, now apparently flattered by his visit. "I am very well. Thank you!"

"What mud puddle?" came a crisp voice from the doorway. A man, shorter than John, with balding hair and dark blue eyes, dressed in an expensive suit, came into the room. "I'm Terrance Colby. Who are you?"

"John Jacobs," he introduced himself. He wasn't certain how to go on. "I own a ranch outside town…" he began.

"Oh, you're here about quail hunting," Colby said immediately. He smiled, to John's astonishment, and went forward to shake hands. "But I'm afraid you're a few minutes too late. I've already procured an invitation to the Four Aces Ranch to hunt antelope and quail. You know it, I expect?"

"Certainly I do, sir," John replied. And he did. That ranch was the sort John wanted desperately to own one day, a huge property with purebred cattle and horses, known all over the country—in fact, all over the world! "I'm sure you'll find the accommodations superior."

The older man eyed him curiously. "Thank you for the offer."

John nodded. "My pleasure, sir. But I had another purpose in coming. A passerby mentioned that the young lady here was staying at this hotel. She, uh, had a bad fall on her way inside. I assisted her. I only wanted to assure myself that she was uninjured. Her companion was less than helpful," he added with honest irritation.

"Sir Sydney drove off and left me there," the woman said angrily with flashing eyes.

Colby gave her an unsympathetic glance. "If you will be clumsy and throw yourself into mud puddles, Ellen, you can expect to be ignored by any normal man."

Ellen! This unfortunate little hen was the very heiress John had come to town to woo, and he was having more good fortune than he'd dreamed! Lady Luck was tossing offerings into his path with every word he spoke.

He smiled at Ellen Colby with deliberate interest. "On the contrary, sir, I find her enchanting," he murmured.

Colby looked at him as if he expected men with nets to storm the room.

Ellen gave him a harsh glare. She might have been flattered by the visit, but she knew a line when she heard one. Too many men had sought access to her father through her. Here was another, when she'd hoped he might like her for herself. But when had that ever happened? Disappointed, she drew herself up to her full height. "Please excuse me. I am in the middle of important work." She lifted her chin and added deliberately, "My father's dog is having her bath."

She turned and stalked toward a door between rooms, while John threw back his head and laughed with genuine glee.

Colby had to chuckle, himself, at his daughter's audacity. She never raised her voice, as a rule, and he'd long since come to think of her as a doormat. But this man pricked her temper and made her eyes flash.

"An interesting reaction," he told John. "She is never rude, and I cannot remember a time when she raised her voice."

John grinned. "A gentleman likes to think that he has made an impression, sir," he said respectfully. "Your daughter is far more interesting with a temper than without one. To me, at least."

"You have a ranch, you said?" Colby asked.

John nodded. "A small one, but growing. I have begun to cross breeds to good effect. I have a long-horn seed bull and a small herd of Hereford cattle. I hope to raise a better sort of beef to suit Eastern tastes and ship it to market in Chicago."

The older man sized up his guest, from the worn, but still useful, shoes and suit and the well-worn gunbelt and pistol worn unobtrusively under the open jacket.

"You have a Southern accent," Colby said.

John nodded again. "I am a Georgian, by birth."

Colby actually winced.

John laughed without humor. "You know, then, what Sherman and his men did to my state."

"Slavery is against everything I believe in," Colby said. His face grew hard. "Sherman's conduct was justified."

John had to bite his tongue to keep back a sharp reply. He could feel the heat of the fire, hear his mother and sister screaming as they fell in the maelstrom of crackling flames....

"You owned slaves?" Colby persisted curtly.

John gritted his teeth. "Sir, my mother and sisters and I worked on a farm outside Atlanta," he said, almost choking on memories despite the years between himself and the memory. "Only rich planters could afford

slaves. My people were Irish immigrants. You might recall the signs placed at the front gates of estates in the
North, which read, No Colored Or Irish Need Apply."

Colby swallowed hard. He had, indeed, seen those
signs.

John seemed to grow another inch. "To answer your
question, had I been a rich planter, I would have hired
my labor, not bought it, for I do not feel that one man of
any color has the right to own another." His green eyes
flashed. "There were many other small landowners and
sharecroppers like my family who paid the price for the
greed and luxury of plantation owners. Sherman's army
did not discriminate between the two."

"Excuse me," Colby said at once. "One of my laun-
dresses back home had been a slave. Her arms were
livid with scars from a mistress who cut her when she
burned a dress she was told to iron."

"I have seen similar scars," John replied, without
adding that one of the co-owners of his ranch had such
unsightly scars, as well as his wife and even their eldest daughter.

"Your mother and sisters live with you?" Colby
asked.

John didn't reply for a few seconds. "No, sir. Except for a married sister in North Carolina, my people
are all dead."

Colby nodded, his eyes narrow and assessing. "But,
then, you have done well for yourself in Texas, have
you not?" He smiled.

John forced himself to return the smile and forget
the insults. "I will do better, sir," he said with unshake-
able confidence. "Far better."

Colby chuckled. "You remind me of myself, when I

was a young man. I left home to make my fortune, and had the good sense to look toward trains as the means."

John twirled his hat in his big hands. He wanted to approach Colby about his spur, which would give him the opportunity to ship his cattle without having to take the risk of driving them north to railheads in Kansas. But that would be pushing his luck. Colby might feel that John was overstepping his place in society and being "uppity." He couldn't risk alienating Colby.

He shifted his weight. "I should go," he said absently. "I had no intention of taking up so much of your time, sir. I wanted only to offer you the freedom of my ranch for hunting, and to inquire about the health of your daughter after her unfortunate accident."

"Unfortunate accident." Colby shook his head. "She is the clumsiest woman I have ever known," he said coldly, "and I have found not one single gentleman who lasted more than a day as a suitor."

"But she is charming," John countered gallantly, his eyes dancing. "She has a sense of humor, the ability to laugh at herself, and despite her companion's rudeness, she behaved with dignity."

Colby was listening intently. "You find her... attractive?"

"Sir, she is the most attractive woman I have ever met," John replied without choosing his words.

Colby laughed and shook his head. "You want something," he mused. "But I'm damned if I don't find you a breath of fresh air, sir. You have style and dash."

John grinned at him. "Thank you, sir."

"I may take you up on that invitation at a later date, young man. In the meantime, I have accepted the other offer. But you could do me a favor, if you're inclined."

"Anything within my power, sir," John assured him.

"Since you find my daughter so alluring, I would like you to keep an eye on her during my absence."

"Sir, there would not be adequate chaperones at my ranch," John began quickly, seeing disaster ahead if the old man or his daughter got a glimpse of the true state of affairs at the Jacobs ranch.

"Oh, for heaven's sake, man, I'm not proposing having her live with you in sin!" Colby burst out. "She will stay here at the hotel, and I have told her not to venture out of town. I meant only that I would like you to check on her from time to time, to make sure that she is safe. She will be on her own, except for the maid we have retained here."

"I see." John let out the breath he'd been holding. "In that case, I would be delighted. But what of her companion, Sir Sydney?" he added.

"Sir Sydney will be with me, to my cost," Colby groaned. "The man is an utter pain, but he has a tract of land that I need very badly for a new roundhouse near Chicago," he confessed. "So I must humor him, to some extent. I assure you, my daughter will not mourn his absence. She only went to drive with him at my request. She finds him repulsive."

So did John, but he didn't want to rock the boat.

"I'm glad you came, young man." Colby offered his hand, and John shook it.

"So am I, sir," he replied. "If you don't mind, I would like to take my leave of your daughter."

"Be my guest."

"Thank you."

John walked toward the open door that contained a maid, Miss Ellen Colby and a very mad wet dog of un-

certain age and pedigree. It was a shaggy dog, black
and white, with very long ears. It was barking pitifully
and shaking soapy water everywhere.

"Oh, Miss Colby, this doggy don't want no bath," the
maid wailed as she tried to right her cap.

"Never you mind, Lizzie, we're going to bathe her
or die in the attempt." Ellen blew back a strand of loose
hair, holding the dog down with both hands while the
maid laved water on it with a cup.

"A watering trough might be a better proposition,
Miss Colby," John drawled from the doorway.

His voice shocked her. She jerked her head in his
direction and loosened the hold she had on the dog. In
the few seconds that followed, the animal gave a yelp
of pure joy, leaped out of the pan, off the table, and
scattered the rugs as it clawed its way to the freedom
of the parlor.

"Oh, my goodness!" Ellen yelled. "Catch her, Lizzie,
before she gets to the bedroom! She'll go right up on
Papa's bed, like she usually does!"

"Yes, ma'am!"

The maid ran for all she was worth. Ellen Colby put
her soapy hands on her hips and glared daggers at the
tall green-eyed man in the doorway.

"Now see what you've done!" Ellen raged at John.

"Me?" John's eyebrows arched. "I assure you, I
meant only to say goodbye."

"You diverted my attention at a critical moment!"

He smiled slowly, liking the way her blue eyes
flashed in anger. He liked the thickness of her hair.
It looked very long. He wondered if she let it down at
bedtime.

That thought disturbed him. He straightened. "If

your entire social life consists of bathing the dog, miss, you are missing out."

"I have a social life!"

"Falling into mud puddles?"

She grabbed up the soaking brush they'd used on the dog and considered heaving it.

John threw back his head and laughed uproariously.

"Do be quiet!" she muttered.

"You have hidden fires," he commented with delight. "Your father has asked me to keep an eye on you, Miss Colby, while he's off on his hunting trip. I find the prospect delightful."

"I can think of nothing I would enjoy less!"

"I'm quite a good companion," he assured her. "I know where birds' nests are and where flowers grow, and I can even sing and play the guitar if asked."

She hesitated, wet splotches all over her lacy dress and soap in her upswept hair. She looked at him with open curiosity. "You are wearing a gun," she pointed out. "Do you shoot people with it?"

"Only the worst sort of people," he told her. "And I have yet to shoot a woman."

"I am reassured."

"I have a cattle ranch not too far a ride from here," he continued. "In the past, I have had infrequently to help defend my cattle from Comanche raiding parties."

"Indians!"

He laughed at her expression. "Yes. Indians. They have long since gone to live in the Indian Territory. But there are still rustlers and raiders from across the Mexican border, as well as deserting soldiers and layabouts from town hoping to steal my cattle and make a quick profit by selling them to the army."

"How do you stop them?"

"With vigilance," he said simply. "I have men who work for me on shares."

"Shares?" She frowned. "Not for wages?"

He could have bitten his tongue. He hadn't meant to let that slip out.

She knew that he'd let his guard down. She found him mysterious and charming and shrewd. But he had attractions. He was the first man she'd met who made her want to know more about him.

"I might take you for a ride in my buggy," he mused.

"I might go," she replied.

He chuckled, liking her pert response. She wasn't much to look at, truly, but she had qualities he'd yet to find in other women.

He turned to go. "I won't take the dog along," he said.

"Papa's dog goes with me everywhere," she lied, wanting to be contrary.

He glanced at her over his shoulder. "You were alone in the mud puddle, as I recall."

She glared at him.

He gave her a long, curious scrutiny. He smiled slowly. "We can discuss it at a later date. I will see you again in a day or two." He lifted his hat respectfully. "Good day, Miss Colby."

"Good day, Mr....?" It only then occurred to her that she didn't even know his name.

"John," he replied. "John Jackson Jacobs. But most people just call me 'Big John.'"

"You are rather large," she had to agree.

He grinned. "And you are rather small. But I like your spirit, Miss Colby. I like it a lot."

She sighed and her eyes began to glow faintly as they met his green ones.

He winked at her and she blushed scarlet. But before he could say anything, the maid passed him with the struggling wet dog.

"Excuse me, sir, this parcel is quite maddeningly wet," the maid grumbled as she headed toward the bowl on the table.

"So I see. Good day, ladies." He tipped his hat again, and he was gone in a jingle of spurs.

Ellen Colby looked after him with curiosity and an odd feeling of loss. Strange that a man she'd only just met could be so familiar to her, and that she could feel such joy in his presence.

Her life had been a lonely one, a life of service, helping to act as a hostess for her father and care for her grandmother. But with her grandmother off traveling, Ellen was now more of a hindrance than a help to her family, and it was no secret that her father wanted badly to see her married and off his hands.

But chance would be a fine thing, she thought. She turned back to the dog with faint sadness, wishing she were prettier.

CHAPTER TWO

JOHN RODE BACK to his ranch, past the newfangled barbed wire which contained his prize longhorn bull, past the second fence that held his Hereford bull and his small herd of Hereford cows with their spring calves, to the cabin where he and his foremen's families lived together. He had hundreds of head of beef steers, but they ranged widely, free of fences, identified only by his 3J brand, burned into their thick coats. The calves had been branded in the spring.

Mary Brown was at the door, watching him approach. It was early June, and hot in south Texas. Her sweaty black hair was contained under a kerchief, and her brown eyes smiled at him. "Me and Juana washed your old clothes, Mister John," she said. "Isaac and Luis went fishing with the boys down to the river for supper, and the girls are making bread."

"Good," he said. "Do I have anything dry and pressed to put on?" he added.

Mary nodded her head. "Such as it is, Mister John. A few more holes, and no amount of sewing is gonna save you a red face in company."

"I'm working on that, Mary," he told her, chuckling. He bent to lift her youngest son, Joe, a toddler, up into his arms. "You get to growing fast, young feller, you got to help me herd cattle."

The little boy gurgled at him. John grinned at him and set him back down.

Isaac came in the back door just then, with a string of fish. "You back?" He grinned. "Any luck?"

"A lot, all of it unexpected," he told the tall, lithe black man. He glanced at Luis Rodriguez, his head vaquero, who was short and stout and also carrying a string of fish. He took Isaac's and handed both to the young boys. "You boys go clean these fish for Mary, you hear?"

"Yes, Papa," the taller black boy said. His shorter Latino companion grinned and followed him out the door.

"We have another calf missing, *señor*," Luis said irritably. "Isaac and I only came to bring the boys and the fish to the house." He pulled out his pistol and checked it. "We will go and track the calf."

"I'll go with you," John said. "Give me a minute to change."

He carried his clothing to the single room that had a makeshift door and got out of his best clothes, leaving them hanging over a handmade chair he'd provided for Mary. He whipped his gunbelt back around his lean hips and checked his pistol. Rustlers were the bane of any rancher, but in these hard times, when a single calf meant the difference between keeping his land or losing it, he couldn't afford to let it slide.

He went back out to the men, grim-faced. "Let's do some tracking."

THEY FOUND THE CALF, butchered. Signs around it told them it wasn't rustlers, but a couple of Indians—Comanches, in fact, judging from the broken arrow shaft and footprints they found nearby.

"Damn the luck!" John growled. "What are Comanches doing this far south? And if they're hungry, why can't they hunt rabbits or quail?"

"They all prefer buffalo, *señor,* but the herds have long gone, and game is even scarce here. That is why we had to fish for supper."

"They could go the hell back to the Indian Territory, couldn't they, instead of riding around here, harassing us poor people!" John pursed his lips thoughtfully, remembering what he'd heard in Sutherland Springs. "I wonder," he mused aloud, "if these could be the two renegades from Indian Territory being chased by the army?"

"What?" Isaac asked.

"Nothing," John said, clapping him on the shoulder affectionately. "Just thinking to myself. Let's get back to work."

THE NEXT DAY, he put on his good suit and went back to the Springs to check on Ellen Colby. He expected to find her reclining in her suite, or playing with her father's dog. What he did find was vaguely shocking.

Far from being in her room, Ellen was on the sidewalk with one arm around a frightened young black boy who'd apparently been knocked down by an angry man.

"…he got in my way. He's got no business walking on the sidewalk anyway. He should be in the street. He should be dead. They should all be dead! We lost everything because of them, and then they got protected by the very army that burned down our homes! You get away from him, lady, he's not going anywhere until I teach him a lesson!"

She stuck out her chin. "I have no intention of moving, sir. If you strike him, you must strike me, also!"

John moved up onto the sidewalk. He didn't look at Ellen. His eyes were on the angry man, and they didn't waver. He didn't say a word. He simply flipped back the lapel of his jacket to disclose the holstered pistol he was carrying.

"Another one!" the angry man railed. "You damned Yankees should get the hell out of Texas and go back up north where you belong!"

"I'm from Georgia," John drawled. "But this is where I belong now."

The man was taken aback. He straightened and glared at John, his fists clenched. "You'd draw on a fellow Southerner?" he exclaimed.

"I'm partial to brown skin," John told him with a honeyed drawl. His tall, lithe figure bent just enough to make an older man nearby catch his breath. "But you do what you think you have to," he added deliberately.

"There," Ellen Colby said haughtily, helping the young man to his feet. "See what you get when you act out of ignoble motives?" she lashed at the threatening man. "A child is a child, regardless of his heritage, sir!"

"That is no child," the man said. "It is an abomination…."

"I beg to disagree." The voice came from a newcomer, wearing a star on his shirt, just making his way through the small crowd. It was Deputy Marshal James Graham, well known locally because he was impartially fair. "Is there a problem, madam?" he asked Ellen, tipping his hat to her.

"That man kicked this young man off the sidewalk and attacked him," Ellen said, glaring daggers at the antagonist. "I interfered and Mr. Jacobs came along in time to prevent any further violence."

"Are you all right, son?" the marshal asked the young boy, who was openmouthed at his unexpected defense.

"Uh, yes, sir. I ain't hurt," he stammered.

Ellen Colby took a coin from her purse and placed it in the young man's hand. "You go get yourself a stick of peppermint," she told him.

He looked at the coin and grinned. "Thank you kindly, miss, but I'll buy my mama a sack of flour instead. Thank you, too," he told the marshal and John Jacobs, before he cut his losses and rushed down the sidewalk.

Graham turned to the man who'd started the trouble. "I don't like troublemakers," he said in a voice curt with command. "If I see you again, in a similar situation, I'll lock you up. That's a promise."

The man spat onto the ground and gave all three of the boy's defenders a cold glare before he turned and stomped off in the opposite direction.

"I'm obliged to both of you," Ellen Colby told them.

John shrugged. "It was no bother."

The deputy marshal chuckled. "A Georgian defending a black boy." He shook his head. "I am astonished."

John laughed. "I have a former slave family working with me," he explained. His face tautened. "If you could see the scars they carry, even the children, you might understand my position even better."

The deputy nodded. "I do understand. If you have any further trouble," he told Ellen, "I am at your service." He tipped his hat and went back to his horse.

"You are a man of parts, Mr. Jacobs," Ellen told

John, her blue eyes soft and approving. "Thank you for your help."

He shrugged. "I was thinking of Isaac's oldest boy who died in Georgia," he confessed, moving closer as the crowd melted away. "Isaac is my wrangler," he added. "His first son was beaten to death by an overseer just before the end of the war."

She stood staring up into his lean, hard face with utter curiosity. "I understood that all Southerners hated colored people."

"Most of us common Southerners were in the fields working right beside them," John said coldly. "We were little more than slaves ourselves, while the rich lived in luxury and turned a blind eye to the abuse."

"I had no idea," she said hesitantly.

"Very few northern people do," he said flatly. "Yet there was a county in Georgia that flew the Union flag all through the war, and every attempt by the confederacy to press-gang them into the army was met with open resistance. They ran away and the army got tired of going back to get them again and again." He chuckled at her surprise. "I will tell you all about it over tea, if you like."

She blushed. "I would like that very much, Mr. Jacobs."

He offered his arm. She placed her small hand in the crook of his elbow and let him escort her into the hotel's immaculate dining room. He wondered if he should have told Graham about the Comanche tracks he'd found on his place. He made a note to mention it to the man when he next saw him.

ELLEN LIKED THE LITHE, rawboned man who sat across from her sipping tea and eating tea cakes as if he were born to high society. But she knew that he wasn't. He still had rough edges, but even those were endearing. She couldn't forget the image she had of him, standing in front of the frightened boy, daring the attacker to try again. He was brave. She admired courage.

"Did you really come to see my father to inquire about my welfare?" she asked after they'd discussed the war.

He looked up at her, surprised by her boldness. He put his teacup down. "No," he said honestly.

She laughed self-consciously. "Forgive me, but I knew that wasn't the real reason. I appreciate your honesty."

He leaned back in his chair and studied her without pretense. His green gaze slid over her plain face, down to the faint thrust of her breasts under the green and white striped bodice of her dress and up to the wealth of dark hair piled atop her head. "Lies come hard to me," he told her. "Shall I be completely honest about my motives and risk alienating you?"

She smiled. "Please do. I have lost count of the men who pretended to admire me only as a means to my father's wealth. I much prefer an open approach."

"I inherited a very small holding from my uncle, who died some time ago." He toyed with the teacup. "I have worked for wages in the past, to buy more land and cattle. But just recently I've started to experiment with crossing breeds. I am raising a new sort of beef steer with which I hope to tempt the eastern population's hunger for range-fed beef." His eyes lifted to hers. "It's a long, slow process to drive cattle to a railhead up in Kansas, fraught with danger and risk, more now than ever since the fear of Texas fever in cattle has caused so much resistance to be placed in the path of the cattle drives. My finances are so tight now that the loss of a single calf is a major setback to me."

She was interested. "You have a plan."

He smiled. "I have a plan. I want to bring a railroad to this area of south Texas. More precisely, I want a spur to run to my ranch, so that I can ship cattle to Chicago without having to drive them to Kansas first."

Her eyes brightened. "Then you had no real purpose of inviting my father to hunt quail on your ranch."

"Miss Colby," he said heavily, "my two foremen and their families live with me in a one-room cabin. It looks all right at a distance, but close up, it's very primitive. It is a pretend mansion. As I am a pretend aristocrat." He gestured at his suit coat. "I used the last of my ready cash to disguise myself and I came into town because I had heard that your father was here, and that he had a marriageable daughter." His expression became self-mocking when she blinked. "But I'm not enough of a scoundrel to pretend an affection I do not feel." He studied her quietly, toying with a spoon beside his cup and saucer. "So let me make you a business proposition. Marry me and let your father give us a railroad spur as a wedding present."

She gulped, swallowed a mouthful of hot tea, sat back and expelled a shocked breath. "Sir, you are blunt!"

"Ma'am, I am honest," he replied. He leaned forward quickly and fixed her with his green eyes. "Listen to me. I have little more than land and prospects. But I have a good head for business, and I know cattle. Given the opportunity, I will build an empire such as Texas has never seen. I have good help, and I've learned much about raising cattle from them. Marry me."

"And…what would I obtain from such a liaison?" she stammered.

"Freedom."

"Excuse me?"

"Your father cares for you, I think, but he treats you as a liability. That gentleman," he spat the word, "who was escorting you stood idly by when you fell in a mud puddle and didn't even offer a hand. You are under-valued."

She laughed nervously. "And I would not be, if I married a poor stranger and went to live in the wilds where rustlers raid?"

He grinned. "You could wear pants and learn to ride a horse and herd cattle," he said, tempting her. "I would even teach you to brand cattle and shoot a gun."

Her whole demeanor changed. She just stared at him for a minute. "I have spent my entire life under the care of my mother's mother, having lost my own mother when I was only a child. My grandmother Greene be-lieves that a lady should never soil her hands in any way. She insists on absolute decorum in all situations. She would not hear of my learning to ride a horse or shoot a gun because such things are only for men. I have lived in a cage all my life." Her blue eyes began to gleam. "I should love to be a tomboy!"

He laughed. "Then marry me."

She hesitated once again. "Sir, I know very little of men. Having been sheltered in all ways, I am un-easy with the thought of…with having a stranger…with being…"

He held up a hand. "I offer you a marriage of friends. In truth, anything more would require a miracle, as there is no privacy where I live. We are all under the single roof. And," he added, "my foremen and their families are black and Mexican, not white." He watched for her reactions. "So, as you can see, there is a further difficulty in regard to public opinion hereabouts."

She clasped her hands before her on the table. "I would like to think about it a little. Not because of any prejudice," she added quickly, and smiled. "But because I would like to know you a little better. I have a friend who married in haste at the age of fifteen. She is now twenty-four, as I am. She has seven living children and her husband treats her like property. It is not a condition which I envy her."

"I understand," he said.

The oddest thing, was that she thought he really did understand. He was a complex man. She had a sudden vision of him years down the road, in an elegant suit, in an elegant setting. He had potential. She'd never met anyone like him.

She sighed. "But my father must not know the entire truth," she cautioned. "He has prejudices, and he would not willingly let me go to a man he considered a social inferior."

His thin lips pursed amusedly. "Then I'll do my utmost to convince him that I am actually the illegitimate grandson of an Irish earl."

She leaned forward. "Are there Irish earls?"

He shrugged. "I have no idea. But, then, he probably has no idea, either." His eyes twinkled.

She laughed delightedly. It changed her face, her eyes, her whole look. She was pretty when she laughed.

"There is one more complication," he said in a half-serious tone.

"Which is?"

His smile was outrageous. "We have lots of mud puddles at the ranch."

"Oh, you!" she exclaimed, reaching for the teapot.

"If you throw it, the morning papers will have a more interesting front page."

"Will it? And what would you do?" she challenged brightly.

"I am uncivilized," he informed her. "I would put you across my knee and paddle your backside, after which I would toss you over my shoulder and carry you home with me."

"How very exciting!" she exclaimed. "I have never done anything especially outrageous. I think I might like being the object of a scandal!"

He beamed. "Tempting," he proclaimed. "But I have great plans and no desire to start tongues wagging. Yet."

"Very well. I'll restrain my less civilized impulses for the time being."

He lifted his teacup and toasted her. "To unholy alliances," he teased.

She lifted hers as well. "And madcap plots!"

They clicked teacups together and drank deeply.

IT WAS UNSEEMLY for them to be seen going out of town alone, so Ellen was prevented from visiting John's ranch. But he took her to church on Sunday—a new habit that he felt obliged to acquire—and promenading along the sidewalk after a leisurely lunch in the hotel.

The following week, John was a frequent visitor. He and Ellen became friends with an elegant Scottish gentleman and his wife who were staying at the hotel and taking the waters, while they toured the American West.

"It is a grand country," the Scotsman, Robert Maxwell, told Ellen and John. "Edith and I have been longing to ride out into the country, but we are told that it is dangerous."

"It is," John assured him grimly. "My partners and I have been tracking rustlers all week," he added, to Ellen's surprise, because he hadn't told her. "There are dangerous men in these parts, and we have rustlers from across the border, also."

"Do you have Red Indians?" Maxwell exclaimed. His eyes twinkled. "I would like to meet one."

"They're all in the Indian Territory now, and no, you wouldn't like to meet one," John said. "The Comanches who used to live hereabouts didn't encourage foreign visitors, and they had a well-deserved reputation for opposing any people who tried to invade their land."

"Their land?" the Scotsman queried, curiously.

"Their land," John said firmly. "They roamed this country long before the first white man set foot here. They intermarried with the Mexican population...."

Maxwell seemed very confused, as he interrupted, "Surely there were no people here at all when you arrived," he said.

"Perhaps they don't know it back East, but Texas was part of Mexico just a few decades back," John informed him. "That's why we went to war with Mexico, because Texas wanted independence from it. Our brave boys died in the Alamo in San Antonio, and at Goliad and San Jacinto, to bring Texas into the union. But the Mexican boys fought to keep from losing their territory, is how they saw it. They considered us invaders."

Ellen was watching John covertly, with quiet admiration.

"Ah, now I understand," the Scot chuckled. "It's like us and England. We've been fighting centuries to govern ourselves, like the Irish. But the British are stubborn folk."

"So are Texans," John chuckled.

"I don't suppose you'd go riding with us, young man?" Maxwell asked him wistfully. "We should love to see a little of the area, and I see that you wear a great pistol at your hip. I assume you can shoot any two-legged threats to our safety."

John glanced at Ellen and saw such appreciation in her blue eyes that he lost his train of thought for a few seconds.

Finally he blinked and darted his green gaze back to the foreigners, hoping his heartbeat wasn't audible.

"I think I'd like that," John replied, "as long as Ellen comes with us."

"Your young lady," the Scotswoman, Nell Maxwell, added with a gentle, indulgent smile.

"Yes," John said, his eyes going back to Ellen's involuntarily. "My young lady."

Ellen blushed red and lowered her eyes, which caused the foreign couple to laugh charmingly. She was so excited that she forgot her father's admonition that she was not to leave the hotel and go out of town. In fact, when she recalled it, she simply ignored it.

THEY RENTED A surrey and John helped Ellen into the back seat before he climbed up nimbly beside her. He noted that it was the best surrey the stable had, with fringe hanging all the way around, and the horses' livery was silver and black leather.

"I suppose this is nothing special for you," John murmured to her, looking keenly at the horses' adornments, "but it's something of a treat for me."

Ellen smoothed the skirt of her nice blue suit with its black piping. "It's a treat for me, too," she confessed. "I had very much wanted to drive out in the country, but my father only thinks of hunting, not sightseeing, and he dislikes my company."

"I like your company very much," John said in a deep, soft tone.

She looked up at him, surprised by the warmth in his deep voice. She was lost in the sudden intensity of his green eyes under the wide brim of his dress hat. She felt her whole world shift in the slow delight it provoked.

He smiled, feeling as if he could fly all of a sudden. Impulsively his big, lean hand caught hers on the seat between them and curled her small fingers into it.

She caught her breath, entranced.

"Are you two young people comfortable?" Maxwell asked.

"Quite comfortable, thank you, sir," John replied, and he looked at Ellen with possession.

"So am I, thank you," Ellen managed through her tight throat.

"We'll away, then," Maxwell said with a grin at his wife, and he flicked the reins.

The surrey bounded forward, the horses obviously well chosen for their task, because the ride was as smooth as silk.

"Which way shall we go?" Maxwell asked.

"Just follow the road you're on," John told him. "I know this way best. It runs past my own land up to Quail Run, the next little town along the road. I can show you the ruins of a log cabin where a white woman

and her Comanche husband held off a company of soldiers a few years back. He was a renegade. She was a
widow with a young son, and expecting another when
her husband was killed by a robber. Soon after, the Comanche was part of a war party that encountered a company of soldiers trailing them. He was wounded and she
found him and nursed him back to health. It was winter.
She couldn't hunt or fish, or chop wood, and she had
no family at all. He undertook her support. They both
ran from the soldiers, up into the Indian Territory. She's
there now, people say. Nobody knows where he is."

"What a fascinating story!" Maxwell exclaimed. "Is
it true?"

"From what I hear, it is," John replied.

"What a courageous young woman," Ellen murmured.

"To have contact with a Red Indian, she would have
to be," Mrs. Maxwell replied. "I have heard many people speak of Indians. None of what they say is good."

"I think all people are good and bad," Ellen ventured.
"I have never thought heritage should decide which is
which."

John chuckled and squeezed her hand. "We think
alike."

The Maxwells exchanged a complicated look and
laughed, too.

THE LOG CABIN was pointed out. It was nothing much
to look at. There was a well tucked into high grass and
briar bushes, and a single tree in what must once have
been the front yard.

"What sort of tree is that?" Mrs. Maxwell asked.
"What an odd shape."

"It's a chinaberry tree," John recalled. "We have them in Georgia, where I'm from. My sisters and I used to throw the green berries that grow on them back and forth, playing." He became somber.

"You have family back in Georgia?" Ellen asked pointedly, softly.

He sighed. "I have a married sister in North Carolina. No one else."

Ellen knew there was more to it than just that, and she had a feeling the war had cost him more than his home. She stroked the back of his callused hand gently. "Mama died of typhoid when I was just five. So except for Papa and Grandmother, I have no one, either."

He caught his breath. He hadn't thought about her circumstances, her family, her background. All he'd known was that she was rich. He began to see her with different eyes.

"I'm sorry, about your family," she said quietly.

He sighed. He didn't look at her. Memories tore at his heart. He looked out beyond the horses drawing the surrey at the yellow sand of the dirt road, leading to the slightly rolling land ahead. The familiar *clop-clop* of the horses' hooves and the faint creak of leather and wood and the swishing sound of the rolling wheels seemed very loud in the silence that followed. The dust came up into the carriage, but they were all used to it, since dirt roads were somewhat universal. The boards that made the seats of the surrey were hard on the backside during a long trip, but not less comfortable than the saddle of a horse, John supposed.

"Do you ride at all?" he asked Ellen.

"I was never allowed to," she confessed. "My grandmother thought it wasn't ladylike."

"I ride to the hounds," Mrs. Maxwell said, eavesdropping, and turned to face them with a grin. "My father himself put me on my first horse when I was no more than a girl. I rode sidesaddle, of course, but I could outdistance any man I met on a horse. Well, except for Robert," she conceded, with an affectionate look at her husband. "We raced and I lost. Then and there, I determined that I needed to marry him."

"And she did," he added with a chuckle, darting a look over his broad shoulder. "Her father told me I must keep her occupied to keep her happy, so I turned the stables over to her."

"Quite a revolution of sorts in our part of the country, I must add," Mrs. Maxwell confessed. "But the lads finally learned who had the whip hand, and now they do what I say."

"We have the finest stable around," Maxwell agreed. "We haven't lost a race yet."

"When I have more horses, you must come and teach my partners how to train them," John told Mrs. Maxwell.

"And didn't I tell you that people would not be stuffy and arrogant here in Texas?" she asked her husband.

"I must agree, they are not."

"Well, two of them, at least," John murmured dryly. "There," he said suddenly, pointing out across a grassy pasture. "That is my land."

All three heads turned. In the distance was the big cabin, surrounded by pecan and oak trees and not very visible. But around it were red-and-white-coated cattle, grazing in between barbed wire fences.

"It is fenced!" Maxwell exclaimed.

"Fencing is what keeps the outlaws out and my cattle in," John said, used to defending his fences. "Many people dislike this new barbed wire, but it is the most economical way to contain my herds. And I don't have a great deal of capital to work with."

"You are an honest man," Maxwell said. "You did not have to admit such a thing to a stranger."

"It is because you are a stranger that I can do it," John said amusedly. "I would never admit to being poor around my own countrymen. A man has his pride. However, I intend to be the richest landowner hereabouts in a few years. So you must plan to come back to Texas. I can promise you will be very welcome as houseguests."

"If I am able, I will," Maxwell agreed. "So we must keep in touch."

"Indeed we must. We will trade addresses before you leave town. But for now," John added, "make a left turn at this next crossroads, and I will show you a mill, where we take our corn to be ground into meal."

"We have mills at home, but I should like to see yours," Mrs. Maxwell enthused.

"And so you shall," John promised.

CHAPTER THREE

Two HOURS LATER, tired and thirsty, the tourists returned to the livery stable to return the horses and surrey.

"It has been a pleasure," John told the Maxwells, shaking hands.

"And for me, as well," Ellen added.

The older couple smiled indulgently. "We leave for New York in the morning," Maxwell said regretfully, "and then we sail to Scotland. It has been a pleasure to meet you both, although I wish we could have done so sooner."

"Yes," Mrs. Maxwell said solemnly. "How sad to make friends just as we must say goodbye to them."

"We will keep in touch," John said.

"Indeed we will. You must leave your address for us at the desk, and we will leave ours for you," Maxwell told John. "When you have made your fortune, I hope very much to return with my wife to visit you both."

Ellen flushed, because she had a sudden vivid picture of herself with John and several children on a grand estate. John was seeing the same picture. He grinned broadly. "We will look forward to it," he said to them both.

The Maxwells went up to their rooms and John stopped with Ellen at the foot of the stairs, because it would have been unseemly for a gentleman to accompany a lady all the way to her bedroom.

He took her hand in his and held it firmly. "I enjoyed today," he said. "Even in company, you are unique."

"As you are." She smiled up at him from a radiant face surrounded by wisps of loose dark hair that had escaped her bun and the hatpins that held on her wide-brimmed hat.

"We must make sure that we build a proper empire," he teased, "so that the Maxwells can come back to visit."

"I shall do my utmost to assist you," she replied with teasing eyes.

He chuckled. "I have no doubt of that."

"I will see you tomorrow?" she fished.

"Indeed you will. It will be in the afternoon, though," he added regretfully. "I must help move cattle into a new pasture first. It is very dry and we must shift them closer to water."

"Good evening, then," she said gently.

"Good evening." He lifted her hand to his lips in a gesture he'd learned in polite company during his travels.

It had a giddy effect on Ellen. She blushed and laughed nervously and almost stumbled over her own feet going up the staircase.

"Oh, dear," she said, righting herself.

"Not to worry," John assured her, hat in hand, green eyes brimming with mirth. "See?" He looked around his feet and back up at her. "No mud puddles!"

She gave him an exasperated, but amused, look, and went quickly up the staircase. When she made the landing, he was still there, watching.

JOHN AND ELLEN saw each other daily for a week, during which they grew closer. Ellen waited for John in the hotel dining room late the next Friday afternoon, but to her dismay, it was not John who walked directly to her table. It was her father, home unexpectedly early. Nor was he smiling.

He pulled out a chair and sat down, motioning imperiously to a waiter, from whom he ordered coffee and nothing else.

"You are home early," Ellen stammered.

"I am home to prevent a scandal!" he replied curtly. "I've had word from an acquaintance of Sir Sydney's that you were seen flagrantly defying my instructions that you should stay in this hotel during my absence! You have been riding, in the country, alone, with Mr. Jacobs! How dare you create a scandal here!"

The Ellen of only a week ago would have bowed her head meekly and agreed never to disobey him again. But her association with John Jacobs had already stiffened her backbone. He had offered her a new life, a free life, away from the endless social conventions and rules of conduct that kept her father so occupied.

She lifted her eyebrows with hauteur. "And what business of Sir Sydney's friend is my behavior?" she wanted to know.

Her father's eyes widened in surprise. "I beg your pardon?"

"I have no intention of being coupled with Sir Sydney in any way whatsoever," she informed him. "In fact, the man is repulsive and ill-mannered."

It was a rare hint of rebellion, one of just a few he had ever seen in Ellen. He just stared at her, confused and amused, all at once.

"It would seem that your acquaintance with Mr. Jacobs is corrupting you."

"I intend to be further corrupted," she replied coolly. "He has asked me to marry him."

"Child, that is out of the question," he said sharply.

She held up a dainty hand. "I am no child," she informed him, blue eyes flashing. "I am a woman grown. Most of my friends are married with families of their own. I am a spinster, an encumbrance to hear you tell it, of a sort whom men do not rush to escort. I am neither pretty nor accomplished…"

"You are quite wealthy," he inserted bluntly. "Which is, no doubt, why Mr. Jacobs finds you so attractive."

In fact, it was a railroad spur, not money, that John wanted, but she wasn't ready to tell her father that. Let him think what he liked. She knew that John Jacobs found her attractive. It gave her confidence to stand up to her parent for the first time in memory.

"You may disinherit me whenever you like," she said easily, sipping coffee with a steady hand. Her eyes twinkled. "I promise you, it will make no difference to him. He is the sort of man who builds empires from nothing more than hard work and determination. In time, his fortune will rival yours, I daresay."

Terrance Colby was listening now, not blustering. "You are considering his proposal."

She nodded, smiling. "He has painted me a delightful picture of muddy roads, kitchen gardens, heavy labor, cooking over open fires and branding cattle." She chuckled. "In fact, he has offered to let me help him brand cattle in the fall when his second crop of calves drop."

Terrance caught his breath. He waited to speak until

the waiter brought his coffee. He glowered after the retreating figure. "I should have asked for a teacup of whiskey instead," he muttered to himself. His eyes went back to his daughter's face. "Brand cattle?"

She nodded. "Ride horses, shoot a gun…he offered to teach me no end of disgusting and socially unacceptable forms of recreation."

He sat back with an expulsion of breath. "I could have him arrested."

"For what?" she replied.

He was disconcerted by the question. "I haven't decided yet. Corrupting a minor," he ventured.

"I am far beyond the age of consent, Father," she reminded him. She sipped coffee again. "You may disinherit me at will. I will not even need the elegant wardrobes you have purchased for me. I will wear dungarees and high-heeled boots."

His look of horror was now all-consuming. "You will not! Remember your place, Ellen!"

Her eyes narrowed. "My place is what I say it is. I am not property, to be sold or bartered for material gain!"

He was formulating a reply when the sound of heavy footfalls disturbed him into looking up. John Jacobs was standing just to his side, wearing his working gear, including that sinister revolver slung low in a holster slanted across his lean hips.

"Ah," Colby said curtly. "The villain of the piece!"

"I am no villain," John replied tersely. He glanced at Ellen with budding feelings of protectiveness. She looked flushed and angry. "Certainly, I have never given Ellen such pain as that I see now on her face." He looked back at Colby with a cold glare.

Colby began to be impressed. This steely young man

was not impressed by either his wealth or position when Ellen was distressed.

"Do you intend to call me out?" he asked John.

The younger man glanced again at Ellen. "It would be high folly to kill the father of my prospective bride," he said finally. "Of course, I don't have to kill you," he added, pursing his lips and giving Colby's shoulder a quiet scrutiny. "I could simply wing you."

Colby's gaze went to that worn pistol butt. "Do you know how to shoot that hog leg?"

"I could give you references," John drawled. "Or a demonstration, if you prefer."

Colby actually laughed. "I imagine you could. Stop bristling like an angry dog and sit down, Mr. Jacobs. I have ridden hard to get here, thinking my daughter was about to be seduced by a bounder. And I find only an honest suitor who would fight even her own father to protect her. I am quite impressed. Do sit down," he emphasized. "That gentleman by the window looks fit to jump through it. He has not taken his eyes off your gun since you approached me!"

John's hard face broke into a sheepish grin. He pulled out a chair and sat down close to Ellen, his green eyes soft now and possessive as they sketched her flushed, happy face. He smiled at her, tenderly.

Colby ordered coffee for John as well and then sat back to study the determined young man.

"She said you wish to teach her to shoot a gun and brand cattle," Colby began.

"If she wants to, yes," John replied. "I assume you would object...?"

Colby chuckled. "My grandmother shot a gun and

once chased a would-be robber down the streets of a North Carolina town with it. She was a local legend."

"You never told me!" Ellen exclaimed.

He grimaced. "Your mother was very straitlaced, Ellen, like your grandmother Greene," he said. "She wanted no image of my unconventional mother to tempt you into indiscretion." He pursed his lips and chuckled. "Apparently blood will out, as they say." He looked at her with kind eyes. "You have been pampered all your life. Nothing that money could buy has ever been beyond your pocket. It will not be such a life with this man," he indicated John. "Not for a few years, at least," he added with a chuckle. "You remind me of myself, Mr. Jacobs. I did not inherit my wealth. I worked as a farm laborer in my youth," he added, shocking his daughter. "I mucked out stables and slopped hogs for a rich man in our small North Carolina town. There were eight of us children, and no money to be handed down. When I was twelve, I jumped on a freight train and was arrested in New York when I was found in a stock car. I was taken to the manager's office where the owner of the railroad had chanced to venture on a matter of business. I was rude and arrogant, but he must have seen something in me that impressed him. He had a wife, but no children. He took me home with him, had his wife clean me up and dress me properly, and I became his adoptive child. When he died, he left the business to me. By then, I was more than capable of running it."

"Father!" Ellen exclaimed. "You never spoke of your parents. I had no idea…!"

"My parents died of typhoid soon after I left the farm," he confessed. "My brothers and sisters were taken in by cousins. When I made my own fortune, I made sure that they were provided for."

"You wanted a son," she said sorrowfully, "to inherit what you had. And all you got was me."

"Your mother died giving birth to a stillborn son," he confessed. "You were told that she died of a fever, which is partially correct. I felt that you were too young for the whole truth. And your maternal grandmother was horrified when I thought to tell you. Grandmother Greene is very correct and formal." He sighed. "When she knows what you have done, I expect she will be here on the next train to save you, along with however many grandsons she can convince to accompany her."

She nodded slowly, feeling nervous. "She is formidable."

"I wouldn't mind a son, but I do like little girls," John said with a warm smile. "I won't mind if we have daughters."

She flushed, embarrassed.

"Let us speak first of marriage, if you please," Colby said with a wry smile. "What would you like for a wedding present, Mr. Jacobs?"

John was overwhelmed. He hesitated.

"*We* would like a spur line run down to *our* ranch," Ellen said for him, with a wicked grin. "So that we don't have to drive our cattle all the way to Kansas to get them shipped to Chicago. We are going to raise extraordinary beef."

John sighed. "Indeed we are," he nodded, watching her with delight.

"That may take some little time," Colby mused. "What would you like in the meantime?"

"A sidesaddle rig for Ellen, so that she can be comfortable in the saddle," John said surprisingly.

"I do not want a sidesaddle," she informed him curtly. "I intend to ride astride, as I have seen other women do since I came here."

"I have never seen a woman ride in such a manner!" Colby exploded.

"She's thinking of Tess Wallace," John confessed. "She's the wife of old man Tick Wallace, who owns the stagecoach line here. She drives the team and even rides shotgun sometimes. He's twenty years older than she is, but nobody doubts what they feel for each other. She's crazy for him."

"An unconventional woman," Colby muttered.

"As I intend to become. You may give me away at the wedding, and it must be a small, intimate one, and very soon," she added. "I do not wish my husband embarrassed by a gathering of snobby aristocrats."

Her father's jaw dropped. "But the suddenness of the wedding…!"

"I am sorry, Father, but it will be my wedding, and I feel I have a right to ask for what I wish," Ellen said stubbornly. "I have done nothing wrong, so I have nothing to fear. Besides," she added logically, "none of our friends live here, or are in attendance here at the Springs."

Her father sighed. "As you wish, my dear," he said finally, and his real affection for her was evident in the smile he gave her.

John was tremendously impressed, not only by her show of spirit, but by her consideration for him. He was getting quite a bargain, he thought. Then he stopped to ask himself what she was getting, save for a hard life that would age her prematurely, maybe even kill her. He began to frown.

"It will be a harder life than you realize now," John said abruptly, and with a scowl. "We have no conveniences at all...."

"I am not afraid of hard work," Ellen interrupted.

John and Colby exchanged concerned glances. They both knew deprivation intimately. Ellen had never been without a maid or the most luxurious accommodations in her entire life.

"I'll spare you as much as I can," John said after a minute. "But most empires operate sparsely at first."

"I will learn to cook," Ellen said with a chuckle.

"Can you clean a game hen?" her father wanted to know.

She didn't waver. "I can learn."

"Can you haul water from the river and hoe in a garden?" her father persisted. "Because I have no doubt that you will have to do it."

"There will be men to do the lifting," John promised him. "And we will take excellent care of her, sir."

Her father hesitated, but Ellen's face was stiff with determination. She wasn't backing down an inch.

"Very well," he said on a heavy breath. "But if it becomes too much for you, I want to know," he added firmly. "You must promise that, or I cannot sanction your wedding."

"I promise," she said at once, knowing that she would never go to him for help.

He relaxed a little. "Then I will give you a wedding present that will not make your prospective bridegroom chafe too much," he continued. "I'll open an account for you both at the mercantile store. You will need dry goods to furnish your home."

"Oh, Father, thank you!" Ellen exclaimed.

John chuckled. "Thank you, indeed. Ellen will be grateful, but I'll consider it a loan."

"Of course, my boy," Colby replied complacently.

John knew the man didn't believe him. But he was capable of building an empire, even if he was the only one at the table who knew it at that moment. He reached over to shake hands with the older man.

"Within ten years," he told Colby, "we will entertain you in the style to which you are accustomed."

Colby nodded, but he still had reservations. He only hoped he wasn't doing Ellen a disservice. And he still had to explain this to her maternal grandmother, who was going to have a heart attack when she knew what he'd let Ellen do.

But all he said to the couple was, "We shall see."

THEY WERE MARRIED by a justice of the peace, with Terrance Colby and the minister's wife as witnesses. Colby had found a logical reason for the haste of the wedding, pleading his forthcoming trip home and Ellen's refusal to leave Sutherland Springs. The minister, an easygoing, romantic man, was willing to defy convention for a good cause. Colby congratulated John, kissed Ellen, and led them to a buckboard which he'd already had filled with enough provisions to last a month. He'd even included a treadle sewing machine, cloth for dresses and the sewing notions that went with them. Nor had he forgotten Ellen's precious knitting needles and wool yarn, with which she whiled away quiet evenings.

"Father, thank you very much!" Ellen exclaimed when she saw the rig.

"Thank you very much, indeed," John added with a handshake. "I shall take excellent care of her," he promised.

"I'm sure you'll do your best," Colby replied, but he was worried, and it showed.

Ellen kissed him. "You must not be concerned for me," she said firmly, her blue eyes full of censure. "You think I am a lily, but I mean to prove to you that I am like a cactus flower, able to bloom in the most unlikely places."

He kissed her cheek. "If you ever need me…"

"I do know where to send a telegram," she interrupted, and chuckled. "Have a safe trip home."

"I will have your trunks sent out before I leave town," he added.

John helped Ellen into the buckboard in the lacy white dress and veil she'd worn for her wedding, and he climbed up beside her in the only good suit he owned. They were an odd couple, he thought. And considering the shock she was likely to get when she saw where she must live, it would only get worse. He felt guilty for what he was doing. He prayed that the ends would justify the means. He had promised little, and she had asked for nothing. But many couples had started with even less and made a go of their marriages. He meant to keep Ellen happy, whatever it took.

ELLEN JACOBS'S FIRST glimpse of her future home would have been enough to discourage many a young woman from getting out of the buckboard. The shade trees shaded a large, rough log cabin with only one door and a single window and a chimney. Nearby were cactus plants and brush. But there were tiny pink climbing roses in full bloom, and John confessed that he'd brought the bushes here from Georgia planted in a syrup can. The roses delighted her, and made the wilderness look less wild.

Outside the cabin stood a Mexican couple and a black couple, surrounded by children of all ages. They stared and looked very nervous as John helped Ellen down out of the buckboard.

She had rarely interacted with people of color, except as servants in the homes she had visited most of her life. It was new, and rather exciting, to live among them.

"I am Ellen Colby," she introduced herself, and then colored. "I do beg your pardon! I am Ellen Jacobs!"

She laughed, and then they laughed as well.

"We're pleased to meet you, *señora,*" the Mexican man said, holding his broad sombrero in front of him. He grinned as he introduced himself and his small family. "I am Luis Rodriguez. This is my family—my wife Juana, my son Alvaro and my daughters Juanita, Elena and Lupita." They all nodded and smiled.

"And I am Mary Brown," the black woman said gently. "My husband is Isaac. These are my boys, Ben, the oldest, and Joe, the youngest, and my little girl Libby, who is the middle child. We are glad to have you here."

"I am glad to be here," Ellen said.

"But right now, you need to get into some comfortable clothing, Mrs. Jacobs," Mary said. "Come along in. You men go to work and leave us to our own chores," she said, shooing them off.

"Mary, I can't work in these!" John exclaimed defensively.

She reached into a box and pulled out a freshly ironed shirt and patched pants. "You go off behind a tree and put those on, and I'll do my best to chase the moths out of this box so's I can put your suit in it. And mind you don't get red mud in this shirt!"

"Yes, ma'am," he said with a sheepish grin. "See you later, Ellen."

Mary shut the door on him, grinning widely at Ellen. "He is a good man," she told Ellen in all seriousness as she produced the best dress she had and offered it to Ellen.

"No," Ellen said gently, smiling. "I thank you very much for the offer of your dress, but I not only brought a cotton dress of my own—I have brought bolts of fabric and a sewing machine."

There were looks of unadulterated pleasure on all the feminine faces. "New…fabric?" Mary asked haltingly.

"Sewing machine?" her daughter exclaimed.

"In the buckboard," Ellen assured them with a grin.

They vanished like summer mist, out the door. Ellen followed behind them, still laughing at their delight. She'd done the right thing, it seemed—rather, her father had. She might have thought of it first if she'd had the opportunity.

The women and girls went wild over the material, tearing it out of its brown paper wrapping without even bothering to cut the string that held it.

"Alvaro, you and Ben get this sewing machine and Mrs. Jacobs's suitcase into the house right this minute! Girls, bring the notions and the fabric! I'll get the coffee and sugar, but Ben will have to come back for the lard bucket and the flour sack."

"Yes, ma'am," they echoed, and burst out laughing.

THREE HOURS LATER, Ellen was wearing a simple navy skirt with an indigo blouse, fastened high at the neck. She had on lace-up shoes, but she could see that she was going to have to have boots if she was to be any help to John. The cabin was very small, and all of the families would sleep inside, because there were varmints out at night. And not just crawly ones or four-legged ones, she suspected. Mary had told her about the Comanches John and Luis and Isaac had been hunting when a calf was taken. She noted that a loaded shotgun was kept in a corner of the room, and she had no doubt that either of her companions could wield it if necessary. But she would ask John to teach her to shoot it, as well.

"You will have very pretty dresses from this material," Mary sighed as she touched the colored cottons of many prints and designs.

"*We* will have many pretty dresses," Ellen said, busily filling a bobbin for the sewing machine. She looked up at stunned expressions. "Surely you did not think I could use this much fabric by myself? There is enough here for all of us, I should imagine. And it will take less for the girls," she added, with a warm smile at them.

Mary actually turned away, and Ellen was horrified that she'd hurt the other woman's feelings. She jumped up from the makeshift chair John had cobbled together from tree limbs. "Mary, I'm sorry, I…!"

Mary turned back to her, tears running down her cheeks. "It's just, I haven't had a dress of my own, a new dress, in my whole life. Only hand-me-downs from my mistress, and they had to be torn up or used up first."

Ellen didn't know what to say. Her face was shocked.

Mary wiped away the tears. She looked at the other

woman curiously. "You don't know about slaves, do you, Mrs. Ellen?"

"I know enough to be very sorry that some people think they can own other people," she replied carefully. "My family never did."

Mary forced a smile. "Mr. John brought us out here after the war. We been lucky. Two of our kids are lost forever, you know," she added matter-of-factly. "They got sold just before the war. And one of them got beat to death."

Ellen's eyes closed. She shuddered. It was overwhelming. Tears ran down her cheeks.

"Oh, now, Mrs., don't you...don't you do that!" Mary gathered her close and rocked her. "Don't you cry. Wherever my babies gone, they free now, don't you see. Alive or dead, they free."

The tears ran even harder.

"It was just as bad for Juana," Mary said through her own tears. "Two of her little boys got shot. This man got drunk and thought they was Indians. He just killed them right there in the road where they was playing, and he didn't even look back. He rode off laughing. Luis told the *federales,* but they couldn't find the man. That was years ago, before Mr. John's uncle hired Luis to work here, but Juana never forgot them little boys."

Ellen drew back and pulled a handkerchief out of her sleeve. She wiped Mary's eyes and smiled sadly. "We live in a bad world."

Mary smiled. "It's gonna get better," she said. "You wait and see."

"Better," Juana echoed, nodding, smiling. *"Mas bueno."*

"Mas...bueno?" Ellen repeated.

Juana chuckled. "¡!Vaya! Muy bien! Very good!"

Mary smiled. "You just spoke your first words of Spanish!"

"Perhaps you can teach me to speak Spanish," Ellen said to Juana.

"Señora, it will be my pleasure!" the woman answered, and smiled beautifully.

"I expect to learn a great deal, and very soon," Ellen replied.

THAT WAS AN UNDERSTATEMENT. During her first week of residence, she became an integral part of John's extended family. She learned quite a few words of Spanish, including some range language that shocked John when she repeated it to him with a wicked grin.

"You stop that," he chastised. "Your father will have me shot if he hears you!"

She only chuckled, helping Mary put bread on the table. She was learning to make bread that didn't bounce, but it was early days yet. "My father thinks I will be begging him to come and get me within two weeks. He is in for a surprise!"

"I got the surprise," John had to admit, smiling at her. "You fit right in that first day." He looked from her to the other women, all wearing new dresses that they'd pieced on Ellen's sewing machine. He shook his head. "You three ought to open a dress shop in town."

Ellen glanced at Mary and Juana with pursed lips and twinkling eyes. "You know, that's not really such a bad idea, John," she said after a minute. "It would make us a little extra money. We could buy more barbed wire and we might even be able to afford a milk cow!"

John started to speak, but Mary and Juana jumped right in, and before he ate the first piece of bread, the women were already making plans.

CHAPTER FOUR

ELLEN HAD JOHN drive her into town the following Saturday, to the dry goods store. She spoke with Mr. Alton, the owner.

"I know there must be a market for inexpensive dresses in town, Mr. Alton," she said, bright-eyed. "You order them and keep them in stock, but the ones you buy are very expensive, and most ranch women can't afford them. Suppose I could supply you with simple cotton dresses, ready-made, at half the price of the ones you special order for customers?"

He lifted both eyebrows. "But, Mrs. Jacobs, your father is a wealthy man…!"

"My husband is not," she replied simply. "I must help him as I can." She smiled. "I have a knack for sewing, Mr. Alton, and I think I do quite good work. I also have two helpers who are learning how to use the machine. Would you let me try?"

He hesitated, adding up figures in his head. "All right," he said finally. "You bring me about six dresses, two each of small, medium and large ones, and we will see how they sell."

She grinned. "Done!" She went to the bolts of fabric he kept. "You must allow me credit, so that I can buy the material to make them with, and I will pay you back from my first orders."

He hesitated again. Then he laughed. She was very shrewd. But, he noticed that the dress she was wearing was quite well-made. His women customers had complained about the lack of variety and simplicity in his ready-made dresses, which were mostly for evening and not everyday.

"I will give you credit," he said after a minute. He shook his head as he went to cut the cloth she wanted. "You are a shrewd businesswoman, Mrs. Jacobs," he said. "I'll have to watch myself, or I may end up working for you!"

Which amused her no end.

John was dubious about his wife's enterprise, but Ellen knew what she was doing. Within three weeks, she and the women had earned enough money with their dressmaking to buy not one, but two Jersey milk cows with nursing calves. These John was careful to keep separate from his Hereford bull. But besides the milk, they made butter and buttermilk, which they took into town with their dresses and sold to the local restaurant.

"I told you it would work," Ellen said to John one afternoon when she'd walked out to the makeshift corral where he and the men were branding new calves.

He smiled down at her, wiping sweat from his face with the sleeve of his shirt. "You are a wonder," he murmured with pride. "We're almost finished here. Want to learn to ride?"

"Yes!" she exclaimed. But she looked down at her cotton dress with a sigh. "But not in this, I fear."

John's eyes twinkled. "Come with me."

He led her to the back of the cabin, where he pulled out a sack he'd hidden there. He offered it to her.

She opened it and looked inside. There was a man's cotton shirt, a pair of boots, and a pair of dungarees in it. She unfolded the dungarees and held them up to herself. "They'll just fit!" she exclaimed.

"I had Mr. Alton at the dry goods store measure one of your dresses for the size. He said they should fit even after shrinkage when you wash them."

"Oh, John, thank you!" she exclaimed. She stood on tiptoe and kissed him on the cheek.

He chuckled. "Get them on, then, and I'll teach you to mount a horse. I've got a nice old one that Luis brought with him. He's gentle."

"I won't be a minute!" she promised, darting back into the cabin.

John was at the corral when she came back out. She'd borrowed one of John's old hats and it covered most of her face as well as her bundled-up hair. She looked like a young boy in the rig, and he chuckled.

"Do I look ridiculous?" she worried.

"You look fine," he said diplomatically, his eyes twinkling. "Come along and meet Jorge."

He brought forward a gentle-looking old chestnut horse who lowered his head and nudged at her hand when she extended it. She stroked his forehead and smiled.

"Hello, old fellow," she said softly. "We're going to be great friends, aren't we?"

John pulled the horse around by its bridle and taught Ellen how to mount like a cowboy. Then, holding the reins, he led her around the yard, scattering their new flock of chickens along the way.

"They won't lay if we frighten them," Ellen worried.

He looked up at her with a grin. "How did you know that?"

"Mary taught me."

"She and Juana are teaching you a lot of new skills," he mused. "I liked the biscuits this morning, by the way."

Her heart skipped. "How did you know that I made them?"

"Because you watched every bite I took."

"Oh, dear."

He only laughed. "I am constantly amazed by you," he confessed as they turned away from the cabin and went toward the path that led through the brush to a large oak tree. "Honestly, I never thought you'd be able to live in such deprivation. Especially after... Ellen?"

He'd heard a faint scraping sound, followed by a thud. When he turned around, Ellen was sitting up in the dirt, looking stunned.

He threw the reins over the horse's head and ran to where she was sitting, his heart in his throat. "Ellen, are you hurt?!"

She glared up at him. "Did you not notice the tree limb, John?" she asked with a meaningful glance in its direction.

"Obviously not," he murmured sheepishly. "Did you?" he added.

She burst out laughing. "Only when it hit me."

He chuckled as he reached down and lifted her up into his arms. It was the first time she'd been picked up in her adult life, and she gasped, locking her hands behind his neck so that she didn't fall.

His green eyes met her blue ones at point blank range. The laughter vanished as suddenly as it had come. He studied her pert little nose, her high cheek-bones, her pretty bow of a mouth. She was looking, too, her gaze faintly possessive as she noted the hard, strong lines of his face and the faint scars she found there. His eyes were very green at the proximity, and his mouth looked hard and firm. He had high cheekbones, too, and a broad forehead. His hair was thick under the wide-brimmed hat he wore, and black. His ears were, like his nose, of imposing size. The hands supporting her were big, too, like his booted feet.

"I have never been carried since I was a child," she said in a hushed, fascinated tone.

"Well, I don't usually make a practice of carrying women, either," he confessed. His chiseled lips split in a smile. "You don't weigh much."

"I am far too busy becoming an entrepreneur to gain weight," she confessed.

"A what?"

She explained the word.

"You finished school, I reckon," he guessed.

She nodded. "I wanted to go to college, but Father does not think a woman should be overeducated."

"Bull," John said inelegantly. "My mother educated herself and even learned Latin, which she taught me. If we have daughters, they'll go to college."

She beamed, thinking of children. "I should like to have children."

He pursed his lips and lifted an eyebrow. His smile was sheer wickedness.

She laughed and buried her face in his throat, embarrassed. But he didn't draw back. His arms contracted around her and she felt his breath catch as he enveloped her soft breasts against the hard wall of his chest.

She felt unsettled. Her arms tightened around his strong neck and she shivered. She had never been held so close to a man's body. It was disconcerting. It was… delightful.

His cheek slid against hers so that he could find her soft lips with his mouth. He kissed her slowly, gently, with aching respect. When he pulled back, her lips followed. With a rough groan, he kissed her again. This time, there was less respect and more blatant hunger in the mouth that ravished hers.

She moaned softly, which brought him to his senses immediately. He drew back, his green eyes glittering with feeling. He wasn't breathing steadily anymore. Neither was she.

"We would have to climb a tree to find much privacy, and even then, the boys would probably be sitting in the branches," he said in a hunted tone.

She understood what he meant and flushed. But she laughed, too, because it was very obvious that he found her as attractive as she found him. She smiled into his eyes.

"One day, we will have a house as big as a barn, with doors that lock!" she assured him.

He chuckled softly. "Yes. But for now, we must be patient." He put her back on her feet with a long sigh. "Not that I feel patient," he added rakishly.

She laughed. "Nor I." She looked up at him demurely. "I suppose you have kissed a great many girls."

"Not so many," he replied. "And none as unique as you." His eyes were intent on her flushed face. "I made the best bargain of my life when I enticed you into marriage, Ellen Colby."

"Thank you," she said, stumbling over the words.

He pushed back a lock of disheveled dark hair that had escaped from under her hat. "It never occurred to me that a city woman, an aristocrat, would be able to survive living like this. I have felt guilty any number of times when I watched you carry water to the house, and wash clothes as the other women do. I know that you had maids to do such hard labor when you lived at home."

"I am young and very strong," she pointed out. "Besides, I have never found a man whom I respected enough to marry, until now. I believe you will make an empire here, in these wilds. But even if I didn't believe it, I would still be proud to take your name. You are unique, also."

His eyes narrowed. He bent again and kissed her eyelids shut, with breathless tenderness. "I will work hard to be worthy of your trust, Ellen. I will try never to disappoint you."

She smiled. "And you will promise never to run me under oak limbs again?" she teased.

"You imp!" He laughed uproariously, hugging her to him like a big brother. "You scamp! What joy you bring to my days."

"And you to mine," she replied, hugging him back.

"Daddy! Mr. John and Mrs. Ellen are spooning right here in the middle of the road!" one of Isaac and Mary's boys yelled.

"Scatter, you varmints, I'm kissing my wife!" John called in mock-rage.

There was amused laughter and the sound of brush rustling.

"So much for the illusion of privacy," Ellen said,

pulling back from him with a wistful sigh. "Shall we get back to the business at hand? Where's my horse?"

John spied him in the brush, munching on some small green growth of grass he had found there. "He's found something nice to eat, I'll wager," he said.

"I'll fetch him," Ellen laughed, and started into the brush.

"Ellen, stop!"

John's voice, full of authority and fear, halted her with one foot in the act of rising. She stopped and stood very still. He was cursing, using words Ellen had never heard in her life. "Isaac!" he tacked onto the end, "fetch my shotgun! Hurry!"

Ellen closed her eyes. She didn't have to look down to know why he was so upset. She could hear a rustling sound, like crackling leaves, like softly frying bacon. She had never seen a rattlesnake, but during her visit to Texas with her father, she had heard plenty about them from local people. Apparently they liked to lie in wait and strike out at unsuspecting people who came near them. They could cause death with a bite, or extreme pain and sickness. Ellen was mortally afraid of snakes, in any event. But John would save her. She knew he would.

There were running feet. Crashing brush. The sound of something being thrown and caught, and then the unmistakable sound of a hammer being pulled back.

"Stand very still, darling," John told her huskily. "Don't move…a muscle!"

She swallowed, her eyes still closed. She held her breath. There was a horrifying report, like the sound of thunder and lightning striking, near her feet. Flying dirt hit her dungarees. She heard furious thrashing and opened her eyes. For the first time, she looked down. A huge rattlesnake lay dismembered nearby, still writhing in the hot sun.

"Ellen, it didn't strike you?" John asked at once, wrapping her up in the arm that wasn't supporting the shotgun. "You're all right?"

"I am, thanks to you," she whispered, almost collapsing against him. "What a scare!"

"For both of us," he said curtly. He bent and kissed the breath out of her, still shaken from the experience. "Don't ever march into the brush without looking first!"

She smiled under his lips. "You could have caught the brush on fire with that language," she murmured reproachfully. "Indeed, I think the snake was shocked to death by it!"

He laughed, and kissed her harder. She kissed him back, only belatedly aware of running feet and exclamations when the snake was spotted.

He linked his big hand into her small one. "Luis, bring the horse, if you please. I think we've had enough riding practice for one day!"

"Si, señor," Juan agreed with a chuckle.

THAT EVENING AROUND the campfire all the talk was of the close call Ellen had with the snake.

"You're on your way to being a living legend," John told her as they roasted the victim of his shotgun over the darting orange and yellow tongues of flame. "Not to mention the provider of this delicious delicacy. Roasted rattler."

Ellen, game as ever, was soon nibbling on her own chunk of it. "It tastes surprisingly like chicken," she remarked.

John glowered at her. "It does not."

She grinned at him, and his heart soared. He grinned back.

"If you want another such treat, you will have to teach me how to shoot a gun," she proposed. "I am never walking into a rattler's mouth again, not even to provide you with supper!"

"Fair deal," he responded, while the others laughed uproariously.

IN THE DAYS that followed, Ellen learned with hard work and sore muscles the rudiments of staying on a horse through the long days of watching over John's growing herd of cattle.

She also learned how not to shoot a shotgun. Her first acquaintance with the heavy double-barreled gun was a calamity. Having shouldered it too lightly, the report slammed the butt back into her shoulder and gave her a large, uncomfortable bruise. They had to wait until it healed before she could try again. The one good thing was that it made churning butter almost impossible, and she grinned as she watched Mary shoulder that chore.

"You hurt your shoulder on purpose," Mary chided with laughing dark eyes. "So you wouldn't have to push this dasher up and down in the churn."

"You can always get Isaac to teach you how to shoot, and use the same excuse," Ellen pointed out.

Mary grinned. "Not me. I am not going near a shotgun, not even to get out of such chores!"

Juana agreed wholeheartedly. "Too much bang!"

"I'll amen that," Mary agreed.

"I like it," Ellen mused. She liked even more knowing that John was afraid for her, that he cared about her.

He'd even called her "darling" when he'd shot the snake. He wasn't a man to use endearments normally, which made the verbal slip even more pleasurable. She'd been walking around in a fog of pleasure ever since the rattler almost bit her. She was in love. She hoped that he was feeling something similar, but he'd been much too busy with work to hang around her, except at night. And then there was a very large audience. She sighed, thinking that privacy must be the most valuable commodity on earth. Although she was growing every day fonder of her companions, she often wished them a hundred miles away, so that she had even an hour alone with her husband. But patience was golden, she reminded herself. She must wait and hope for that to happen. Right now, survival itself was a struggle.

So was the shotgun. Her shoulder was well enough for a second try a week later. Two new complications, unbeknownst to Ellen, had just presented themselves. There were new mud puddles in the front yard, and her father had come to town and rented a buggy to ride out to visit his only child.

Ellen aimed the shotgun at a tree. The resulting kick made the barrel fly up. A wild turkey, which had been sitting on a limb, suddenly fell to the ground in a limp heap. And Ellen went backward right into the deepest mud puddle the saturated yard could boast.

At that particular moment, her father pulled up in front of the cabin.

Her father looked from Ellen to the turkey to the mud puddle to John. "I see that you are teaching my daughter to bathe and hunt at the same time," he remarked.

Ellen scrambled to her feet, wiping her hair back with a muddy hand. She was so disheveled, and so dirty, that it was hard for her immaculate father to find her face at all.

He grimaced. "Ellen, darling, I think it might not be a bad idea if you came home with me," he began uneasily.

She tossed her head, slinging mud onto John, who was standing next to her looking concerned. "I'm only just learning to shoot, Father," she remarked proudly. "No one is proficient at first. Isn't that so, John?"

"Uh, yes," John replied, but without his usual confidence.

Her father looked from one to the other and then to the turkey. "I suppose buying meat from the market in town is too expensive?" he asked.

"I like variety. We had rattlesnake last week, in fact," Ellen informed him. "It was delicious."

Her father shook his head. "Your grandmother is going to have heart failure if I tell her what I've seen here. And young man, this house of yours…!" He spread an expansive hand helplessly.

"The sooner we get *our* spur line," Ellen told her father, "the quicker we will have a real house instead of merely a cabin."

John nodded hopefully.

Terrance Colby sighed heavily. "I'll see what I can do," he promised.

They both smiled. "Will you stay for dinner?" Ellen invited, glancing behind her. She grinned. "We're having turkey!"

Her father declined, unwilling to share the sad surroundings that his daughter seemed to find so exciting. There were three families living in that one cabin, he noted, and he wasn't certain that he was democratic enough to appreciate such close quarters. It didn't take a mind reader to note that Ellen and John had no privacy. That might be an advantage, he mused, if Ellen decided to come home. There would be no complications. But she seemed happy as a lark, and unless he was badly mistaken, that young man John Jacobs was delighted with her company. His wife's mother was not going to be happy when he got up enough nerve to tell her what had happened to Ellen. She was just on her way home from a vacation in Italy. Perhaps the ship would be blown off course and she would not get home for several months, he mused. Otherwise, Ellen was going to have a very unhappy visitor in the near future.

He did make time to see John's growing herd of cattle, and he noticed that the young man had a fine lot of very healthy steers. He'd already seen how enterprising Ellen was with her dressmaking and dairy sales. Now he saw a way to help John become quickly self-sufficient.

WORD CAME THE following week that Ellen's father was busy buying up right of way for the spur that would run to John's ranch. Not only that, he had become a customer for John's yearling steers, which he planned to feed to the laborers who were already hard at work on another stretch of his railroad. The only difficulty was that John was going to have to drive the steers north to San Antonio for Terrance Colby. Colby would be there waiting for him in a week. That wasn't a long cattle drive, certainly not as far as Kansas, but south Texas was still untamed and dangerous country. It would be risky. But John knew it would be worth the risk if he could deliver the beef.

So John and his men left, reluctantly on John's part,

to drive the steers north. He and his fellow cowhands went around to all the other ranches, gathering up their steers, making sure they appropriated only the cattle that bore their 3J brand for the drive.

"I don't want to go," John told Ellen as they stood together, briefly alone, at the corral. "But I must protect our investment. There will be six of us to drive the herd, and we are all armed and well able to handle any trouble. Isaac and the older boys are going with me, but Luis will stay here to look after the livestock and all of you."

She sighed, smoothing her arms over the sleeves of his shirt, enjoying the feel of the smooth muscles under it. "I do not like the idea of you going away. But I know that it is necessary, so I'll be brave."

"I don't like leaving you, either," he said bluntly. He bent and kissed her hungrily. "When I return, perhaps we can afford a single night away from here," he whispered roughly. "I am going mad to have you in my arms without a potential audience!"

"As I am," she choked, kissing him back hungrily.

He lifted her clear of the ground in his embrace, flying as they kissed without restraint. Finally, he forced himself to put her back down and he stepped away. There was a ruddy flush on his high cheekbones, and his green eyes were fierce. Her face was equally flushed, but her eyes were soft and dreamy, and her mouth was swollen.

She smiled up at him bravely, despite her concern. "Don't get shot."

He grimaced. "I'll do my best. You stay within sight of the cabin and Luis, even when you're milking those infernal cows. And don't go to town without him."

She didn't mention that it would be suicide to take Luis away from guarding the cattle, even for that long. She and the women would have to work something out, so that they could sell their dresses and butter and milk in town. But she would spare him the worry.

"We'll be very careful," she promised.

He sighed, his hand resting on the worn butt of his .45 caliber pistol. "We'll be back as soon as humanly possible. Your father…"

"If he comes to town, I'll go there to wait for you," she promised, a lie, because she'd never leave Mary and Juana by themselves, even with Luis and a shotgun around.

"Possibly that's what you should do, anyway," he murmured thoughtfully.

"I can't leave here now," she replied. "There's too much at stake. I'll help take care of our ranch. You take care of our profit margin."

He chuckled, surprised out of his worries. "I'll be back before you miss me too much," he said, bending to kiss her again, briefly. "Stay close to the cabin."

"I will. Have a safe trip."

He swung into the saddle, shouting for Isaac and the boys. The women watched them ride away. The cattle had already been pooled in a nearby valley, and the drovers were ready to get underway. As Ellen watched her tall husband ride away, she realized why he'd wanted his railroad spur so badly. Not only was it dangerous to drive cattle a long way to a railhead, but the potential risk to the men and animals was great. Not only was there a constant threat from thieves, there were floods and thunderstorms that could decimate herds. She prayed that John and Isaac and the men going with them would be safe. It was just as well that Luis was staying at the ranch to help safeguard the breeding bulls and cows, and the calves that were too young for market. Not that she was going to shirk her own responsibilities, Ellen thought stubbornly. Nobody was stealing anything around here while she could get her hands on a gun!

THE THREAT CAME unexpectedly just two days after John and the others had left south Texas for San Antonio on the cattle drive.

Ellen had just carried a bucketful of milk to the kitchen when she peered out the open, glassless window at two figures on horseback, watching the cabin. She called softly to Juana and Mary.

Juana crossed herself. "It is Comanches!" she exclaimed. "They come to raid the cattle!"

"Well, they're not raiding them today," Ellen said angrily. "I'll have to ride out and get Luis and the boys," she said. "There's nothing else for it, and I'll have to go bareback. I'll never have time to saddle a horse with them sitting out there."

"It is too dangerous," Juana exclaimed. "You can hardly ride a saddled horse, and those men are Comanches. They are the finest riders of any men, even my Luis. You will never outrun them!"

Ellen muttered under her breath. They had so few cattle that even the loss of one or two could mean the difference between bankruptcy and survival. Well, she decided, there was only one thing to do. She grabbed up the shotgun, loaded it, and started out the back door, still in her dress and apron.

"No!" Mary almost screamed. "Are you crazy? Do you know what they do to white women?!"

Ellen didn't say a word. She kept walking, her steps firm and sure.

She heard frantic calls behind her, but she didn't listen. She and John had a ranch. These were her cattle as much as his. She wasn't about to let any thieves come and carry off her precious livestock!

The two Comanches saw her coming and gaped. They didn't speak. They sat on their horses with their eyes fixed, wide, at the young woman lugging a shotgun toward them.

One of them said something to the other one, who laughed and nodded.

She stopped right in front of them, lifted the shotgun, sighted along it and cocked it.

"This is my ranch," she said in a firm, stubborn tone. "You aren't stealing my cattle!"

There was pure admiration in their eyes. They didn't reach for the rifles lying across their buckskinned laps. They didn't try to ride her down. They simply watched her.

The younger of the two Indians had long pigtails and a lean, handsome face. His eyes, she noted curiously, were light.

"We have not come to steal cattle," the young one said in passable English. "We have come to ask Big John for work."

"Work?" she stammered.

He nodded. "We felt guilty that we butchered one of his calves. We had come far and were very hungry. We will work to pay for the calf. We hear from the Mexican people that he is also fair," he added surprisingly. "We know that he looks only at a man's work. He does not consider himself better than men of other colors. This is very strange. We do not understand it. Your people have just fought a terrible war because you wanted to own other people who had dark skin. Yet Big John lives with these people. Even with the Mexicans. He treats them as family."

"Yes," she said. She slowly uncocked the shotgun and lowered it to her side. "That is true."

The younger one smiled at her. "We know more about horses than even his vaquero, who knows much," he said without conceit. "We will work hard. When we pay back the cost of the calf, he can pay us what he thinks is fair."

She chuckled. "It's not really a big cabin, and it has three families living in it," she began.

They laughed. "We can make a teepee," the older one said, his English only a little less accented than the younger one's.

"I say," she exclaimed, "can you teach me to shoot a bow?!"

The younger one threw back his head and laughed uproariously. "Even his woman is brave," he told the older one. "Now do you believe me? This man is not as others with white skin."

"I believe you."

"Come along, then," Ellen said, turning. "I'll introduce you to... Luis! Put that gun down!" she exclaimed angrily when she saw the smaller man coming toward them with two pistols leveled. "These are our two new horse wranglers," she began. She stopped. "What are your names?" she asked.

"I am called Thunder," the young one said. "He is Red Wing."

"I am Ellen Jacobs," she said, "and that is Luis. Say hello, Luis."

The Mexican lowered his pistols and reholstered them with a blank stare at Ellen.

"Say hello," she repeated.

"Hello," he obliged, and he nodded.

The Comanches nodded back. They rode up to the cabin and dismounted. The women in the cabin peered out nervously.

"Luis will show you where to put your horses," Ellen told them. "We have a lean-to. Someday, we will have a barn!"

"Need bigger teepee first," Red Wing murmured, eyeing the cabin. "Bad place to live. Can't move house when floor get dirty."

"Yes, well, it's warm," Ellen said helplessly.

The young Comanche, Thunder, turned to look at her. "You are brave," he said with narrow light eyes. "Like my woman."

"She doesn't live with you?" she asked hesitantly.

He smiled gently. "She is stubborn, and wants to live in a cabin far away," he replied. "But I will bring her back here one day." He nodded and followed after Luis with his friend.

Juana and Mary came out of the cabin with worried expressions. "You going to let Indians live with us?" Juana exclaimed. "They kill us all!"

"No, they won't," Ellen assured them. "You'll see. They're going to be an asset!"

CHAPTER FIVE

THE COMANCHES DID know more about horses than even Luis did, and they were handy around the place. They hunted game, taught Luis how to tan hides, and set about building a teepee out behind the cabin.

"Very nice," Ellen remarked when it was finished. "It's much roomier than the cabin."

"Easy to keep clean," Red Wing agreed. "Floor get dirty, move teepee."

She laughed. He smiled, going off to help Thunder with a new corral Juan was building.

JOHN RODE BACK in with Isaac and stopped short at the sight of a towering teepee next to the cabin he'd left two weeks earlier.

His hand went to his pistol as he thought of terrible possibilities that would explain its presence.

But Ellen came running out of the cabin, followed by Mary and Juana, laughing and waving.

John kicked his foot out of the stirrup of his new saddle and held his arm down to welcome Ellen as she leaped up into his arms. He kissed her hungrily, feeling as if he'd come home for the first time in his life.

He didn't realize how long that kiss lasted until he felt eyes all around him. He lifted his head to find two tall Comanches standing shoulder to shoulder with Juan and the younger boys and girls of the group, along with Juana and Mary.

"Bad habit," Thunder remarked disapprovingly.

"Bound to upset horse," Red Wing agreed, nodding.

"What the hell…!" John exclaimed.

"They're our new horse wranglers," Ellen said quickly. "That's Thunder, and that's Red Wing."

"They taught us how to make parfleche bags," Juana's eldest daughter exclaimed, showing one with beautiful beadwork.

"And how to make bows and arrows!" the next youngest of Isaac's sons seconded, showing his.

"And quivers," Luis said, resigned to being fired for what John would surely consider bad judgment in letting two Comanches near the women. He stood with his sombrero against his chest. "You may fire me if you wish."

"If you fire me, I'm going with them," Isaac's second son replied, pointing toward the Indians.

John shook his head, laughing uproariously. "I expect there'll be a lynch mob out here any day now," he sighed.

Everybody grinned.

Ellen beamed up at him. "Well, they certainly do know how to train horses, John," she said.

"Your woman meet us with loaded shotgun," Red Wing informed him. "She has strong spirit."

"And great heart," Thunder added. "She says we can work for you. We stay?"

John sighed. "By all means. All we need now is an Eskimo," he murmured to Ellen under his breath.

She looped her arms around his neck and kissed him. "Babies would be nice," she whispered.

He went scarlet, and everyone laughed.

"I GOT ENOUGH for the steers to buy a new bull," John told her. "Saddles for the horses we have, and four new horses," he added. "They're coming in with the rest of the drovers. I rode ahead to make sure you were all right."

She cuddled close to him as they stood out behind the cabin in a rare moment alone. "We had no trouble at all. Well, except for the Comanches, but they turned out to be friends anyway."

"You could have blown me over when I saw that teepee," he confessed. "We've had some hard battles with Comanches in the past, over stolen livestock. And I know for a fact that two Comanches ate one of my calves…"

"They explained that," she told him contentedly. "They were hungry, but they didn't want to steal. They came here to work out the cost of the calf, and then to stay on, if you'll keep them. I think they decided that it's better to join a strong foe than oppose him. That was the reason they gave me, at least."

"Well, I must admit, these two Comanches are unusual."

"The younger one has light eyes."

"I noticed." He didn't add what he was certain of—that these two Comanches were the fugitives that the deputy marshal in Sutherland Springs had been looking for. Fortunately for them, James Graham had headed up beyond San Antonio to pursue them, acting on what now seemed to be a very bad tip.

She lifted her head and looked up at him. "They rode up and just sat there. I loaded my shotgun and went out to see what they wanted."

"You could have been killed," he pointed out.

"It's what you would have done, in my place," she reminded him, smiling gently. "I'm not afraid of much. And I've learned from you that appearances can be deceptive."

"You take chances."

"So do you."

He sighed. "You're learning bad habits from me."

She smiled and snuggled close. "Red Wing is going to make us a teepee of our own very soon." She kissed him, and was kissed back hungrily.

"Yesterday not be soon enough for that teepee," came a droll accented voice from nearby.

Red Wing was on the receiving end of two pairs of glaring eyes. He shrugged and walked off noiselessly, chuckling to himself.

John laughed. "Amen," he murmured.

"John, there's just one other little thing," Ellen murmured as she stood close to him.

"What now? You hired a gunslinger to feed the chickens?"

"I don't know any gunslingers. Be serious."

"All right. What?"

"My grandmother sent me a telegram. She's coming out here to save me from a life of misery and poverty."

He lifted his head. "Really!"

She drew in a soft breath. "I suppose she'll faint dead away when she sees this place, but I'm not going to be dragged back East by her or an army. I belong here."

"Yes, you do," John replied. "Although you certainly deserve better than this, Ellen," he said softly. He touched her disheveled hair. "I promise you, it's only going to get better."

She smiled. "I know that. We're going to have an empire, all our own."

"You bet we are."

"Built with our own two hands," she murmured, reaching up to kiss him, "and the help of our friends. All we need is each other."

"Need teepee worse," came Red Wing's voice again.

"Listen here," John began.

"Your horse got colic," the elder of the Comanches stood his ground. "What you feed him?"

"He ate corn," John said belligerently. "I gave him a feed bucket full!"

The older man scoffed. "No wonder he got colic. I fix."

"Corn is good for horses, and I know what to do for colic!"

"Sure. Not feed horse corn. Feed him grass. We build teepee tomorrow."

John still had his mouth open when the older man stalked off again.

"Indian ponies only eat grass," Ellen informed him brightly. "They think grain is bad for horses."

"You've learned a lot," he remarked.

"More than you might realize," she said dryly. She reached up to John's ear. "These two Comanches are running from the army. But I don't think they did anything bad, and I told Mr. Alton that I saw two Comanches heading north at a dead run. He told the..."

"...deputy marshal," he finished for her, exasperated.

"When you get to know them, you'll think they're good people, too," she assured him. "Besides, they're teaching me things I can't learn anywhere else. I can track a deer," she counted off her new skills, "weave a mat, make a bed out of pine straw, do beadwork, shoot a bow and arrow, and tan a hide."

"Good Lord, woman!" he exclaimed, impressed.

She grinned. "And I'm going to learn to hunt just as soon as you take me out with my shotgun."

He sighed. This was going to become difficult if any of her people stopped by to check on her. He didn't want to alienate them, but this couldn't continue.

"Ellen, what do you think about schooling?" he asked gently.

She blinked. "Excuse me?"

"Well, do any of the children know how to read and write?"

She hadn't considered that. "I haven't asked, but I don't expect they can. It was not legal for slaves to be taught such things, and I know that Juana can't even read Spanish, although it is her native tongue."

"The world we build will need educated people," he said thoughtfully. "It must start with the children, with this new generation. Don't you agree?"

"Yes," she said, warming quickly to the idea. "Educated people will no longer have to work at menial jobs, where they are at the mercy of others."

"That is exactly what I think. So, why don't you start giving the children a little book learning, in the evenings, after supper?" he suggested.

She smiled brightly. "You know, that's a very good idea. But, I have no experience as a teacher."

"All you will need are some elementary books and determination," he said. "I believe there is a retired schoolteacher in Victoria, living near the blacksmith. Shall I take you to see him?"

She beamed. "Would you?"

"Indeed I would. We'll go up there tomorrow," he replied, watching her consider the idea. If nothing else, it would spare her the astonished surprise of her people if they ever came to visit and found Ellen in dungarees and muddy boots skinning out a deer.

He drove her to Victoria the next morning in the small, dilapidated buggy he'd managed to afford from his cattle sales, hitched to one of the good horses he'd also acquired. Fortunately it took to pulling a buggy right away. Some horses didn't, and people died in accidents when they panicked and ran away.

The schoolteacher was long retired, but he taught Ellen the fundamentals she would need to educate small children. He also had a basic reader, a grammar book and a spelling book, which he gave to Ellen with his blessing. She clutched them like priceless treasure all the way back down the dusty road to the 3J Ranch.

"Do you think the Brown and the Rodriguez families will let me teach the children?" she wondered, a little worried after the fact. "They might not believe in education."

"Luis and Isaac can't even sign a paper," he told her. "They have to make an 'x' on a piece of paper and have me witness it. If they ever leave the ranch, they need to know how to read and write so that nobody will take advantage of them."

She looked at him with even more admiration than usual. He was very handsome to her, very capable and strong. She counted her blessings every single day that he'd thought her marriageable.

"You really care for them, don't you?" she asked softly.

"When the Union Army came through Atlanta, they

burned everything in sight," he recalled, his face hardening. "Not just the big plantations where slaves were kept. They burned poor white people's houses, because they thought we all had slaves down south." He laughed coldly. "Sharecroppers don't own anything. Even the house we lived in belonged to the plantation owner. They set it ablaze and my sister and mother were trapped inside. They burned to death while my other sister and I stood outside and watched." He touched his lean cheek, where the old scars were still noticeable. "I tried to kill the cavalry officer responsible, but his men saved him. They gave me these," he touched his cheek. "I never kept slaves. I hid Isaac and Mary in the root cellar when they ran away from the overseer. I couldn't save their oldest son, but Mary was pregnant. She and Isaac saved me from the Union Army," he said with a sigh. "They pleaded for my life. Shocked the cavalry into sparing me and my oldest sister. Isaac helped me bury my mother and my younger sister." He looked down at her soft, compassionate expression. "My sister went to North Carolina to live with a cousin, but I wanted to go to my uncle in Texas. Isaac and Mary had no place else to go, so they traveled with me. They said they wanted to start over, but they didn't fool me. They came with me to save me from the Union Army if I got in trouble. Those two never forget a debt. I owe them everything. My life. That's why they're partners with me."

"And how did you meet Luis and Juana?" she asked.

"Luis was the only cowboy my uncle had who wasn't robbing him blind. Luis told me what the others had done, and I fired the lot. I took care of my uncle, with their help, and rounded up stray calves to start my herd." He chuckled. "The cabin was the only structure on the place. It got real crowded when Isaac and Mary moved in with me. Juana and Luis were going to live in the brush, but I insisted that we could all manage. We have. But it hasn't been easy."

"And now the Comanches are building teepees for us," she told him. "They've been hunting constantly to get enough skins. We're going to have privacy for the very first time. I mean…" She flushed at her own forwardness.

He reached for her small hand and held it tight. His eyes burned into hers. "I want nothing more in the world than to be alone with you, Camellia Ellen Jacobs," he said huskily. "The finest thing I ever did in my life was have the good sense to marry you!"

"Do you really think so?" she asked happily. "I am no beauty…"

"You have a heart as big as all outdoors and the courage of a wolf. I wouldn't trade you for a debutante."

She beamed, leaning against his broad shoulder. "And I would not trade you for the grandest gentleman who ever lived. Although I expect you will make a fine gentleman, when we have made our fortune."

He kissed her forehead tenderly. "You are my fortune," he said huskily.

"You mean, because my father is giving us a railroad spur for a wedding present," she said, confused.

He shook his head. "Because you are my most prized treasure," he whispered, and bent to kiss her mouth tenderly.

She kissed him back, shyly. "I had never kissed anyone until you came along," she whispered.

He chuckled. "You improve with practice!"

"John!" she chided.

He only laughed, letting her go to pay attention to the road. "We must get on down the road. It looks like rain." He gave her a roguish glance. "We would not want you to tumble into a mud puddle, Mrs. Jacobs."

"Are you ever going to forget that?" she moaned.

"In twenty years or so, perhaps," he said. "But I cannot promise. That is one of my most delightful memories. You were so game, and Sir Sydney was such a boor!"

"Indeed he was. I hope he marries for money and discovers that she has none."

"Evil girl," he teased.

She laughed. "Well, you will never be able to accuse ME of marrying you for your money," she said contentedly. "In twenty years or so," she added, repeating his own phrase, "you will be exceedingly rich. I just know it."

"I hope to break even, at least, and be able to pay my debts," he said. "But I would love to have a ranch as big as a state, Ellen, and the money to breed fine cattle, and even fine horses." He glanced at her. "Now that we have two extra horse wranglers, we can start building up our herd."

She only smiled. She was glad that she'd stood up to the Comanches. She wondered if they'd ever have wanted to work for them if she'd run away and hid.

THE TEEPEE THE Comanches built for the couple was remarkably warm and clean. No sooner was it up than Ellen built a small cooking fire near its center and put on a black iron pot of stew to cook. Red Wing had already taught her how to turn the pole in the center to work the flap for letting smoke out while she cooked.

She also learned that she was born to be a rancher's wife. Every chore came easily to her. She wasn't afraid of hard work, and she fell more in love with her roguish, unconventional husband every day. She did still worry about her grandmother coming down to rescue her. She had no intention of being carted off back East, where she would have to dress and act with decorum.

She sat the children down in the cabin one evening after she and the other women and older girls had cleared away the precious iron cookware and swished the tin plates and few utensils in a basin of soapy water and wiped them with a dishrag.

"What are we going to do?" one of Juana's daughters asked.

Ellen produced the books that the retired Victoria schoolteacher had given her, handling them like treasure.

"I'm going to teach you children to read and write," she told them.

Mary and Juana stood quietly by, so still that Ellen was made uneasy.

"Is it all right?" she asked the adults, concerned, because she'd worried that they might think education superfluous.

"Nobody ever taught me to write my name," Mary said. "Nor Isaac, either. We can only make an x. Could you teach me to write? And read?"

"Me, too!" Juana exclaimed.

Their husbands looked as if they might bite their tongues off trying not to ask if they could learn, too, but they managed.

"You can all gather around and we'll let the older folk help show the young ones how to do it," she said, managing a way to spare the pride of the men in the process of teaching them as well.

"Yes, we can show them, *señora*," Luis said brightly.

"Sure we can," Isaac added with a big grin.

"Gather around, then." She opened the book with a huge smile and began the first lesson.

SHE LOOKED DOWN at the dungarees she was wearing with boots that John had bought her. She had on one of his big checked long-sleeved shirts, with the sleeves rolled up, and her hair was caught in a ponytail down her back. She checked the stew in her black cooking pot and wiped sweat from her brow with a weary hand. The Comanches had gathered pine straw from under the short-leafed pines in the thicket to make beds, which Ellen covered with quilts she and the other women had made in their precious free time. It wasn't a mansion, but she and John would have privacy for the first time that night. She thought of the prospect with joy and a certain amount of trepidation. Like most young women of her generation, her upbringing had been very strict and moral. She knew almost nothing of what happened between married people in the dark. What she didn't know made her nervous.

The sudden noise outside penetrated her thoughts. She heard voices, one raised and strident, and she ran out of the teepee and to the cabin to discover a well-dressed, elderly woman with two young men in immaculate suits exchanging heated words with Juana, who couldn't follow a thing they were saying. Mary was out with the others collecting more wood for the fireplace in the small cabin.

"Do you understand me?" the old woman was shouting. "I am looking for Ellen Colby!"

"Grandmother!" Ellen exclaimed when she recognized the woman.

Her grandmother Amelia Greene was standing beside the buggy beside two tall young men whom Ellen recognized as her cousins.

Amelia turned stiffly, her whole expression one of utter disapproval when she saw the way her granddaughter was dressed.

"Camellia Ellen Colby!" she exclaimed. "What has become of you!"

"Now, Grandmother," Ellen said gently, "you can't expect a pioneer wife to dress and act as a lady in a drawing room."

The older woman was not convinced. She was bristling with indignation. "You will get your things together and come home with me right away!" she demanded. "I am not leaving you here in the dirt with these peasants!"

Ellen's demeanor changed at once from one of welcome and uneasiness to one of pure outrage. She stuck both hands on her slender hips and glared at her grandmother.

"How dare you call my friends peasants!" she exclaimed furiously. She went to stand beside Juana. "Juana's husband, Luis, and Mary's husband, Isaac, are our partners in this ranching enterprise. They are no one's servants!"

Mary came to stand beside her as well, and the children gathered around them. While the old woman and her companions were getting over that shock, John came striding up, with his gunbelt on, accompanied by Luis and Isaac and the two Comanche men.

Amelia Greene screeched loudly and jumped behind the tallest of her grandchildren.

"How much you want for old woman?" Red Wing asked deliberately, pointing at Amelia.

Amelia looked near to fainting.

Ellen laughed helplessly. "He's not serious," she assured her grandmother.

"I should hope not!" the tallest of her cousins muttered, glaring at him. "The very idea! Why do you allow Indians here?"

"These are our horse wranglers," Ellen said pointedly. "Red Wing and Thunder. And those are our partners, Luis Rodriguez and Isaac Brown. Gentlemen, my grandmother, Amelia Greene of New York City."

Nobody spoke.

John came forward to slide his arm around Ellen's waist. He was furious at the way her relatives were treating the people nearby.

"Hospitality is almost a religion to us out here in Texas," John drawled, although his green eyes were flashing like green diamonds. "But as you may notice, we have no facilities to accommodate visitors yet."

"You cannot expect that we would want to stay?" the shorter cousin asked indignantly. "Come, Grandmother, let us go back to town. Ellen is lost to us. Surely you can see that?"

Ellen glared at him. "Five years from now, cousin, you will not recognize this place. A lot of hard work is going to turn it into a showplace...."

"Of mongrels!" her grandmother said haughtily.

"I'm sorry you feel that way, but I find your company equally taxing," Ellen shot back. "Now will you all please leave? I have chores, as do the others. Unlike you, I do not sit in the parlor waiting for other people to fetch and carry at my instructions."

The old woman glowered. "Very well, then, live out here in the wilds with savages! I only came to try and save you from a life of drudgery!"

"Pickles and bread," Ellen retorted haughtily. "You came hoping to entice me back into household slavery. Until I escaped you and came west with my father, I was your unpaid maidservant for most of my life."

"What else are you fit for?" her grandmother demanded. "You have no looks, no talent, no...!"

"She is lovely," John interrupted. "Gentle and kind and brave. She is no one's servant here, and she has freedom of a sort you will never know."

The old woman's eyes were poisonously intent. "She will die of hard work here, for certain!"

"On her own land, making her own empire," John replied tersely. "The road is that way," he added, pointing.

She tossed her head and sashayed back to the buggy, to be helped in by her grandsons, one of whom gave Ellen a wicked grin before he climbed in and took the reins.

"Drive on," Amelia said curtly. "We have no kinfolk here!"

"Truer words were never spoken," Ellen said sweetly. "Do have a safe trip back to town. Except for cattle thieves from Mexico and the bordering counties of Texas, and bank robbers, there should be nothing dangerous in your path. But I would drive very fast, if I were you!"

There were muttered, excited exchanges of conversation in the buggy before the tallest grandson used the buggy whip and the small vehicle raced forward down the dusty dirt road in the general direction of town.

"You wicked girl!" John exclaimed on a burst of laughter, hugging her close.

"So much for my rescuers," she murmured contentedly, hugging him back. "Now we can get back to work!"

THAT NIGHT, Ellen and John spent their first night alone, without prying eyes or ears, in the teepee the Comanches had provided for them.

"I am a little nervous," she confessed when John had put out the small fire and they were together in the darkness.

"That will not last," he promised, drawing her close. "We are both young, and we have all the years ahead to become more accustomed to each other. All you must remember is that I care more for you than for any woman I have ever known. You are my most prized treasure. I love you. I will spend my life trying to make you happy."

"John!" She pressed close to him and raised her face. "I will do the same. I adore you!"

He bent and kissed her softly, and then not so softly. Tender caresses gave way to stormy, devouring kisses. They sank to the makeshift mattress and there, locked tight in each others' arms, they gave way to the smoldering passion that had grown between them for long weeks. At first she was inhibited, but he was skillful and slow and tender. Very soon, her passion rose to meet his. The sharpness of passion was new between them, and as it grew, they became playful together.

They laughed, and then the laughing stopped as they tasted the first sweet sting of mutual delight in the soft, enveloping darkness.

When Ellen finally fell asleep in John's arms, she thought that there had never been a happier bride in the history of Texas.

CHAPTER SIX

ELLEN'S GRANDMOTHER AND cousins went back East. Her father came regularly to visit them in their tee-pee, finding it touching and amusing at once that they were happy with so little. He even offered to loan them enough to build a bigger cabin, but they refused politely. All they wanted, Ellen reminded him, was a spur of the railroad.

That, too, was finally finished. John loaded his beef cattle into the cattle cars bound for the stockyards of the Midwest. The residents of the ranch settled into hard work and camaraderie, and all their efforts eventually resulted in increasing prosperity.

The first thing they did with their newfound funds was to add to the cattle herd. The second was to build individual cabins for the Rodriguez and Brown clans, replacing the teepees the Comanches had built for them. The Comanches, offered a handsome log cabin of their own, declined abruptly, although politely. They could never understand the white man's interest in a stationary house that had to be cleaned constantly, when it was so much easier to move the teepee to a clean spot! However, John and Ellen continued to live in their own teepee for the time being, as well, to save money.

A barn was the next project. As in all young communities, a barbecue and a quilting bee were arranged along with a barnraising. All the strong young men of the area turned out and the resulting barn and corral were quick fruit of their efforts. Other ranches were springing up around the 3J Ranch, although not as large and certainly not with the number of cattle and horses that John's now boasted.

The railroad spur, when it came, brought instant prosperity to the area it served. It grew and prospered even as some smaller towns in the area became ghost towns. Local citizens decided that they needed a name for their small town, which had actually grown up around the ranch itself even before the railroad came. They decided to call it Jacobsville, for John Jacobs, despite his protests. His hard work and lack of prejudice had made him good friends and dangerous enemies in the surrounding area. But when cattle were rustled and houses robbed, his was never among them. Bandits from over the border made a wide route around the ranch.

As the cattle herd grew and its refinement continued, the demand for Jacobs's beef grew as well. John bought other properties to go along with his own, along with barbed wire to fence in his ranges. He hired on new men as well, black drovers as well as Mexican and white. There was even a Chinese drover who had heard of the Jacobs ranch far away in Arizona and had come to it looking for a job. Each new addition to the ranch workforce was placed under the orders of either Luis or Isaac, and the number of outbuildings and line camps grew steadily.

Ellen worked right alongside the other women, adding new women to her dressmaking enterprise, until she had enough workers and enough stock to open a dress shop in their new town of Jacobsville. Mary and

Juana took turns as proprietors while Ellen confined herself to sewing chair and sofa covers for the furniture in the new white clapboard house John had built her. She and her handsome husband grew closer by the day, but one thing was still missing from her happiness. Their marriage was entering into its second year with no hope of a child.

John never spoke of it, but Ellen knew he wanted children. So did she. It was a curious thing that their passion for each other was ever growing, but bore no fruit. Still, they had a good marriage and Ellen was happier than she ever dreamed of being.

In the second year of their marriage, his sister Jeanette came west on the train with her husband and four children to visit. Only then did Ellen learn the extent of the tragedy that had sent John west in the first place. The attack by the Union troops had mistakenly been aimed at the sharecroppers' cabin John and his mother and sisters occupied, instead of the house where the owner's vicious overseer lived. The house had caught fire and John's mother and elder sister had burned to death. John had not been able to save them. The attack had been meant for the overseer who had beaten Isaac and Mary's son to death, along with many other slaves. John was told, afterward, but his grief was so sweeping that he hardly understood what was said to him. His sister made sure that he did know. The cavalry officer had apologized to her, and given her money for the trip to North Carolina, unbeknownst to John. His sister obviously adored him, and he was a doting uncle to her children.

She understood John's dark moods better after that, the times when he wanted to be alone, when he went hunting and never brought any wild game home with him. Ellen and Jeanette became close almost at once, and wrote to each other regularly even when Jeanette and her family went home to North Carolina.

Deputy Marshal James Graham had come by unexpectedly and mentioned to John that he hadn't been able to find the two Comanche fugitives who were supposed to have shot a white man over a horse. It turned out that the white man had cheated the Comanches and had later been accused of cheating several army officers in horse trading deals. He was arrested, tried and sent to prison. So, Graham told John, the Comanches weren't in trouble anymore. Just in case John ever came across them.

Thunder and Red Wing, told of the white man's arrest, worked a few months longer for John and then headed north with their wages. Ellen was sad to see them go, but Thunder had promised that they would meet again one day.

The Maxwells came to visit often from Scotland, staying in the beautiful white Victorian house John later built for his beloved wife. They gave the couple the benefit of their extensive experience of horses, and John branched out into raising thoroughbreds. Eventually a thoroughbred of the lineage from his ranch would win the Triple Crown.

YEARS PASSED WITH each year bringing new prosperity to the 3J Ranch. One May morning, Ellen unexpectedly fainted at a church social. John carried her to the office of their new doctor, who had moved in just down the boardwalk from the new restaurant and hotel.

The doctor examined her and, when John had been invited into the examination room, grinned at him. "You are to be a father, young man," he said. "Congratulations!"

John looked at Ellen as if she'd just solved the great mystery of life. He lifted her clear of the floor and kissed her with aching tenderness. His happiness was complete, now.

Almost immediately, he began to worry about labor. He remembered when Luis's and Isaac's wives had given birth, and he turned pale.

The doctor patted him on the back. "You'll survive the birth of your children, Mr. Jacobs, we all do. Yes, even me. I have had to deliver mine. Something, I daresay, you will be spared!"

John laughed with relief, thanked the doctor for his perception, and kissed Ellen again.

She bore him three sons and two daughters in the years that followed, although only two of their children, their son Bass and their daughter Rose Ellen, lived to adulthood. The family grew and prospered in Jacobsville. Later, the entire county, Jacobs, was named for John as well. He diversified his holdings into mining and real estate and banking. He was the first in south Texas to try new techniques in cattle ranching and to use mechanization to improve his land.

The Brown family produced six children in all. Their youngest, Caleb, would move to Chicago and become a famous trial lawyer. His son would be elected to the United States Senate.

The Rodriguez family produced ten children. One of their sons became a Texas Ranger, beginning a family tradition that lived on through subsequent generations.

John Jacobs founded the first bank in Jacobs County, along with the first dry goods store. He worked hard at breeding good cattle, but he made his fortune in the terrible blizzard of 1885-86 in which so many cattlemen lost their shirts. He endowed a college and an orphanage, and, always active in local politics, he was elected to the U.S. Senate at the age of fifty. He and Ellen never parted for fifty years.

His son, Bass Jacobs, married twice. By his young second wife, he had a son, Bass, Jr., and a daughter, Violet Ellen. Bass Jacobs, Jr., was the last of the Jacobs family to own land in Jacobs County. The 3J Ranch was sold after his death. His son, Ty, born in 1955, eventually moved to Arizona and married and settled there. His daughter, Shelby, born in 1961, stayed in Jacobsville and married a local man, Justin Ballenger. They produced three sons. One of them was named John Jackson Jacobs Ballenger, so that the founding father of Shelby's family name would live on in memory.

A bronze statue of Big John Jacobs, mounted on one of the Arabian stallions his ranch became famous for, was erected in the town square of Jacobsville just after the first world war.

Portraits of the Rodriguez family and the Brown family are prominently displayed in the Jacobs County Museum, alongside a portrait of Camellia Ellen Jacobs, dressed in an elegant blue gown, but with a shotgun in a fringed sheath at her feet and a twinkle in her blue eyes. All three portraits, which had belonged to Bass Jacobs, Jr., were donated to the museum by Shelby Jacobs Ballenger. In a glass case nearby are a bow and arrow in a beaded rawhide quiver, in which also resides a black-and-white photograph of a Comanche warrior with a blond woman and five children, two of whom are also blond. But that is another story…

* * * * *